Praise for the novels of Laurell K. Hamilton featuring Anita Blake, Vampire Hunter

Obsidian Butterfly

"An erotic, demonic thrill ride. Her sexy, edgy, wickedly ironic style sweeps the reader into her unique world and delivers red-hot entertainment. Hamilton's marvelous storytelling can be summed up in three words: over the top. She blends the genres of romance, horror and adventure with stunning panache. Great fun!"
—Jayne Ann Krentz

"Just when I think that Laurell K. Hamilton can't possibly get any further out on the edge, along she comes with yet another eye-popping blend of hilarious sex, violence, and stuff that makes your hair stand on end. I've never read a writer with a more fertile imagination—and fewer inhibitions about using it!"
—Diana Gabaldon

"A monstrously entertaining read."—*Publishers Weekly*

"Hamilton sets a good pace and weaves a nifty tapestry of glowy-eyed monsters against a background of blood."
—*Kirkus Reviews*

"A fast-paced, high-fire power mix, a nice grisly vacation from Anita's usual relationship problems."—*Locus*

"An abundance of thrills, chills, violence, and sexual innuendo. Recommended."
—*Library Journal*

"An R-rated *Buffy the Vampire Slayer* . . . the action never stops . . . the climax is an edge-of-your-seat cliffhanger . . . dessert for the mind, with sprinkles!"
—*The New York Review of Science Fiction*

Continued . . .

"*Obsidian*'s greater attention to continuity and detail sharpens Hamilton's trademark intensity and nonstop action." —*Crescent Blues Book Views*

Guilty Pleasures

"I was enthralled—a departure from the usual type of vampire tale which will have a wide appeal to any reader hunting for both chills and fun."

—Andre Norton

The Laughing Corpse

"Supernatural bad guys beware, night-prowling Anita Blake is savvy, sassy, and tough."
—P. N. Elrod, author of *The Vampire Files*

Circus of the Damned

"Ms. Hamilton's intriguing blend of fantasy, mystery and a touch of romance is great fun indeed."
—*Romantic Times*

The Lunatic Cafe

"A well-written, stylish, and imaginative work . . . a wonderful set to read." —*Kliatt*

Bloody Bones

"This fast-paced, tough-edged supernatural thriller is mesmerizing reading indeed." —*Romantic Times*

The Killing Dance

"As usual, the plot is full of red herrings . . . also, as usual, it's a lot of fun, with some significant new developments in Anita's personal life fans of the series won't want to miss." —*Locus*

Burnt Offerings

"Filled with nonstop action, witty dialog, and steamy sex, this title will appeal to fans of Anne Rice and Tanya Huff." —*Library Journal*

Blue Moon

"[This] series has to rank as one of the most addictive substances on earth . . . *Blue Moon* is the best book Laurell Hamilton has produced recently." —*SF Site*

NIGHTSEER

Laurell K. Hamilton

A ROC BOOK

ROC
Published by New American Library, a division of
Penguin Group (USA) Inc., 375 Hudson Street,
New York, New York 10014, U.S.A.
Penguin Books Ltd, 80 Strand,
London WC2R 0RL, England
Penguin Books Australia Ltd, 250 Camberwell Road,
Camberwell, Victoria 3124, Australia
Penguin Books Canada Ltd, 10 Alcorn Avenue,
Toronto, Ontario, Canada M4V 3B2
Penguin Books (N.Z.) Ltd, Cnr Rosedale and Airborne Roads,
Albany, Auckland 1310, New Zealand

Penguin Books Ltd, Registered Offices:
80 Strand, London WC2R 0RL, England

First published by Roc, an imprint of New American Library,
a division of Penguin Group (USA) Inc.

First Printing, March 1992
20 19 18 17 16 15 14

*To Laura Gentry, my grandmother,
who read to me as often as I asked.*

ACKNOWLEDGMENTS

Gary W. Hamilton, my husband, my first reader, and my best friend. Greer Barnard-Pressgrove, who told me I would sell. Deborah Millitello, who kept me from panicking. And all the members of my writer's group, The Alternate Historians, Stan and Brenda Ward, Jim Tourville, and Mary-Dale Amison. To all those who attended the first NameThatCon Writer's Workshop.

Also to Emma Bull, Will Shetterly, and Steven Gould, a little thunder to share.

Prologue

Prophecy begins with a child's nightmare.

Keleios did not know the dream was prophetic; she only knew it felt different from other dreams.

Mother, Elwine the Gentle, stood at the top of a stairway. She smiled and beckoned with a slender white hand. Keleios, the child, ran to her. Keleios saw her as very tall and very beautiful, as only a mother can be. A blemish appeared on the woman's face, a mere darkening of the skin, but it grew. The blackness burst the skin in an oozing sore. A second blackness raised on her forehead, and another, and another. Keleios held the white hand, saying, "Mother what's wrong?"

The woman screamed and fell to her knees, jerking her hand free from Keleios. Her mother whispered, "Run."

Keleios ran. The hallways were dark with flickering torches sending twisted shadows in her path. And from one shadow stepped a woman. Harque the Witch formed from the darkness. Keleios knew Harque did not like her mother, and the child had always been afraid of the witch without knowing why. Harque said, "Where is the fair Elwine the Gentle? Where is she now?"

Keleios screamed and ran back the way she had come. She ran, but the voice kept asking, "Where is the fair Elwine the Gentle? Where is she now?"

Harque came from every shadow, she was always there. Keleios ran into a wall—a dead end, nowhere to go. Harque stood behind her, tall and severe. "Do you want to see your mother?"

Keleios stared at her, too frightened to speak, too tired to move.

The witch repeated her question. "Do you want to see your mother?"

Keleios nodded and couldn't stop herself from taking the woman's hand. The witch's hand was cool to her sweating flesh. Harque led her up a narrow-walled stairway. At the top there was a narrow landing and one door. Harque smiled down at Keleios, smiled with her vision-befuddled eyes, and the child shrank back. She dragged Keleios to the door. "Don't you want to see your mother?"

There was an odor now, faint but growing stronger. The stench of sickness and uncleaned clothes soured with sweat. Keleios tried to pull away, but the grip was like iron. The door opened so slowly. The smell washed over the child, and she vomited on the stones. Harque held her forehead, gently, and helped her stand afterwards.

Keleios balked, not wanting to enter the room. Harque dragged her along the floor, screaming, dragged her over the doorsill into the stinking room. She was jerked to her feet and told, "Look."

The room was narrow with only a rickety bed in it. Something was tied to that bed. It was black, and pus oozed from it. The skin was cracked and bleeding as if the sickness were too much for the skin to hold. Keleios stared at the thing for a time, not understanding. Her eyes wouldn't make sense of it.

The small girl realized a person was tied to the bed. Keleios began to cry. There was no hint of who it had been, only that it had been a person.

The black face turned toward them and opened its eyes—brown eyes, her mother's eyes.

Keleios screamed.

Harque's voice came. "Where is the fair Elwine the Gentle? Where is she now?"

The nightmare faded to the sounds of her own screams.

She woke, panting and sweat drenched. Magda, her nursemaid, was there, brought by her screams. "Keleios, child, what is it?"

Keleios cried into Magda's plump bosom, sobbing, unable to talk. The fear was still there, horrible and complete. She could not breathe around the terror of it. She could not think for the sight of her mother's eyes, her mother's death.

There was a soft footstep and the rustling of silk in the reeds that covered the floor. Elwine was there, tall and slender, dressed in white. Keleios fought free of the nurse and scrambled for her mother.

Elwine held her and stroked her hair until her breathing calmed and her sobs quieted. "Now, little one, what has happened to upset you so?"

Keleios whispered, "I dreamed."

"But we've talked before, Keleios; dreams cannot hurt you."

Keleios prided herself on being brave and would not look at her mother, but stared at the silver thread worked into her mother's bodice. It formed a silver line of leaves and common flowers, the sort of things that went into an herb spell. Mother smelled like peppermint and faded apple blossoms. She had been working a spell when Keleios screamed.

Elwine forced the child away from her and said, "Look at me, Keleios."

The child did, half-afraid.

"Are you still afraid?"

Keleios nodded. "It isn't gone, Mother."

"What isn't gone?"

"The dream, the bad dream. It's still here." She touched her forehead. "It's still here."

Elwine motioned the nurse to leave and crawled up on the bed with Keleios. She snuggled the child to her and said, "Now tell me about this dream that won't leave."

Keleios told her everything. Her mother listened and

nodded and made all the comforting noises she was supposed to. There had never been a dream prophet on either side of Keleios' bloodline; magic talents just didn't appear by themselves.

Elwine comforted her child, and Keleios felt better. With the telling of the dream, a weight seemed to have moved. She could breathe again, and that horrible fear was gone.

"Mother, why does Harque not like you?"

Elwine sighed and hugged the child. "Do you understand what it means to be challenged to walk the sands?"

Keleios frowned. "It means you fight with someone and you win."

Elwine smiled. "Not always, but you have the idea. Harque challenged me years ago, when you were very small. She lost and felt humiliated. Do you understand what humiliated means?"

"It means when you're embarrassed."

"Very good. Harque feels I humiliated her, and that is why she doesn't like me."

"She scares me, Mother."

Elwine stiffened. "Has she ever hurt you or frightened you in any way?"

It wasn't anything Harque had done, but Keleios had no word for it. "No, mother."

Elwine hugged the child. "You must always speak freely to me, Keleios. If anything frightens you, you must tell me about it."

"I will."

"Good. Do you feel better now?"

Keleios smiled and nodded.

At five, Keleios was easily comforted by her beloved mother. Elwine tucked the child into the large four-poster bed. She kissed Keleios on the forehead and said, "Would you like to have a lamp?"

Keleios was a brave little girl. "No, I'm fine."

Elwine smiled, pleased. "Sleep tight, little one."

"Good night, Mother. I hope I didn't spoil your spell."

Elwine laughed, a rich throaty sound. "No, little one, the spell keeps well." With that she was gone. Keleios was left alone with the wind moaning round the castle, but she slept because Mother had said there was nothing to fear.

Three days later Harque the Witch kidnapped Elwine and her daughters, Keleios and Methia. Five days after that Harque forced Keleios to make the walk of her nightmare to the room where her mother lay. What the dream had withheld had been the horror in her mother's eyes, the madness that the disease had forced upon her. She died that way, the life slipping from her eyes without knowing that Keleios was there to see and to remember.

Two days after that, Harque's keep was raided; Keleios and her sister were rescued. Harque the Witch escaped. And Keleios found that true nightmares had their horrors, also.

1

A Reluctant Dreamer

Keleios had come to the rose garden and hidden behind its wall to work her magic. The warm summer darkness was thick with the fragrance of roses and the song of crickets. A stray frog had wandered into the garden's centerpiece, a fountain. It gave its shrill song alone. Keleios laughed. She was not sure if she had ever heard just one frog. They usually went in chorus.

Soon her magic would quiet the crickets and the lonely frog. It was strange how the presence of active magic silenced the world.

Keleios' brown-gold hair lay in a loose braid down her back. Any mirror Keleios passed told her she was like a ghost of her mother. The only thing that saved her was her father's elven blood, which thinned her face and let Keleios look like herself. She was dressed all in brown, except for the glimpse of snowy linen at the collar of her tunic. She wore trousers laced close to her legs with crisscrossing bandages. Boots came to her knees, hardened leather soles and soft hide. Keleios knew her mother, ever feminine, would have been horrified. But her mother had been dead for eighteen years. It was a long time to worry about someone's opinion.

Keleios touched the small pile of dry bark shavings and twigs. Fire had been the first sorcery she had ever called; it was still the easiest. It flared like a falling star and landed in the wood. The flames leapt and crackled round the dry kindling. She placed two slightly larger sticks on top of the flame, and the fire slowed to work on the thicker wood.

The world had fallen into silence. Only the wind still blew through the roses.

Keleios poured water in a small empty pot. She had not been able to get the right kind of wood for this particular fire, so she planned to cheat. She placed a fire-protect spell on her hands. It glimmered briefly just behind her eyes, then she could not see it. It was a matter of trust that when she picked up the fire, it would not burn her. A matter of trust and confidence in her own sorcery.

She scooped up the fire in one hand. The blaze flared in the wind, sparking against the darkness. Keleios looked at the fire, concentrating on its wavering orange-red depths, studying its heat without fearing it. She concentrated, and it flared a tiny column of burning. Another thought and it burned to the low orange of embers. It flickered stronger, following her thoughts.

She nearly lost concentration, distracted by the fire's dance in the shining surface of her arm guards. She drew her mind back to the work at hand. It was a bad sign, being distracted by light. It spoke of dream sickness. She was vision prophet as well as dream, so she was doubly at risk.

Keleios touched the flame briefly, curling it to her will. Her concentration was pure. She was ready for the levitation.

It was a different sort of spell from calling fire. Instead of calling something out of nowhere, one touched an object with nothing and made it move. There were no lines of power, no dim glows, to let one know that one was on the right track. The thing either moved or it didn't.

The water-filled pot floated upward, then hovered above the flame. She waited. Even with magic fire it took time.

The water began to simmer. Keleios reached her free hand to the small earthenware bowl. She took tiny but equal amounts of anise seed and fragrant valerian root from it. She placed them gently in the bubbling water.

Keleios checked the time by the clock tower and its striking of the quarter hour.

More waiting. Keleios had had potion to ward off nightmares, nearly a week's supply, but she had run out last night. A potion that merely allowed a peaceful night for a frightened child blocked prophecy in a dream prophet.

Keleios was courting dream sickness and knew it. Too much fragrant valerian was poisonous, and she knew that, too. She had the beginnings of dream sickness already. She was easily distracted at odd moments and caught herself listening to voices that were not there. She was being foolish. Fear makes a person foolish from time to time.

An evil dream was waiting for her. She was afraid to sleep, afraid to dream, afraid not to dream. Keleios hated prophecy. From its first touch prophecy had never helped her. It was the most useless of magics.

Whatever waited for her was something awful. She had never felt such a crashing on her mind, not even when she dreamed of her mother's death. This would be worse; she wasn't sure she could face it. It was a child's fear and she cursed herself for it, but she could not bring herself to have the dream.

The tower clock struck. She set the pot on the white gravel pathway to cool. She flung the fire into the darkness, and it vanished in a cascade of sparks. She canceled the fire-protect spell. Conserve sorcery—it had been a rule drummed into her mind these last three years. Though sorcery was instant magic and powerful, it was easily depleted and left the spellcaster drained and magicless.

She thought of cold, the cool autumn cold that first blows near the door in November. Not too cold, or she would freeze the potion solid and ruin it. She wanted only to cool it.

Keleios secured cheesecloth over the pot with a string and strained the liquid into the cup. A little water from the fountain restored the volume lost in simmering.

Keleios held the cup in her hands. Another dreamless night lay in her hands. The moon rose free of the castle towers. It bathed the rose garden in silver and grey and blackest black. The towers were midnight silhouettes against the rising moon.

The tallest tower soared black and perfect, velvet in the moonlight: the tower of prophecy. It mocked her, tall and menacing, a challenge.

Keleios squeezed the wooden cup in her hands, and it cracked, spilling the potion down her hands and forearms. Her decision was made. She would go to the tower tonight, unguarded, with nothing but her skill to protect her. Anything was better than this cowardice.

Keleios rinsed the potion from her golden bracers. The water would not rust them. They were magic and never needed polishing. Stains ran from them like the water that sparkled down them now. They were a good piece of enchantment. She half-whispered, "I am a master enchanter and master dreamer, regardless of what council says." Tonight the words seemed empty.

Three years ago she had been a master. Then she had discovered she was a sorcerer. At the age of twenty a totally new magic poured out of her hands. It was unprecedented, impossible, but true. And the Council of Seven, ruling body of Astrantha, had seen fit to strip her of master rank, until she mastered this new talent. They had sent her back to Zeln's school. She was a journeyman again, and had been for three long years.

Was one little word so very important? Did she need to be called master to be one? Keleios knelt and plunged her arms into the fountain's bowl. She splashed water on her face and gasped from the sudden cold.

The small frog dived frantically with a wet plop.

Keleios blinked up at the moon. Water trailed down her neck into the linen undershirt. She felt better, her mind cleared. These doubts were their own poison. To doubt one's magic at all was a very dangerous thing.

She wiped the water from her eyes and smoothed some of it back into the loose braid of her hair. She dried her hand on her pants. It was one of the benefits of wearing the inexpensive hide. She began gathering up her spell components.

The second moon had risen small and dim, yellow beside the white mother moon. This time of year it would be the small hours of the morning before the red moon rose.

Three moons for three faces of the great Mother, or so some of the very ancient legends said. The All-Mother was Cia, the healer, all that was good; Ardath, she who balances the scale of heaven; and Ivel, destruction incarnate and hatred made real. Astrantha and its neighbor across the sea, Meltaan, were countries that believed in all faces of the Mother equally. They called it the law of balance. If you were registered as a follower of Ivel, or one of her dark children, you could literally get away with murder.

Keleios had come to understand the law of balance but never to agree with it. There were a handful of times when Keleios had sought blood price in secret, because some acts were not to be tolerated no matter what land you lived in.

Keleios had spent much of the last three years in research. She had hunted for the reason that the goddess was one in three, three parts, but not a whole. Only the legend of how the moon had broken into three pieces seemed to hint at it. It said that the goddess had gone mad with a pain in her head. When the pain cleared, she was split asunder, and so was the moon. The legend hinted that the goddess could be healed and made one again, but it never said whether that would be a good thing or a bad thing.

Keleios had seen the moons through Zeln's telescope. They were dead rock, nothing more, worlds of shining light and shadows. Keleios found it hard to believe that the moons were tied to the goddess. She did believe that the Mother could have split the moon in a fit of anger.

Keleios laughed. "I am wasting time staring at the moons. My fear seeks to trick me." She would delay no longer. There was freedom in the decision. Now that she would go to the tower and have her dream, the fear had lessened.

She had discovered that most fears shrank when confronted. Not all fears, though. Keleois pushed the thought back before it could grow.

Keleios opened the small leather pouch at her belt. It glowed softly with enchantment. She had not made this but had purchased it in Meltaan. The pot slipped through the impossibly small opening, followed by the bowl. She scattered the remnants of the wood and tossed the cracked cup off the path.

She took the simple golden ring off her right hand and placed it in the enchanted pouch also. She unlaced each of the bracers and slipped them through. They were four times as long as the pouch appeared, but they slipped out of sight. Her waist dagger and the two hidden knives followed after. Luckweaver, her short sword, lay in her room. Zeln had tried to outlaw knives in the keep, but there were too many other uses for them besides as weapons. Swords were nothing but weapons, and one must get special permission to wear them openly.

Keleios agreed with the rule in part. There were many who had carried swords who would have been alive today if they simply had been unarmed. For herself she disliked the rule, but she obeyed it.

It was not Zeln's rules that kept enchantments and weapons out of the dreaming rooms. Dreamers had been known to do themselves, or others, harm with weapons. The tower of prophecy did not like foreign magic. For whatever reason enchantments seemed to anger the tower.

Keleios herself had forgotten the ring of protection once but only once. The tower had tried to trick her into cutting off her own finger.

The opening to the leather pouch was spelled so that only her own hand could open it. Regardless of who was prophet keeper tonight, it would be safe from tampering.

She had done all she could to prepare. It was time to go to the tower. Keleios walked through the trellised arch and passed into the herb garden. The intricate beds of plants led up to the steps of Zeln's castle. Zeln the Just had once been a rich Astranthian noble, and the castle showed that, but Zeln had changed. It was from him that Keleios learned her love of simple clothing and a feel for equality of all people. Anyone could come to Zeln's school, all they had to have was talent. And every student learned what it was to do manual labor. Some of the noble children found that a very hard concept indeed. Keleios thought it was normal.

The castle towered above her in the dark. Its square shape had been designed for defense, but centuries of softer living had widened the windows and brought gardens up to the very door.

The inner corridors of the castle were darker than the summer night. Keleios paused to let her eyes adjust. She could see in the dark, like a cat, or a demon. She was demon-named Nightseer, but she still had to wait for her eyes to adjust to the darkness.

The libraries were in the center of the castle, and in the center of the libraries was the tower of prophecy. Keleios walked up the narrow, winding stair. She could taste her heart thudding in her throat. She did not want this dream.

The dreaming rooms circled an open space that held the stairs and a fireplace. Here the prophet keepers kept guard.

Eduard, the journeyman herb-witch, sat in front of the fire, knees clasped to his chest. The fire caught vague highlights in his raven-black hair. The emeralds on his tunic glimmered with green fire. The tunic was the stylish above-the-waist cut, leaving most of his lower body in nothing but green tights. His eyes were the crystalline blue of sapphires. "Keleois the Enchanter, I am honored to guard your prophecy."

The smirk on his face gave the lie to his courtesy.

Eduard and Keleios had an understanding between them. He didn't like her, and she didn't like him. He was a follower of Ivel.

"Surely you do not stand guard alone, Eduard the Witch."

"My companion had to take a piss."

Keleios' face remained impassive. If he hoped to anger her with vulgarities, he would fail. If someone could provoke you to anger without good cause, they controlled you. She would never give Eduard that satisfaction again. She disliked Eduard, but he had lost the ability to anger her, and that angered him.

"Your little follower is in the dreaming rooms tonight."

Keleios knew who he meant. Alys was the youngest apprentice to ever be allowed at Zeln's school. She was five and had come plagued with nightmares that were truly powerful prophetic dreams. Whenever Alys wasn't doing chores or studies, she was tagging behind Keleios. It was sometimes bothersome to have a child in such constant attendance, but Keleios could not tell her no. The child reminded Keleios of herself at five, and you must be kind to shadows of your own childhood.

"How was she when she went in?"

He shrugged. "Nervous, but who wouldn't be? I hear the tower can eat a person's soul."

Keleios ignored his attempt to frighten her. "Is there a dreaming room open?"

"Three."

She waited, but he didn't offer to show her which were empty. "Which ones are empty, Eduard?"

He pushed himself upward with his arms and directed her to three doors. He gave a courtly bow and said, "It is your choice, my lovely coquette."

It was a nice word for slut, but that was what it meant. "Eduard, you're being childish."

It was not the reaction he had hoped for. "I will find something that will break through that calm stoic face of yours. I've heard rumors that you have a violent temper.''

''When I was a child, I did. But I am no longer a child.''

He caught the emphasis and his face darkened. ''I will find something that bothers you.''

Keleios stepped close to him; they were almost the same height. ''If you ever find something to truly anger me, Eduard, it will mean a duel on the sands. And I will kill you.''

He didn't move back, but his hands tightened into fists.

For a moment Keleios thought he would strike her. She let a slow smile dance on her lips. It was a mocking smile. ''As you constantly remind me, I am only a journeyman. And by Astranthian law I can challenge any other journeyman to battle.''

His blue eyes had gone wide. Taunting a fallen master was one thing. Fighting her on the sands was another. His anger discolored his face and made his eyes glint like hard rock, but he took a step back. ''Take any of the rooms that you like.''

''Thank you.'' She held out the leather pouch.

He took it reluctantly. ''Your weapons?''

''Yes, all that I was carrying with me.''

He looked perplexed then at being trusted with so much of her power.

She laughed. ''Don't look so worried, Eduard. There is a spell on the opening that I think you would find less than pleasant.''

''I will leave on journeyman quest this year. You think I cannot undo a simple locking spell?''

''Whoever said it was a simple locking spell?'' At the puzzled look on his face, she decided to elaborate. Keleios had no desire for the young man to try the pouch and be killed. Fidelis the Witch would be angry. It was considered very impolite to kill someone's journeyman. ''The pouch is easily opened, but if any but my hand open it . . . Let us say that it is an unpleasant way to die.''

"You did not make this."

"No, but the guardian spell was worked into it at its making. So it can't be dispelled or disarmed. It is one with the substance of the pouch."

"There is always a way to undo a spell; that is a law of magic."

"I didn't say there wasn't."

He held the pouch awkwardly.

Keleios could read his thoughts on his face, but she knew how to make sure there wasn't an accident. "Eduard the Witch, I charge you not to open that pouch. To do so is death, so I have spoken, and now my guilt is ended."

"There really is a death spell on here, isn't there?"

"Have you ever known me to bluff?"

He shook his head and held the pouch carefully between three fingers.

Keleios was satisfied. Her weapons were safe, and she would not be explaining to Fidelis why her journeyman had been eaten.

She chose a door and pushed it open. The air was cool and dry. Through the room's only window the last rays of an orange sunset were dying. The dreaming rooms kept to a different time than the outside world.

The night blackness of Astrantha had been left behind. Some said the windows reflected dreams, but Keleios did not think so. There were many theories, but Keleios did not believe any of them. No one remembered why the builders had even given windows to the tower. It was a mystery, and that was enough. The light faded, dying in golden oblongs on the floor.

There was a rich smell through the window, like honeysuckle or the jasmine in the greenhouses, yet that wasn't it either. It was sweet and rich, and made her think of magic and hidden places. Keleios had smelled it many times but had yet to see the flower that gave off such perfume.

Dreamers were advised not to look out the windows. Keleios often did, just a glance. She had become almost familiar with the alien stars that glittered so brightly and the calls of birds that never saw Astrantha.

Tonight the dream fought for attention, and Keleios did not go to the window. The tower's magic was already beginning to work upon her. Keleios belonged to the tower until her prophecy came.

Without sight she would have known where she was. The tower of prophecy was a slow ponderous building of spells, stone by stone, death by death, prophecy by prophecy, for this tower had been one of the first built. In those long-ago days the golden Astranthians had served fiercer gods. They had killed to aid their magic; blood had gone into the tower. Dreams, especially the dreams, reflected that.

The room held only a narrow bed, a small table, a dark lamp, and a carved stone basin full of water. Darkness had fallen on the land of the window. A velvet blackness swallowed the dreaming room.

Flint and tinder were near at hand. Perhaps through the heavy air she could have thrown a spell to light the lamp, but it was not always wise to flaunt magic in the tower. Keleios had no real need of light. She still felt attracted to it like a frightened child cheers at the dancing flames. She was Keleios Incantare, called Nightseer, and true need for light was a thing of the past.

Keleios stripped off her tunic and boots. The boots were soft brown hide with hardened soles, an elfish thing. She hated the clopping noise the new wooden heels made. Most of the hunters and scouts still wore the soft boots. Elfish boots were highly prized, and she had watched her Wrythian cousins make them. Even a human could make them, if he knew the techniques, but Keleios, like all Wrythians, enjoyed keeping a secret.

She undid the single braid that held her hair back. It came free in a wavy mass, and she ran her fingers through it briefly.

Keleios slipped between the sheets and almost immediately felt the tower's need. She lay on her back, staring up at the ceiling, trying to fight the pull of sleep. The magic was too strong. Her eyelids began to close; the need for sleep was a terribly physical thing. She fought it until she was nauseous and her head ached. Sleep pulled her under and the sickness vanished.

Images flashed in her mind: vivid colors, feelings, dreams demanding that she enter, but they were old dreams, memories of people long gone. Keleios evaded them with long-practiced ease. It was her own dream that she had come to find, not someone else's outdated prophecy.

The true dream that she had come to find began quietly with memories like all dreams. Master Poula, teacher of herbs and prophecy at the school, was walking down the hallway that led across the front of the keep. And in the way of dreams the figure changed to other faces that Keleios knew. It was Alys, the school's youngest prophet, whom Keleios comforted when she cried from homesickness. It was apprentice Melandra, she with the scarred face and the timid heart. Keleios had more or less adopted the frightened girl, the younger sister that Keleios had never had. Keleios knew that someday Melandra would be a great enchanter, but Melandra did not know it yet. Face after face flowed through the dream, all walking down the hall toward the windows that looked out over the courtyard. The fear began.

It gripped her chest until she fought to breathe at all. It was Belor, her friend since childhood and the keep's greatest illusionist, who turned to the windows. One window was filled with darkness. A silver light that wasn't light shone round the blackness.

"No!" Keleios fought the dream. Against all her training, she tried to change the dream, but prophecy cannot be changed. Belor could not step into the darkness, for if he did, he would die. It was Feltan, the peasant child Keleios herself had brought to the keep for training, who fell through the window into the dark, his small body swept away.

Something else was in the darkness, someone standing. Fidelis the Witch, teacher of herbs and illusion at the school, and follower of the dark gods, stood wrapped in black. A bloody dagger slipped from her hand and fell winking in the dark like a fading star. The walls of the keep stood in the dark, and someone walked atop them, a tall woman dressed in grey. Keleios knew who would turn to face her. Harque strode the walls of the school. That wall began to crumble. Harque turned her back and threw her hands skyward. When she turned to face Keleios again it was Fidelis who stood on the crumbling wall. The wall blew inward, spraying rock into the growing darkness.

The dream faded.

Chaos came.

Keleios found herself in a place she had never dreamt of, never imagined. She was surrounded by nothing, and something. Colours half-sensed wove through shades of grey. Forms twisted into shapes that could only be half-remembered. She was standing, but there was nothing to stand on, nothing to hold to, nothing. Keleios screamed and fell to her knees, covering her eyes. If this had been a dream, she might have been unable to move, but it was not a dream.

She knelt, screaming until her throat burned and her voice sounded ragged. Tears were streaming down her face, and she had not even known she was crying.

There was a whisper of sound, but Keleios did not search for it. She pressed the palms of her hands against her eyes until white flowers exploded against her closed lids. The whisper became a word, then another. The sound was as if many sighs had been sewn together into one voice, the faintest of sounds, the barest of humanity left in it.

"A prophet, a prophet, look upon us, prophet. See what you shall become."

Keleios ignored the summons, praying to Urle, god of prophecy. She concentrated on the prayer, each word important, each syllable a shield against the madness. "Urle, god of good dreams, god of favored prophecy, aid me, your child. A prophet cries to you for help. A prophet cries to you in great need. Hear me, Urle, god of the forge, hear me, and do not leave me desolate. Help your prophet child.'' Keleios recited the ancient prayer over and over until the hissing sighs became quiet screams.

''Hear us, prophet. You must obey. Look up at us and see true power. We who have gone before you command you to look up; look upon us.''

Keleios stumbled over the words; her tongue seemed to forget how to form them. It was an effort to remember, an effort to cover her eyes, an effort not to look up.

Keleios knew what it was: a phantasm, an eater of souls. They preyed upon dream prophets and were minions of the Grey Lady herself, goddess of evil dreams and treachery. They were attracted to dark prophecy like vultures to the newly dead.

The prayer to Urle had died on her lips. She could not think of it anymore. There was something that kept phantasms out of the tower. She knew what it was. She knew, but she could not think.

The sighing voices whispered, ''Prophet, prophet, look upon us. You cannot escape this place, and you cannot survive in this place. Look up and end your suffering.''

Keleios found herself rising to her knees, eyes still pressed shut. She spoke to it, ''No, no.'' She sat back down, hiding her eyes against her knees. It was said that one glance at a phantasm and sanity was snuffed like a candle, one's soul ripped away. So alien were they that only a glance was needed. Keleios fought not to give that glance.

How were the phantasms kept from the tower? She had known the answer only minutes before, but she could not think. Sorcery, something of sorcery, yes. A symbol of sorcery.

''Prophet, hear us. You cannot escape. You are ours. Do not torment yourself. Give up and you shall be free of all cares.''

Sorcery, a symbol, a symbol . . . of law. Phantasms are kept out by a symbol of law. Every apprentice dreamer knew that. The symbol of law was replaced every day, but someone had taken the symbol. Someone had opened the tower to the phantasm, and she was helpless.

"No." There had to be a way.

"Little prophet, aren't you tired yet? Don't you weary of this game?"

She screamed at it, voice breaking, "Shut up!"

"In dream you have power, but we are not a dream to be shaped and controlled. We are not prophecy to vanish when complete. We are your destiny. You are to join with us. You shall be power with us."

Power, that was it, power. She was a sorcerer now, and sorcery made the symbol of law. She didn't know how to wield the symbols of making yet. The symbols were high sorcery, beyond a journeyman, beyond Keleios, unless . . . unless it was like any other sorcery: Once she formed an image in her mind, knew its name, and was unafraid of it, then the power was hers. To hesitate was to be worse than dead. If she called it and couldn't control it, then she would die cleanly and cheat the soul-eater.

Without thinking more, she called it. She stood, eyes closed, hands out in front of her, the whispers gone distant, that neck-ruffling flash of power that was sorcery sweeping through her, but stronger until she could not breathe, waiting for power to level off, waiting for it to be controlled. The magic swelled until Keleios thought that her skin would burst with light and power.

The phantasm shrieked, "What is that, what is that? Dirty thing, filthy thing, take it away! Take it away!"

The radiance beat against her closed eyelids, forming red shadows. Her entire body tingled with the nearness of so powerful a sorcery. She drew a shaky breath and opened her eyes carefully, a slit at a time. The symbol hung just in front of her eyes, beautiful in its straight lines, its simplicity. She could see nothing else but the shining of it.

The phantasm called just beyond its glowing circle. "Prophet, prophet, hear me. Cast that thing aside. Join with us. Free yourself of that frail shell and become as one with us."

Keleios stared at the symbol of law, reading its power and understanding some of it, and she understood something that her teachers had not told her. They had said that no journeyman had the strength to call a symbol, but that was a lie. Any sorcerer could call them, but very few could deal with them. She had called the symbol to herself, but its power overwhelmed her. She was but an empty shell before it, waiting for its command. So quickly and so completely was she possessed that Keleios did not even have time to be afraid.

Keleios heard herself speak, but it was not her choice. "Here me, Methostos, third of three. By true name, by sorcery, word, will, and gesture, I cast you out. I close this tower to you."

The thing shrieked. Against the blaze of the magic she was blind; the symbol flared yet brighter, feeding off the phantasm's pain.

As the phantasm vanished in distant screams, the symbol of law left also, burning after images in her eyes. Keleios was blessed that the symbol of law was not a greedy rune. There were other symbols that would have kept what they had touched.

2

A Spell of Binding

Keleios woke instantly, staring up into the darkness, gasping for air. A scream, half-formed, died as she recognized her surroundings.

"Safe," she whispered, "safe, only a dream." Even as she said it, she knew better. The last had been very real. There was still something wrong. Her magic sense pulsed with the nearness of magic, and not her own. The tower room was bare of human magic. The thought came to her: if it wasn't in the room, there was one more place it could be.

Keleios pressed fingers to her chest and searched herself. A touch of magic was there, someone else's magic. There had been a spell tied to the phantasm like a tail on a kite. Fear slid down her spine like ice. Keleios had not known such a spell was possible. How could she protect herself against something she did not understand? Keleios forced herself to breathe past the fear.

"I am alive and sane. I conquered the phantasm. I am all right," Keleios whispered. She was not all right, and she knew it. The spell was dormant, but it was still there, and Keleios could not tell exactly what spell it was. She swallowed hard, and refused to be afraid. Fear would not help her now.

So there was a spell inside of her coiled like a snake, but she was alive and sane. She had her dream. Unlike most dreams this one would remain vivid, each retelling bringing the terror fresh and horrible. She had to tell someone. Already, the compulsion to share her prophecy was upon her. It would only grow worse.

She sat up in the narrow bed. The night breeze from the open window played coolly on her sweat-soaked body. The covers were drenched as if she had had fever in the night.

She swung her legs over the edge of the bed. Her feet dangled helplessly above the floor. There were good points and bad points to being half-elven. In most households she would have had no problem, but the Astranthians were a tall race.

Her clothes were wrinkled from the hours of sleep. Most dreamers wore gowns or bed shirts, but Keleios felt unprepared in nightclothes.

Most dream prophets strode the hallways, spouting prophecy to all who were near. Keleios appeared in rumpled men's clothing, quiet, waiting to tell only a select few. She was unimpressed with hysterical dreamers. Visionaries could sometimes be excused; the immediacy of vision was often too much even for the trained prophet. Visions did not stay with the prophet the way dreams did, but evaporated into wisps of sun-ruined fog. There was no excuse for lack of control in dreams.

She retrieved her boots from beside the bed and sat down to put them on. In another room was a five-year-old girl who dreamed. For such an age with such a talent there were excuses. Keleios frowned; there was something wrong. She should have been worried about Alys but couldn't think why.

She padded over the cool stone floor to the water-filled basin. She spoke, "Thanks be to Urle, god of prophecy, that I have pierced the veils once more and seen that which is to be, that which has been, and that which is now." She splashed the water on her face and arms. It fell in cool splendor down her chest. Keleios hesitated, feeling especially reluctant to finish the ritual tonight. "Thanks be to the Shadow Lady, god of evil dreams, that I have pierced the veils once more and seen that which is to be, that which has been, and that which is now." She splashed more water upon herself and added as she turned away, "Even the shadows deserve their duty."

It was an ancient phrase used without meaning or magic in the world. In the tower, magic is different. There was a quiet surge, as if the stones drew a breath. The air was suddenly cool. A pleasing dampness touched her skin as if of unseen fog. Her pulse pounded in her throat, and she couldn't breathe the cool air.

Something was here, something beside the stinging shadow of prophecy and long-cast spells, something powerful.

A woman's voice entered the silence, a deep rich alto, not unpleasant. "Thanks be to the prophet who worships the shadows still."

Keleios tried to say, "I don't," but she could not speak.

Warmth began to creep into the room, and the unnatural dampness stole away. The spells of the tower resumed with a rush, a surge, that she could hear with the inner ear of magic. Keleios leaned against the table, suddenly weak. It was not easy to be brushed by the minion of a god. Even a dethroned god had her power.

Keleios drew in careful breaths of the dry, warm air. The smell of jasmine was still strong through the window. She stood away from the table, afraid. Keleios shook as if with fever, her breath coming in gasps. The Lady's messenger had been preventing her from thinking, and it had not even been a spell, only will and power. Shadow messengers were not that uncommon in unprotected towers. Until the symbol of law was placed upon the tower, many things could come and go. She had to spread the alarm before more monsters came.

Alys had been in the tower with a phantasm loose. What chance did a five-year-old have? How many others had been in the tower when it came?

The dream struggled with her fear. It tried to force itself upon her. She had to waste time in calming herself, fighting for control of the dream. If she started prophesying now, she would be useless for a time. There was no time for weakness.

Keleios listened to her own breathing, concentrating on the simple flow of her own body. When she opened her eyes, she was no longer trembling. The dream was contained, for now.

She opened the outer door, but the dream struggled beneath the calm. It was a calm not of placid waters but of carved steel.

The outer chamber was dark; the dying embers of the fire glowed, popped, and flared. The flash of light shone on Selene's hair, crow-wing black, and Melandra's upturned face. Selene was a journeyman herbwitch and card prophet. Neither girl stirred at her entrance. The prophet keepers had changed, perhaps many times tonight. Keleios stopped just in front of a ward sprinkled in a semi-circle before her door. It would not let her pass. The wards protected the prophet keepers from surprises from the dreaming rooms. It allowed them to get some sleep without having to set watches. Sometimes a prophet came out temporarily mad, without aid of a phantasm. Once they had only had sound wards but a journeyman dreamer killed one of the keepers and a ward of enclosure was added.

The prophecy spoke to her sorcery, her magic, and it whispered, "Cross the barrier. We are powerful; we will not be harmed."

Keleios knew the feeling of invincibility was a delusion. The power offered was real enough. Her left hand itched and burned, it too felt the power of dream. The palm of her hand was safely covered by stiff leather, the thongs that held it in place traced a webbing across the back of her hand to encircle her wrist. It was a mark of power to some; to others, corruption; to Keleios, an unfortunate accident. The left hand reached for the ward. She clinched it into a fist and placed it rigid at her side. Most of the time she could ignore it, but after dreaming, all power was magnified. Though she had once held the rank of master dreamer, her control was strained and leaked round the edges. Tiny sparks of magic flitted through the room.

She called to them, trying to swallow past the building power. Sorcery was the worst for a dreamer to have for it was so much easier to have accidents. Melandra woke first, rolling onto her side and blinking into the near-dark. She clutched a knit shawl across the shoulders of her brown dress. She scrambled to her feet, thick golden-brown hair floating in disarray over her scarred face. She was only thirteen and still had baby fat to lose. Her face was an old face, broken and battered. She was a Calthuian, and they outlawed magic there. So there had been no healer to fix the damage her father and mother inflicted. They had tried to beat the evil magic out of her. Magic will come out one way or another. She was an enchanter and worked in flour, sugar, and spices.

Selene was awake, brown eyes searching the dark, as if this wasn't where she expected to be when she woke up. She stood tall for a Zairdian noble, and slender. The square-cut bodice of her dress was covered in white lace that formed a frill around her neck, traced by black velvet. The only skin that showed was face and hands.

Melandra was already kneeling by the ward, having sensed Keleios' haste, but paused and looked up at the older girl. "Was it the sign of ending, or of infinity that allows safe passage?"

"Could you really trace a symbol of infinity in such a small space? I don't think I could."

Melandra shook her head and mumbled, "No, I suppose not."

The symbol of ending traced through the reddish powder and made the warding neutral until the symbol was wiped away. Keleios stepped over the line, careful not to smudge it. A shudder ran down her spine.

Selene asked, "Are you all right?"

"No, there was a phantasm in the tower tonight."

Both girls gasped. Melandra said, "Keleios, how?"

"There's no time. Is anyone else in the tower besides myself?" She prayed that Alys had gone long ago.

"The child Alys is still here." Selene paled. "Oh, Keleios, do you think?"

"Melandra, go find a healer, preferably a white-robed."

The girl nodded and was gone, running down the stairs. A tic had begun just under Keleios' right eye, a sign of stress. The dream tugged at her to be gone; *no time,* it cried, *no time.* Her back rippled, and she covered her face with her hands. "I control my powers; they do not control me." When she felt steady once more, she put down her hands.

"Keleios, you are too full of dream tonight."

"If she isn't already gone, time is precious. Open the ward to me."

Selene did as she was told even though as a fellow journeyman she could have argued. Keleios stepped in front of the child's room and paused with her hand upon the doorknob. She gathered her will one last time. There was no way to tell what sort of power lurked in the room. The visit from the Shadow messenger was still vivid and close. Evil was abroad tonight, and if one spell could enter the tower, there could be others.

She pushed the door forward, fighting an urge to use magic on it. She was constantly urging the apprentice sorcerers not to use their power on trivialities like opening doors.

The room was as dark as her own had been. The furniture was the same. Almost lost in a full-size bed, a small figure tossed, crying out, one tiny hand flung upward as if avoiding a blow.

Keleios hurried to her side. The wavy froth of pale brown hair was plastered darkly to Alys' head. The child murmured words in her sleep, words she couldn't know, ancient phrases of great power. She was fighting with magic she did not yet possess, in a battle fought long ago.

The phantasm had not gotten her. Alys had hidden herself in one of the tower's dreams. It had taken great talent for that. Now she was trapped. The important question was: How long had she been like this? How long had she been fighting to break free? If it were too long, it could be fatal.

Keleios sat upon the bed and grabbed the flailing hands, her own delicate hands encircling the tiny fists. She spoke quietly at first. "Alys, Alys, can you hear me?"

The child whimpered and called out, "Keleios! Keleios, help me, save me!"

"Wake up, Alys, it is a dream. Awake!"

The child struggled, the effort showing on face and flowing in tension through her hands. She was trying, but something was holding her. It took only a moment to find the twist of spell on the child, not a full binding, not even active. It was not holding her to the dream yet, but it was there.

Where were all the Verm-cursed spells coming from?

Keleios dragged the child into her arms and shuddered, holding the girl to her. There was too much power tonight. She was going to have to use sorcery, but an awakening spell was simple enough. She calmed herself and held tightly to her straining power. Too much, and she would wake all the sleepers in the keep. "Awake, Awake!"

Alys moved fitfully in her sleep but did not obey.

"Loth's blood, I'm going to have to enter her mind."

The small body writhed in her arms as if trying to escape, but her struggles were not much. She was tired and losing the battle. If she should give up or die in the dream, unable to break it . . .

"Selene!"

The girl rushed through the door, questions ready, but there was no time.

"Sit on the bed." Selene did as she was told, staring at the thrashing form of the child. Keleios shoved the unresisting girl into Selene's arms. "Hold her tightly." Even as they watched, the struggles grew less. She was shivering, limbs twitching, skin cooling.

Selene said, "Keleios, you aren't going to enter her mind? It isn't your best spell."

"There is no time for anyone else to come. May Zardok guide my power this night, but we're out of time."

Keleios pressed her fingertips against Alys' skull. Sorcery came to her, neck-ruffling, stomach-tightening power. She concentrated and held back. Lightly, lightly, or you shatter the mind you probe.

She entered Alys' mind, the child's thoughts tumbling round but through all was fear. Keleios called quietly, "Alys, do you hear me?"

A soft sobbing came from far away. "Keleios, help me."

"Show me the dream, Alys."

A touch, a butterfly's wing of power, and she entered. The world was the chaos of battle, weapons ringing, magic blazing. Keleios knew this dream. It was the battle of Ohi-elle. The shorter blond natives fought mostly with weapons. The conquering Astranthians used both. A fireball threw the field into high relief, screams. It was twilight; the old gods would soon be released. She had to find Alys before that. She stood perfectly still, only her eyes searching for the child. As she didn't draw attention to herself, no one noticed her. Alys must have interfered somehow.

Then in the distance over a litter of bodies was a small shape in a white nightgown, valiantly defending herself with sorcerous powers that she never possessed outside of dream.

Keleios started forward slowly. She was a ghost that screaming figures fell through; she was mist until she chose to act. So she waited until she could be close enough to grab Alys.

Dusk fell and with it the scaled gods of the natives.

They rushed onto the battlefield, shrieking and throwing magic to match the invaders. A horned devil at least seven feet high approached Alys. The sword that he wielded shone magic to Keleios' eyes. She hurried forward, tripping on a body that hung spitted on a broken spear. Keleios paused, willing the panic to pass. If she lost control, she would be caught in the fighting and never reach the child in time. She went, carefully holding herself in. The creature approached the child faster. Keleios was almost there, just a few feet. She could clasp Alys to her and they would disappear to the sight of the dream beings. The sword the thing carried was powerful, shattering the bolts of energy Alys threw at it.

Keleios could almost reach out and touch her when the sword came crashing downward, and there was no time left.

The twist of spell inside Keleios flared to life. Real, it said; pain, it said. If she hesitated, Alys would die; if she went forward, they might both die, or not. Keleios took the 'or not' and flung herself forward, suddenly appearing to the demon. The blow was heavy and he couldn't change course. Though it was only a dream, Keleios screamed as the blade broke her collarbone. The spell forced her to stay for the pain. She screamed and lashed outward with power. She released a burst to the thread that bound her to this dream as surely as it bound Alys. As she lay there, impossibly still alive in the dream, she saw the grey threads going up into the sky. "I am not bleeding," she told herself. "This is only a dream." Her heart pumped frantically, wounded by the sword. Shrill piercing screams came from just behind her. Alys of course, poor child. Keleios drew power, all that she could find. Reaching outward and inward, she blasted the threads. The threads in the sky shriveled as with fire. The dream broke.

Keleios knew darkness for a time, the sort her night vision did not touch. Velvety soft it was, and comforting. Tired, she was tired, but something nagged at her, pulled at her. Magic seeping through her mind, someone else's magic. She lashed out at the touch, and it broke abruptly. There were other things to do besides floating in the dark. Alys had to be found and helped. Yes, helped. "Help me, Keleios, help me." And there was the dream, that urgent awful dream that needed telling.

Keleios opened her eyes to look at Bertog, the journeyman healer. There was a tightness about her blue eyes and Keleios knew where that second burst of magic had come from. The healer had used a deep probe to waken her, and Keleios had harmed Bertog. She tried to speak, but a hoarse rasp was all that would come.

Bertog spoke carefully, hurting. "Don't try to talk or move, Journeyman Keleios. You are now out of immediate danger, and Selene has gone to fetch a full healer."

Keleios made a protesting sound.

The girl sat very stiff, every inch an Astranthian noble. The yellow silk of her dress was almost the same color as her hair. "I met Selene in the hall. I came up to see what I could do."

Keleios reached up to grab the healer's flowing sleeve, but her hand would not do it. There was a fading pain from her left shoulder to the middle of her back. It was an angle of dull throbbing.

Bertog went on as if reluctant to have Keleios speak. "Alys is fine. She is asleep, a deep exhausted one. I have studied dream sickness thoroughly. She will sleep for hours, not dreaming, except the dreams that normal little girls have."

Keleios had her voice. "Correct." She coughed to clear the hoarseness from it and tried to remember why she couldn't speak easily. A glint of silver as the sword descended—yes, it had been something of a neck cut. Throat wounds sometimes affected the speech. She remembered the threads tying them to the dream.

Having come so near death, Keleios would have

spoken to Bertog about the spells and the phantasm, but she distrusted the healer. The healer's vows prevented her from harming anyone, but she could still bear secrets. For a white healer the girl spent entirely too much time associating with the followers of Mother Bane. The door swung inward.

Jodda, in the shapeless white robe of a full healer, came, and a breath of healing came with her. Her black hair was a rich length against the snowy cloth. Her blue eyes were concerned, her face professionally blank but pleasant. Behind her was Belor the Dreammaker.

His blue eyes were clouded with sleep or magic. He was short, broad-shouldered, yellow-haired. A firm, square jaw saved his face from being soft and boyish. He wore a pair of baggy trousers stuffed into over-the-knee boots. A blue tunic gaped open and beltless over his bare chest. The tunic and trousers did not match. Belor's illusions were the envy of the rest. Even the school's High-master illusionist was learning from them.

Only Belor and Keleios suspected the source of his gift: demonmark, demon magic that flowed through their veins. As her hand behind its leather prison, so with his inborn magic—contaminated.

His eyes searched hers now, and a glance was enough between them. She was all right. His fear lessened.

Melandra came last, quietly, head hung low so her hair would hide her face. She had a girl's crush on Belor, but she thought herself hideous and so was awkward in the role.

Jodda traced a red line from Keleios' left shoulder near the neck, to disappear into the cloth of the tunic she wore. "You got this in a dream?"

Keleios managed a yes.

The healer's face cleared, becoming clean of all emotion. Jodda spread her hands, palms down, at the beginning and the end of the wound. Warmth spread from her hands to Keleios, then Jodda began to jerk and thrash, never loosing contact with the body of her patient. A breath-stealing scream reverberated through the tower room, and a crimson slash spread slowly across the white robe. The throbbing pain left Keleios. Jodda drew back to sit cross-legged in deep meditation. Only for severe wounds did a white healer need trance afterwards. Keleios wondered how bad the internal damage had been, or if it were more a wound of the soul.

"Someday, I will do that," Bertog said quietly.

Keleios looked at the girl in her fashionable silk dress. The sleeves were tapered and flowing nearly to the floor. Jewels decorated the belt that wrapped her waist. The yellow hair was coiled and wrapped by gold thread. Many of the journeyman healers copied their masters and wore shapeless robes of pale blue. When they became full healers, blue would be exchanged for white. Bertog would not look nearly as fetching in the baggy healer's robes. Keleios smiled; it was a cheering thought.

Belor knelt on the other side of Keleios. "What went wrong?"

She spoke softly for his ears alone. "A phantasm and a spell of binding."

His whisper was a hiss of shock. "Phantasm—but how? And a spell in the tower, how?" She struggled up on her elbows; Belor moved to help.

"I'm all right." She could see Alys now, curled against the far wall. "Someone here opened the tower. The symbol of law is no longer protecting this tower. It must be replaced before other monsters come in."

Jodda shooed Belor away and began exploring her patient with firm professional hands.

Keleios called Melandra to her. "Melandra, I need a favor."

"Of course." She knelt close, keeping her thick hair like a veil on the side near Belor.

Jodda told her, "Please stop talking so I can examine you."

"Jodda, the tower has to be closed to the night seekers. I think all the sorcerers below journeyman should be checked. Let me send Melandra to waken the dorm mother and father and alert one of the master sorcerers so they can close the tower. I will be quiet after that.''

''The tower being opened I understand, but what is wrong with the sorcerers?'' Jodda asked.

''When I was trying to free Alys, after I was hurt, I reached outward for power. I fear that I used the power of at least one other sorcerer without their consent.''

Bertog said, ''That is evil sorcery.''

''It was not done on purpose, but out of lack of control.''

Jodda said, ''Very well. Bertog, go with the apprentice in case there is need of healing.''

''No,'' Keleios said. ''I hurt her accidentally when she entered my mind to heal.''

''Come here, Bertog.'' The girl stepped forward hesitantly. Jodda touched her body and closed her eyes for a moment. ''You certainly did. Go to your room and rest; heal thyself. Melandra, get Feldspar the healer. Do you know him on sight?'' The girl nodded. ''Good. Now go.''

The girl bowed to Master Jodda and ran out. Selene entered breathlessly. ''Healer, we need you downstairs.''

''What is it this time?''

''Master Fidelis—she was found unconscious. Apparently, something went wrong in the middle of a spell.''

Jodda rose. ''I am not through with you, Keleios, so rest.'' She turned warning eyes to Belor. ''I am charging you with seeing that she rests and does herself no more injury tonight.''

He half-bowed. ''As you say, healer.''

''I can't rest yet, Jodda. My prophecy cannot wait until tomorrow.''

Jodda's eyes were angry, almost black. ''Why do I heal you? You abuse yourself constantly. Go prophesy, but I will not heal you if you collapse tonight. It will do you good to be bedridden for a day or two.''

She turned with a swish of skirts and scooped up Alys. ''The child's injury is one of the mind and will take longer. She will likely sleep tomorrow away, or rather today.''

Keleios said quietly, ''I had to enter her mind to free her from the dream. Did I harm her? When I fought to free us, I was still inside her mind, calling on sorcery.''

''She is injured, Keleios, but she will heal. You did no permanent damage. You saved her life. If she had died while in dream, the tower would have taken her soul. There would have been no chance of resurrection.''

''You will come get me when she wakens.''

She hesitated, then nodded. ''Yes, I will come get you. Alys will probably need to see you, alive and whole. Try to stay that way until she wakens.''

Keleios smiled. ''I'll do my best.''

Jodda departed, her skirts whispering on the stones. The light from the single lamp flickered in a breeze that began inside the room. Keleios spoke quietly so her voice would not echo in the room. ''How did you come to be here?''

''The sound of running woke me. Selene told me only that you had been hurt and were in the tower,'' Belor said.

''So you came to rescue me.''

''To guard your back. You'd do the same for me.''

''True.'' She stood, feeling a lingering stiffness that would pass. The shadows seemed to thicken. The lamp's flame streamed in the growing wind.

Belor searched the room uneasily. ''What is that?''

''Wind. Let us leave the tower to itself.'' Keleios picked up her pouch from its spot near the wall. She slipped the throwing daggers into their sheaths. The golden bracers slipped on her forearms; the strength spell glimmered through them. She felt better already.

The ring of protection was last. She tied the leather pouch to her belt.

She walked through the door and he followed.

"What about the lamp?" As he asked, the flame vanished, giving the room to the dark. He stood a moment with the wind ruffling his hair until Keleios laid a hand on his arm and drew him out.

The fire in the outer room had faded to a sullen blue glow.

He asked again, "What is that?"

She walked towards the stairs. "The tower wishes to be left alone, Belor. Let us give it what it wants."

He followed with many backward glances. She stood impatiently, watching him back up. The hilt of his long sword peeked through hair and tunic collar. He had fastened it bare across his chest and waist.

"Belor, we must leave now."

He came to her, and they entered the close walls of the stairway. Its small narrow steps and too-close walls seemed worse tonight. They pressed with a great weight that Keleios had never noticed before.

"You could have dressed before you strapped on your sword, Belor."

"Oriona is lucky I threw on pants, boots, and tunic." He continued in a near perfect imitation of the girl's dorm keeper. "You be running around half-naked to the world, in front of my girls."

Keleios laughed. "You've been practicing."

The stones caught their laughter and intensified it until the narrow stair seemed to be laughing back. Belor's grin faded. He shrugged. "News of you hurt means little time to dress and the need of a sword."

"Your sword could not have helped me tonight, Belor."

The stair continued its winding without aid of walls. The air seemed cooler and welcome. "But Luckweaver could have helped you."

"Enchanted items are not allowed in the tower." The tower's shell ended in four archways leading to the points of the earth. Through each arch the library's books glimmered, jewels spilled in the darkness.

Keleios found herself drawn to the books. She wanted to caress each glowing binding and each dark one, too. But even the nonmagic books deserved to be saved; the three-volume herbal, though not magic itself, was one of a kind. "So much knowledge, and it must burn."

"Keleios, what do you mean, 'It must burn'?"

She turned to him in the dark and continued talking as if their first conversation had not stopped. "I know you are concerned. But a phantasm cannot be fought with a sword."

Keleios walked through the south arch. Belor followed. "Do you have any idea of whose magic it was?"

"The spell of binding was herb-witchery. And it was powerful. Only two people in this keep could do it: Poula and Fidelis. Poula would not do it, but Fidelis would. She worships Mother Bane and the Shadow Lady. But I have no proof to take before council."

"There are other ways to handle such things."

"Why, Belor, you've gone bloodthirsty on me."

He grinned. "I've been around you too many years. You've taken a law-abiding illusionist and made him into a warrior." His smile faded. "I don't believe in killing when there are other answers. But Fidelis has no scruples. Waiting for proof to take before council could get you killed. Keleios, you aren't listening to me. Why are you are touching the books?"

She turned, surprised. "I am, aren't I? Belor, if there is anything in here you value, take it, save it."

"From what?"

"My prophecy."

"Keleios?"

She laughed. She felt so strange, exhilarated, as if dream and vision were combining, yet she was conscious. "No, Belor, I am not in trance, but my dream will not leave me tonight. The keep will fall, and everything in it be lost. The strength of the prophecy is tugging at me tonight.'' She took the black pouch off her belt and opened it. It too shimmered softly to the enchanter's eye. She dumped out the spell paraphernalia. *Enchantments Incredible* vanished into it, as did the three-volume herbal. She paused at *The Great Book,* her fingers tracing its runes. ''No, you must remain, but you will not burn. Relic that you will be, it is not my hand that will save you.''

She chose a thick volume of peasant folktales, the only one of its kind for Astranthian peasants. Much of the culture that had bred them was now gone. ''If you could choose only one book to save, what would it be?''

It was so hopeless, so very many books and so little room or time. Belor chose the *Book of Illusions*; it pulsed pink-white under his arm. As befit a book of that name it appeared to change in size and color, even texture—one minute fine leather, the next coarse leaves. He handed it to her without a word, and she stuffed it into the impossibly small opening.

''How do you know which books to take?''

''I see them through a film of flame. The ones I take do not burn. And there is a feeling of rightness.'' She shivered. ''I must speak soon; the dream builds.'' She turned abruptly, and he followed. ''No, Belor, I need to finish this walk alone.''

''Why?''

''Don't question me!'' The prophetic vision swirled before her eyes. The library was afire; smoke formed a haze that rose toward the ceiling, explosions as the magic books caught and burned. A vision snatching her down. Keleios screamed at him over the roaring in her ears, ''Get out! Get out! Leave me!''

He would not go. She drove him back with flame and fear, her vision nearly complete. She could not guarantee his safety once she was taken. When he was safely away, Keleios gave herself to the vision. Impossibly, a thin strand of spell wrapped round her, like an anchoring rope.

There was no time to fight it; the immediacy of the vision was too real.

Flames licked up the walls, the books crumpling, flaring, the shelves blackening. She stood in the burning rubble, which was not there, and screamed, "Fire!"

Embers were like stinging wasps on her hair and skin. She shrieked, "Burning, burning!" until her throat went dry.

A voice called to her through the flames, a voice shouting her name.

3

Prophecy

"Keleios, Keleios!"

The smoke-hazed air clogged her throat. She huddled on the floor, letting the smoke rise to the ceiling, trying to breathe. Pieces of the floor erupted in flame. Shelves crashed, crumpling in flames to meet the floor.

The voice called urgently, "Keleios, hear me!"

The heat seared her skin, too near. Her eyes teared, and breath was agony.

A cool wind brushed her cheek, a slim white hand reaching out to her. She grasped the hand as the roof groaned and began to bend fire-eaten beams to the floor.

Cool thoughts came to her. "Not real, it is not real. Vision cannot harm you. You are safe."

Keleios stood in the fire and did not burn. A vision—now she remembered. This had not come to pass yet and could not truly harm.

The spectacle began to fade. The fire was a dim orange mist. A last wisp of acrid smoke, a flash of burning, and it was gone.

Keleios found herself lying in the dark; strong arms pinned her against a cloth-covered chest. The cloth was silk and black as darkness. Only one person in the entire keep would be so blatant as to wear the color of Loth, god of bloodshed: Lothor. Lothor the Black Healer. Keleios wanted to move away from his touch, but she shivered in reaction to vision, so cold. She was so tired, and yet the dream remained. She could not afford another vision like that.

She struggled away from the restraining arms, still

shaking. Keleios crawled to the end of the shelf row; she didn't have strength to go further. Her arms encircled her knees in an effort to stop shivering. A flexing of right arm and left calf showed that both daggers were still in place. A red witchlight sprang to life over the man's shoulder and cast his high-boned face in crimson relief.

"Don't you ever sleep, Lothor?" she asked.

"Not often," he said without a trace of a smile. "When you can walk, I will help you to your destination."

Keleios opened her mouth, ready to say, "But I don't need help." Truth was truth, but why did it have to be him? "It was you calling me. How did you know what to do? I thought prophecy was rare in Lolth."

"My brother was a visionary. I am accustomed to assassination attempts in Lolth, but not here in Zeln's school."

"What do you mean assassination attempt?"

He made a sharp sound, half-laugh, half-snort. "Still don't trust me? Well, Keleios, someone put a binding spell on you, and I had to break it to free you from your vision. If it had been I that wanted you dead, I could have stood and watched."

Keleios leaned against the books and closed her eyes for a moment. "Thank you for saving me."

"It was my . . . pleasure." And the last word rolled off his tongue full of obscene suggestion.

She opened her eyes and stared at him. He came closer; the red witchlight gave fiery highlights to the fur at his throat.

"Why do you do that?"

"Do what?" His face didn't achieve innocence, but he looked puzzled.

Keleios shook her head. "It doesn't matter." She stood, forcing herself not to cling to the shelves. "I believe we can go now."

He made no protest, did not try to question her further. He knew the sound in her voice and it meant that the subject had been changed. It irritated her that Lothor could read her so well.

He had spent the last three months learning about her. He had questioned everyone who would talk to him and had made every effort to court her properly. Keleios wished him gone.

She staggered, and he caught her, his arm like iron under her hand. Keleios looked up at him. He was impossibly tall for a Varellian, but then he was half-human. Under the dark silk of a black healer prince were broad shoulders and a body too slender for a human of the same height and girth. Black fur edged his collar and decorated the hem of his jerkin, which fell just above his knees. The only color was the glimpse of red on red-patterned silk that told the color of his doublet, hidden under all that blackness. His hair fell straight and thick, baby fine, past his shoulders. It was the color of fresh-fallen snow. His skin was frost, and his eyes were the silver of old ice in the winter sun. He was an ice elf stretched out of shape, but still showing why they were considered one of the most beautiful of races.

Of course, the word *elf* was an insult to a Varellian. Keleios had never understood why, but the white elves considered themselves better than that. Calling a Varellian an elf to his or her face could get a person killed. Lothor knew nothing of being a Varellian. He would not know *ice elf* was an insult. Blood alone didn't make one an elf of any kind.

She looked down and felt a blush creep up her face. She had been staring at him.

He laughed, a rich throaty sound that threw his pale face into friendly lines. Keleios tried to pull away but he held her and said, "I am sorry, but it is so seldom that you show interest. For weeks I have waited. Your favorite color is green. Your best sorceries are those dealing with fire and cold. Even though you can do many things with a flexing of mind, you prefer to use herb-witchery. You like the slow building of power. You feel more in control that way." His arms wrapped across her back, and she glared at him. "I have studied you like a rare book. I know you, but you ignore me. Tonight you felt the drawing of my body as I feel yours."

Anger lent her strength, and she pulled away from him, enchanted might against enchanted might. "What do you want, black healer?"

"You, to be my wife."

"I am not ready to give you an answer."

His silver eyes traced her body, and he said, "You should decide soon." He stepped close and stared down at her. "Royal marriages are so often a matter of borders, especially when the two countries in question . . . touch."

"Don't threaten me, or pressure me." She swayed, putting a hand in front of her face. The power was back, nagging, tricking. She smiled at him, unpleasantly, and reached a hand to caress his face.

The touch of the leather glove made him jump back. Fear showed for a moment. Then a sickly smile crossed his lips. "You wouldn't dare."

"Tonight, Lothor, I might." She walked past him and scooped up her enchanted pouch from where it had fallen.

"I have something for that pouch of yours."

Keleios turned reluctantly. He held out a thick black book. It was surrounded by dark flames. The first creepings of returned power strengthened at the sight of that book.

"Do you make a habit of overhearing other people's conversations?"

"Yes." He smiled and extended his arm. His fingers were like white roots against the black covers, as if when she reached to take it, the hand would come with it like a parasite, drawing strength.

He stood patiently as if he could stand offering her evil forever. The red glow of his sorcery turned his white hair to blood, and she touched the dagger in its arm sheath for reassurance.

She went to him.

Her hand closed on the binding, and it sent a shock through the leather glove, a burning over the mark on her palm. She knew this book, or one like it. A pale shadow of it had resided on the Grey Isle. Six years ago that slim copy, a bare handful of this book's worth, had been used against Belor and her. It had conjured demons and opened the way to the pit. Harque the Witch had valued it above all other powers. Yet, her prophecy told her this one must be guarded. Those who come after could do great harm with it. The enchanted pouch quenched the black flames, and the book slid from sight. The burning in her hand did not stop, and she rubbed it against her leg. She had a strong desire to uncover her hand and rub the pain. There was a need to feel cool air on it. There was a great sense of rightness to her taking the book, but it was dangerous. It was peril in a way she could not define.

As if aware of the dark volume passing through her hands a cry came from nearby. "Keleios!"

She stepped from between the shelves, and she could feel Lothor following close behind. A circle of flame licked and wavered, casting orange shadows on the shelves. Glimpsed between the flames was Belor. Her last thoughts had been to keep him safe, but the flames had been so close. He was imprisoned, but not harmed, safe from her vision, but trapped.

Lothor spoke quietly. "He doesn't look happy."

"The vision came without proper warning. I was afraid I would harm him by accident."

"I suppose he's safe enough, but he isn't going to be pleased with you."

A shiver ran up her spine, and her left hand demanded attention. "He isn't happy, but if I free him now, he'll ask questions, waste time with concern and answers, and apologies." There wasn't time for all that, and Keleios turned and walked down the main aisle. Belor did not yell after her; perhaps he could not see through the flames.

Lothor followed witchlight bobbing ahead of them like a bloated will o' wisp.

When they stood in the open hallway, she turned to him. "I thank you for your help, but I am feeling much better now. My destination lies only a few steps away."

"I am not so easily dismissed. You are still weak. I will see you through the door."

"I do not need your protection, Prince Lothor."

"But I have already protected all your prophecies tonight."

"All my prophecies?"

"I was prophet keeper tonight."

Anger and something close to fear flashed through her. "You do not belong to this school. You are only a guest, albeit a long-staying one."

He smiled, and his silver eyes glittered. "I have been here so long, I have been granted privileges."

The power was returning. Her skin crawled with it, and a tic began in her left cheek. She wanted to be rid of him and his cursed question. So easy—just say it was accidental, too much power and one veiled insult too many. Keleios shook her head to clear such thoughts away. It was the sorcery talking; it wanted use. The dream was urgent, and something had to give soon.

She clenched her fists and spoke carefully. "Are you here merely to torment or is there a purpose to it?"

"I have had but one purpose since I arrived." He moved beside her smoothly, with a fencer's grace. His silver eyes met hers, and she would not look away. "Will you marry me?"

"I have told you many times that you must be patient."

"I have been patient. I believe that you would answer no if I were not a prince and heir to a throne. It is not polite to refuse a prince hurriedly." Anger showed on his face. His whiteness flushed slightly, eyes sparking.

"If you believe that is your answer, then go, leave me in peace." She turned from him.

He called after her, "You will not be rid of me that easily, Keleios Nightseer."

She stopped, trying to breathe through the power. It choked her, demanding to be freed. He would choose to use a demon-got name, reminding her that he had ties with them, too. She dared not move, only breathe in and out.

He stepped round her and brought her left hand upward. His angry eyes watched hers, saw the struggle in them. He turned it palm upward and kissed the leather glove softly. "My poor little enchanter, half-good and half-bad, how confusing."

"Lothor, please."

"We could end it now. Fight, and you would be rid of me."

She stared at him, the magic pulsing close. "You would give me such a way out?"

"I, yes; my father who sent me, no." He touched her shoulder, and an answering sorcery welled in his fingers. "I would spare us both an unhappy marriage if I were allowed to." His hand fell to his side. "But I am not my master."

"Everyone should be their own master at least part of the time, Lothor." She walked around him, breathing carefully through the magic that threatened to spill over. Tiny bits of magic flitted through the hallway.

She stood in front of Master Poula's door, but before she could speak, a voice called, "Come in, dear."

Keleios pushed the door inward with magic and stepped into the dark room like a storm about to break.

The room was as dark as the tower had been. Rushes squeaked underfoot, each step pressing the strewing herbs to fragrance. The pine scent of rosemary, spearmint, peppermint, and some fruit mint, perhaps apple, filled the air. Mint and rosemary were old favorites of Master Poula's. The smells calmed Keleios. No lights and the soothing spell upon the floor showed Poula had been prepared for a dream-heavy Keleios. She too was a prophet, if only of cards.

The master sat very still at a small round table. It was formed of ash and dark with polish. It was mildly enchanted to strengthen her card prophecies and her healing teas. She wore a loose belted robe that Keleios had seen before. It was deep forest green with white edging it round. Herbs were embroidered on the white border, but there was nothing of magic in it, not even for an herb-witch. It was just a pretty robe.

In the gloom Poula's face bore terrible scars: one eye nearly shut with scar tissue, the other an empty blackness. Her long brown hair, turning grey, was unbound. The smooth blank mask that she usually wore lay beside her on the table. Keleios was privileged to be one of a handful who ever saw her unmasked.

She was blind, but through the enchanted necklace that she wore objects were outlined with color like auras. It was a singular joy to Poula that Keleios did not need lights. Even though it did not hide her scars from the half-elven, Poula was more comfortable in the dark.

Once, a much younger Keleios had asked how she came to have those scars. It was of endless debate among the apprentices and journeymen, of what she hid and why, and how. Poula looked past the child and seemed to be looking at other things, then said, "Once I was young and foolish. I was challenged by a sorceress and I met her in the arena. I could have killed her. She lay at my feet and could not move but I worshipped Mother Blessen and gave mercy." She turned her blind eyes to Keleios and said, "But she was evil, and because I left her alive, she did this to me."

As far as Keleios knew, she was the only apprentice to be honored with the story, and she told no one. It was this story that had given Keleios the courage, or the fear, to kill in the arena. Two challenges, two deaths, both as a journeyman. No one had challenged her since she returned from her quest and became a master. There had been one challenge after she was stripped of her master's rank, but official rank or not, she had been a master, and the sorcerer had died.

"Come in, child. I have a cup of tea ready for you."

"Master Poula, I have come to prophesy."

"I am aware of that. The tea will help you control your powers. Bits of magic, like colored fireflies, dance round you. Drink, then prophesy."

Keleios held out her hand; the cup and saucer flew to her. The movement was too fast, and the amber-green liquid spilled over the rim. "Loth's blood, can I do nothing right tonight?"

"Be eased, child; the tea will remove the last lingering touches of the spell that nearly killed you twice tonight."

The cup was delicate white with sprigs of blue lavender painted on its side. Its curved handle fit her fingers nicely, small. She took a deep breath of the tea's steam. Peppermint, so strong that it made one think of summer and fresh-crushed leaves. The fruity fragrance of camomile, like faint summer apples. Keleios raised the gilt edge to her mouth and sipped the liquid. It was hot, but not scalding, and it carried magic. There was the faint sweetness of lavender flowers, the familiar fragrant valerian root, fennel, and milfoil. Keleios knew the spell well. Each draught hardened her calm; each drop chased back one of the flitting spells. When it was finished, she levitated it carefully back to the table and sat it next to the small round teapot.

"Do you feel better?"

"Much, thank you, master."

She chuckled. "That's what I'm here for." She settled back in her chair and did not offer one to Keleios—she knew better. "Well, child, tell your dream."

Keleios stood and stared at the darkened walls. Deep breaths for control, channel the power, and she touched the steel calm that held the dream back. The steel split, and the dream came free like a butterfly winter long imprisoned.

"And the dream ended." She blinked, slumping and

drawing in a deep shuddering breath. When she looked up, Poula still sat unmoved. "Master, what are we to do?"

"Come, child, sit and have a second cup of tea while we think."

Keleios sat gratefully. If it were not for the spell in the tea, she would be good only for sleep now. She poured a second cup and asked, "Poula?"

"No, thank you, the spell is all for you." The herb-witch sat very still and said, "You are prophet; this message was yours. What do you say about it?"

Keleios took a sip of tea and spoke carefully. "It is frightfully clear, Poula. The great blackness, whether a hole or a window, is my symbol for death. I am sure of one death: Feltan's."

"I sorrow with you, Keleios. Will you tell him?"

"How do you tell an eight-year-old boy that you have seen his death?"

"Then you won't tell him?"

"I don't know yet. I brought him here to the school so he could train. He had already attracted a familiar. You know how rare that is in an untrained herb-witch."

Poula nodded. "He has great potential."

"I brought him here, perhaps to his death."

"You cannot think that way."

Keleios stared at the tabletop. "But I do think that way."

"I cannot offer you comfort, Keleios. I have seen death in the cards before. It is not an easy or simple thing to know what to do with the knowledge."

Keleios nodded and sipped her tea, thinking.

"And the rest of the dream?" Poula asked.

Keleios took a deep breath and let it out slowly. "The keep walls will be breached. Whether by magic or force of arms, I am not sure. Fidelis the Witch will aid the treachery that allows us to fall. As she aided it tonight."

Poula stared at her and said nothing.

Keleios said, "You know as well as I that it had to

be Fidelis. No other herb-witch in the school could have done such a spell. Except for you, of course.''

"You have never liked Fidelis."

Keleios wasn't sure that it was a question, but she answered it. "No, I don't approve of black magic. I believe there are some spells that are not meant to be used."

"Then why are they in the tomes? Someone had to create them."

"I know, I know. It is the same old argument."

'You and she have shared a room for over two years."

"And I appreciate you fighting for me. It would have been worse somehow to go back to the journeymen dorms."

"I knew it would be." Poula paused, blind eyes staring at her own folded hands. "Has it occurred to you that the binding spell might have been a personal attempt on your life."

"No, I believe it was to keep the prophecy a secret."

"And the phantasm's purpose?"

"The same . . . to keep the news of the keep's impending doom secret."

"Do you really think that Alys could have hidden from a phantasm?"

"She must have!"

"Not if a spell of binding was placed on her first. It would have tied her to the first dream that came along."

"But to what purpose?"

"Keleios."

"So I would save her? But that makes no sense. Surely the phantasm would finish off most prophets."

"Yes, but you are here, alive, sane. And you closed the tower to the phantasm—no easy feat."

"You're saying that tonight was meant for me, the only sorcerous dreamer in the keep, the only one with a chance of escaping the phantasm."

"Yes, my dear."

"So Fidelis planned to kill me and keep the dream secret one way or another. Even if it meant killing Alys in the process."

"Perhaps there was another reason for her to make sure of your death."

"What do you know that I don't?"

"She worships Mother Bane, Keleios, and it would not be against her vows to kill you. Especially if it were her questing debt."

"Her questing debt? Who would waste their questing task on my death?"

"Fidelis quested with Harque the Witch."

Keleios slumped back in her chair and just stared. "How could Zeln and you have allowed that? Harque is mad, a danger, and you sent a journeyman to quest with her."

"Fidelis requested it. And Harque was herb-witch, shadow priest, and prophet. It is a rare combination, and it matched Fidelis."

"Fidelis is also an illusionist."

"Be reasonable, Keleios. Perfect matches are hard to find."

Harque—the name took her back to being five years old and to her mother's murder. "She haunts me like some spectre. I had my old nightmare tonight, with her chasing me through the halls."

"Do you still hold to the vow you made so long ago?"

"Yes, Poula." She smiled, and her brown-gold eyes darkened as she spoke. "We must all have goals. My first was to be a full journeyman. My second was to kill Harque. I accomplished the first and failed the second, six years ago."

"Both you and Belor nearly died in that attempt."

Keleios waved it away as if of no importance. "Belor knew as well as I what we attempted; we took our chances." She turned nearly black eyes to Poula. "Belor wanted to feed her to the pit as she had done to us."

"But you said no. Why?"

"I want to watch the light die in her eyes the way it died in my mother's eyes. Do you know that the only recognizable part, at the end, were her eyes? My mother's brown eyes, lost in a face that was decaying away. The running sores had become bloated, splitting flesh; she was eaten alive. And for eighteen years Harque has taunted my nightmares. 'Where is the fair Elwine the Gentle? Where did she go?' and that insane laughter." Keleios shook her head and sat up very straight. Her hands gripped the chair arms, and the wood began to protest. Keleios stopped herself and gripped her hands together in her lap. "I will see her die at my hand."

Poula asked quietly, "The same way your mother died?"

Keleios flexed her left hand, touching leather glove to her cheek. "No, I've thought about it, but no. Steel would be a preference."

"Hatred is self-destructive."

"Yes, but someone needs to destroy her. She was crazier six years ago than eighteen years ago. Harque must be stopped. I see no reason why I can't be the one to stop her."

"And you wonder why she wants your death from a safe distance."

"Poula, we escaped with demon aid and luck. The gods were with us. She could have killed us easily and quickly days before. Why should she fear me enough to waste her questing task on me? For that matter, why not challenge me to the arena?"

Poula sighed. "I don't know, child. Perhaps it was losing to your mother all those years ago that frightened her. Or your escaping from the pit with that mark on you."

Keleios stared at the hand, rubbing it behind the leather.

"Perhaps she fears ending as Elwine did."

"That I can believe. She has always feared her own methods of punishment. Harque sent us down in the pit to die, but we surfaced and gained power, of a sort.

Power that she was too terrified to try." Keleios searched the herb-witch's face carefully. "Poula, why did you put Fidelis and me in the same room?"

She gave a rich throaty laugh, and Keleios always imagined the face that went with that laugh. It was young and full with sparkling eyes, and desirable, and gone. "Child, it was the only open room. We meant to change it when the next teacher left, but you did not complain, nor did she."

"That's why you questioned me off and on about how we got along?"

"Yes, we did not know Fidelis meant you harm. And who else would we put with her, evil that she is? Jodda, a white healer, no. Allanna, she refused to be housed with a commoner. But you, you would keep her in her place and"—Poula hesitated and then continued softly—"and being already demon marked, evil was not unknown to you."

"But now she's trying to kill me."

"I believe so."

"Should I challenge her to the arena, get it out in the open?"

"No, don't challenge her."

"Why not?"

The blind eyes stared at her. "Because I fear for you. Fidelis knows your reputation and has even seen you fight. She is illusionist and one of the most powerful herb-witches I have ever trained."

"You expect me to go back to my room, knowing she may try to kill me again."

Poula nodded. "We need proof to take before council."

Keleios said nothing, but all knew that Poula was sand-shy. She was like Zeln. She preferred to work out problems in the legal system rather than on the sands of the arena. If they and some others had their way, the challenge system would be abolished, and murder would be murder.

"Guard yourself well, though."

"Without letting her catch on."

"Preferably."

"There is an old warding on my bed, from practice sorceries. I'll activate it. If anyone disrupts my sleep, it will shriek to wake the dead. If Fidelis asks, I'll tell her I was curious to see if it was still working."

"Your sorcerous wards are unusually long lived, perhaps because you are also an enchanter."

Keleios shrugged. "I don't question it. I just use it." She sipped the cooling tea. "I would invoke prophet's right and have the wards up. Seal the keep off for three days, and the danger will be passed."

"And?"

"And I had a vision in the library. The books were burning, except for ones I saved. I believe this school, this keep, will burn." Keleios held the thin china cup in her hands as if it had no handle and stared at the tea, breathing in the fumes of strength and calm.

Poula said, "I will contact one of the master sorcerers and have her raise the shielding. Now what else can we do to protect the school?"

"Send for Master Zeln and the rest. Alert Carrick to double the watch. Have someone watch Fidelis. I believe she is the key." Keleios spread her hands on the tabletop. "But none of it may help. In fact it may harm."

Poula nodded.

That was the crux of prophecy of any kind. What one saw was valid for the future but would one's actions prevent it or cause it? "Right or wrong, Poula, we must do something."

"Agreed. I will alert Zeln and the others using the communications tower. No other magic messages are allowed into Nesbit's castle."

Keleios laughed. "The High Councilman of Astrantha is very afraid of assassination and plotting behind his back."

"Is he still with your sister Methia?" Poula asked.

Keleios flinched and could not hide it. "He no longer visits my sister or their child."

"Did he truly challenge you to the sands?"

Keleios nodded. "On the day I leave this school as a master sorcerer, he plans to kill me."

"What did you do to him, Keleios?"

She stared at Poula. "I, what did I do to him? Poula, he treated my sister worse than the lowest whore."

"Did you bring this to his attention, my hot-tempered journeyman?"

Keleios almost smiled. "Yes. I shoved a knife between his ribs during one of those silly Meltaanian duels."

"If I remember correctly, it is considered bad manners to kill someone during one of those silly Meltaanian duels."

"He didn't die."

"Why do I believe it wasn't for lack of trying on your part?"

Keleios shrugged. "Our host, Duke Cartlon, had a very good white healer."

"What am I to do with you?"

Keleios grinned and changed the subject. "Nesbit believes that the only reason Zeln is allowing Astranthian peasants into the school is to become High Councilman."

Poula said, "We know Zeln. He wishes to prove that the peasants are human and have rights. To do that, they must have magic. This year will prove him right as three peasants graduate. What changes will that make in Astrantha?"

Keleios answered, curious about the new line of questioning. "The peasants will all be able to vote in the next council elections." Keleios stared at her. "He wouldn't dare. He wouldn't dare attack a keep in his own country."

"Frightened men do many foolish things."

"Not even Nesbit would do that."

"Do you think it an accident that we have only a handful of masters left here? Zeln left me in charge. We have one master enchanter, one master conjuror, one master illusionist, and two master sorcerers. Fidelis is a master of both illusion and herb-witchery, but if she will betray us, I doubt we can depend upon her help. The rest are in Altmirth, attending this impromptu council meeting. Zeln did not want to take so many from the school, but it is only for two more days. If I were attacking this keep, it would be before they returned.''

"Then sometime between now and day after tomorrow.''

Another thought came to Poula. "Were Zeln and the others under attack in your dream?''

"No, come to that they weren't in my dream at all. If my dream were true, they are safe.''

"Do you think your dream could be clouded?''

"The Lady of Shadows had her minions in the tower tonight. It is possible, but I don't think so.''

"We will warn them anyway.''

"If you can get a private message to them.''

Poula laughed. "That has not been an easy thing with Nesbit's spies, but I have managed.''

"I'll bet you have.'' Keleios stretched her shoulders and back. She was beginning to feel like sleeping. "The strength spell seems to be wearing off. I feel tired.'' She stood and pushed the chair under the table.

"It was of limited use. I only knew you were coming an hour before you came. I didn't have time for anything fancier.''

Keleios smiled and stretched again. "It was fancy enough. I'll bid you good dreams and pleasant prophecies.''

"And to you. Warn Carrick or his lieutenant before you go to bed, if you would.''

"Done, but first I must take care of something.''

Poula's eyes widened. "What sort of something?''

Keleios grinned. "Let us say that Belor will not be happy with me.''

Poula laughed again. "You have no idea how to be boring, do you?''

Keleios made no answer but left the room to the sound of Poula's laughter. The torchlit hall seemed very bright. And the silence of the sleeping keep pressed very close.

She reentered the library corridor. The flames were a beacon down the narrow way. Belor was no longer visible, and as she neared the circle, Kelcios wondered if he had escaped somehow. If he had gone to all that trouble, how angry would he be?

She approached as close as the heat would allow and peered over. Belor the Dreammaker sat, ankles tucked under, one elbow propped on his right knee. His tunic lay crumpled beside him. The hilt of his sword and the metal fittings on his sheath glimmered in the firelight. A sheen of sweat glistened on his back and shoulders. Keleios raised her hands upward and drew inward. The reverse of spells always felt strange, as if you were trying to breathe air you'd already used. The flames hesitated and paled until they were colorless as melted glass. With a rush the fire vanished.

It left them in a velvet darkness with the scattered glow of books only emphasizing it. Keleios called a witchlight to her hand and set it shining above them. It was white light, so Belor could see normally, a peace offering. The night had been busy and the effort brought a bead of sweat to her forehead. She could feel the energy draining away.

Keleios found herself looking into a pair of hostile eyes. She stepped close and offered a hand; Belor stared at it coldly. He rose in a single motion, using only his legs. His pale blue eyes had turned nearly grey, a very bad sign.

"Belor, please, I had no choice."

He said nothing, having discovered long ago that silence made her more uncomfortable than accusations.

"I was afraid I would harm you. You know that." She picked up his fallen tunic and said, "Here, let me wipe your back. I am sorry I was gone so long."

He turned without a word, and she tried to soak the sweat from his back.

Belor took the robe from her and mopped his chest.

"I was worried about you," he said without meeting her eyes. "I've never seen you so close to losing control of a vision before. What happened? I heard you screaming and a man yelling your name."

She smiled. As long as he was willing to talk, he wasn't that mad. "I'll tell you all on the way to alert the guard."

He shook the robe out and held it gingerly in his right hand. "Alert them to what?"

"I'll tell you that on the way."

She spoke quietly as they turned down the west corridor. The white witchlight floated steadily some eight inches above Keleios' left shoulder. She told him everything except that she carried the book commonly known as *The Book of Demons*. Over the centuries since its creation it had gone by many names: *Black Death, Pit Opener, Demon Summoner*.

Belor stopped her before they came to the outer hall, gripping her arm loosely. His eyes grew distant. "You're lying, hiding something."

She could have broken his grip, but there would have been no purpose to it. "Belor, I carry another book."

His hand dropped to his side. "*The Book of Demons*."

"Yes."

"Why, in the name of Cia, why?"

"I can't leave it behind to be found by whoever. It's too dangerous to be floating free."

"And it's safe with you carrying it?" He stared at the floor and took a deep breath. "Keleios, you and I are contaminated. You endanger yourself by carrying that thing. It has a mind of its own, as most of the books of power do."

"You don't need to lecture me on enchanted times."

"No, but on common sense, yes. Get rid of it, please."

"I can't. It won't burn. Someone will find it. Someone searches for it, and they must not have it."

"Searches for it? It's common knowledge it's here."

"But with restrictive spells lacing it. It can't be taken

out as long as this keep stands. And it is stunted in power until the sorceries and herbs binding it are broken. Belor, if the keep falls, it is free. You know what it can do.''

"Carry it, if you must, but I'm not finished arguing against it.''

"I know.'' They stepped out into the torchlit hall and Keleios extinguished the witchlight thankfully. A keep guard stood at attention at the door to the teleportation room. It was a permanent spell enabling the nonmagic soldiers to come and go to the outer wall. Keleios recognized the guard in his gold and black livery. Bundie was a tall Calthuian, young and overly ambitious but good with a weapon. He put his hand on his sword hilt and said, "Keleios, Belor, what keeps you up so late?''

"Prophecy, Bundie.''

One pale brown eyebrow raised. "Oh, grim news?''

"Grim enough for the guard to be doubled. The wards should go up soon. The keep is to be sealed for three days, starting tonight.''

"What did you see?''

"Death.'' At his grim expression she smiled. "But I think it can be fought with steel as well as magic.''

He grinned. "Then we will be ready. Carrick runs the best-trained guards on the island, and who has more magic than Zeln's school?''

Keleios did not disillusion him but agreed. "Pass the word along.''

She turned to go and Bundie called, "I'll see you on the practice grounds tomorrow morning, prophet.''

It was a sly insult. Carrick, the weapons master, had often said, "Spellcasters are poor swordsmen and prophets worst of all, because most of them are mad.''

Keleios ignored the insult, almost. "I'll be there, Bundie, and you had better watch your back.''

He laughed. "With you and the illusionist around, always.''

They paced the silent halls and felt the magic seep

from under the doors. The very stones seemed to breathe spells. She knew the feeling was caused from lack of sleep and too much magic but everything was hushed, as if the world held its breath.

Belor spoke in a whisper. "What is wrong tonight?"

"You feel it also."

He nodded.

She whispered back, "The gods walk among us. It's a bad sign."

They stood in front of her room.

"I don't feel their presence. I know I'm only an illusionist and not a sorcerer, but my magic sense isn't that blunt."

"It was just an expression, you know. When things go really wrong, the gods are abroad."

He let it go at that, stifling a yawn. "Fair dreaming, Keleios, and be careful."

"And to you. And I will be careful."

She watched him go until he vanished round the corner. She shivered as from a sudden chill. Keleios wasn't sure what had made her speak of the gods, but the words had rung in the air like a bell. Prophecy spoken in jest, perhaps. She knew the gods could hide their presence if it suited their needs. She whispered into the magic-laden air, "The gods walk among us. It is a bad sign."

4

An Answer

The door opened with the slightest of sighs. Keleios paused, thinking of murder.

The room was silvered darkness. Fidelis lay quietly on her side, pale brown hair flung across her pillow, one slender hand half-clinched on her hip. When she was six, Keleios had tagged after the older girl, as Alys followed Keleios now. One bright summer day Keleios had been playing near the water garden with a kitten. Fidelis had asked to hold it. Keleios had been so proud that the older girl noticed her. Fidelis had held and petted the tiny cat. Then with a wonderful smile that reached all the way up into her eyes, Fidelis shoved the kitten underwater and held it there while Keleios beat on her with tiny fists. Keleios had learned hatred from Fidelis. It was she who taught Keleios that all her fear and rage for Harque's murder of her mother could be turned into something else. Fear crippled, rage blinded, but hatred could be formed into revenge. With revenge could come satisfaction.

When Keleios was a little older she and Belor had ambushed the older girl. They had beat her bloody. Fidelis had asked, ''Why?''

''The kitten you drowned,'' Keleios said.

''You never forget, do you?''

''No,'' Keleios said, ''I never forget.''

Was Fidelis trying to kill her now? It was better to be cautious. The spell tonight had been a blatant attempt; perhaps there would be others—although being a shadow worshipper, Fidelis was more inclined to treachery than frontal attack.

Keleios searched the room with her night vision. The cool, seeking breath of the night wind touched her through the open windows. It rustled the papers on the two worktables and sent rows of hanging herbs scritching against the wall. She gave over to her suspicions and searched the chamber with the other sense that could not be tricked by silvered shadows; even night vision had its faults. The air currents moved around familiar things. The shelves lining the walls were stacked thick with books and papers, jars and bottles, and the strange miscellany that spell casters of any sort seem to collect. There was evil in the room, but again familiar evil. A large gallon bottle, carefully blown and enchanted, sat on the third shelf of Fidelis' side of the room. A demon swirled softly, bound by magic and hating. Oh, how demons hated to be used.

A scuttling under Fidelis' bed attracted her attention, and pinpricks of many eyes stared back at her.

Fas, Fidelis' familiar, was awake. The spider was only as large as a medium-sized dog, small for a wish spider, but he gave Fidelis the power of illusion.

The wind blew stronger, and the papers on Keleios' table struggled against the lead-lined weight of the demon's skull that held them down. The bare white skull was a trophy she had carried away from the Grey Isle. It had been one of the lesser demons, but not many people lived through encounters with the devilkin. All one needed was a magic weapon and a great deal of luck; her sword had given her both. Now the horned skull acted as a paperweight and a reminder that she had done the nearly impossible. A chunk of raw ore sat nearby, waiting to be forged if only Keleios could decide what it most wanted to be. The herb press sat smelling of crushed thyme and verdis. She wondered briefly if one of the apprentices had forgotten to clean it again, but for once was too tired to care.

Something fluttered in the far corner, but it was only the dark cloth hiding Fidelis' mirror—a beautiful thing in itself, lovingly carved of polished oak, a floor-length oval of unblemished glass. It had power as all enchanted objects did, and it was evil.

Fidelis had hidden it from Keleios' view since the day Keleios had looked at it and said, "I see you standing in a chamber with a blond man. I can almost see his face."

"How can you do that?" she asked, suddenly pale.

Keleios smiled. "Remember, I am an enchanter. I can divine the uses of enchanted items much more thoroughly than an illusionist/herb-witch."

"It is evil. You shouldn't be able to use it."

Keleios shrugged. "It is also demon-aided magic, and like it or not, so am I."

"Demonmonger!" Fidelis hissed, "How long have you been watching the mirror?"

Keleios had toyed with the thought of lying, making her sweat, but Fidelis was a little too dangerous to play with. "Not long, Fidelis. Your secrets are safe, for the most part. And before you start calling names, remember, my demon alliance was accidental; yours was not."

So the mirror had been covered.

Keleios sat down on the edge of her bed, back to Fidelis and Fas. If it were the herb-witch, she would not want to bring blame upon herself. Most likely attacks would continue outside of the room. She was probably safe for tonight, or was it tomorrow already? The sword, Luckweaver, slid along the slanting mattress to touch her. Keleios reached back and drew the cool golden hilt to her. The hilt was carved simply for gripping but its one jewel was not simple. That orange jewel was a luckstone nearly as large as her fist. It rode the end of the hilt and pulsed magic to her touch. It was an elementary enchantment, her first shaped weapon. It would be just as powerful in anyone else's hands, if they knew how to use it. There was no blood, or soul binding in it, so she had to touch it for the magic to shift things in her favor. If she had worn Luckweaver tonight, the damage would have been less or avoided completely. One did not take alien magic into the tower. She caressed the sword and resisted the idea of unsheathing it. Perhaps it was time to go openly armed. She sighed, stretched, and set the weapon carefully on the bed.

She pulled off one boot. A cat materialized through the door. It was a spell they had worked out between them. The door was enchanted to be soft near the bottom, but only Poth's touch would activate it. Keleios didn't want just any cat-sized creature crawling into the room. Gilstorpoth, who had many names around the school—Mistress Poth, or just plain Poth—came to rub against her ankles. Keleios picked up the cat. She trusted her hands to tell her that the cat was all right. Though Poth was not her familiar, she was more than a pet and sometimes sensed what only a familiar, or another sorcerer, should have felt.

The cat's mother had been a shapeshifted elf who had become trapped. The beautiful white, silver-eyed cat had finally taken a true cat mate, and Poth had been one of her first and only litter. It is said that after a while one forgets one's old shape; Keleios always hoped that was true. There had been a look in those silver cat eyes that had frightened her. Regardless of the pain it may have caused the mother cat, the mixed ancestry had given Poth sorcery. Poth meowed up at her, and Keleios cupped the small chin in her palm. She stared into those gold eyes, the color of well-worn gold pieces. They communed quietly for several minutes until the cat purred in a long contented line. Though there was no need for words, Keleios spoke softly. "I'm glad to see you, too." She sighed. She had been too long among humans and had picked up the habit of talking when it wasn't necessary. It was past time for a visit to her elven kin. Elves knew the value of silence.

A soft thump from the far corner announced that Piker was awake. Encouraged by her gaze, the half-grown white mutt ambled toward her. She smiled, and her thoughts turned to Piker's owner, or rather master. Feltan was the youngest untrained witch ever to attract a familiar, and he was a peasant. Keleios herself had brought them to the school. If her dream came to pass, Feltan would die. She let the thought go, for she had learned not to dwell on death prophecies. She had been wrong once. Piker stayed with Keleios because no animals were allowed in the apprentice dorms. If they made an exception, even for a familiar, the place would turn into a zoo, or so said Toran, head of the boy apprentices. Personally, Keleios thought Toran just didn't understand children and their need for animals. Fidelis had complained that their room was turning into a zoo.

The moon shadow of the canary's cage placed huge bars on the floor. Keleios smiled. Perhaps there were enough animals in the room.

Fidelis' familiar, the wishing spider Fas, had tried ridding the room of some of its occupants. Keleios had entered the chamber in time to see Fas enclosing the canary's cage with his hairy legs. "Fas! No!" The chain holding the cage to the ceiling snapped, toppling the spider and freeing the tiny bird, which flew to the highest shelf, panting.

Keleios had been about to fry the vile thing when Fidelis had entered screaming. She convinced Keleios that she would punish the spider. Keleios let it be, for it was a very serious offense to kill someone's familiar. Secretly, she thought that Fidelis herself had ordered the animals killed.

The canary's cage once more hung from the ceiling, and Poth the cat slept where she would, and Piker slept in the corner, all unmolested. To those who could see it, the cage, the dog's blankets, and Poth herself glowed magic.

Fidelis had protested the severity of the wards. Later Keleios admitted to Zeln that perhaps a fifth circle fire ward was too much, but to change it would have been to admit she was wrong. She was excessive, not wrong.

Fas was intelligent enough to leave well enough alone, so Zeln had let it stand.

Keleios sat on the bed, the dog's head sunk on her

leg, and scratched his ear. Poth clambered up her back and curled round her neck. A precarious perch for a cat, but she liked it, and her purrs rumbled through the back of Keleios' neck.

Keleios' skin prickled, and Poth jumped down with a squall. Piker whined softly.

Fidelis called sleepily from her bed. "What is it?"

"The wards have gone up. Prophet's right."

"Why did they go up?"

Keleios turned to watch Fidelis grope out of sleep. "I told you: prophet's right."

"You being the prophet."

"Yes, go back to sleep. We can argue in the morning if you want."

Fidelis opened her mouth to speak, changed her mind, and settled back into her covers.

A few minutes and the woman's even breathing filled the room.

Keleios rubbed the dog's head, making his ears flap, and sent him to his bed.

Poth walked along Keleios' covers, trying to find a comfortable spot.

"We're safe now," she whispered to the cat. But as she finished undressing, she wondered just how safe one could be with traitors on this side of the wards.

She placed a hand to her bedpost and activated the spell. It gave a pulse, a mere spark of power. Keleios lay back gratefully. There would be no more magic tonight, no matter what the need. Poth curled into a black and white ball beside her shoulder, her plumed tail resting just under Keleios' chin.

She checked briefly to assure herself the wrist sheath dagger was in place, and placing a hand over Luckweaver, she gave herself to sleep.

Keleios lay snuggled into the warmth of her sheets, tired, very tired. Something was tapping at her hair. She batted it away but the tentative touch returned. She opened her eyes just enough to catch a black and white blur.

Keleios groaned. "Poth, what is it?" Then she noticed the angle of the sunlight. "Urle's forge, I'm late."

Poth jumped to the floor with a startled cry as Keleios tore back the covers. The cat swatted at her foot, claws carefully sheathed.

"I'm sorry, and thank you for waking me."

The cat sat very straight, looking virtuous and patient. Keleios laughed and picked her up. Poth tried to remain unmoved but consented and began to purr. Keleios put her on the bed and began to undress. "I haven't slept in this late in months."

She was alive, the ward was intact, and Fidelis was gone. A note was pinned to the clothes she had taken off last night. It read simply:

KELEIOS,
WE CAN ARGUE LATER TODAY. I HAD
EARLY AND URGENT BUSINESS TO TEND TO.
THE WITCH

She smiled. They had been leaving notes to each other for two years. Keleios signed hers 'the half-elf' and Fidelis was always 'the witch.' The smile faded when she realized that the urgent business could be the planning of her own death.

Keleios felt a light touch on her mind. She opened to it and Allanna asked for permission to enter her room. The woman appeared in the middle of the floor. As always, Keleios was taken with Allanna's beauty. She was the heroine of an old legend, or should have been. Being Astranthian, she was tall and slender with straight yellow-gold hair that fell to her knees. Her eyes were the surprised blue of cornflowers, and her skin had never known the touch of sun, white and pure like a wax doll. She was dressed in blue today, which emphasized everything—the eyes, the skin, the golden hair. Her gown was blue on blue-patterned silk. It gapped below her fitted waist to reveal a pale blue dress. A necklace of pearls and sapphires adorned her slender neck. Allanna of the Golden Hair was a princess waiting for her prince, and no one was more aware of it than Allanna herself. Her beauty would have been breath-stealing if it had been an unconscious beauty, but it was affected, like the dress that matched her eyes and the refined gestures. It was a self-conscious show.

She began her sentence with a sweep of long tapered hand. "Belor bid me hurry you."

Keleios pulled her gown over her head. "How late am I?"

"An hour."

"Carrick will skin me alive."

The impossibly red lips smiled. "It is a possibility."

"You think it's amusing; I do not." Keleios poured water from the pitcher into the basin, tepid cold. She gasped at the feel of the chill water.

Allanna said, "Here, let me warm it for you."

"No, thank you."

Allanna shrugged. She wasted sorcery on minor things like warming water without thinking it a waste.

Allanna sighed gracefully. "I'm sorry. I know you are in trouble but why do you put yourself at the mercy of a man like that?"

Keleios dried herself on a small towel. "A man like what?"

Allanna shifted uncomfortably. "Oh, come, you know what I mean."

"No, tell me."

Allanna stamped a delicate foot and sent the blue silk whispering over the floor. "He isn't magic, not even an herb-witch."

"True, but then he doesn't need magic to be the best swordsman in the islands." It was an old argument between them. Allanna had very Astranthian ideas about people without magic. Without magic one was less than human, and it was this idea that had kept the peasants in thrall for so many years. "When you have exhausted your spells, what is left? You can't even use a dagger, let alone a sword. What happens when you've run out of spells?''

She stood perfectly straight, hands loose at her sides. "I do not run out of spells.''

It was true, in a way. Allanna was perhaps the most powerful sorcerer to come out of Astrantha since Zeln and his sister Sile.

"You are powerful, Allanna, but everyone, everyone, will eventually run out of spells. Or at least the strength to use them.''

The pale face was haughty; her opinion of her magic was very high. Unfortunately, up until now the opinion was deserved. She was one of four people who could enter the arena with Zeln and stand a chance of coming out alive.

Keleios watched Allanna's face until her linen shirt blocked her view. It was useless to argue. Until someone stronger than Allanna challenged the girl, she would think herself unbeatable. The frightening thing was she just might be right.

Keleios pulled her hair from the shirt collar. "Perhaps you are a special case, Allanna, but I with my more humble talents feel the need for more.''

Allanna gave a small laugh. "You, humble? My father is only a viscount; yours was a prince and your mother, a princess.''

"Such things are much more important in Astrantha than in Wrythe. And as for my mother's family, they consider me a bastard child.''

She sniffed. "The Calthuians are a barbaric people, no offense intended. Your mother was far above most of her countrymen.''

Keleios, being half-Calthuian, wasn't sure what was compliment and what wasn't, but she said, "Thank you, Allanna.''

"I do not profess to understand the ways of elves, but in Astrantha you are not humble.''

A torso of Belor floated through the window. Ghostlike they could see through it. Keleios whispered to it, "I'm hurrying.''

Keleios started to put on the vest she had discarded last night.

Allanna's delicate lips curled slightly, a look of disgust touching her face.

Keleios held it up at arms length. Allanna did have a point. She opened the chest at the end of her bed and began rummaging through it. "I haven't even fed the animals yet."

"I'll do that."

Keleios' voice came muffled from inside the trunk. "Remember to chop parsley for the canary."

As if in answer to it, the tiny bird sang an ear-thrumming trill.

Allanna said, "I will see that the dog gets to Feltan, and Mistress Poth will dine in the kitchen under my watchful eye."

"Thank you."

She blinked, long gold eyelashes curling downward. "Your haste is my only reward."

Keleios stood, a rather pale green vest clutched in her hand. It fit rather snug but would have to do. There didn't seem to be any other clean ones. Poth circled round her ankles. Keleios picked the cat up and cuddled her. "Allanna will tend you, Poth. If you don't mind?" The cat didn't, perhaps because Allanna was somewhat catlike herself. They got along very well. And she cautioned the dog, "Behave or Allanna will turn you into a rabbit."

The dog gave an apologetic tail thump.

Keleios put Poth down and ran a hasty brush through her thick hair. She began to braid it. Allanna stepped forward. "Here, let me." The swift delicate hands wove her brownish gold hair into a single braid. The fingers lingered on a somewhat pointed ear. "How lovely they would be if you would let me put earrings in them."

"Thank you for the thought, but they're fine the way they are." Keleios scooped up her short sword and belt. She fastened Luckweaver in place.

"Perhaps, Keleios, you should take a more direct route today."

"Direct?"

She motioned toward the windows.

"You mean levitate down. I think not."

"Oh, come now, Keleios, you are a journeyman sorcerer. Surely you can levitate yourself to the courtyard."

"It is not a matter of can, or can't, but a waste of magic."

Allanna sniffed. "I will levitate you myself if you are so stingy with your spells."

Keleios sighed, resigned. She strode forward, touching the middle window to release the sound-muffling spell. Steel on steel rang through the courtyard.

The green-brown canary hopped from perch to perch, the wooden cage swaying gently with his movement. She smiled at his inquiring chirp. "Be a good bird, Shotzi, and Auntie Allanna will give you a surprise."

The Astranthian laughed, and the sound was like wind chimes or feast bells. Surely the woman had to sit and practice. Keleios hesitated, staring down at the courtyard below. It was too much for Allanna's patience. Keleios vanished with a startled cry and reappeared on the stones below. She frowned up at the slim hands that were closing her window, but she dared not draw more attention to herself. Carrick did not approve of magic anywhere near his practices. A summer breeze swept up, tugging wisps of hair.

She stood in the center of one of the gigantic blocks of square-cut stone. They had been magic-lifted to their places and were magic-supported still. In the middle of the vast stony expanse huddled the weapons practice. Most sat in a wide circle. Carrick strode round the inside of that circle. He wore a sleeveless brown jerkin and baggy trousers stuffed into knee-high boots. He was large, with a beefy, muscled body. He looked slow, but it was deceptive. Keleios had felt his lightning-quick blows too many times to be fooled. His muscles were the kind that hid in a disguise of bulk, no shapely definition for Carrick's body. His black hair was cut close to the round balding head. His quick brown eyes caught every mistake. The stick he carried poked, prodded, and tripped, so you would notice your mistake also.

Two fighters danced round each other. The wooden practice swords had been left behind for blunt steel— blunt steel that was two or three times the weight of most ordinary weapons. Tobin was one; the other was a blond guardsman.

Tobin was short, but at sixteen, he hadn't yet attained his full height. His hair was a dark copper-red and his skin flushed with gold highlights. Somewhere back in his ancestry was a faerie of some sort. It was a common heritage in Meltaan. Only his amber eyes showed ordinary and young. His linen shirt trailed over a pair of bright red trousers. His boots were shiny black with polish, and since Zeln considered it an excess for the servants to do such things, Tobin had shined his own boots. He was heir to the entire province of Ferrian. He was a prince, and someday he would be a king.

The guardsman towered over Tobin; and his reach was twice the boy's. The man possessed superior strength as well. Yet Tobin circled, feinting. The boy opened wide his arms, giving Darius his chest and stomach as a target. Darius reached forward with his long arm; it would be a gut slice. Snake-quick, Tobin's sword slid under the arm and got in a heart blow with inches to spare for his own life. It was an elven thing, and Tobin had sweated and worked to acquire the strength of wrist to do it. His quickness was still not elven, but it was close.

Keleios made it safely to the group without being noticed by any except Belor. She quickly moved to take her place.

Carrick ignored her arrival and she slid in between Tobin and Belor. Tobin's auburn hair clung in dark strands round his face. He smiled, and his eyes sparkled. He had never beaten Darius before.

Belor frowned at her. He seemed ready to speak but didn't dare with the weapons master so close.

Five people down to the left sat Lothor, shirtless, sweating, and staring at her with his strange silver eyes.

She laid Luckweaver and the magic bracers on the ground beside her. Carrick did not allow any magic weapons at his practices. Those with magic weapons held a practice on their own in the afternoon or early evening. The guard had begun to come and watch and to use some of the magic weapons. Carrick had finally consented to let Bellenore, his second in command, direct the practice.

The next match finished early, one guard tripping and nearly getting his nose smashed. Carrick turned to Keleios like a great dark cloud. She felt that uncomfortable urge to shrink back. But she sat straight and met his angry eyes.

His voice was deep and thick with emotion, each word a whip. ''Zeln forced me to let magic users in my training sessions. I said it would be a waste of time to train nonguards. He countered with let them be part-time guards then. He willed it; I obeyed. But I told him that spell casters don't make good soldiers; they distract too easily. Magic is more important than steel to them. But I take you magicmongers seriously. I will train you, and you will learn. You will learn that these practices are important and come first.''

He barked out her name.

Keleios stood.

He called out, ''Bellenore to the circle.''

Bellenore was tall with wide shoulders. The braid of her brown hair was streaked with grey, though she couldn't have been past her thirtieth year. She was dressed as Carrick was, brown sleeveless jerkin and trousers. Scars decorated her bare arms. Her face was plain until she smiled, and then it was beautiful. Pale brown eyes regarded Keleios without smiling.

Carrick handed them each a shield and sword. The

shield was weighted for fighting, and the sword was edged. Edged weapons were not an uncommon punishment. It was a compliment of sorts. He trusted only the best of his fighters with edged weapons during practice. His glittering eyes challenged Keleios to protest. She did not, even though Bellenore was a better fighter than she was. They would fight with short sword and shield, Keleios' own favorite method, and Bellenore would beat her. It was meant to be a humbling experience.

Carrick bawled out, "To third blood; a nick is as good as a wound."

As they faced off, Lothor's pale flesh seemed to glimmer, like carved alabaster. Keleios shook her head to clear her vision and Bellenore withheld asking, "Are you fit for the circle?"

Keleios nodded, and they began the dance. They had fought before, and Keleios had even won twice, but not with an edged weapon, and not to draw blood. Even with blunt weapons Bellenore won nine out of ten times.

A lesson would have worked better on others because Keleios did not consider it embarrassing to be beaten in practice, by the guards' second in command. Carrick knew this, but it was one of his standard punishments. He had not come up with a satisfactory punishment for the half-elf. Though he had found he could make her angry, he could not make her truly repentant.

They circled, wary, shields held close covering upper bodies and stomach, tensed to move up or down. Bellenore's preferred weapon was the two-handed sword. She was one of only two women who Keleios had seen with the strength to use it properly. For that matter, she hadn't seen many men who could use the two-handed well. More of them carried it but only a handful had the strength, stamina, and mind-set for the weapon.

They tested each other with some half-hearted feints, which neither fell for. Then Bellenore grinned, and

Keleios did too. The fight began in earnest with a clang of steel. Bellenore rushed inward, sword slashing. The tension was not there; it was a ruse. Keleios let the blow go past but countered with a smash of shield against Bellenore's body. It set the woman off balance, but before Keleios could bring sword into play, she had recovered.

As they circled, Keleios found her eyes drawn to Lothor. His hand as it swept up his arm fascinated her. Bellenore was upon her, blade flashing downward. Keleios threw her steel upward; the swords sang down each other, with a shower of sparks. As they broke from each other a thin line of crimson began to wend down Keleios' forehead. The point of the blade had found her before she reacted. With the knowledge of blood, the cut began to sting.

Worse, the thin stream of blood dripped across her left eye, hampering her vision.

Blade met blade, blocking. Blade, shield, met straining against each other. Without magical aid, Keleios could not hold Bellenore. Knowing this, feeling it, she collapsed downward. It was a great gamble, and if she had been fighting for her life, she might not have done it. Bellenore staggered forward, and Keleios' sword caught her across the stomach. Elven quickness allowed her to roll away and stand ready for the next rush.

Every time the circle showed her Lothor, her concentration wavered. Something was wrong. Keleios decided before the dance turned her to Lothor once more to try another dangerous move. It was a disarming technique more favored in elven circles than human. The blades met. Keleios forced her steel down the length of Bellenore's and twisted point along the haft. It should have disarmed her and nicked the wrist. But this was Bellenore. She bled but kept her sword.

The blood welled out of the slice and would make the hilt slippery in a short time. Keleios moved away to give it that time. The woman knew that, too, and pressed the fight. Keleios shook blood from her left eye, but the eye was useless until cleaned. Nothing bled like a shallow scalp wound.

For whatever reason she was being distracted, Bellenore had noticed and began moving her to gaze that way. It worked like a charm. Keleios' eyes were drawn away to Lothor, and she found herself on the ground with Bellenore's sword at her throat. She had not dropped her sword. The point bit into her neck twice, one nearly atop the other.

Carrick strode forward. "Winner."

Bellenore offered Keleios a hand up and she accepted. "What was of such interest over there?"

Keleios touched her neck and her fingers came away crimson. "I am not sure."

Keleios went back and sat beside Belor. The healer attending the practice session this morning knelt and pressed an herb mixture into her face cut. He began cleaning the blood from her face. She contacted Belor by mind. *Belor, is Lothor wearing anything new, different? A ring, a piece of rope, a necklace?*

* Yes, a silver chain with a large ball cage. It's magic of some sort.*

The herbs absorbed the blood, and the healer began salving cream for pain and to speed healing.

Belor, I can't see that necklace.

So a charm for, or against, you.

Keleios did not answer; there was no need. Belor stood and walked to Carrick. Carrick gave the prodding stick to Bellenore and went to speak quietly to Lothor. Belor resumed his seat. Lothor protested. Keleios watched him from across the circle, gripping the silver charm, still invisible to her.

Reluctantly, Lothor moved to undo the unseen chain. He handed it to Carrick, and it became visible to Keleios' eyes. The two fighters had sat down, and the circle was empty. The weapons master strode into the circle and said, "Our visitor here was wearing a magical charm, which is against the rules for my practices. He claims it to be a charm against the unusually cool weather of our island." He let the chain slide into his big palm—a pool of silver chain. "Keleios, what is this?" And he tossed it through the air. Lothor sprang forward and the guard's reflexes took over as they covered him.

Keleios caught it and nearly choked with its closeness.

Until Belor knelt beside her, she didn't realize she had fallen to the ground in a near faint. He had to pry her fingers from the chain.

Carrick knelt beside her, all anger forgotten. "Girl, girl, are you all right?"

She managed to speak, "Yes, master, I am . . . fine."

Belor was carefully dissecting the ball of herbs. The empty metal ball lay near at hand. Keleios allowed Carrick to help her sit and watched Belor tear the woven herbs apart and place them in neat piles. When all else was cleared away, two locks of hair remained. One was the white of fresh snow; the other a golden brown.

Lothor stood very straight, anger bringing a flush to his death-pallor cheeks. He was ringed round by guards, uncertain yet if he was to be prisoner. No one had been comfortable with a black healer in the school; they were quite willing to believe he had done something evil.

Keleios got to her feet, shaking off the well-wishing hands. She walked through the ring of guards to face Lothor. "I suppose I should ask where you got it, but only three people in this keep could have made such a charm. I didn't do it; Poula wouldn't do it. That leaves Fidelis." She stood very close to him and said, "You wanted my answer, well here it is—no. No, not if you were my only chance out of the seven hells."

His voice was low, calm with menace. "Do not say in anger what you will regret later."

"Don't caution me."

Carrick interrupted, "Keleios, what is that thing? Is it a magic weapon of some kind?"

"Not in the way you mean, Carrick. It was a charm of lust."

He half-laughed. "Then how did it harm you? You fell when you touched it."

"It was that powerful, too powerful. It gave itself away."

Carrick waved the guards back. "Many a man's turned to magic to acquire a lady's favor. 'Tis no crime."

Keleios was forced to agree with him. "No, but it is grounds for a refusal."

Lothor stood isolated, alone. He bowed slowly. "You have refused me, very well. I challenge you."

"To what?"

"The arena."

Someone gasped. "If that will satisfy you, Lothor, you have it."

He smiled, his gaze roaming over her body, stripping her in his mind. "It will not satisfy, but it will do."

She stepped close and nearly hissed. "Stop that."

"Stop what?"

"Looking at me like I'm something to eat."

His smile broadened. "I wasn't aware of it. So sorry."

"Insincerity becomes you. As the one being challenged, I choose tonight, just after dusk, and magic." She turned, picked up Luckweaver, slipped the bracers on, and strode up the main steps of the castle. Belor and Tobin caught up with her in the corridor outside one of the classrooms. The murmur of voices floated into the hallway. A sharp snap of magic and a burst of childish laughter said a spell had gone awry.

Belor jogged to catch up with Keleios. "Where are you going?"

"The stillroom."

Tobin caught up with them. "You aren't going to challenge Fidelis as well?"

She smiled, but her eyes remained dark. "What a marvelous idea."

Belor laid a hand on her arm, but she would not stop. "Keleios, do you think it wise to make two challenges in one day? By law you could end up fighting both today. You'd surely lose the second."

She stopped and turned to them. "I am almost certain that Fidelis nearly killed me last night. I'm tired of waiting for proof while she plots behind my back. I want my enemies in front of me across the sands." She shook off Belor's hand and started walking again.

Belor tried reasoning with her as they passed through the south arch into the keep's gardens. "This is not wise. You are letting your anger best you."

"Perhaps, but it is my mistake to make, not yours."

Tobin said quietly, "Keleios, don't do this." His usually mocking grin was gone; his face was sober.

The herb garden was a thousand shades of green, from the silver-grey of lambsquarter to the pine dark of rosemary leaves. Keleios led them through the white-painted trellis and into the rose garden. The scent of roses was a close sweetness that clung to the summer air. The white gravel paths formed a cross round the fountain, each path leading to a boxwood hedge and a gate.

Belor said, "You know I don't agree with the council rule about waiting for proof. I've said before that it would get you killed—but two challenges in one day, Keleios. It is madness."

The far gate led into the healer's garden. The plants stood alone in their circular patterns, knotted and bordered by stone paths. The white marble and gold sundial stood in the center of the garden, a reminder against wasted time. Digging tools lay discarded along the path as if the tenders had left in haste. The far gate opened, and a trio of apprentices entered, Melandra among them.

Keleios took time to notice the dark circles under the girl's eyes. Then the ever-masking hair fell over the scarred face. "Keleios, what is wrong?"

The other two, a girl and a boy, stood silent and

round-eyed. Something was up. One master and two journeymen straight from practice—it was news.

"Is Master Fidelis in the stillroom?"

Melandra hesitated, then nodded, feeling that she had done something vaguely wrong. The apprentices parted like frightened birds to let them pass. They followed at a discreet distance.

Keleios turned and said, "Don't follow us."

The apprentices stood very still. Melandra said in a small voice, "As you wish, Keleios."

By the time they came to the door, Belor and Tobin had fallen back to either side. They jumped her from behind, knowing that the bracers made pinning her a lost cause.

Belor spoke through gritted teeth as they struggled. "Keleios, think, think, control your anger. Behave like a master, not a journeyman."

She froze for an instant, staring up at the sky. Her breathing came harsh, but she stopped fighting them. "Let me go."

They rose slowly and offered to help her up.

She took their hands and said, "I will confront her but not challenge her. Is that satisfactory?"

Belor smiled one of his gentle smiles. "Very."

They fell back like a guard of honor and followed her.

The building was framed in the golden eastern light, but inside all was cool and shadow-dark. Firelight and lamplight cast yellow pools in the gloom. The rich perfume of herbs filled the place. The thick dryness of hanging herbs, the rich dampness of herbs boiled down in a pot, made the air almost solid with their smells. As always, the scent of a well-run stillroom reminded Keleios of her mother, but it was here that she found the witch.

Fidelis stood feeding herbs into a grinder. Her plain grey dress clung to her body, almost like a slip, more seductive than any of the full-petticoated skirts. A single strand of pearls was her only ornament.

A small apprentice turned manfully at the handle of

the grinder. It was he who saw them enter, and his face paled, leaving his brown eyes like islands. Fidelis asked, "What is it?" She turned, irritated, and saw Keleios. Something flashed over her face—fear, perhaps, but not quite. A small pot bubbling on the fire spat into the flames, and the drop sizzled, making the fire pop.

The boy jumped, and Fidelis said, "That will be all."

The boy walked slowly between the two women, and once clear of Keleios, he ran.

A rustling from the side of the room, and two girls stepped hesitantly into sight.

Keleios said, quietly, "Get out."

They fled

"We are alone now, Keleios, save for your cortege and my familiar." Fas the spider clicked from the top of a nearby shelf. Belor and Tobin were a solid reassurance at Keleios' back. "State your business, half-elf."

"You wrote we could fight later; well, it's later."

The witch blinked and smiled. "What should we fight about?"

"Belor." He stepped forward and showed Fidelis the dismantled charm.

"Why, Fidelis, why?"

"You've come about that." She began to laugh. She leaned against the table and cackled until tears ran down her face.

They weren't sure how to take that. Keleios had planned for almost any reaction but not laughter.

"I don't think this is a laughing matter, witch."

Fidelis nodded, wiping her eyes with her fingers. "No, no. You asked why." She straightened, a strange half smirk still on her thin lips. "The black prince wanted something to attract you, and I needed his help with spells."

"His help? He knows no herb-craft. What help could he give you?"

The smile widened, the eyes hooded with the long-lashed eyelids. "The help any man could give me." She moved closer to them, her slender frame seeming to glide over the stone floor. "I asked the illusionist for help, but he follows Cia and would not aid me."

Belor blushed.

"I almost had the journeyman convinced, but at the last he would have asked your opinion, and I knew what that opinion would be."

Tobin simply stared at her, amber eyes glittering.

"But Lothor wanted something from me. A willing man for a charm, that was the bargain."

Keleios' face paled. "The Landien Cycle. Urle's forge, Fidelis, how could you?"

Her eyes darkened, anger rising. "Power, half-elf, power."

"How many times did he help you?"

Lothor answered from the doorway, "Twice."

Keleios backed to the side of the room in order to watch them both. "Are you bargained for one more?"

He nodded.

"You need a child's heart for the last spell. Where were you planning to get it?"

Fidelis began to laugh again; the sound bubbled up and filled the room. "Keleios, don't be naive."

"You give witches a bad name, Fidelis."

The laughter stopped abruptly, "Perhaps, but it was worth it for power, and he is a wonderful lover. I envy you with him for your bedmate."

Lothor bowed. "And may I return the compliment, my lady."

Keleios had a great desire to scream. "It seems I will never know; we fight in the arena tonight."

"Too bad, and if you have no more business with me, I have work to do."

"One more thing. You were amazed that I should confront you over this charm. Well, it's all I have solid proof of. But I know that you are up to something treacherous."

"Was I in your dreams last night, prophet? But even so, you have no proof."

"You have been very careful. Without proof I can't go before council, but there are other ways to deal with it."

"Yes, half-elf, there are other ways to deal with it. A knife in the dark, perhaps."

"Are you threatening me?"

"Oh, no, not me. I don't use knives as weapons, that's much more your area."

"Then what did you mean?"

"Why, whatever you want it to mean." The witch smiled sweetly, flashing a dimple to one side of her lips.

Keleios stared at her for the space of three heart-beats then said, "This is not over between us, witch."

"On that at least, half-elf, we can agree." Fidelis turned back to her table of herbs and began sorting them. "My first class is soon, if that is all?"

"For now, witch." And Keleios turned abruptly. She brushed past Lothor with the words, "I'll see you tonight."

"I look forward to it."

Belor and Tobin left with her. Tobin glanced back and only Fidelis was smiling.

They walked quietly for a few paces, then Belor said softly, "She plans to kill you, Keleios."

Tobin shook his head and said, " 'A knife in the dark' means an assassin. Why would she warn you?"

"Maybe she hopes to frighten me."

Tobin gave a rough snort. "Doesn't she know you better than that by now?"

"I don't think Fidelis has ever understood me, or I her."

Belor touched her arm. "I don't think you should worry about assassins until after tonight."

"You mean that Fidelis may wait and see if Lothor kills me."

"If I were her, that is what I would hope for." He squeezed her arm. "It's done now, but you should make plans, strategy. He is an enchanter/sorcerer, the same as yourself. You've never faced anyone who matched you.''

"He is not an herb-witch.''

"No, but you may not get to use herbs tonight.''

She shook her head. "I will plan, Belor. Meet me in my room in half an hour. I must tell Master Tally I cannot help him today in the forge.''

Tobin asked, "What can I do?''

"Come dressed for battle to dinner tonight; do your duties as if everything were normal.''

"Am I to be your second then?''

She smiled at him. "No, Tobin, but I fight a follower of Verm and Ivel, and that may mean treachery. I would want us all on our guard tonight. Now you are almost late for your first class. Allanna is not kind to late arrivals.''

He grinned. "No, but someday maybe she'll be kind to one young Meltaanian prince.''

Keleios shoved him. "Oh, go to class, skirt chaser.''

"Battlemonger.'' And he jogged off towards the classrooms.

Belor spoke softly. "I want to know your plans.''

She clapped him on the back and smiled, much too cheerily. "My second has to know.''

"I am honored to second you, but you don't have a plan, do you?''

"Not yet. Better make it an hour before you meet me.'' And with that she turned towards the main keep and the blacksmith workshops.

Belor yelled after her, "I hope you know what you're doing.''

A delicate touch of sorcery brought her thoughts to his mind.

So do I.

The thought did not comfort him in the least.

5

Into the Darkness

The smithy area was under the keep near the kitchens. It was doubly warded. One ward would contain the magic in case of a mistake. A good explosion could bring down half the castle. It had happened at other smithies that handled the repair of relics. A second ward would keep the stench of fire and burned metal from leaking into the kitchens and ruining the food.

Only a few small windows gave sunlight to the forge. Most of the light was fire. Metal glowed in the near dark, blue, straw yellow, white, and cherry red. The giant bellows whooshed air into the main forge, and over all, the clang of hammers.

The heat was skin stripping, air stealing. The constant heat, darkness—it was not a place to look for an elf, or even a half-elf.

She passed through to the back with its glimmering shield spell keeping it separate from the rest of the forge. Keleios had had Allanna place the shield, because if it failed, it wouldn't be mere explosions. Tally, master smith, had been given a gift. It was a remnant of a sword and handle, with numerous blackened pieces along with it. It had been a gift from the High Councilman himself. He wanted a sword made of the pieces, but no one else would touch the job.

It was rumored to be the remains of the sword, Elf Killer. It had been made by a renegade elven smith. He, fittingly enough, was its first victim. It had been a soul-stealer among other things. Keleios had no desire to put a relic in Nesbit's hands, but she could not resist the challenge to discover some of the secrets of making that the elves had lost through the war. If they could manage to save the metal, the blade would not be Elf Killer risen from the grave. This sword promised to be a marriage of evil magic and Keleios and Tally.

Tally did not turn around as she entered the warding. He was the shortest Astranthian Keleios had ever met, and his nearly bald head with its fringe of fine blond hair gave him a peculiar look. "Good," he said, still bent over the sword's main piece. "You're here. Today we will finish saving the last piece." He turned then with the largest whole piece in his hand, and his smile faded. "You are not dressed for the forge."

"No, Master, I am to duel tonight."

His fingers tightened on the metal. "That black healer, isn't it?"

She nodded.

"Well, it had to come, I suppose." He set the metal down on the work stand and then grabbed a handful of saw dust from a bucket where it was kept. He threw it on the embers and soon a blaze was going.

"Tally, I can't help you today. I must prepare."

"I know, I know. Send in Jarick."

"Do you think that wise?"

He frowned and snapped at her, "He'll just man the bellows. I won't do anything but purge the steel."

Seeing the look on her face, he said, "I promise."

"All right, I'll send him in as I go out."

"You be careful tonight, Keleios. I may not like the man's religion, but he's careful and meticulous when he forges, and his enchantments are strong. And if anything happened to you, who could I trust to stand beside me on this?"

She laughed. "No one else is crazy enough, Tally."

When she told Jarick, his freckles stood out against suddenly white skin. "Don't worry. He's just going to restore the metal; you man the bellows." She clapped him on the back. "Besides, Jarick, you've been wanting more responsibility."

He stared at her, brown eyes wide. "Not that kind."

Journeyman Nerine stopped her on the way out. "Keleios, our ice elemental is about to be loosed. Could you redo the entrapment spells?"

The elemental stood by the main forge. It was glittering white ice with vague eyes and mouth. Nothing could temper steel like a captive ice elemental.

Flickers of white crossed the bounders of the entrapment spell. "You're right; someone should have seen to it days ago. Ask Allanna to do it. If she protests entering the forge tell her I asked."

The girl looked cautious, considering. "I will, but why can't you do it yourself? You are right here."

"I walk the sands tonight."

Being Nerine, her face did not give away her emotions. "You will need all your energy then. Thank you for looking at it. And, Keleios, have a care tonight."

"I will, Nerine."

Nerine said softly, in a neutral voice, "And if you fight the black healer, kill him."

The voice betrayed nothing, but there was a look in the eyes.

Keleios said, "That is my intention."

Nerine smiled, a very rare thing for her. She left the forge area, presumably to find Allanna, but Keleios wondered what harm the black healer had done to the girl.

Just outside the smithy doors a white envelope floated at eye level. The outside was marked 'Keleios' and sealed with wax. It bore Poula's seal: crossed sprigs of mint with a ring at the bottom. The note requested that Keleios go to Poula's room, and she did as the note asked.

Poula was sitting in the familiar dark with her back to the door. She did not turn as Keleios stepped in the room. "So you go on the sands tonight."

"It would seem so, Master Poula."

The silence stretched outward, and Keleios let it stand untouched. Poula stood, her chair scraping backwards. "I think this was ill advised, Keleios."

"Perhaps it was, but he challenged me."

Poula turned swift and angry, striding down on her. "But you berated him in front of witnesses. You gave him a reason to challenge you. And you let your anger best you. Do you know what your chances are of winning against the black healer?"

"I think my chances are good."

"How could you be so foolish? Don't you understand, Keleios? He is a black healer, completely treacherous. You have never faced such as that in the arena."

"I am prepared, Poula."

"You cannot be prepared. Nothing prepares you for dealing with true evil."

Keleios raised her left hand, with its leather covering, to Poula's eye level. "I know what evil is, Poula."

Poula turned from her and walked a few steps. Without turning around, she asked, "Who is your second?"

"Belor."

"Find him. I'll rearrange the afternoon classes. You and he are excused for the rest of the day to prepare. Go on; get out."

Keleios stepped forward, one hand reaching then dropping to her side. "I had to answer challenge."

"Remember what I taught you."

Keleios stepped through the darkness and embraced her.

Poula stiffened then gripped the arms that held her.

Keleios whispered, "I remember everything you ever taught me."

Poula released her first, and Keleios stepped back.

Keleios started to say something, but it would all have been lies. There was no real comfort when death was near.

Keleios realized then that Poula had worn her mask. For the first time since Keleios was ten, Poula had hidden from her. Keleios hesitated at the door, wanting to say something, anything, but she left, closing the door quietly behind her.

The apprentice dorms were empty, each bed carefully made, every one like every other. At the end of the long room Alys lay in bed. A journeyman in healer's blue sat in a chair beside the bed, reading to herself. Alys' laughter filled the dim room. Poth was patiently chasing a piece of yellow yarn over the coverlet. She crouched, furred tail tense, and pounced. The child giggled.

It was Poth who saw her first, giving a loud meow. Alys yelled, "Keleios, Keleios!"

The journeyman stood and swept back long blond hair. "Keleios, how good of you to visit. Do you wish me to leave?"

"Sit down—Valira, isn't it?"

"Yes, I am honored that you remember."

"Sit down. There is no need for you to leave."

Keleios sat on the edge of the bed. "And how are you doing this morning?"

"Oh, much better."

"Do you remember what happened last night?"

A frown crossed the small face, and she would not meet Keleios' eyes. "No, no, I don't 'memember."

Keleios corrected her. "Remember—you don't remember. You must have clear diction or you'll never be able to cast herb spells."

"I know."

"I didn't come here for a lesson, apprentice. I came to see how you were."

The girl looked up, eyes shining. "Poth came to visit me."

"I see that." Keleios picked the cat up and stroked her. "She attends to my duties better than I do sometimes."

Alys tossed the yarn at the cat. Poth threw a reproachful glance to Keleios then went to chase it. Poth hadn't even liked chasing yarn when she was a kitten. Keleios hid her smile as best she could. It was terribly obvious to Keleios that the cat was only pretending to enjoy herself. But the child was fooled.

"Alys, we must talk about last night, but it can wait until you feel like talking about it."

Again she wouldn't look at Keleios. "I don't want to talk 'bout it right now." She looked up quickly. "I mean about, about it."

"All right, apprentice, get some rest, and I'll try to look in on you just before dinner. Come along, Poth."

"Oh, can't she stay?"

"No, we have work to do." Seeing the look on the child's face, Keleios added, "But perhaps she'll come visit again soon." The cat looked thoroughly disgusted but gave Alys a last body rub and then hopped down to the floor. She padded noiselessly at Keleios' heels.

When they were out in the hall, Keleios said, "That was a very nice gesture on your part."

The cat didn't answer but bounded ahead, white-tipped tail held high. She vanished through the door to Keleios' room without waiting.

Keleios opened the door and went after her. "All right, what's wrong with you?"

The cat sat on the bed and licked a delicate forepaw and stared at Keleios.

"You think I could have avoided the challenge with Lothor."

The cat concentrated on grooming her back and pointedly ignored Keleios.

"You think I'm going to get myself killed. We can win tonight." Keleios went down on her knees by the bed, eye level with the cat. The golden eyes stared at her, hostile, distant.

"I will win tonight," Keleios said.

The cat gave a small sneeze and went back to grooming, swiping one paw over her face.

There was a knock at the door. Belor entered without being asked. He wore a charcoal-grey jerkin, cut short, over brown trousers. White linen showed at rounded collar and sleeve. He stopped. "What's wrong? Not more exciting news, I hope."

"No, Poth's mad at me. She thinks I was foolish, like Poula, and you."

Belor said nothing but leaned against the bedpost. His blue eyes said everything for him.

Keleios stood and paced the room. "All right, all right, I let my anger best me. But who could have known he would challenge me? He did come here to marry me, after all."

"It was not entirely unexpected."

"All right, he has had two duels since he entered Astrantha. But he lost the second; if Glairstran hadn't taken a vow of mercy, we might have been rid of him then."

"That is awfully cold for a follower of Cia."

"Our vows say only we cannot murder. When someone is trying to take our life, we are not bound to give mercy." It was a matter of disagreement between them. He had fought in the arena twice, once by steel and once by magic. He had been victor both times. He had killed both times, but he was not comfortable with it.

"What are your plans, Keleios?"

"To use what herb spells I already have made up. To strike viciously and completely."

"What spells do you have made up?"

"At least two sleep spells, a ward of pain, a ward of fire, a spell of dragon summoning that I've been working on, and one for demon summoning."

He raised a pale eyebrow. "Do you think it wise?"

"I was curious; I haven't used it yet."

"Curiosity such as that, you do not need."

She ignored him and went on. "I have a potion to bring pleasant dreams and some powder of illusion. The powder is very unpredictable, though."

"There's no substitute for a good illusionist."

Keleios smiled. "Not yet, anyway."

"The sleep spells, yes; the ward of pain and fire, yes. I don't know what good dragon summoning will do. He might be able to gate in a demon of his own, so demon summoning may be useful. But for Magnus' sake be careful what you bring in. The illusion powder could be useful as a distraction."

Keleios agreed with his assessment. "So much for planning."

"Now wait, Keleios. You need more of a plan. Remember, if he kills you, I fight him."

"I absolve you of it, Belor. You are my second, but this is not your fight."

He stepped close to her and spoke softly. "If he kills you, it will be my fight."

She smiled. "I suppose if things were reversed, I'd do the same."

"You know you would." He pulled a slip of paper from the bed where it had been pinned. It was a note from Fidelis. She had retired to the stillroom for the rest of the day. She would not be interrupting them. Belor said, "That was very considerate of her."

"Very. She plans on killing me tomorrow night, so why should she worry?"

Keleios stretched arms over head and said, "I must spend some time in the hall of gods this afternoon."

"Quite a bit of time. How many gods do you normally worship now, four?"

"Three, but I will have to waste something on Zardok and Loth."

Belor raised a pale eyebrow. "You are going to make an offering to the black prince's god?"

"He doesn't own him personally; he is merely a priest. And Loth is the god of war, bloodshed, and battles. You do not enter the arena without first offering something to the god who can control it."

Belor shrugged; he didn't make sacrifice to Loth, regardless of circumstance.

As if reading his mind, Keleios said, "And before you go all self-righteous on me, illusionist, you worship the Shadow Lady. She isn't exactly good."

He shifted uncomfortably. "No, but she is the only illusionist among the gods."

"That is not true. There is Shalinelle, the elven goddess of beauty, truth, and music. She is an illusionist."

He smiled. "And you have to be at least partly elven to worship her."

"Not always."

Keleios left it at that. If Shalinelle wanted him, she would have him. If not, all the sacrifices on the island wouldn't make him a worshipper.

The midday meal was tense and short. Rumors like wind moved round the dining hall. All the voices fell silent as Keleios passed, but the wind of buzzing voices trailed her.

The hall of gods stretched cool and shadowed. A thick haze of incense nearly choked her as she entered. The vast pillared hall was cluttered with altars and carven figures of gods.

It had been Zeln's idea that people would prefer to send their children to a school where they could worship as their parents chose. He had been right.

There was something about the hall of gods. Perhaps it was the presence of so many holy items, or the magic, or just the emotions of the worshippers, coming in their endless line. Or the presence of lonely students first away from home, crying to their gods. The place had a claustrophobic feel to it, the stones weighed down, the pillars looked too frail to support. The chanting and the cloying sweet incense tried to hide it, but underneath was the neck-ruffling scent of blood. This was a place of sacrifice, and things died here. Everyone passed through the double doors, everyone. When the gods can reach out and punish, there is no disbelief.

The elven gods were here, tucked away in a cramped corner, nearly touching one another. Keleios made her first sacrifice to Elventir, god of agriculture. He had been the first god that she had chosen for herself.

When Keleios was seven, a sprig of mint that she had grown herself sprouted on his altar and grew into a tremendous plant before her eyes. People had come for miles around to get a start off of that mint plant. Keleios had worshipped Elventir ever since, even if she was not an earth-witch and had little time for gardening.

She placed one half-open white rose, a sprig of thyme, and a ripe red tomato on his altar.

He was the only elven god she regularly worshipped. The human pantheon seemed more forgiving of her dual nature. One goddess shared both pantheons. She was the goddess of the hunt, archery, and wild things; and she had a vindictive nature. She was half-elven daughter of Urle, human smithy god, and Shalinelle, elven goddess of beauty. She stood with the humans in the hall of gods.

Keleios laid a short dagger she had made herself, and a rabbit skin that had been killed and cured with her own hands. Urelle or Wolelle always demanded sacrifices that had been done by the hands of her worshippers.

Urle, god of the smithy, was next. He was Keleios' personal god, for she was a minor priestess in his temple, as were most enchanters. She laid a plain gold ring on his altar. It was the ring of protection she commonly wore and had made with her own hands. She did not usually give such rare magic to the altar. Urle understood what work went into such a simple thing. He was content with less for all but one day a year. If this were to be the last time she worshipped him, Keleios wanted it to be special. The ring was all shining magic, and she felt good about giving it to her god.

Zardok, consort to the All-Mother, was next. He was the sorcerer among the gods, and Keleios would need all her sorcerous powers tonight. She placed a flawless opal, the size of her middle fingernail, on his altar. Zardok was the god of wealth and would accept only jewels and precious metals. He was not a poor man's god. He was also the god of madness, and for that reason alone Keleios worshipped him as little as possible. He was too unpredictable and too powerful.

She knelt before Loth's altar, god of bloodshed, war, and violence. She came empty-handed and drew her dagger. She made a diagonal cut across her left forearm and let the blood drip onto the altar. She laid her bleeding arm directly on the cool stone and said, "I do not often come to you, great god that you are. But I come to you now, offering myself as sacrifice, my own blood to coat your altar. Guide me tonight; let my blows be swift and sure, let my enemies hide themselves in terror. Give me victory tonight as I give you blood today."

There was a small sound behind her, and she whirled, knife held ready in her right hand. Lothor stood there, a strange half-smile on his face and a tied but living hawk under his arm. Keleios could see the bird's frantic heartbeat as its chest rose up and down.

He wore a priest's garment over his clothes; perfect blackness with the blood-tipped sword of Loth sewn across the chest. "Well, Keleios, Loth's two favorite sacrifices, a bird of prey and his follower's blood. I wonder which he will favor?"

She said nothing but cleaned her dagger and put it away. She walked past him without a word, and he called, "Keleios."

She stopped and half-turned.

He strode toward her and made a lightning grab for her right wrist. She pulled back, but he was quick, almost elf-quick. His pale face flushed and he said, "Your arm, show me your arm."

There was something about his voice, a note of urgency; she did what he asked. She held out her left arm.

"The wound."

He seemed almost afraid, and she showed him the underside of her arm without a word. He brushed the blood away with his long fingers, but there was no wound. He hissed through clenched teeth. "You are a woman; he would not honor you."

Keleios stared at the unblemished flesh. She was shaken, a sign of favoritism from an evil god was not always a good sign. But she spoke boldly, calmly. "You say it is an honor. What does it mean?"

He stared at her, angry.

"You are a priest of Loth; act like one. Perform your priestly duties; interpret this sign for me."

He nodded and spoke. "Any sign that the god Loth has deigned to use his powers is an honor. It could mean that he is well pleased with your offering and nothing more. It could mean he will grant what you asked—victory over me tonight, I would think. It could mean that he will lay a heavy hand on your life in the next few days. That is what it could mean."

"Thank you, priest. May your sacrifice be as blest."

She turned to go, and he did not call after her.

Keleios walked into her room to find a crowd. Melandra sat on the bed, stroking Poth. Her dress was forest green and flattered her thick gold-brown hair. Keleios had helped her pick out the cloth. It was time the girl stopped dressing like a peasant.

Tobin and Belor stood quietly talking. The younger man's bright orange-red clothing was a sharp contrast to Belor's casual grey and brown. They had laid her armor, weapons, and spells out on the bed. Keleios crossed to the water basin and poured water from the pitcher to the bowl. She cleansed her bloodied arm hurriedly. Tobin stepped close to her and said quietly for only her ears, "What's wrong?"

"I sacrificed to Loth."

He stared at the smooth unbroken skin of her arms. "An animal?"

"No."

He smiled. "Then it means victory. You will triumph over Lothor tonight."

"Over a high priest of Loth? Over the crown prince of Loth's pet country? Something is wrong with that."

"You worry too much, Keleios. Take it for a good sign and let it go."

"When the gods are near, trouble is never far behind."

"If you are determined to think badly of this, then I can't help you. But by Magnus' red hand, don't let it spoil your concentration."

Belor had heard some, and she had to repeat the tale

for the entire room. Melandra's brown eyes were a sparkling glint from her veil of hair. Both she and Tobin should have been elsewhere, and Keleios knew how much favor swapping had gone into it.

"I'm glad you are all here."

Tobin grinned, and Melandra dipped her head even lower. Keleios had spent a great deal of time helping the girl gain some sense of worth. Now she looked up, and the scar that twisted her mouth made the smile an uncomfortable thing to see.

Melandra was very brave to do it with her beloved Belor in the room.

They dressed Keleios in the leather armor with its gold-plated studding; it was a familiar snugness. The magic bracers went on over the arms of the leather. A long knife for in fighting was fastened at her right hip. Luckweaver was secured at her left-hand side. The golden helm, a gift from her elven grandfather, she laid back on the bed. It was a thing of great craftsmanship. It was the sculptured head of a bird, each feather etched, the eyeholes in the center like an owl, so she could see. The nosepiece was a small hooked bill. Her chin and mouth came where a lower mandible would have been. The feathers covered to her collarbone, carved to fluff at the edges as if real feathers rested on her shoulders. The helm was a thing of beauty but no magic. The spells lay encased in cloth bags, a clay vessel, all enchanted and secure against breakage. They would hang on a cross strap across her chest attaching to her sword belt. The last thing to lie on the bed was a golden shield. It had been a gift from her journeyman smithy master Edan. The shield held a small magic dweomer. It had cost him dearly to magic the shield.

Keleios unbound her hair, and Melandra brushed every tangle from it. It was a wavy frothy mass. Keleios braided only the hair on either side of her face, leaving most of it free but holding it back from her eyes. It was an elfish custom, something the half-elven

Loltun wouldn't recognize. For all he knew of elves, he might as well be wholly human.

She asked them to leave then. They did, all but Poth. The cat rolled onto her side and stared at Keleios with lazy golden eyes. Only Poth watched the last few weapons go into place. It was a rule among the Nagosidhe that no one but a fellow warrior watch you. The Nagosidhe were a tiny sect of the Wrythian army. Men called them assassins. Though Keleios had only brushed the surface of the dark and efficiently violent way of the Nagosidhe, she did not break the rules. Her elfish uncle, Balasaros, said Keleios did not have the temperament for true Nagosidhe. Keleios was never sure if he was complimenting or insulting her.

The wrist sheath was useless with the bracers on and she changed that throwing knife to a sheath that went down her back. The hilt brushed against her neck. The second stayed in its boot sheath. Inside the neck of her armor she tucked a garrote. The thin double strand of wire with its gripping places on both ends fitted snugly and invisibly into place.

She was sitting with Poth on her lap when there was a knock on the door. It would be Tobin to fetch her for the evening meal. "Come in."

Most boys didn't get their first set of plate mail until they had ascended to title or reached their full growth, but being a prince, Tobin had been an exception. For his last birthday he had received a suit of plate mail. It was glittering and gold like so much of Meltaanian armorwork, with flowers and beasts etched along it. The helmet tucked under his arm was scrolled with vines, and two lions battled on its top. Tobin was very proud of the gaudy suit, for he, like most Meltaanians, liked sparkle and glitter. It had a small magic dweomer on it because no wizard could wear that much normal metal and still be able to cast spells.

Keleios slipped on the helmet, cool, constricting, protecting. She hefted the shield to her left arm and tested its balance. A wrist strap needed tightening.

Tobin's shield was large, almost as big as he, and

strapped to his back. A short sword and dagger hung at his belt.

Lastly, she settled her spells and pouches round her belt. When it was as comfortable as it would get, she said, "Let's go," and led the way out the door. Poth trailed after them.

Neither spoke as they turned toward the stairs. Someone was running through the library, someone whose breathing was ragged and loud, a voice saying, "Mother help us. Mother help us."

Tobin slipped on his helmet, and Keleios crouched forward, motioning him to stay put in his clanking armor.

She hunted through the shelves, shadowing the gasping stranger. It was Selene, leaning against a shelf, tears trailing quietly down her cheeks. "Selene?"

She jumped as if struck then turned and flattened herself against the books, moving away from Keleios. She muttered, "I didn't know, I didn't know."

"Selene, what has happened?"

"I didn't understand, how . . ."

"Journeyman, tell me what has happened."

"I . . . I gave tea to Master Dracen, the conjure master, drugged tea, spelled tea."

"Selene, what sort of spell was in the tea?"

"I didn't know."

"You didn't know the tea was drugged?"

She shook her head.

"Who gave you the tea?"

"Master Fidelis."

"Where is Dracen now?"

"She took him."

"Fidelis? How, Selene, how?"

"She had a wand, and she changed him into a large black snake. He didn't even wake up after he was shapechanged."

Selene turned wide brown eyes to Keleios and said, "And Poula . . ."

"What about Poula?"

The girl turned away and began to walk down the

shelf isle. Keleios caught her and spun her round. "What about Poula?"

Tobin stood behind them, all gold and unseen.

Selene said, "She's dead, she's dead." Once having said it, she kept saying it over and over again. Tears and laughter came in torrents. Keleios shoved Selene into Tobin's arms. "Get her to a healer and send a healer to Master Poula's room. Have Fidelis stopped and detained."

Before he could answer, she was running toward Poula's room.

Luckweaver snicked from his sheath as she eased open the door. Just this side of the table Poula lay face down. A wide pool of darkness was spreading from her back across the floor. The reeds had been scuffed clear, and the blood traced along the bare stones.

Her first instinct was to run to her, protect her somehow, but it wouldn't help if she fell victim too. Keleios forced herself to search the room and see that nothing lurked. She sent a frantic call to Jodda, nearly knocking the healer into a wall with the force of the summons. All she could do was wait.

Keleios stood beside Poula and carefully knelt, setting her sword on clean reeds near at hand. The bird helmet she took off and placed by the sword. She swept back the graying hair and touched the mask, but her fingers couldn't find a pulse in the throat. Keleios' chest tightened, her throat closing around unshed tears. She would not cry, not yet. Had Fidelis done this, too?

The flesh was still warm. The wound flowed slow but had not begun to clot. From the angle and size she judged the murder weapon to be a knife, straight to the heart. Not everyone could knife someone in the back and strike the heart; you had to know just where to enter.

She resisted the urge to hold the body; nothing must be disturbed. Healers were coming, but it was really too late.

Tears sparkled in the candlelight. Whoever had come had needed light, been welcomed in, betrayed her.

The light glinted off something—a small oval mirror that was propped on Poula's table. What did a blind woman need with a mirror? Keleios sheathed her sword and went to the mirror. An envelope sat in front of it, sealed with wax and bearing Keleios' name.

She hesitated. Where was Jodda? Keleios picked the envelope up; on the back was written, "Answers are inside." She recognized the long swirled handwriting: Fidelis.

Keleios broke the seal and found one sheet of paper. "Half-Elf, If you want to know the how and why of it, repeat the words written below. The mirror will answer all your questions. The Witch." There was a spell written on the bottom half of the paper. Keleios recognized it as a triggering spell; speak the words, add a little sorcery, and presto, magic. Keleios had to do it, had to know.

She placed hands on either side of the mirror and spoke, "Mirror, hear me. Pane of glass, oval seer of this room, hear me. I enchant thee; I adorn thee with magic. Show me what I seek, show me what I need to know."

Nothing happened at first, then the clear surface clouded as if her breath were fogging it.

Jodda entered the room with two journeyman healers in tow. Tobin was behind them, and he came to stand near Keleios and watch the mirror.

The fog vanished as if sucked away, leaving a mirror image of the room. The reeds on the floor were undisturbed, no body lay in the image.

Tobin called to the journeyman Feldspar. "We need two witnesses for this."

Jodda nodded her permission, and the Zairdian healer stood and watched the images.

Fidelis passed in view bearing a tray with tea on it. Poula met her saying, "A new blending of mints. I'll try it, but I believe I've tried them all." Then they passed from the mirror's sight.

The quiet murmur of their voices; the tea was good, but Poula had something similar.

Fidelis' voice next, admiring the completeness of Poula's herb racks. "May I borrow a pinch of dried tarrow root?"

"Certainly." Poula, being blind, had a different system for knowing what was in the jars, so she would have to get it.

They came into sight, Poula walking to the herb shelves, her back to the woman. Fidelis brought a dagger that flashed in the light. Keleios whispered, "Poula, Poula, please see it, please see it."

The tall, slender woman stepped close, peering over her shoulder. "How do you tell what is in all these?" Fidelis was almost leaning against the woman. An arm swung round Poula's chest, the dagger flashing upward. Poula's spine stiffened, and everything froze for an instant. The candlelight flickered over the scene. Poula's hand stretched outward as if reaching for something, her spine bending backward, her leather mask. Fidelis' grey dress, shimmered like silk, face buried in Poula's unbound hair. Then she stepped back and pulled out the knife.

Poula stood for a moment, heart blood pumping down her back, black and rich with life, then she fell forward. She struggled barely at all. Fidelis knelt and stirred the reeds away from her, making the struggle look worse.

The woman passed from sight, then returned with her tea tray and left.

Jodda came quietly up behind them, eyes on the mirror, and said, "I can do nothing for her."

Keleios didn't react for a moment then she turned slowly. "You cannot raise her?"

"No, there was a curse on the weapon used. Whoever dies by it is dead once and for all."

"A soul-eater?"

"I don't know."

"She's dead then?"

"Yes."

Keleios walked past her and knelt by the body. Tears slid silently down her face. She stroked the hair and said, "Poula, I swear to you that you will rest easy with Fidelis beside you."

A voice spoke in the room. "Keleios Incantare."

She looked up to find Fidelis' face staring out at her from the mirror. Keleios stood and went to it. "Fidelis?"

The face smiled. "For you, half-elf, a present, from your old friend, Harque." Fidelis turned away from the mirror, then back, laughing. "And from me, of course. A knife in the dark, half-elf." The mirror cracked. Keleios threw an arm in front of her face and turned. The mirror exploded outward in a shower of glass. Keleios staggered and found herself standing in a ring of glass slivers, like solid rain. For a moment she was stunned, numb; she thought she had escaped unhurt, then two points of sharp pain touched her. A piece of glass in her left cheek and the left side of her neck. The neck wound covered her fingers with blood.

Jodda touched her shoulder. "Keleios, let me remove the glass." The healer's gentle fingers removed the slivers. Keleios gasped at the neck wound. It was deep. Just a touch deeper and it might have killed her, but armor and Luckweaver had protected her.

"You failed, Fidelis," she whispered.

Jodda gave a small cry and dropped the last piece of glass. She was cradling her hand. Blisters covered her fingers. She stared up at Keleios, blue eyes wide. "Poison, Dermog. Keleios . . ."

Keleios understood. Dermog was a derivative of demon venom; no white healer could touch it, let alone cure it. Only a black healer could save her now. The only black healer in the keep had challenged her to the sands, and hoped to kill her.

"I've summoned Lothor," Tobin said.

She stared at the young man, in his gaudy plate mail. "It won't help."

"Only a black healer can save you."

"Lothor hopes to kill me tonight, Tobin. Why would he save me now?"

The boy shifted uncomfortably. "He answers my summons. He is coming."

As if conjured by Tobin's words, the black healer entered the room. He was dressed in full plate armor, black as the night, plain and unadorned. Only the helmet sported two long horns as decoration. His double-headed battle-ax, Gore, was belted at his side. He was an enchanter in his full power and had bound the ax to his soul. "How may I be of service?"

Keleios glared at him. "Didn't Tobin tell you?"

He nodded, black helmet moving ever so slightly.

"Then why ask?"

His silver eyes stood out like jewels in the ebony of his helmet.

"Zardok's crown, you two, get on with it. Heal her, Lothor." Tobin stared from one to the other.

Keleios swallowed hard. The wounds were beginning to burn, as if someone had shoved a piece of red-hot metal into her skin. Her voice came out breathy. "Perhaps he came to watch me die."

"Lothor?" Tobin said. He took a step toward the man, then stood undecided.

Lothor stripped off his gauntlets. "I did not come to watch you die, Keleios." He strode over the broken glass, grinding it underfoot. His voice came whisper soft from behind the helmet. "What if I would not heal you unless you promised to marry me?"

The burning was spreading down into her chest. Each breath was becoming painful. She took as deep a breath as she could manage and said, "Then I would die."

He laughed softly and laid long white fingers on her neck. "I thought you would say that."

A soothing coolness spread from his hands through her skin. She took a deep shaking breath. The burning was chased away by the cool healing magic. There were two tiny bursts of warmth as he healed the outer wounds as well.

Keleios stared at him. "Thank you, black healer."

"You are welcome." His hand lingered on her neck, and she was forced to step back out of reach.

"Why, black healer?" she asked.

He pulled on his gauntlets. "Why did I save you?"

"Yes."

"I have my reasons."

She could feel the weight of his gaze on her, an almost physical touch. Keleios shivered before she could stop it. "What reasons?"

An explosion sounded far off, muffled. Keleios staggered as a journeyman sorcery blared through her mind. "Carrick bids everyone to their posts. We are under attack. The communications tower was just destroyed."

Keleios blinked and found Tobin staring at her. He had had the same message. Jodda was pale. Feldspar murmured a prayer to Mother Blessen.

Only Lothor stood apart. "What was that explosion?"

Keleios answered, "The communications tower." She retrieved her helmet where it lay by Poula's body. "I will kill Fidelis for you, Poula, I swear it." The lamplight swam in tears. Keleios shoved the helmet on and stood. There was no time to cry, but Keleios was glad of the masking gold helmet. She strode out the door, with Tobin behind her.

Lothor called, "Where are you going?"

"To our posts, to defend this keep," she called back.

Lothor caught up with them. "I will help you."

She glanced at him. "Suit yourself, black healer, but if you hinder us in any way, you become the enemy."

"Of course."

Keleios led the way to the cellars. A narrow doorway was nearly lost in the wall by the boys' dormitory. A spider web hung across its top, and Lothor brushed it away. Cool, damp air flowed up the stairs against them. The stairs allowed two abreast, but barely. They came to the lower corridor stretching off into the cool darkness.

Around the first corner the darkness stretched velvet and whole. A second explosion sounded and the keep shuddered above their heads. For a moment Keleios could feel the weight of the castle on top of her, making the air stale and her chest tight. The feeling passed, as it always did. An elf underground in the dark, what a wonderfully dwarfish joke. Keleios unsheathed her sword and led the way into the dark.

6

Blood Oath

Tobin conjured a blue witchlight. It bobbed just behind Keleios so as not to ruin her night vision. They had come this way before, in practice.

"Where are the other guards?" Lothor asked.

"There are no others," Keleios said.

"The three of us to defend all the lower reaches of the castle. Are you mad?"

Keleios glanced back at him. "You are free to go back."

Tobin said, "The lower reaches are designed for just a sorcerer and a enchanter to guard. A crystal ward guards everything in the lower reaches. If anyone dares to dig under or breech the lower areas, it would kill them."

"Crystal wards are very rare," Lothor said. "It is indeed the ultimate warding."

Tobin nodded. "That is why only the two of us. Someone on this side would have to remove the crystal ward for anyone to gain entrance."

"And what is to stop someone from doing just that?" Lothor asked.

"No one would betray this keep," Tobin said.

Keleios realized what he meant a moment before Tobin said, "Fidelis, but even she wouldn't betray the entire keep."

"Mother Blessen save us," Keleios whispered.

A scream shattered the quiet. It froze them for a heartbeat, then Keleios cursed, "Urle's forge, they couldn't have broken through." They broke into a jog, weapons held close and pointing out and down.

The sound of many men came from up ahead, and Keleios slowed, waving them back. She crept forward, willing herself unseen. It was not magic, and thus not detectable, an elfish ability to blend with surroundings to simply be overlooked. She came to the huge doorway that led to the main cellar. Light flowed from it, bright and golden, lamplight, and torchlight. Keleios peered round the edge of the doorway and found a sea of men. They stood in silence like good soldiers, but their clothes spoke of the sea. Armor was almost nonexistent among them. Five men in the group did not belong. They were dressed all in black. Torchlight fluttered off the device sewn on their chests: a decaying skull with green eyes. It was the symbol of Verm, god of corruption, Loth's twin brother. All five gave off a magic aura and they were black healers. If she hadn't seen Fidelis' treachery herself, she might have accused Lothor of being an accomplice. The thought came to her that he still might be.

Struggling in the grips of one of the black-robed was Melandra. Keleios bit her lip to keep from crying out. She would not loose Melandra, too. A basket of carrots lay spilled at the girl's feet. Melandra had been a favorite of the cook's and was often in charge of the kitchen crew. Three others were captured with her. The tall boy had his arms bound behind him. The smallest girl was crying and huddling against a black-haired girl. Keleios ought to have known the Zairdian girl but couldn't place the name.

The black healer jerked on Melandra's arm, but she did not cry out. She had spent years enduring much worse than that. Keleois forced her hands to unclench. Anger would not help them; planning would.

Keleios stood and searched the room for some way to save them, but three couldn't fight a hundred. All they could do was keep the fighters from gaining the upper areas. They could not rush in and save the children and let these men through. She had to defend her post, to defend this keep, no matter the cost. Her duty was clear but she cursed it.

One black healer in particular seemed to shine unbelievably bright. If he was as magic as he appeared, they would find out just how powerful the lower reaches' defenses were. The only course was to whittle them down on the way—the only way—to the higher levels and hope that they didn't kill the prisoners. Keleios took one of the fire ward pouches from her belt and sprinkled it lightly in front of the doorway. She sent a silent prayer to Urle that she would remain unseen.

Two men were dispatched to see if that flicker of movement had meant anything. They hit the ward at almost the same time and the fire roared round them. Their shrieks chased Keleios back to the others.

She whispered her findings to Lothor and Tobin, then pulled them farther into the darkness away from the screams.

Keleios stared at Lothor in his night-black armor. "I thought about killing you, prince. And if I find you've betrayed us I still might."

"Why should I betray you?"

"Five below are black healers or dressed as such."

He was so silent that Keleios knew he was hiding something. When he spoke, it did not help him. "So Velen has won."

"Who is Velen?"

"My brother. There is no time for more now. But I did not betray this keep."

She turned from him because there wasn't time. "I set a fire ward that should keep them busy for a while." But as if her words had cursed it, a dull explosion sounded. "Urle's forge, the ward's down." They ran back up the corridor.

"That isn't the only ward down. Feel," Tobin said.

The tingling of the keep's main ward was gone.

"Lothor, set a ward across the hall, something damaging. Tobin, set a second just behind his; make yours inconspicuous."

"If they merge . . ."

"You could be killed, I know. But it will work, and

I haven't the skill to do it. My control of wardings isn't fine enough for it."

Tobin had seen enough of her classwork to know it was true.

Lothor asked, standing on the other side of his glowing ward, "And what will you be doing while he risks his life?" His ward was perfect, large and showy, as she knew it would be. They could not miss it. She ignored the insult and simply replied, "Something only I can do."

She turned and pressed her body against the left-hand wall. The spells were there, in the walls themselves, waiting to be activated. She called enchantment first, and it was a welcome familiar heaviness of magic. Then she called sorcery to her as well, and it was a light tingling magic, like caged lightning. She wound them together into a single rope of power. The makers of the spell had intended two people to call the spell, for enchantment and sorcery were a rare combination in one person. Keleios knew her own magic as she knew her own hand or face in the mirror. If she failed, it would be the sorcery that would betray her. If you failed at instant enchantment, you simply failed to enchant your item. Failed sorcery could lash back upon the spellcaster, and that possibility was why she didn't often combine her talents.

It felt like the tingling rush of sorcery but quieter, stronger, controlled.

She whispered to the stones, "Walls, hear me; do as I bid. Stop the wicked, help the good, protect your own safety and those up above. Be my strong arms for this day." Keleois stood away from the wall and touched it gently. The stones hummed with enchantment. She turned to the right-hand wall and merged her power with it, also.

Sweat beaded her face, but she smiled. The spell was a combination of Bellarion's strong-arm enchantment and Venna's trip spell. Master Tally and Zeln the Just had invented it together.

Keleios turned her attention to Tobin. He was

pressed inches from the white glare of the first ward. She could see his sorcery tracing outward, delicate, possessing a restraint that the black healer did not even understand. The lines of yellow-gold power spread outward framed by the walls, floor, and ceiling. His ward was a phantom, lost against the glare of Lothor's.

She smiled at Tobin's relieved and proud grin. "I knew you could," she whispered, and motioned them both farther down the hall.

The second fire ward was poured along the floor.

Keleios decided that the warding of pain would go just before the turn to the stairs but not yet. There was scouting to be done.

A second dull explosion came, followed by screams.

"How are they breaking through those wards so quickly?"

Lothor said, "You show contempt toward my sorcery because it lacks delicacy." She stared at him, for the thoughts were her own. "But we are taught to use raw power to overcome any obstacle."

"So you are all taught the same way?"

He nodded.

She began to have an idea.

When next she scouted, only two of the black healers strode in front.

Walking a horse-length in front of them was a prisoner. Keleios couldn't put a name to the blond girl. She was six or seven and in Fidelis' beginning herbwitchery class. Her blue eyes stood out in a very pale face.

She stopped, uncertain, looking back toward her captors for reassurance. One in front, black hood thrown back to show him every bit as blond and blue-eyed as she, motioned her forward.

Keleios could almost feel the child's pulse racing.

Keleios took one step away from the wall to warn the child but a soldier stepped into the enchantment.

Arms of stone shot from the walls. They grabbed the man and began to crush and tear. The yellow-haired black healer stopped the fighters from rushing in. He stood arms wide and shot magic out toward the walls.

Keleois flinched at the power in the dispelling. If it had been only sorcery, it would have worked, but enchantment is a stouter thing.

The soldier hung limp and bloodied. The man tried again to dispel it as if he couldn't believe he had failed.

His next attempt was at destruction, and power like red lightning played along the hall.

The child, waiting alone, stumbled back in fright and fell into the fire ward. Flame roared up her legs, drowning out her screams. Her small frame was engulfed in fire. It rushed outward a sheet of flame, orange death. It filled the hallway with burning.

When the fire cleared, the men stood untouched. The girl had done her duty. She had set off the ward with them safely out of range. Her bones were twisted and black, a charcoal heap.

The magic-user tried once more, and this time Keleios leaned against the wall. It was the sorcery that tripped the enchantment like a string on a snare. She reached outward through the cold stone toward that sorcery. Keleios wasn't sure how to absorb it, so she held it in by brute will. The stone arms on the left side vanished.

The blond spellcaster smiled, pleased with himself.

They entered the cleared way, the right-hand wall straining after them. When as many as possible were there, Keleios released her control. The arms shot out and grappled. Metal screamed on stone to little effect.

"You would have used that on me?"

Keleios whirled, sword half-rising from its sheath. Lothor stood there and repeated his question. "You planned to use that fire ward on me, didn't you?"

"You challenged me to the arena. What did you expect? And what are you doing here?"

"You have been gone a long time."

They backed away, leaving the men to the carnage of the stones.

Keleios poured out the warding of pain at the bend to the stairs.

Lothor said quietly, "I know the magic-user who leads them."

"Who is he and how powerful?"

"Tranisome the Smiler, and very."

"The smiler—what does that mean?"

"If the gods are not with us, you'll see soon enough."

"You are his prince. Can you talk to him?"

Lothor considered it. "Perhaps, but doubtful."

"Doubtful is better than facing seventy to eighty men and a powerful sorcerer."

Again Keleios crept forward and spied upon them. Another child walked before them. This time Keleios could put a name to her.

She was Bella, daughter to a Zairdian earl. She was eleven and a sorcerer of some promise. The girl paced forward nervously, sweeping long black hair from her face, eyes concentrating on the floor. Bella was good.

She stopped and flinched; she had seen it. The girl looked backward and licked her lips; she was planning something.

Tranisome came within sight and called to her, "Girl, get on with it."

"I . . . have found one."

Bella stepped a little back from it. He approached and peered at the powder line. She was standing just behind him, and it was a small matter to give a tiny push. The ward flared brighter and vanished, his screams echoing in the hall. Bella ran past him over the now-useless ward.

Tranisome writhed on the floor and shrieked, "Kill her!"

Two guards moved to obey and Keleois simply appeared before them. Luckweaver sliced one's neck and took the other in the side. The blade pulled free with a sound of breaking bone, and Keleios ran up the stairs after Bella.

The fighters were in full chase. Here was something they could fight, something to bleed and die.

Keleios let her still-bloody sword fall to the steps and touched the wall. A warding of destruction was in the walls; all it needed was a spark of sorcery. The warding blinked into place. Two fighters hit it seconds later.

Lightning exploded in blinding white fire. It raised the hair on head and arms like a secret wind. The bolt blazed down the stairway. Men screamed, ran, burned, and died.

Tranisome was still writhing and shouting, "Idiots, they want you to chase them!"

The smell of burned flesh was strong, and Keleios swallowed past it. Smoke curled from the bodies. It was not the complete incineration of a fire but as if a great lightning whip had torn along them.

Tranisome called for the boy to be brought to him. Keleios knew this one, also, briefly. It was Tobin who exclaimed, "Brion!"

Some of the fighters glanced their way. Keleios understood the frustration, the horrible helplessness of it all.

Brion was a journeyman herb-witch and fighter. His hands were bound behind his back, and they forced him to kneel by the writhing black healer.

Keleios whispered to Lothor, "What is he doing with the boy?"

"Healing himself."

"How will the boy help him?"

Lothor said nothing, only stared down at the scene below.

Bella had been quietly sick in a corner, the stench of burning hair and flesh too much for her.

The healer put hands on Brion's shoulders and the boy started to scream.

Keleios swallowed hard, fighting sickness. She knew what he was doing now. "He's using him like a grey healer uses an animal, but the boy can't take that much damage."

"His life force, no; his dead body, yes."

"This isn't healing, it's murder."

He chose not to argue.

The boy's screams stopped abruptly, and he sagged to the floor. Tranisome never lost contact with him. The body quivered, then lay very still. But it was long after that that Tranisome released the body. Then he stood and looked up the stairs, smiling.

Lothor stood in front of the ward's bare glow without his helmet and waited. It was the last ward fixed into the walls themselves. After this, it would be their magic alone.

Tranisome walked slowly, deliberately, through the bodies and stopped on the other side. The smile spread across his face. It was large and cheerful but it never reached his eyes. They remained pale and empty like a corpse's.

He bowed from the neck, still smiling. "Your brother, Velen, sends greetings, my prince."

"And what are those greetings, Tranisome?"

"Death, my prince. She must die."

"So in my absence my father's mind was changed."

The smile brightened. "Did you expect it would be otherwise, my prince?"

"No." Lothor stared at him for a moment and asked, "Am I to die also?"

"Regrettably, my prince."

"And will you do it, Tranisome?"

The smile waxed and waned, eyes never changing. "There is a bonus for your death. Someone will claim it before dawn."

Keleois stepped into sight. "But it won't be you, smiler."

Tranisome looked surprised. "I am flattered that you spoke of me, prince." His blue eyes searched her from golden helm to leather armor and shining sword hilt. "Ah, this must be . . . your intended."

"Yes."

"I am honored, but this warding will not stop me

from slaying you.'' He glanced along it. ''It is strong, but not strong enough.''

She said, ''Let us test how strong it is.'' She placed her hands flat against the surface. It glowed and shimmered through her body as she connected with it. Tobin gasped. What was a rather childish test of wills in the classroom could be deadly in combat. Though Tobin's control was better, Keleios could not ask him to do this test. It was hers to succeed or fail.

A smile of pure delight shaped Tranisome's lips but left the rest of his face untouched, like a partial mask.

Lothor understood also, and was horrified. ''Keleios, no.''

Tranisome spoke, a lilt to his voice. ''Oh, what a bonus I will make tonight.'' He matched his hands to hers.

The world narrowed to a glowing wall and hands that she could almost feel pressed against her own. He would use great force against her, that's what she was counting on.

The first surge came. Testing the strength of the ward and her. It was a careful swat of power, pure and concentrated. His smile widened, for she had not added to the force. She refused to waste energy against anything but attack. Sweat began to trickle down her face. He had more control than she had wanted him to have.

He tried again, a mere feint. He shot power through the warding, forcing her to put power into it to hold. Keleios felt him gathering strength, and she gathered hers to answer it. At the last moment, with sorcery nearly blazing in the air, she threw, not to strengthen the ward, but to burn Tranisome.

His force hit the ward unchecked, and it vanished with a dull boom. For a moment their hands met. His eyes flew open wide, and he began to burn. As the fire rushed up him and consumed him, he screamed, ''Kill her!''

As he passed, he set the partially burned bodies afire. The stair was soon filled with choking acrid smoke. His own men began to run, for he did not burn as he should have, but continued to stumble down the stairs as he flared.

"Why isn't he dead?" Keleios asked in a whisper.

"He is healing himself as he burns. Whether he dies or not will depend on whether your fire does more damage than he can heal."

Keleios swallowed very hard, bile threatening to come up. "White healing is strange enough, but this—this is abomination."

"He may live through this; your white healers would be dead by now."

The fighters down below were backing off from him; a few began to run. The fighter who gripped Melandra's arm began pulling her back with him. She struggled, trying to break free, and he hit her a backhanded blow. She staggered and was dragged off.

Keleois whispered, "Melandra." She went after them, following the cries of the burning man. The stones shuddered underfoot. Keleios paused, then ran on with Tobin and Lothor following her.

Tranisome no longer burned, and two men dragged him along. His yellow hair was gone from one side of his head, blisters and blackened skin covered his face, his clothing turned to ash in places. He moaned but no longer screamed.

Tobin shot a bolt of power and another. Two men went down and did not rise again. Keleios called her own sorcery and felt the hair on her head creep with the nearness of it. A bolt took a man in the back. Cries of, "Attack, attack," and the men turned to face them. Bows were brought to the front, and Keleios flattened herself to the ground. Tobin rushed to her, taking her behind his great shield.

Lothor, shieldless, strode toward them. He pointed the blade of his ax at them, and a roaring bolt of red energy poured out. Arrows bounced off his ebony armor, and the red waves cut swaths of death in their ranks. A round ball rolled down toward him and exploded into thick grey smoke. When the smoke cleared, they were gone. Lothor led the way now.

There was a hissing sound, and Keleios called it to their attention. Tobin spotted a tiny spark on one side of the hall; its twin sparkled across from it.

Lothor yelled, "Back, run!"

They ran. Bella, waiting at the foot of the stairs, came out of hiding to question what was wrong. An explosion rocked the stones and threw them all forward. They scrambled up and ran as the second explosion echoed the first, and the walls began to crumble.

The world was full of roaring falling rocks, and there was no air to breathe. Keleois felt deafened by the rushing force, her head vibrating with the rumbling.

It was impossible to stand, and she crawled along the buckling floor. Rocks bounced down on her, bruising her body. She didn't know where the others were; she was alone in the crashing world.

The world ended in jagged stone, and she could crawl no further. She tried to protect herself, using arms and curling her body, but the stones rained down. She tried to huddle underneath her shield, but the world was full of crashing stone.

Slowly, the overwhelming cacophony of sound quieted. Keleios was buried in a dark, dust-choking space. Rock touched her, enclosed her. There was no air. She panicked, arms scrambling through the rocks. Her shield buried her left arm, pinned it. She calmed herself enough to feel down her arm until she found the straps that trapped her arm to the metal. Keleios undid the straps and carefully pulled her arm free. More rocks cascaded down on top of the shield, burying it. She fought against the rock and freed herself to the waist, half-sitting but still trapped in the rock. She could breathe; nothing was broken. She would be all right unless more rock fell.

A haze of grey dust hung in the air. A second mound of rubble was in front of her and partially blocked the passageway. From what she could see there was no passageway left behind her.

She began to move cautiously, afraid of bringing more rocks down. Enchanted strength allowed her to push the larger pieces away from her. A block almost as large as her own body rested against her right leg. A hand's breadth more and she might have lost the leg.

A red glow came over the mound in front of her, and Lothor crawled into view. His witchlight glinted on something metal. He said, "I cannot find the Meltaanian prince, or the girl."

She swallowed, her throat suddenly tight. "I saw a glint of metal there." She pointed and Lothor slid down to investigate.

He cleared a shoulder in gleaming armor and stopped.

"What are you waiting for? He'll suffocate." She pressed hands to the large stone block and began to push. Her back pressed against another pile of rubble, and small stones slid down it. She stopped, worried that she would bury herself again. She needed more leverage for something this big. "What are you waiting for? Dig him out."

"I think I am getting an answer."

"What are you talking about?"

"The answer I came for these many weeks ago."

She stared up at him. "You have had your answer."

"I am asking again."

"Surely there will be a more appropriate time to discuss this."

"But this is the perfect time, Keleios. The keep falls tonight, as you predicted. I will not try to bargain with your own life, but your friend's life—that we will bargain with."

"Black healer, I'm warning you." She pressed her back into the rubble pile and pushed, cursing softly between her teeth. Rocks began sliding faster, cascading down about her shoulders and head.

"No, by the time you free yourself and drag him to the surface, it will be too late. I can heal him."

The boulder shifted the wrong way as the debris moved underneath it. Now she was holding it just to keep it from rolling on top of her. "Cursed rock. I will teleport with him."

He seemed unconcerned with her plight.

"Where? You have no idea where the fighting is or how much of the keep is still standing. You could teleport both of you into a rubble pile."

She pressed her forehead against the gritty rock. "Black healer, I would come closer killing you than marrying you. Loltun customs are too severe. I would give my life for Tobin but not my soul and the souls of my unborn children."

"Be my consort then."

"Verm's curse on you and this rock!" She called power to her hands. Too much power and she might bring down the rest of the hallway, but at least Lothor would be buried, too. Sorcery hit the rock and shattered it. When dust had settled, Lothor was staring at her, his hands spread wide, ready for battle if she chose. "Only I can heal him in time, Keleios."

She stood carefully, hands ready, sorcery bubbling just below the surface. "If Tobin dies, you die."

"And you will die in killing me. And we will all be dead, including the little girl."

Keleios cursed quietly, "Urle's holy fire, Loth's blood! You know I can't let them die."

Lothor allowed himself a small smile.

She glared at him. "Know this, black healer, if we bargain, you may get what you want, but I will make your life a living hell."

His eyes grew cold. "I expected nothing less out of this."

Keleios continued, "I will not be your consort but you be mine. For the life of my friend and the child, you be my consort, according to Astranthian laws."

He nodded. "If our child is a boy, he goes with me; a girl, she stays with you."

"No, we raise the child together according to my customs, or at least not Loltun customs."

"That isn't acceptable, Keleios. If it is a girl, I will have no use for it."

"But I will have a use for my child, male or female."

"It will be my child, too."

"If you keep reminding me of that, I will let them die before I consent."

A rumbling sounded far off, and Lothor shifted nervously. "Agreed. I will be your consort, and we will raise the child together."

She added, "And not according to Loltun customs."

He nodded. "Not according to Loltun customs. You must swear, Keleios Nightseer, swear that we will be consorts after we escape." He drew a large hunting knife. "I want a blood oath for it. That way you can't kill me without destroying yourself."

She started to argue but the very floor shuddered. "Agreed, but get on with it. And remember, this oath covers our entire bargain; you can't run away with our son if we swear this. You will be just as bound as I."

He drew off his left gauntlet and sliced his palm. He stared at the bright red blood and sliced her right hand. They clasped hands, and he spoke slowly, "By our mingled blood let us swear, and if we lie, let the gods beware of it. Let the hounds of Verm and the birds of Loth circle us if we bear false oath."

With a few simple words they were bound.

7

Demon's Edge

A small flash of healing stopped the blood but left a fresh pink scar. She looked a question at him. He answered, "A blood oath always leaves something behind, no matter who heals it."

He began to clear rock from the glinting patch of gold.

Lothor laid the still form on the cracked floor and reached back into the hole. Bella came up, weeping. When he stood her on the ground, she gasped, favoring her right leg. Lothor eased her to a sitting position and turned back to the unconscious prince.

He removed the boy's cracked helmet, exposing a horribly pale face. Blood trickled down it from a deep cut.

Lothor removed his own gauntlets and helm, laying them carefully beside the body. He spread pale long-fingered hands over the wound. Healing was a quieter magic than most, and it barely touched Keleios' magic sense.

She herself had only bruises. Luckweaver had stood her well.

Lothor sat back in meditation while Tobin blinked into the gloom. He was confused, disoriented. She knelt beside him.

He asked, "What happened?"

"They destroyed the tunnel with some kind of spell. The roof and some wall fell in on top of you." Keleios hesitated, then said, "Lothor healed you."

Blood dripped down Lothor's white skin, and slowly the wound began to close.

His silver eyes opened and he stared at her for a moment; she did not drop her gaze. He blinked and wiped the blood from his face. He turned to Bella and laid hands upon her ankle. He drew a sharp breath as he took her wound. There was no need for meditation over a broken bone.

He said, "It wasn't a spell that brought down the walls."

"Then what was it?"

"An exploding powder."

"A what?"

He started to say more, but she silenced him. A touch flitted against her mind, waiting for permission to enter. It was one of the journeyman sorcerers. Keleios opened to it. *Keleios: Carrick says, "Where are you, girl? Are the lower regions secure? If yes, get up here now. We need more sorcery." Do you have an answer?*

Yes, the lower reaches are secure, caved in, in fact. I will be there as soon as possible.

The contact snapped, and Keleios turned to tell the others. She wondered to herself how a journeyman had ended as the sorcerous backup to Carrick's men. The girl was only a first-year journeyman sorcerer. Keleios wondered just how many were already dead.

It was Tobin who voiced it, as they crawled over the rubble. "What of Melandra?"

Keleios' stomach tightened, but what could she do? The tunnel was completely blocked, and Melandra was on the other side. There was no way to get to her, nothing Keleios could do, but go up and help Carrick. Helpless to save Poula, helpless to save Melandra, helpless to save her own mother. Useless. No. Keleios shoved the thoughts back with an almost physical wave of anger. She could help save this keep. She could save other lives. She was not helpless, not by a long amount. Keleios' voice came out even, no hint of her anger, or her sorrow. "She is lost to us, for now." Keleios vowed to herself, "I will find you, Melandra. I swear."

They came to the top of the stairs and found no clatter of sword on sword, but it was war nonetheless. The singing of arrows rained down and was returned. The screams of the wounded, the stillness of the dead, filled the hallway as far as the eye could follow.

Carrick paced behind his archers. He wore leather and metal-studded armor. A large shield rode his right arm, sword in his left hand. Long poles were propped along the wall to push back the invaders' ladders. Jodda knelt over the fallen; three apprentices or journeyman healers aided her. She was a white pool of soothing in the midst of pain. Keleios experienced what no other healer could do, a wave of calm healing coating the mind within a certain distance of the white healer.

Carrick bellowed, "Ready, loose arrows." Bows thrummed throughout the hall. "Down, everyone, down."

The archers hid behind the walls, tucking heads down. Even Carrick knelt behind his shield. And when the returning arrows came, they flamed. Where they struck the stone floor, the rock burned. The journeyman sorcerer, a red-haired girl, vanquished the flames, but sweat drenched her.

Without looking, Keleios could feel the evil reaching outward, the mad joy in destruction. A demon was outside the walls.

Keleios sat Bella by the healer, telling the girl to help and stay out of the way. She went forward to Carrick. "I am here, weapons master."

"Keleios, what is this magic fire that eats stone? Can you do anything about it?"

"It is illusion."

He stared at her. "Illusion? But it burns. Illusions don't harm."

"It is demon illusion, Carrick. If you believe, then it can do real harm."

The journeyman fell to her knees, gasping. "Not illusion, doesn't feel right for that." Keleios knelt by the girl. "Trust me; I have dealt with demons before. It is illusion."

The girl shook her head stubbornly. The healers came and took the exhausted sorcerer away, still protesting.

Keleios went back to Carrick. "You must disbelieve the fire. The arrows are probably real, but not the fire. No fire, even demon fire, burns stone."

She could feel their fear. A body lay against one wall, skin blackened by fire. A woman leaned against the far wall with an arm covered in blisters. Carrick ordered them to return fire. They crouched and hid. Keleios watched the flame eating into the stone, collecting in pools that spread. The fire would actually feed off of the guards' belief. Their belief would make it real. It could eat holes through the stones, destroy the entire keep, if enough people believed.

Keleios took a deep breath and crawled into the nearest pool of fire. She sat in it, untouched. She could feel it like a cold wind on her skin, a ghost's touch. Illusion was always a cold magic. One guard yelled, "It is well for you, sorcerer, but we have no magic to protect us."

"It is illusion; your disbelief will protect you." But she had come too late for simple answers. It was not an easy thing to disbelieve something that you have felt and have seen kill. Keleios looked up at Carrick as she sat in the fire. "Am I the most powerful sorcerer you can lay your hands on right now?"

He crouched beside her. "Yes."

She did not ask what had happened to the others. She knew what had happened to Master Dracen, and Poula. Fidelis, and behind that Harque, had done a very thorough job. Curse them both.

Tobin came to crouch beside them. He passed a hand through the flame. His gauntlet showed through it, like it was orange glass. "What are you planning?" he asked.

"They have to disbelieve or the keep is lost."

He whispered, "Mind control without permission is not allowed."

"Should I let everything be destroyed because of some rule?"

Tobin hung his head then looked at her. His amber eyes were very serious. "No. Do you want me to do it?"

She smiled. "You are better at wardings, but I'm better at controlling minds."

"All right, but be careful." He moved away from her, to let her call her magic.

Keleios called power from within herself, that spark of herself. Sometimes she thought sorcery more than any other magic drew on the power of the caster's soul. She conjured calmness, fearlessness, surety, a deep breathing certainty that this was illusion. She hammered her own disbelief into something almost tangible, and flung it outward to the ends of the hallway. The guards cried out and one, his arm still blackened from the fire, said, "Illusion, it is illusion."

Keleios slumped over the floor, sweat beading her forehead.

Tobin knelt beside her. He whispered, "How do you feel?"

"I'll be all right in a moment. The demon is crippled without its illusion. It was worth it."

When the next rain of arrows came, the fire burned for a time but was ignored and faded accordingly.

When Keleios felt well enough to move, she went to Carrick. "How are they shooting arrows? Why hasn't the courtyard been trapped?" The courtyard was designed so any sorcerer could but touch and speak the words, and the stones would become a pit. Whether it was bottomless or not was a point of long debate.

Carrick rubbed a hand across his chin. "We cannot get a sorcerer near enough to drop the stones from beneath them. Three journeyman have gone and died. It is the demon. He sees them, invisible or no. We have no way to protect them."

"I will go next, but I must see what sort of demon it is first."

He nodded, and she crept to the window. The demon floated on black-feathered wings at level with the windows. Its body was fur covered; its head lionlike, with a full midnight-dark mane. Clawed hands held a great whip, which it whirled round about itself. Its eyes were burning red. A short sword swung at its side, flashing silver, a small magic deowmer on it. Its hooves were cloven like a goat's. Across its sculptured belly ran a livid white scar. Keleios' stomach knotted and beads of sweat broke on her body. A blackmane had been one of her tormentors when Harque the Witch captured her six years back. Demons could heal without scarring, so there couldn't be two blackmanes with the same wound. He had been forced to bear a scar as a mark of failure. She bore his mark for a different failure.

She eased back from the window. "It is a blackmane, one of the most powerful of the lower-level demons. Keep on as before; do nothing special to guard me. If I need you to save me, it will be too late."

Lothor stepped up to her. "You aren't going out there."

She stared at the hand that gripped her arm. "Are you volunteering?" She stepped close and whispered to him. "Have you felt the lash of the black whip? Have you screamed in the third darkness?"

He pushed back from her. "Go, then, but take care."

She stared at him a moment. "You haven't been there, have you?" Her voice sounded the surprise she felt. "The great black prince heir to the demon-got throne hasn't even tasted the whip. Many delights await you beyond that."

"It is not wise to speak of such things with it so near."

"True." There were questions she wanted to ask, but there wasn't time. She turned to Carrick. "I will go out through the hidden gate, no magic. I will drop the stones, but that will not stop the blackmane. Do what you can with it after I succeed.''

''Against a demon, we can do little.''

Tobin stepped up. ''How will you stay hidden without magic?''

''Elven concealment.''

''Of course, it is a handy thing to know. Why can't I do it?''

She hesitated then laughed. ''I don't know; you've tried hard enough.''

Carrick saluted her and turned back to ordering his men.

Lothor paced after her. ''You think to escape our bargain by suicide, don't you?''

She started down the stairs before answering him. ''Bedding you is not my idea of pleasure, but it is hardly a fate worse than death, especially at the hands of a demon that has already tasted my blood.''

He tried to stop her then, but she pulled away. He moved to catch up with her. ''If it has already had your blood, then it has certain powers over you.''

''And I have certain powers over it.''

''You may know its true name, but it will bring back the pain it caused you and cripple you.''

''If it is given time.''

The main gate rose before them, barred and guarded. Bellenore was captain of the men on this level. She strode forward. ''Keleios, you go to try?''

''Yes.''

''May the gods smile upon you.''

''And on all within this keep tonight.''

Bellenore motioned two men to the side of the main gate and Keleios stepped up to the wall.

Lothor called behind her, ''Keleios.''

She hesitated. There was a cold weight in her stomach, and her mouth was so dry she couldn't swallow. The demon outside had tortured her for weeks. It was not something you could forget.

''Keleios.''

She shook her head and did not look back. She ran

through a quick calming exercise, and shoved her fear down. You could be afraid but it couldn't eat over your skin like a wind. Fear could attract demons. Keleios built a wall around her fear. The hidden gate swung open, and she stepped outside, the two men pulling frantically to close it behind her.

Keleios stood on the top step leading down into the courtyard. She was elven and melted into the stones; no one saw her. There was no empty space to give away or a spell to puzzle men why they couldn't quite look at a certain spot. She moved down, winding through the men that worked at battering the main door in. Their ram would not touch it for it needed magical things to split that door.

Men stood dressed in leather armor, or no armor. They clustered behind shields waiting patiently for the group of black healers to give them the gate. Even now the three magic-users worked spells over the ram, having finally recognized the need. The ram was set on the stones of the courtyard, and all but a handful of the men stood on those same stones. She sidestepped a man with a gold loop in his ear. Four guards stood on the steps, swords and dagger ready. She would have to fight them if she succeeded and if the demon gave her the time.

As she scanned the yard, she noticed the blackened hulk with a small charcoal lump that could only be a rider. By its size it was the female silver; the dragons were down. A wild dragon would never have believed illusion, but the magic sense was blunted in the tame war dragons. Without the dragons the air belonged to the demons. She moved to the last step.

She knelt, close enough to smell the sweat of the magic-users as they cast. The ram was a dark bulk at her side. She laid hands on the courtyard stones and spoke one word.

A sound of thunder shuddered through the courtyard, and the chanting stopped, all eyes searching for the danger. The courtyard fell away.

The ram slid from sight; men fell screaming into a

deeper dark than night. As she had known it would, the demon took to the air, great wings fanning the night. She was visible to the four men at her back.

They froze long enough for her to stand, then fell upon her to vent anger and shock on something of flesh and blood. The first one closed too fast. She dunked and foot-swept him into the pit. She came up slicing the belly of the second and taking another across the throat. The last one tried a lunging run, and she sidestepped, putting a knife between his ribs. He fell forward and coughed blood until he died. She retrieved her knife and looked upward.

The demon floated just above her, wings still, levitating. His voice was a tenor, musical and still a surprise to the ears even when prepared. "Nightseer." His wings fanned out, arms flexing, and a grin flashed white teeth.

She inclined her head and greeted him. "Barbarros."

He fanned the night with his wings, and the wind pulled at loose strands of her hair. "So you have not forgotten me. How flattering."

"Barbarros, I would never forget you, your black magnificence, your masterful hand with whip or sword."

He flew higher, preening in the praise, and stopped to float almost even with her. "Nightseer, I will not be tricked by mere flattery. A sacrifice, we could talk about."

She stared into his red eyes with their cold fire. "What sacrifice did you have in mind, Barbarros?"

He tried to smile and made a snarl of black jowls and ivory fangs. "Why you, Nightseer."

She took a breath and tensed. They were three namings for three. Whatever protection she gained from it, he had quietly taken away. For though Nightseer wasn't a birth name, it was a name of power and would suffice. She managed a smile in return. "Dear Barbarros, that is not something I am willing to give."

His head drew close, and she could smell the rich

musky sulphur of demon. "The best sacrifices are un-willing, at first." And he laughed. It echoed in the archway where she stood, bouncing round the walls. The laughter died suddenly, ominously. He flew higher, floating above her like a dark god. "Do you remember pain, little elf?"

She whispered it. "Yes."

She did remember after six years; it was still a frequent nightmare: being tied down on her stomach, the floor cold and harsh against her cheek, the sound of ripping cloth as her back was bared, and him snaking the whip along the ground, rustling, alive. The first stinging bite, tiny hooks biting into flesh and tearing out, again and again and again. The feel of blood, her blood flowing, washing over her back. Pain so sharp that it rode her whole body, in one blinding bloody wave. Keleios closed her eyes and breathed. "I control; I control. It cannot harm me; it cannot harm me." She opened her eyes to find the demon still at level with her. It had tricked her with its eyes. She was careful not to look into them a second time.

He hissed and swung into the sky, hovering. "Pain remembered is not the same. Pain is always better fresh."

Keleios threw a sorcerous shield round herself, but there was a feeling of hopelessness to it. It was a simple spell, and she did it well in class. But she had been helpless against the demon for weeks. She knew as she tried to protect herself that she couldn't. The doubt, of course, was her undoing and the demon's edge.

He stretched out one clawed hand and flexed the fingers.

Keleios screamed as scars ripped open and ran red. Blood soaked through the leather of her armor like a flood, all the blood she had lost over a matter of weeks draining out. She dropped to her knees, one hand steadying herself against the steps. One long ragged scream after another was torn from her throat; it echoed in the archway, mocking her.

The screams turned to a word. "No!" She glared up at the thing and screamed, "Barbarros, begone, ahhhh!" Out of nowhere a bolt of red power struck him in the chest. He reeled backwards in the air, flapping wings to regain his balance. A second bolt hit him, and hands closed on Keleios from behind.

A voice said, "Keleios, it is Bellenore." The fighter picked her up under the arms, but when her back slipped against Bellenore, she screamed.

The demon shrieked and dove after them as they crawled through the gate. A red bolt sent him tumbling out of his dive, and he snarled his rage to the night sky as the gate closed behind them.

She lay for a minute, gasping into the cool stone floor, and whispered, "Someday I'm going to kill that son of a bitch."

Martin, the only male white healer the keep could boast, knelt beside her, his square clean-shaven face frowning down at her. His brown hair was held by a strip of cloth. His hands touched her gently and came away stained with blood. "Get this armor off."

Hands moved to obey and Keleios said, "Gently, this armor took me a long time to make."

Someone laughed, and Bellenore stepped close. "Magic-user or not, you have a warrior's concern for your tools." The second-in-command personally helped remove the armor.

The effort left Keleios gasping on the floor. The linen shirt underneath was stuck to her back, and Martin lifted it slowly. Keleios tried not to cry out. It ripped up the back, and the journeyman healer aiding Martin gasped. He admonished the journeyman for showing such lack of tact, but his face was pale, too. "Cia, preserve us. Keleios, your back is shredded."

Lothor was beside her, helm scraping as he set it down. "It is the way these wounds heal."

Martin looked at him with open contempt. "You know something of this sort of wound?"

"I am a black healer. Whether you like that or not,

it makes me something of an expert on demon-got wounds.''

Some of the defiance slipped from the white healer. ''I will not let my patient suffer for my prejudice. What can be done for her?''

''The wounds are ordinary enough, but be careful. I do not know if white healers can heal demon-got wounds with impunity. The worst is the blood loss and resulting weakness. It will be harder to heal.''

''I think I can heal anything a black healer could.'' The 'and more' was left unsaid, but it hung in the air.

Lothor smiled, a tight pleasant smile, and said, ''Be my guest then, white healer. You need no advice from me.''

Outside the demon raved and tore at the keep's face. ''I will not be cheated this time, Nightseer. I will not be cheated again!''

Martin laid hands on her back, searching the damage. He hissed and drew back from her. ''Such pain, such pain, how could you endure it?''

Keleios answered him in a strange distant voice. ''It wasn't torture as we think of it. They wanted nothing from me. No word, or thought, or thing, that I could do or give them would have freed me. They simply asked that I endure. It is simple to endure something when you have no other choice.''

''Mother of us all, greatest healer that has ever been, help me heal this woman.'' And he touched her again.

Blood soaked his white robe to add to the many stains, now dry. It spread slowly, and at last he withdrew and sat back in deep meditation.

His face bore the complete peace that was the only thing she envied the white healers. He opened his eyes to inspect his work and frowned.

The wounds had scabbed and become scars before their eyes. The scars vanished, leaving the back smooth and clean except for one. It was long and thin, stretching from just below her left shoulder to the top of the right. At the end, like a twisted flower, was a starburst of scars from metal hooks.

The journeyman healer sponged her back gently, as if afraid he would harm her further.

Before anyone could stop him, Martin laid a hand at either end of the scar.

Lothor yelled, "It is not a scar; it's a demon mark!"

A wash of crimson exploded along Martin's back and he screamed. Keleios screamed with him, but his hands remained locked to her back as he rocked and fought the pain.

Keleios yelled, "Get him off me, get him off me!"

Lothor gripped Martin's straining wrists, but the journeyman tried to stop him. "If you break his concentration, you could kill him."

"If I don't break his concentration, he will die."

The boy slumped back, still uncertain, but did not protest as Lothor pulled on the healer. A great warm force held the hands down and another force, not so warm, also held. He was forced to pry a finger at a time, a hand at a time. The healer slumped forward over her body. Lothor lifted the unconscious healer and laid him against a wall. The journeyman laid hands on him, timidly. "He is barely alive, but his magic tries to heal him." He ripped the white robe from Martin's back. Keleios had to turn away. She remembered every lash that his back showed, even to the tiny gouging bites of metal hooks.

The boy asked, "How can we help him? You said it was a demon mark."

"Yes, it only looks like a scar or wound. No healer, be he white, black, or grey, can heal it away. Your white healer must be very strong to still be alive."

The boy touched him, tears shining in his eyes. "Master Martin is that."

Keleios drew a deep breath and waited for pain, but with the contact broken she felt healed. Like six years ago, she couldn't think about the pain. Her mind shied from it, tried to convince itself that it was safe.

Lothor came back to her side. "Do you hurt still?"

"No."

Tobin helped her stand. She tore the ruin of linen

from her without thinking and reached for her armor. Lothor's silver eyes stared at her bare breasts, and she found herself covering her bareness with her armor. She resisted an urge to spit at him, but remembered that soon enough, if they lived, he would be seeing more than bare breasts. The thought saved her from embarrassment. She glared at him and began putting the armor on with Tobin's help. The look in her eyes told Lothor not even to offer to help.

His eyes found the dagger sheath at her neck, and he wondered for the first time if any bargain would keep her from putting a dagger in him one dark night.

The journeyman sorcerer attached to this level tensed and nearly swayed. "They are overrun. The south wall falls, unless help is forthcoming." He tensed again. "Carrick orders half the men on this level to the south wall. If Keleios is well enough, she is to go too, and Tobin goes with or without her."

Keleios stood, flexing muscles and casually touching to make sure all weapons were in place. "I'm ready."

Bellenore looked doubtful, but chose the men quickly. She put Davin, a senior guard, in charge. He was dependable without much flare for leadership. They were at the south wall soon after.

The sounds of battle were here. Shrieks, the clash of metal on metal, the roaring ozone smell of sorcery, hung heavy on the air. Davin sent Keleios and a young blond guard, named Torgen, to the windows to scout. The south wall was the only one not guarded by enchantment. The stones would not fall here and the battle was waged on the courtyard stones rather than from windows.

The courtyard was littered with bodies, dark shapes that sprang into shadow with each burst of lightning or fire. Allanna stood nearly alone, white fire building in her hands, washing all color from her yellow hair and pale skin. Her blue dress was dimmed to grey by the growing light. Her hair shifted and crackled from her own power being so close. The vain woman was gone; this was Allanna in her power—tall, deadly, and wondrous.

Both hands went forward, and the glowing ball shot outward to land a dark shape. A second blackmane shrieked and fanned the air with its great dark wings. The white fire exploded like a net of lightning, and the demon began to fall earthward. But Allanna dropped to her knees. An arrow arched toward her, and a guard leapt forward, putting his shield before her. The remaining guards formed a wedge round her and waited shields outward for a last stand.

A small dark figure knelt by the lightning-enrobed demon. From the window Keleios could feel the power. The skyfire drained away and fell sparkling over the man. Keleios got a brief glimpse of pale face before she and Torgen went back to report.

Davin led them to the nearest door, the east door. It led out into the rose garden. Keleios and Torgen again scouted forward through the whispering roses. The coiled thorny vines reached for them but stopped just short of binding round them. It was as if the animated plants could smell the difference between friend and foe. They entered and moved as swiftly as possible. Torgen nervously gripped his weapons as the hedges grew to block their paths, then parted when they had almost touched them. Everywhere was a rustling, grasping, coiling of vines. In the herb garden they found hacked vegetation and two dead intruders nearly covered in leaves.

Just outside the gate to the south court lay the male silver dragon. Half of him smashed the struggling plants of the healers' garden down, forcing a hole through the bay hedge. The courtyard and the dragon runs lay visible through the broken hedge. The battle flashed like a multicolored storm against the night.

The dragon's rider, a dark-haired girl, slumped in the saddle, curiously straight. Keleios motioned Torgen back to wait for the others before following, and she went on. She knelt in the shadow of the dragon and found no light in his eyes, dead. She moved to the rider and found why she was so straight. Arrows pinned left leg; right arm and the broken shaft of a spear made rider and dragon one. Keleios knelt in the shadow of their death and fought a desire to scream to the gods. If Verm could send his demons, then where was the help for the defenders? "May the Mother keep you both."

She pulled an arrow free of the rider's leg, smelled it, and threw it to the ground. She hissed, "Dragon's bane." Trust a Loltun to grow something with only one purpose.

There was no need for scouts now. Davin led them out into the courtyard. The archers readied themselves to kneel and give room to the sorcerers. Davin gave charge of the four journeyman sorcerers to Keleios. They formed a loose double line of thirty men, half the force from the north wall. The demon rose to the air once more and lashed out with a whip of many tails. It flew at the handful of guards crouched around Allanna. It encircled one man's head and neck; he had not hidden far enough behind his shield. The man screamed, and the demon laughed as he dragged the man forward. The guards closed ranks across the hole and waited.

The man was lifted up into the air until the demon held him. The thing laughed in a deep voice and snapped his neck.

Davin whispered an order for the archers to aim at the demon. Keleios stopped him. "Ordinary arrows won't even hit him. You must kill the one that controls it."

"But which one?"

Lothor spoke close at her shoulder. "It is the short man in black robes just under the demon."

She stared at him. "How can you be sure?"

"I can't, but it's the best guess I can make."

They accepted that, though Keleios wasn't sure why. Davin gave his orders.

Arrows arched into the night sky and hit their mark, but bounced harmlessly against an invisible shield.

Keleios said, ''Everyone with me on his shield, now!''

Five lines of power stretched outward, multicolored destruction. The shield gave with a loud pop. Death flew in at their backs. The other demon flew into them, breaking their concentration, sending most to their knees. Two journeymen came up, raked by claws. Barbarros circled, nearly lost against the blackness, but he would come again. The second blackmane snaked its whip for another try.

Keleios knelt on the ground and refused to look up. ''I can't fight two of them. We can't fight two of them.''

Tobin knelt beside her. ''Keleios, what of the demon-summoning spell? Couldn't another demon fight them?''

''You don't understand. The spell is not designed to gate in a higher demon. And if I could do it, I couldn't control it, not here with no protective circle, no charms. We'd end up with three against us instead of two.''

Lothor's voice came silk smooth. ''Use the book. Bare your hand and use the book.''

''What book?'' Tobin asked.

She asked, trying to judge his truth with her eyes, ''Would it work?''

''Yes, with the book, your spell, and your highest demon mark, it will work. I have seen it done with lesser books than the one that you hold.''

Air whistled down about them, and they cowered behind shields. No one could hit the beast except Keleios and Lothor, for no one else bore magic weapons. It hooked talons under the chin of a young guard and drew him upward. Lothor sliced at the thing with his axe and drew dark blood. The guard fell to the ground with his life burbling from a slit throat.

They would be picked off one by one. The easiest thing that could happen was a quick death. Keleios opened the pouch at her side and withdrew the black book. It burned with ebony flame.

Tobin whispered, "What is it?"

Keleios laid the clay bottle of demon summoning beside it on the ground. "It is abomination." She began to unlace the glove on her left hand and found the knots so tight she had to cut it with a dagger. She spoke to Davin. "You must protect me until I have raised and sent the demon back. If I am killed beforehand, it will be freed. And you will have one more demon to fight."

They formed a shield wall round her and waited.

The glove slipped off, and she stuck it in her belt. In the center of her palm was a perfect circle. The circle was only as large as a unicorn gold piece, but inside it was disease. Raw and red, bloody, without running onto the hand, pus struggled among the rawness. She whispered, "Unclean." Keleios was careful to hide the mark from the others. A flat shiny scar was one thing; this corruption was a mark of high favor from the dark gods.

When her bare left hand touched the book, power shot up her arm. Joyous release, evil power, and for a moment she froze, listening to promises that the book whispered. Power like sweet wine flowed through her body. She could almost taste it on her tongue. Evil, corruption, power—but the taste wasn't bitter, it was sweet, comforting. Keleios was tainted, not evil. The book could only persuade, not control. She cleared her mind of its dark promises, but it was a sweet, sour music in her head.

She lifted the book upward and stood with the demon summoning in the other hand. She broke the clay vessel over her left hand, and words poured out of her mouth. No one except Lothor could remember what she said, not even Keleios.

Barbarros dived them desperately, and Lothor cut him once more with his ax. But neither wound was deep, and the demon came again.

The man who controlled the demons was screaming, "Stop her! Bring me that book!"

Barbarros tried, but though he killed others, he

could not reach her. The second blackmane rushed in on them, and a guard screamed as the thing stalked them.

Davin's voice came calm. "Hold your position. If we break now, we die. Hold your position."

The demons closed from either side, both floating just above the ground. Whips lashed out and two guardsmen screamed. Hands held them, but the shield wall broke. Barbarros left his half-strangled man and reached for Keleios. With a muffled clap of thunder and a nose-wrinkling smell, a greater demon stood among them.

The shield wall shattered as the guards ran wildly from the fear spell the demon radiated. Tobin stood trembling at her side, barely able to stand in its presence. Lothor knelt and touched his head to the ground. Barbarros and the other blackmane also knelt, staring upward at the thing. It looked like a praying insect, but with hands where front claws would have been and a great battle-ax gripped in its hands. The thing stood over ten feet tall. It turned round insect eyes this way and that, rotating its triangular head almost completely round. Its voice rolled out of its thin insectlike body. "Who summons me?"

Keleios said, "I do."

"What task will you have me do?"

"Defeat the demons that the invaders send against us."

"And what am I to be paid for this task?"

"Nothing. You are mine to command, Nezercabukril."

He hissed, mouth parts clacking. "Nothing! You overstep your bounds, woman." He walked over, towering above her. "You stand without circle or charm. It is you who are mine."

"No, Nezercabukril, by the book that summoned you am I protected."

He swung the great white ax with its haft of bone, and it dug into the ground beside her. Her eyes closed, but she did not move. She now stood alone before him. The demon freed his ax from the ground and said, "I am yours to command, for now." He raised the ax, and it flashed in the moon's light. "You will come to me soon; then I will be paid."

She replied, "The future is only possibilities, Nezercabukril; go do as I bid."

The great white demon, seemingly carved of bone, turned to the first blackmane. "Get out and do not return this night."

The demon vanished.

Barbarros groveled before him. "Master, please grant me a death before you send me away."

"Speak."

"The woman, she is Nightseer. Twice I have been cheated of her death; let it not be three times, Master of Bones."

"That is one thing that I cannot grant tonight."

Barbarros screamed, gnashing his teeth, and vanished.

The ground trembled, and the white demon looked down. "I have done your task; send me back."

"They will gate in more demons. I will need you."

The demon laughed deep in its throat. "There will be no more demons here tonight."

"I warn you, Nezercabukril, do not lie to me."

He laughed. "Warn me. You command me tonight, but do not let it give you delusions of grandeur. I do not lie." The ground trembled again, stones buckling on the courtyard. "Where devils come, demons do not. Release me."

"Devils? What do you mean?"

The courtyard exploded upward in a great tower of flame. The leering face of a devil rode the flames and began to form a body from them.

Nezercabukril said, "That is what I mean."

She whispered, "Begone."

The demon gave a mocking bow, and said, "Thank you, and may you enjoy my master's attentions, personally." With that he vanished.

8

The White Dagger

The column of fire roared upward into the dark. Orange cinders arched outward like fireworks, sizzling and crackling on the courtyard. The base twisted and writhed, flaming ropes of orange, yellow, and white. In the flames faces flickered, screaming and being endlessly consumed by the fire. Arms reached outward, flamelets that larger flames blazed round and swallowed. A thin keening wail echoed over the roaring of the flames. A hot parching wind seemed to blow off the thing. It robbed what it touched scalding. It dried hope up and left only terror behind—run, run and hide. But there was nowhere left to hide.

Lothor called to her over the noise. "Hide the book. It will call to him like a signal fire." She stared at him for a moment, half-stupefied by the noise and the presence of the thing. She stuffed the book inside the pouch, quenching the black flames. Keleios pulled the drawstrings tight and stared at Lothor.

He stepped close to her. "Keleios, are you all right?"

She didn't answer but was vaguely aware of Tobin on his knees, eyes riveted to the devil behind her. Over all was the sound of burning and a dark singing in her head. She raised her left hand; it had never itched so much, demanded to be used. She raised it slowly as if unable to stop it. Lothor caught her left wrist just before she touched him. "Keleios?"

The devil spoke. His voice was a burning wind, a forest ablaze. "Who dares summon me?"

Lothor tightened his grip on Keleios, pulled Tobin

to his feet, and began to walk quickly, but not too quickly, for the questionable shelter of the dragon runs.

They, like the smithy, were warded. They hit the magic with a skin-tingling rush, but there was no noise of dragons to greet them. The dragons were dead.

When they had put a building between them and the devil, Lothor let Tobin slide to the ground. The boy began to vomit. Lothor gripped both of Keleios' wrists and shook her. "Keleios!"

She heard him distantly over the song in her blood, in her head, from her hand. It sang of death, and power, and a blacker darkness than any night. He shoved her backwards, slamming her into the barn twice.

Tobin crawled towards him and said, "Let her go."

He kicked Tobin hard enough to roll him along the ground. The boy did not get up but lay moaning. Lothor rocked Keleios against the wall until she fought to get away.

She glared up at him, "What, by Loth's red talons, are you doing?" She jerked free of him and he stepped back.

"You wouldn't answer me. I thought something had possessed you."

She tried to remember and found the song still there bubbling through her blood. Her left hand itched, and she had to force herself not to touch it or rub it against herself. "The book promised power. And I listened." She looked up at him, fear tightening her chest. "I listened."

"It is not your fault that it calls to you; you did not choose evil."

She nodded but remained unconvinced. She reached for her leather glove and began binding it into place. She had lost a finger joint worth of leather thong from cutting the knot, but it would do.

When it was fastened securely, she moved to Tobin's huddled form. She pushed back his sweat-soaked hair and said, "Tobin, can you speak?"

His voice was hoarse with emotion. "I have never

been so afraid. I couldn't think or move. The black one had to drag me to cover."

"The devil gives off a very powerful aura of fear. It is one of his weapons. You stood beside me when all the others ran. Be proud of that."

He nodded.

She helped him stand, then led the way inside the building. It wasn't much protection, but it was better than being in the open. Sprawled in the aisle was the body of a man. He had been clawed and chewed almost beyond recognition. Only his blond hair and shape of body remained.

Lothor spoke quietly. "The raiders?"

She knelt in the blood-stained sawdust. "No, or at least I don't think so. It looks like some kind of beast did it." She looked up at Lothor. "What sort of pets do black healers keep?"

"A small demon, perhaps."

"Perhaps." She covered the body with a saddle blanket. The large double doors at the other end were open. Through them the devil's fire still blazed into the sky. A small figure in black with a pale, clean-shaven face looked up at the devil, bargaining. Lothor stared out at the devil and the man. "If anyone can command the Fire Lord, it will be Velen."

He turned to her. "You must use the dark book again, Keleios. We must conjure a devil to fight this one or all is lost."

"Then all is lost." She sat down on a bale of hay and stared at her leather-entrapped hand. "I am too tired and too frightened of the book. I couldn't control what I could call up. The last thing we need is two devils after us."

"The devil will bring down the keep."

"Once it finds the secret of the keep's magic. We have a little time."

"Time for what, Keleios? Either be stronger than it or die. There are no other choices."

"Lothor, I can't. I have been healed twice tonight; it has its price. I used instant enchantment on those walls; it has its price. My sorcery is still usable, but against that thing, I have nothing. Only my sword remains and this cursed darkness that seeps from my hand. The first demon summoning was aided by herb-witchery, and that is gone now.''

''You only need the book and the power in your veins. Tap your darker half, or we will be destroyed.''

''And if I try and fail, I will be destroyed.'' She began to laugh. ''Where would our bargain be then, black healer?''

''Leave her alone,'' Tobin said.

''You stay out of this, princeling.''

''For my sake, don't fight. We need a plan, but I will not, cannot do what you suggest, black healer.''

''There is no other way to fight the thing.'' He paused, ''Unless.''

''Unless what?''

''Unless we can kill Velen.'' He gave an abrupt, bitter laugh. ''If only it were that easy.''

Velen was walking toward them, a group of warriors and black clerics at his back.

''He knows I am here. He felt your magic; he is priest, sorcerer, and very dangerous.''

''Who is he to you?''

''My brother.''

The man was young, no older than eighteen, with smooth pale skin, but not ice-pale. His hair was like a raven wing, his eyes of some dark color, short, a man in every shape. ''Your half-brother, I take it.''

''His mother was a Zairdian slave.''

Lothor took the left side of the door; Keleios, the right, and Tobin took the rear doors.

Keleios whispered, ''Are you close to your brother?''

''You mean will I be angry if you kill him?''

She didn't answer.

''Kill him if you can, Keleios, but I doubt you can. He has Verm's own luck at escaping things.''

Velen stopped just out of range of missile weapons. ''Brother, I would speak with you.''

"You can speak from there, Velen."

"I would rather not air private matters in front of commoners."

Lothor laughed. "I have no commoners with me, Velen."

The boy's face colored. "Very well. Father has named me heir. You were unsuccessful in your plan, but I will not fail. My plan is better."

"I have not failed, yet. She is to be my consort, Velen."

Keleios hissed, "You, mine."

He whispered, "Don't make me lose face, not now."

She huddled into her corner, unsatisfied but silent.

He spoke to Velen once more. "She is mine; I have succeeded."

Velen smiled, a beautiful smile. "Best wishes to you, brother, but you know now what I must do?"

"Yes, brother, you must kill me."

He nodded. "I am tired of father's indecisiveness: first you, then me, then back. Your success could tip the hands in your favor, and I will not have that."

"I did not think you would, brother dear."

Tobin hissed, "Men moving in from the other side."

Keleios backed away from the front and moved to stand with Tobin at the back.

Lothor kept Velen talking so they could set up their own ambush.

Keleios drew Luckweaver quietly, and Tobin drew his own sword. She outlined a brief and hopefully quiet plan, and he crouched down to stay out of sight until it was time. She mouthed the words, "No magic." He nodded.

Four fighters crept along the wall, two on either side. They sounded ridiculously loud to Keleios. Even Tobin winced as a stray blade scraped against the outer wall. The men's breaths were harsh and loud. They muttered one to the other; one on Keleios' side stumbled and cursed. Keleios drew a dagger for her left hand and waited.

Keleios could feel the man just on the other side of the wall. His body was pressed against the stones, and unconsciously she mirrored him. He peered round the edge, and she moved forward, dagger plunging into his neck. She pulled it free with a spray of blood and took the second man through the belly and chest with her sword. He looked surprised. She rolled and left the sword rather than struggle to free it. Tobin had taken his front man with a slash, opening the man's belly, but he traded sword strokes with the second man. Keleios changed grips on her dagger and threw it. It hit with a meaty thunk. Tobin finished the stumbling man with a thrust to the neck. He turned to grin at her, and his face changed.

She rolled without waiting for the warning. Something fell on her left side, stopping the roll before it was begun. A numbing pain took her left arm. Keleios drove an elbow back and threw with her body and shoulder. The attacker rolled forward off her and was on his feet.

She faced him standing, but her left arm hung useless. Her right hand held the last knife. The man was slender and looked snake quick. His only weapon was a white-bladed dagger that gave off a magic aura. His hair was long and reddish brown, held back by a strip of black rawhide. Elf-pointed ears peeked through the hair. He grinned at her and began to circle. Under normal battle with an unarmored man she might have thrown the blade, but he looked too quick. She figured him for an assassin, and she didn't fancy giving up her only weapon without a plan.

Tobin moved toward him.

Keleios said, "No, stay out of his reach."

Tobin backed off and sheathed his sword, but was clearly unhappy about it.

Whatever the dagger was, it had harmed her. The wound was deep and clean from one side of the arm to the other. The bone had been missed and for that she was grateful. It had bled a great deal at first, but now the blood had almost stopped, save for a trickle.

It shouldn't have. A deep bone-numbing cold was seeping from the wound down her arm and spreading up her shoulder.

She feinted, trying to draw him out and test his fighting style, but he stayed out of reach and smiled. He knew what the dagger was doing to her. The cold was an ache, not the healthy pain of a knife wound, but freezing like a touch of ice. All he had to do was stay out of reach and the cold would take her over, she could feel it. Tobin was not quick enough, even armed with shield and sword, against dagger.

As they circled and put the assassin's back to Tobin, the boy extended a hand and said one word. An explosion of yellow-white light took the assassin in the back. He stumbled forward, and Keleios lunged. He turned at the last moment, spoiling her heart blow. The dagger took him in the upper chest and shoulder. They teetered, pressed together. Keleios fought for his heart and forced her left hand to grab for his dagger.

It cut a shallow wound down the length of her hand from little finger to wrist and sliced through the rawhide bindings. The glove slipped to the ground, and her hand grabbed the man's hand desperately. She dug half-frozen fingers into his flesh, fighting to keep the blade from her. Her own dagger came free, and his hand kept its point from his throat.

A warmth began at the palm of her hand, chasing the coldness. Like a warm summer breeze in a snowstorm, it chased the cold, melting, giving hope. Her grip strengthened, and she bent all her enchanted strength to plunge the dagger in his throat as the warmth spread. His eyes opened wide, surprised. The dagger tip was almost there.

The warmth reached the wound, blood flowed freely, and it hurt like it was supposed to. Her left hand crushed downward, and the white dagger fell to the dirt. He began to scream, eyes staring downward.

A green mold covered his hand, spreading up his sleeve. Keleios watched it climb from his tunic collar to his neck. He panicked, and she plunged the dagger home. His screams were cut short in a gurgle of blood.

The green disease kept spreading as he twitched and died. It ate the flesh as it covered it, bare white bones showing at his hand where it had begun.

So that was how it felt to use the demonmark. It felt good and warm and safe and powerful. Most who passed through the fifth darkness had only a round scar for proof. For a very few, as a sign of high favor, they were given the gift. The wound would never be healed but remained raw, full of pus and blood and death.

The green slime had nearly covered the body. Tobin stood across from her, eyes disbelieving, and he whispered, "How did you do that?"

She raised her left hand and showed him the demonmark. "I did not do it of my own free will." She knelt in the dust and picked up her leather mitt, but it was ruined. A substitute would have to be found. Keleios wondered what would happen if she touched her own flesh accidentally. A laugh caught at the back of her throat and didn't quite come out. She pulled Luckweaver free of the dead body and cleaned and resheathed it. They walked back in the building slowly. Keleios found a pair of riding gloves, leather with the fingers free to work. She slipped one on gingerly, then thought of the dagger. They couldn't just leave something like that lying about. She went cautiously, looking up this time as well as out. It lay shining whitely in the dust beside the remnants of its wielder.

There was a great roaring sound; the devil had returned. Keleios could see the orange flames spreading along the keep, but a larger glow was on the other side of the dragon gates. She touched the dagger's blade tentatively with her left hand. Its blade was the coldness of early winter before the land has given up on life. It was bearable, and she picked it up loosely, carrying it, blade down, into the building.

Lothor and Tobin crouched beside the open doors. She stood behind them, not trying to hide.

The devil had formed from the waist down now, and

its great cloven hooves walked in a shower of fire. Gripped in his hands were Bella and a blond servant girl. Bella had fainted, and he dropped her as if uninterested in prey that was immune to fear. She fell and rolled as if dead, a seep of blood spreading from beneath her. The other girl struggled, screaming, so lost in terror that she tore bloody scratches in her own face.

The devil held the girl away from its body and gripped a struggling arm in its giant fingers and pulled. The arm gave way at the shoulder, a burst of crimson. Like a cruel child with a butterfly, first a wing, then a leg. But butterflies do not scream.

Keleios strode forward, shrieking her frustration, white dagger plunging skyward, a white torch of defiance that the devil found most amusing.

Tobin and Lothor crowded round her, trying to drag her back. Lothor stared at the blood on his hand from her wound.

The devil turned, grinned, and flung the bloody remnants toward them. The body flew end over end, spraying blood in arcs. They scattered and it fell to the pavement with a heavy wet thud. Keleios knelt and struck the dagger against the stones. Sparks like bits of snow showered upward.

The devil began striding toward them. They regrouped and drew weapons; there was no place left to run.

As the ground trembled under each step, Lothor asked, "So I may die happy, how did you get wounded and how did you get that dagger?"

Keleios glanced at it in her left hand paired with Luckweaver in her right. "An assassin, he was good, but not quite good enough. This was his blade. I don't like leaving relics lying about, so I picked it up."

The first wave of fear hit them, and the devil laughed. "Run, and hide, mortals. You cannot escape me. Behold." He spread his great crimson arms skyward. A flash of sorcery thundered over them like a storm, and was gone.

All around the keep, over the ruined walls an orange glow spread; a devil's warding. "A barrier," Lothor said.

The devil roared, "Run, run from me!" He took two giant steps toward them, crashing on the stone. It split into a crevice that widened and spread toward them.

"Run!" the devil shrieked.

They sheathed their weapons and ran. Keleios ran carefully, the naked dagger in her hand. They scrambled over the crushed hedges and the dead dragon. They ran into the gardens with their whispering death, and Keleios led them through the living maze of greenery. She had been leading them back to the keep without thinking about it. When they reached the rose garden, Keleios stopped. She sat on the fountain's edge and stared.

Fire reflected redly into the fountain's basin, blazing from the windows and roof of the keep. The west side of the keep was broken, shattered, and the fire was strongest there. The mostly stone keep was holding its own against the fire.

Keleios fought an urge to scream, or cry. There was no place of safety tonight.

Lothor examined her wounds.

She asked, "How do we kill it?"

"The devil?"

She nodded.

"We don't."

"How do we fight it then?"

"Let me see the dagger." He touched it gently. She let it fall from her fingers to his hand.

He grinned and gripped the thing. "Do you know what this is?"

She shook her head, no.

"It is 'Ice,' one of the seven."

"Then it is a relic."

Lothor handed the dagger to her good hand and continued to probe the wound. "I have no healing left, but I can bind it. What made this wound?"

"The white dagger."

He stopped and looked at her. "It couldn't have."

"Lothor, believe it. The wound felt as cold as a winter ice storm."

"Then how is it healthy now?"

Keleios hesitated, unwilling to share it. "That is none of your business."

He jerked the bindings tight and she gasped. "Keleios, I need to know if you have any special powers over the dagger because it could affect the way we use it."

Tobin's voice came low but clear. "For those of us who aren't enchanters, what are the seven, and what is that dagger?"

Keleios spoke as Lothor cleaned and bound her wound. "Long ago, when Pelrith was but a man and not a demigod, he made seven daggers with the aid of demon magic. Each blade was cooled in blood and flesh, and a demon was imprisoned in each one." Keleios stared at the blade in her hand. "You say that this is 'Ice' from the frozen hells."

"Yes." He finished dressing the wound and took the dagger from her. "With this dagger we can build ourselves a protective circle." He frowned. "But we would need a third person who had been initiated to at least the second darkness."

"If we had such a person," Keleios asked, "could it work? Could we control it?"

"I've seen it done before with another of these."

She hesitated, but the image of the girl flashed across her mind. "Belor is such a person."

"Then we must find him. And you must tell me how you cleansed yourself."

"Do you need to know?"

"It could make the difference between success and failure."

"Very well." She dragged the riding glove off, wincing as the leather caught on the dried blood.

Lothor hissed between his teeth when he saw her palm. "Even Velen lacks that."

"The dagger sliced through my mitt, and the demonmark touched his flesh. As I destroyed him with it, warmth crept up my arm and cleansed me."

He spoke in a low voice. "Demon magic against demon magic."

A mind power crushed through her shields, and Keleios swayed. "Master Eroar. He is with Belor. Great danger, fire, trapped, sorcery almost gone, can't hold out. The devil broke their hold on the west side. Belor is badly injured." Keleios opened her eyes and said, "We must hurry." Keleios was surprised that the assassins had missed Eroar. Of all the remaining masters, he was the most dangerous. His true form was a dragon. Keleios smiled grimly. Perhaps dragons were not so easy to kill as a blind herb-witch.

Keleios stared up at the burning keep. There was no fire directly in front of them, but it was only a matter of time before it spread. "We might want to have some protection from fire spells close in mind."

Tobin nodded, eyes wide.

"Shall we go," Lothor said.

They clattered up the steps leading into the keep. Lothor hesitated before the opened doors, testing the darkness. Keleios came up slightly behind him. There was a hint of smoke over everything, stronger inside than out. Two keep guards lay dead near a third body. No living thing moved.

Keleios whispered back to Tobin, "Do you have the fire-protect spell ready?"

The boy closed his eyes and drew a deep breath. "Yes."

They entered, Keleios taking the lead followed by Tobin, and Lothor guarding the rear. It took some energy to follow toward Eroar, but thankfully not too much. Keleios led them toward the west and the smell of smoke. The harsh clash of battle drew nearer as they approached the central library. Keleios called a halt in the hallway before they reached the library. Something was moving down the main corridor toward them. They flattened themselves against the wall and waited, trapped between the fighting in the libraries and whoever was coming toward them.

The figure appeared around the corner and found Keleios' sword at her stomach. The woman gasped.

"Jodda!" Keleios hissed. She grabbed the healer's arm and drew her into the smaller hallway.

Jodda's white robes were stained with dried blood and soot. Her healing calm was stretched and almost gone. Her eyes looked too large for her face, and her skin was nearly the color of her dress. She leaned against Keleios with a long sigh.

"Jodda?" Keleios said.

The healer stood away from her, straight and proud, but worn around the edges. "I am very glad to see someone alive."

"Belor is still alive and Master Eroar—we are on our way to rescue them. Do you have major healing left?"

She nodded. A tear slid down the dirt on Jodda's face. "Why are they doing this?"

"Jodda, we have a way to stop the devil, but we need Belor whole for it and he needs healing."

She nodded. "You want me to come; I cannot refuse. It is the code."

Eroar the Dragonmage called, *Keleios, we are trapped between the fire and the battle. Belor is weak. I cannot fight and carry him.*

We are coming, Eroar.

We are discovered.

The contact was broken. Keleios forced herself not to reestablish it for fear of breaking his concentration. She could feel the shreds of his power gathering. "Tobin, can you cast a traveling invisibility spell?"

Tobin grinned. "I do that spell much better than you."

Keleios smiled and could almost have hugged him for being himself in the midst of all this . . . chaos.

He closed his eyes and nothing happened. The most unnerving thing about group invisibility was that your group could tell no difference. You just have to trust that it was working. It was one of the reasons Keleios hated the spell. She liked to see her results.

Keleios led the way, with Tobin behind her, Jodda in the middle, and Lothor protecting their backs. As long as they didn't attack anyone, the invisibility would hold, if it held at all. Keleios forced that thought away. She had to trust Tobin's magic.

The great central library was dying, shelves fallen and tossed like a child's toys, irreplaceable books scattered on the floor. Guards and invaders struggled weapon to weapon, finding footholds treacherous on the blood-stained, book-strewn floor. It was all Keleios could do not to lend a hand, but if the devil went unchecked, they would all die. As Carrick had said time and again, "Keep your eye on your objective." She gritted her teeth and led them along as far from the fighting as possible.

A struggling pair fell between Tobin and Jodda. They all froze, watching the daggers come closer to the two throats. The guard gave a mighty yell and plunged the dagger home. When he got up, he left the body. Jodda lifted her white skirts delicately to step over it.

They entered the far corridor, unchallenged. The sounds of battle drew them faster. The west wall was no more. A blasted emptiness full of torn rock and naked support beams was all that was left. Belor lay in a crumpled heap against that emptiness. Poth lay curled beside him on her side, panting. She was not hurt but Keleios could feel the emptiness of no more sorcery. Eroar knelt in front of him, blue fire spilling from his hands to surround a black-robed figure. A man in ebony plate mail moved toward Eroar's back, a naked sword in his hands. The sword was as night black as the armor.

Lothor motioned to Keleios that he would take the armored man. She nodded. That left her the wizard. They began moving toward the men. Tobin stayed behind to guard the entrance from the library and to concentrate on his invisibility spell.

Eroar half-collapsed onto the cracked floor. His arms trembled as they pushed his body away from the floor. Poth hissed at the black-armored man. Eroar half-turned, but before he could cast a spell, the wizard struck. The Dragonmage was enveloped in a red glow. Eroar screamed.

Keleios hesitated, close enough to touch the wizard. Lothor drew Gore from its sheath and nodded. They had to strike together, for if even one of them betrayed the spell, they were all visible. Keleios drew Ice from her belt and did two things at once—she gripped the man's shoulder and shoved the dagger between his ribs. The dagger sank through flesh as if it were silk.

Lothor swung Gore in a great looping curve. The blade sank through the other's black helmet like cracking an egg. The ax buried itself in the man's shoulder bone, the head split in two.

Keleios stared as the black-armored corpse toppled to the floor in a spray of blood, bone, and brains. The axe had cut through the magic plate mail like warm butter.

Lothor stared at her over the body, as if he could read her unease. She knelt and cleaned the dagger on the dead wizard's robes. Lothor walked over and knelt beside her to clean his ax. She glanced up and met his silver eyes. For some reason Keleios didn't want to be this close to him. She stood and went to Master Eroar.

Eroar the Dragonmage was covered in ash, his straight black hair, royal blue robe, the dark skin of his face all white-grey with wood death. It was all he could do to retain his human form. The shadow of his true self lurked in his eyes, leather wings stretching skyward. He smiled at her as she stooped and picked up Poth. The cat gave a weak meow. She stroked the thick fur and asked, "Master, how did the assassins miss you?"

"They did not, completely." His smile widened. "But Eduard was not the expert killer that was needed."

"Eduard was Fidelis' journeyman."

He nodded and said, "It seems she taught more than simple herb-witchery."

Jodda knelt by the emptiness of the ruined wall; the night sky framed her white dress. Her hands were on Belor; he did not move. She sat back in deep meditation, blood flowing from her shoulder. A trail of blood was drying on her forehead.

"We must leave here soon; the fire is near," Keleios said.

Eroar nodded. "I fought long and hard to find a place without flames to make a stand. When the devil came through, it shattered Belor's illusions and blasted and fired the keep." He breathed deeply, then coughed. "These human lungs don't take to smoke properly."

A tongue of flame broke through to the left, a tiny sparkle of orange, promising great things. "We need to get out of here. Can you walk, master?"

Eroar nodded and got to his feet, slow, a little unsteady, but moving.

Jodda blinked at them as if just waking. "He is not well enough yet to help you."

"Heal him later; we must keep ahead of this fire. The smoke will steal our lives as surely as the flames."

Jodda allowed herself to be helped up; Lothor took Belor's still-unconscious body.

A shudder ran through the area and Keleios yelled, "Go, now!"

They ran with her bringing up the rear, Poth clutched to her chest. The fire exploded outward, spraying the room with rocks and fire. Keleios turned her back against the blast, shielding the cat. The fire was free and climbed hungrily toward her.

The others stood uncertain in the midst of the library wreckage. The guards had been defeated, and the invaders circled round the group that had suddenly appeared. Lothor set Belor down to unsheath his ax. The men smiled; ten against one were their kind of odds.

Keleios appeared and contacted Eroar. *Can you teleport all of us to the dragon area?*

He stretched his shoulders. *No, I am too tired. We would just as like end up in a wall as at our destination.*

Keleios cursed, set Poth down on the floor, and drew Luckweaver. The roof overhead gave a long groan, and everyone looked up apprehensively.

The invaders shifted uncomfortably, but one led forward, saying, "I want the white healer. I've never had myself a white healer."

The roof sighed, and a sparkle of orange showed itself. Smoke was beginning to fill the room like grey choking fog. Keleios contacted Tobin. *Can you do another group invisibility spell?*

I think so.

Then do it.

Lothor started forward toward the fighters and Keleios caught his arm. He pulled away, and the men said, "Where did they go? They just disappeared!"

Tobin spoke. *The spell's done. Now what?*

Lothor turned to Keleios. She put her fingers in front of her mouth; if one of them spoke, the fighters would know they had not just disappeared. Eroar and Jodda carried Belor's unconscious form out of the room.

Two fighters advanced within a sword stroke of Lothor and Keleios. She fought an almost overwhelming urge to strike out, but there were too many of them, and the fire was coming. There was no time. Tobin was in the hallway trying to keep everyone in sight. He had to concentrate on the whole group or the spell failed.

Keleios swallowed hard against the smoke and a horrible urge to cough. It was Lothor who coughed. A small sound, but almost in the face of one of the men. The fighter's sword struck outward and reflex took over. Lothor caught the blade with his ax, and smashed his fist into the man's face. The man fell to the floor and did not get up.

Keleios slashed the nearest man across the stomach, and shouted, "Get to the hallway!"

The hall was narrow and Lothor filled the doorway, slashing with Gore. Keleios stood behind him out of the fight. "Keep them busy for just a minute."

He spoke through gritted teeth. "Whatever you are going to do, do it fast." Gore sliced one man's throat, and nearly chopped off the arm of a second. The fighters drew back, wary, but it wouldn't last. Eight against two were good odds.

Tobin stood at the far end of the hallway, sword out, facing the main corridor. A sword swung into view; Tobin turned the blade and chopped downward and retreated back into the doorway. There was more than one.

Keleios called wild sorcery, no concentration, no shaping of a spell, just raw power, and a prayer that it wouldn't backlash on her. Magic raced along her skin and raised the hair on her arms; her stomach twisted with the strength of it. She yelled, "Lothor, get out of the way!"

He didn't ask why but dropped to one knee, ax upraised to deflect a sword stroke.

Blinding white power spilled from Keleios' hands and smashed into the face of the man Lothor was fighting. The man screamed and vanished. Keleios spilled raw power into the fire-touched ceiling. With a scream of dying timbers the roof collapsed on top of the men. Fire whooshed into the room. Heat and smoke drove Keleios and Lothor back along the hall.

Jodda screamed up ahead and they ran toward the sound. A man lay dead near the doorway. Tobin was trying desperately to keep the far wall at his back while three fighters circled him. He blocked two of the swords but the third was coming in for his throat and there was nothing he could do. Keleios raced toward them and knew she would not make it in time. A large white dog leapt on the sword arm and pulled it back with teeth and weight. The man stumbled, cursing as

Piker dug teeth into his arm. Feltan darted forward and shoved a dagger into the man's leg.

Tobin took advantage of the surprise and shoved his sword into one man's chest. His sword caught and wouldn't come free. He dropped to his knees and a sword swished air over his head. Keleios was there slashing at the man, forcing him to turn from Tobin to her.

She faced him with Ice in her left hand, Luckweaver in her right. The man crouched behind a small shield, sword ready. Smoke poured out of the narrow hallway behind them like a chimney. They fought in a choking fog. Someone yelled, "The fire is spreading."

Keleios doubled over coughing, the man's sword sliced toward her bowed neck. She dropped to one knee, Luckweaver coming up, taking the blow. Ice shoved under the shield edge and sank through leather armor into the heart. When she stood up, Tobin was standing over the man who Feltan and Piker had injured. The man's throat had been sliced.

Jodda called from the entryway that led into the garden. She and Eroar had Belor sagging between them. "Hurry!"

Keleios found Piker running at her heels. Feltan stumbled and fell. Keleios stuffed Ice in her belt and picked the boy up by one arm, and they ran. The others were coughing by the fountain in the rose garden, waiting for them. Piker gave a soft snuff, half-sneeze, half-greeting, and nuzzled Keleios' leg. Feltan, face smudged with soot, flung himself upon her, hugging fiercely. "I thought you were dead. I thought everyone was dead."

"Not everyone. Did you think I would leave you alone with just that mongrel for company?"

He grinned up at her, tears shining in his blue eyes.

She petted the dog and found Lothor staring at her. "Thank you for your help in there," she said.

"You didn't seem to need any help."

She started to argue, then stopped. Was it a compliment? Keleios wasn't sure.

Eroar said, "Let us go on to the dragon runs if it is a place of safety."

Keleios nodded. "Safe as we are going to get tonight." She led the way deeper into the gardens, toward the doubtful safety of the dragon runs.

9

Fire and Ice

There was nothing alive between the gardens and the dragon stables, neither enemy nor friend. Keleios stared back at the keep, for the flames had claimed it. Great roaring sheets of fire blazed from the collapsed roof. The library was being consumed. Jodda knelt by Belor, laying hands on him once more.

He stirred and moaned under her touch.

Tobin said, "Keleios, one of the black healers called Velen is bargaining with the devil. The devil is listening."

She turned to Lothor. "What could your brother offer to a free devil?"

"He is an intimate of Verm. Even devils like to stay on the good side of a god."

"An intimate—what does that mean."

Lothor stared at the twin glows in the night sky. The keep blazed brightest, but the devil's glow rivaled it. "Some say his father was Verm."

"So you and Velen don't share either mother or father?"

"If Verm is truly his father, no."

"You don't really believe a god fathered Velen, do you?"

Lothar shrugged. "I don't know."

Keleios shook her head, feeling an argument coming on. "We have little time. Can you make a protective circle with the dagger?"

"I said I could."

"Will it be too dangerous to include all of us in the power circle?"

"It might be too dangerous not to."

Jodda said, "I will not be party to raising a devil for any reason."

Lothor bowed to her. "White healer, you and the young ones will be inside the power circle, protected, but not drawn upon. All the power needed or used will be within a star."

He held out his hand, bare now, and Keleios gave him the white dagger handle first. It seemed to blend with his skin, to belong in his grasp. His helmet had been set on the ground, leaving his white hair and face free. His hair was tied back in a long knot, leaving his elf-pointed ears bare. He began to pace a circle, the white dagger out before him balanced on his outstretched palms.

Belor sat up slowly and Tobin moved to help him. He waved the boy back. "How did we get here?"

Keleios went to him. "We carried you."

He massaged the back of his head. "I remember falling rock. Something exploded my illusions."

"It was a devil."

"What . . ."

"Belor, we need your help to conjure up another devil to turn or fight this one, or we will all die."

He stared at her, mouth slightly agape. "Have you lost your senses? You do not conjure devils without preparation and a sacrifice, and then you still don't do it."

Lothor began his third circuit, the blade pointed downward. When Keleios concentrated, she could see a line of power flowing downward from the blade.

"Belor, I felt the same way, but this thing must be destroyed, or we will die; everyone will die."

His eyes reflected the flames. "Keleios, everyone is dead. They couldn't survive the fire, the explosion."

"Very few are in the keep now."

They turned to Jodda. "The invaders came to the place where the children were kept and took them. They knew where we would hide the children, they knew."

Keleios asked quietly, "Has anyone seen Fidelis since this began?"

Feltan said, "I have."

"Where?"

"By the main gate. She opened the gates to them."

Keleios gripped his arm, too tightly. "You saw her do this?" She released him, but he seemed unsure in the face of her anger. It was as if he read someone's death in her eyes.

"I took Piker out for his last run before bedtime. I saw her standing and letting them pass. She wasn't afraid, and they didn't try to harm her."

"Where were the guards on the outer wall?"

"I don't know. No one tried to stop them. I ran as fast I could to spread the warning." His blue eyes suddenly looked tired beyond their years. "But it was too late."

Keleios hugged him to her. "No, Feltan, know that you saved lives by the early warning."

He looked up at her. "Truly?"

"Truly."

Lothor stepped inside the circle, a faint glow to his skin. Power washed over her when he stood close.

Belor asked, "Where did they take the children?"

Jodda shook her head. "Unknown, but they are slavers. They tried to capture rather than harm the children. I suppose they thought the rest would be less trouble dead."

Eroar used sorcery to trace outward. There should have been a trail of fear and pain, but all he could gather was a continuous buzz like the crackling of a great fire. "It is the devil. Its power clouds subtle magic."

Keleios turned to Belor. "They are alive, your apprentices, students, our friends. We can go after them, trace them if the devil's influence is cleansed from this area."

Belor said, "We can slip away and trail them, physically. Surely a group of children under armed guard will leave a wide enough trail."

"Look at the walls, Belor."

The orange glow was still visible, pulsing against the darkness. "A warding of some kind," he said.

"The devil put it there. We saw him do it."

It was Feltan who pointed and said, "What is that?"

They stared where he pointed and saw a flicker of green. It wavered like flame in the wind, but it moved over the stones of the unburnt corner. Where it moved, the stones crumbled.

Lothor hissed, "It is a minion of Verm. Velen's token. He brought it to impress the devil, and it will impress him." He stared at Belor. "We are running out of time."

Belor's face clouded, struggling within himself. "I don't want to do this. But I will help, if I must. How do we do it?"

Keleios explained briefly about Ice and the book. Belor refused to touch either unless absolutely necessary.

Lothor said, "We will all need to read from the book, touch it, and the dagger will need to taste our blood."

"How much blood?"

"Enough to seal a blood oath."

Eroar stood near the edge of the circle. Jodda, Tobin, Feltan with his arms round Piker's neck, all knelt or sat beside Eroar. Poth started to join the three who would conjure, but Lothor said no. He snapped at Keleios, "Get that animal out of here."

Keleios held down the answering anger and told Poth to leave the star. The cat had to be carried out.

Jodda had to hold Poth the cat, for she was determined to join her mistress. After a time she settled to sulk in the healer's arms.

Lothor traced the pentagram with the white metal, the black book gripped in his other hand. Belor and Keleios stood waiting, watching. The green flame had left a trail of rubble in its wake and was now entering the flames unharmed, devouring them as it had everything else.

The pentagram closed with a spark, and magic played over their skin. It seemed to pull the hair from the scalp and force shivers down the spine. Lothor opened the book and placed the dagger across it using its blade as a reading line. He began the ritual and passed book and dagger to Belor. The illusionist read in his clear voice that served him so well at holy days, making toasts. Keleios held the dark relics. The dark singing began again, and a chill crept into her soul. The book's power song grew with each word. The chill became a deep cold as they passed them back and forth. Power threatened like a coming storm, heavy and close and suffocating.

Each word was forced out through half-frozen lips. The words they spoke were distant to the book's dark singing. The song reached a crescendo of dark promises. The air was so cold it hurt to breathe, each intake like needles in throat and lungs. Movements seemed slowed as if they were freezing in place. The book seemed heavy in her hands, her fingers freezing to the blade of the knife. She spoke the last word, and the cold crackled in their ears, silence.

Into that aching silence a voice came. It whispered and hissed like a winter wind. "Who dares summon me?"

She could not move, or speak.

Lothor answered, "We summon you."

Their vision was a wall of light snow like mist; a tendril of vapor as if a giant had taken a breath came from its center. "Who is we?"

"Prince Lothor Gorewielder of Lolth."

"Belor the Dreammaker."

Keleios found her voice at last. "Princess Keleios Incantare of Calthu and Wyrthe."

"So, two members of royalty, what do you want?"

Lothor said, "For you to battle another devil."

"And what sacrifice do you offer for such a service?"

"We offer you token blood and command you by book, steel, and name, Fraizur."

The wind ruffled their hair and tugged at them. "I have felt the pull of Ice and the book. And you name me rightly. Let me see the color of your blood, and if the blade doesn't kill you, I am yours to command—once."

Keleios passed the book, still open, to Belor. She sliced her right palm, forming an X with the earlier blood oath. Lothor held the book and Belor used the blade. He gasped, teeth chattering, and swayed. Keleios touched him, keeping him to his feet as Lothor took the knife. Lothor's blood was a bright red wash against his hand. He laid the book carefully in front of them and clasped bloody hand to bloody hand with Belor. They formed a linked chain, a chain of flesh, blood, cold. Slowly, a faint warmth spread through them. It began in the demonmarks and flowed upward, outward from the old wounds until it chased the cold back. They stood linked in warmth. The frigid wind hissed and beat around them, growing in strength. The snow flew at them in icy sheets trying to steal breath, warmth, and hope, but they held firm. At the blizzard's raging height the devil stepped out of it, materializing before them.

Fully formed, he stood twenty feet, cloven hooves of ivory, eyes pupiless and white, skin like new-fallen snow, and an evil grin twisting his face. His four clawed hands gleamed in the moonlight as the blizzard faded.

With the dark song still ringing in her head, Keleios found all that white gleaming power beautiful.

The fire devil stood like a mirror image, all red and orange, with eyes of burning flame. The two devils faced each other, both held outside the protective circle.

The ice devil hissed, "Command me."

"Slay or banish this fire devil."

He grinned. "With pleasure."

They stalked toward each other, the ground shuddering under their steps.

The fire devil snarled, "We don't have to fight for these humans. Let us turn and devastate them."

"I am commanded, fire thing, and I will enjoy beating you."

"Come and try it, slush ball. We'll see who gets beaten."

The giants circled each other, baiting. The ice devil threw first a cloud of ice. Fire met it, turning it to water. The water drenched the fire devil and was frozen on him by a blast of freezing air. Water running down his red skin, the fire devil blasted fire and caught the white giant. It screamed, and the scream reverberated through the three still locked. Steam hissed, and the devil leapt forward. Combat was joined in earnest. The red devil's claws racked fire from the other, and the red flesh froze at the white devil's touch. They rolled along the courtyard, flattening the dragon building. A blizzard began to rage; a fire, to consume the building. The two forces blazed bright and brighter, until through the fog of melting ice and the glow of fire, the devils vanished from sight.

The white cloud raised the red off the ground and threw it to the stones. The ragged courtyard groaned and began to crack. The white leapt upon the red and a great fissure began to open up, sending smaller seams along the stone.

One of those cracks came through the magic circle and stole the rocks beneath their feet. Keleios leapt to one side, losing Belor's hand. She rolled and drew sword, for what good it could do, but the devils were too far gone in battle to heed the broken bond. Jodda and the rest were on her side of the fissure; Belor and Lothor, with book and knife, trapped away from them. The cracks kept spreading. Eroar was isolated from them on an island of rocking stone. The ground shifted underfoot until Keleios crouched close to the betraying stones and waited.

A fan of cracks opened up underneath the huddled group. As Jodda tried to get them to safety and Keleios tried to reach them, the cracks widened. Feltan teetered on the edge, then tumbled backward. Piker leapt in after his master. Jodda hesitated; Keleios screamed for her to get back.

Keleios sheathed her sword and began crawling over the heaving ground. Rocks forced upward as other sections buckled under the weight of the fighting giants. She hung, settling her weight as evenly as possible on knees and hands, and peered into the hole. Feltan stood trying to climb the dark earthen walls; Piker whined, nuzzling his leg. A man half-covered in dirt was near them. He looked to be a slaver who had gotten left behind somehow. He moved, and there was the dull gleam of steel. It was too close quarters for a sword. Keleios unstrung her garrote from its hidden pocket and leapt. The man was too close. His sword took the dog between the ribs. He grunted his satisfaction an eyeblink before Keleios landed on him.

The length of steel-braided cord looped round his neck. She allowed her weight to bow him over backward as the cord dug into his neck. The garrote had not landed perfectly, and he was half-turned to her. There was no room to maneuver for a better hold. He did not waste time clawing at the cord but dropped sword and went for a knife. If she let go, she was weaponless. Luckweaver would never be drawn in such a small space. Any sorcery this close to the devils would have to be major, and Feltan was on the other side of the man. She pulled harder, straining; her wounded arm protested, bleeding afresh. She tried to hide behind his own body, but he was a man who knew death and was determined to take his killer with him. Even as his breathing hissed and he began to die, the knife struck backward, cutting through leather armor like it wasn't there.

"An enchanted knife, too many damned enchanted items tonight," she thought. The blade took her. She gasped and gave one last tug. Whether the force of the pull, or the wound, the world spun for a second. The man slumped backward. She let him fall brushing past.

The knife stuck halfway into her side just above the leg joint. She gripped the hilt, trying to control her breathing, to control her own fear, to slow the heart rate, and the blood flow. Sometimes it worked; sometimes it didn't. The blade pulled free, and she gasped for air like a stranded fish. Blood poured in a red wash. Keleios moved the short distance to the dead man's neck. She tried to laugh and ended up coughing. She hoped it was the dust. The last heave had nearly decapitated him. His throat was a gaping wound. She was forced to dig for the garrote in the torn flesh. The garrote didn't want to come and she pulled and caused more bleeding at her side. She laughed and choked again. It didn't really matter if someone found the garrote or not.

There was a small sound. Keleios placed pressure against her side and crawled to Piker. The dog was dead, eyes glazed. Black heart blood pumped from his wound. She stood and stepped over his body to kneel beside the boy. Her hand pressed to her own side was becoming slick with blood. The boy lay on his side. She turned him over gently. His blue eyes stared at the distant sky without blinking. Blood dribbled from his nose and mouth. The death of his familiar had been too much for him to sustain. She checked for his heart, knowing it was useless.

She screamed her helplessness to the night. "Nooo!" The sound was lost in the fighting.

If she could not save Feltan and Piker, there were others up there whom she could save, had to help. "Oh, Urle, god of the forge, help me to help them." With the whispered prayer she began to climb upward.

The black earth, so fertile where it wasn't stone capped, gave deceptive handholds, crumbling under her hands. Her enchanted strength gave her the ability to force her hands inside the earth, but the earth wasn't accustomed to such treatment and crumbled at her disturbance. She hung halfway up, panting, her side and arm on fire, tiredness like an ocean wave threatening to engulf her. A cloth rope snaked past her, and, not caring who held the end, she took it and began to climb. Tobin helped her the last bit. She tumbled and lay still beside him. The rope was strips of white dress tied off on a rock that was stuck on its side. She prayed again, this time to Shendra, goddess of victims. "Oh, Shendra, give me strength to help them." She rose to her knees, then stood. Tobin gasped at the blood at her side. She gripped his shoulder, and they began to cross to the others still huddled on the quaking ground. Lothor and Belor had not been able to bridge the largest crevice. It was a great rift as wide as three horses long. The fiends still battled. Eroar, who was closest to the devils, was forced to place a sorcerous shield around himself.

As Tobin and Keleios moved over the broken courtyard, it shook. The boy was thrown to the ground. Keleios crouched low, trying to ride it out. A cleft widened between them, moving Tobin to a rock island out of reach.

Fire flamed round the red devil. He stood atop the white blizzard until all was orange and the white devil lay still. The flaming beast stood over the still form and screamed its victory. Then it turned blazing eyes to the people. Jodda screamed, but there was nothing she could do. It extended a flame-engulfed hand toward the tiny huddled group.

Keleios screamed at it, "No!"

With a flame-writhed hand, he turned to her and let fly a bolt of orange power.

Keleios dived and came up with Luckweaver between her and it, but a second bolt was already on its way. The orange power hit the blade and flamed along it, turning the metal cherry red with heat. Keleios heard her own screams as her hand burned. She dropped the blade and cradled her right hand against her body. The sword continued to burn brighter and brighter.

Over a sound of roaring fire she heard Lothor screaming, "Keleios, get away from . . ." The sword exploded.

The fire took her on the right side and sent her tumbling backward. She lay, face pressed against crumbling darkness. She whispered, ''It doesn't hurt yet.'' Through the wondrous numbness she saw the white devil grapple the red, and the fight began again. Then darkness flowed around her.

10

The Only Thing More Sad

There was a dragon thundering somewhere high above. A hot close darkness shielded her. She opened her eyes to the muted shade of a cloak hood. A bar of greyish sunlight hinted round the edges. One hand lay free of the covering; it stretched experimentally in the grey-and-white-flecked ash. Ash? The hand squeezed the stuff together and opened, stained with wood death. Ash?

The stink of smoke was everywhere, bitter and acrid. An image flashed in her mind of the keep engulfed in flames. The keep had fallen last night. Beyond that she wasn't sure what she remembered. She did know who she was, and that was an important thing to know. She mouthed the words, "I am Keleios Incantare, and I am not dead."

There was the hum of magic nearby—not her own magic, though. Keleios had been stripped last night of all weapons, enchanted or otherwise. She had no strength left for sorcery, and herb-witchery took more time than she had been permitted last night. Whose magic then? She was inside a protective shield, that much she could feel in the air, a strong one. Keleios rolled slowly onto one side, supporting on an elbow. The day seemed to roll and shimmer. The jagged black beams merged with the rising smoke into a fog untouched by sun. Pain seeped back slowly, and with its touch, she remembered more. Feltan was dead. Poula—she was dead, too.

Dead. Gone. Never coming back. Those were the words that she had heard so long ago, about her own mother. She whispered, "Poula." Her throat tightened. She swallowed hard against the rising tears. "No." There was no time for this, not yet. Grief would make her helpless, and this was no time to be helpless.

She eased to her back, and the sky still rode summer blue overhead. The last clear thing she remembered was being in the dragon yard. The devils were fighting. Luckweaver was gone. Its death was an empty ache. It was as if a part of herself had gone missing. The magic of the bracers had been breached; they no longer hummed. Great white clouds moved above, and smoke rose lazily into the sky. Keleios turned her head slowly. There was a painful stiffness to the right side of her face. Two lengths from her sat Tobin. His golden armor was ripped from one arm, rusted with blood, black with soot and dirt. His reddish-brown hair was stiff with blood on one side, but it was he. His back was to her, and he was hunched cross-legged in a position of power, but even then she began to feel his weariness. Keleios mouthed his name but dared not disturb him. She lay and drifted on the growing wave of pain. She was afraid of how hurt she might be. Tobin was near exhaustion, and the shield would not still be up if danger were past.

Then far off in the ruins she glimpsed something green, moving. It traveled like water with skin, flowing, and yet it flickered and changed like flame. Where it moved, even the charred boards crumbled into dust and clumps of blackened rock were sand. Flames of corruption. She remembered that Velen had brought the thing in as a token to the fire devil. The master was gone, but the hound had not gone home.

Keleios watched the thing flow toward them, destroying everything in its path. Would Tobin's shield hold against it? She should have been terrified, afraid, but the pain was too much for fear. If the shield did not hold, then there was nothing Keleios could do about it.

It flowed over the shield, showing the world through

green glass, glass that flickered and wavered and hungered.

Tobin moaned, and the shield bowed, then steadied. The flame slid off and flowed the direction it had come.

Keleios could not remember using all her sorccry last night, but it was gone. Perhaps she was simply too hurt to use it. Given a day or two of rest and a healer, she might be able to escape the corruptions with sorcery. Tobin would last only hours, not days. The only power left to her was herb-witchery. What ingredients were there? Ash, burned wood, dried blood, and from the feel, fresh blood if she wanted it that badly. She lay on burned stone. Ash for the circle, stone for the base, blood for the symbols, or perhaps soot. It could work.

She levered herself up and sat, cradling her right hand and arm. The hand was blood encrusted; the two smallest fingers looked twisted. Every movement sent sharp pains through it. She didn't need a healer to tell her the hand was badly broken. Tiny pieces of bone ground against each other; the hand was nearly crushed. Try as she would, she couldn't remember it happening. The flesh of arm and leg, glimpsed through the torn and blackened armor, was thick with huge watery blisters. The bracer on her right arm was melted to the armor and the skin beneath. The bracers were a pair, and when one was destroyed, the magic was gone. There was something wrong with the right side of her face, a painful something. It felt too much like the leg and arm to be anything less than a burn. Her good hand rose toward it then stopped. There was time enough later to be horrified. If she didn't find a healer, she would remember Luckweaver's passing in more than just memory. Sitting up had started a trickle of crimson from a shallow belly wound, but it shouldn't have been shallow. The dagger thrust had been deep; she should have bled to death by now. Her fingers told her that the wound was closing. It must have been Jodda.

She had had a brand burned into her skin once. But

this was a new measure of pain. The pain was a nau-
seating, all-consuming thing. She couldn't give over to
it. It hurt just as much lying still as it did moving, so
she could move if she had to.

By the angle of the sun it was afternoon. Tobin had
done very well to maintain his shield. If the spell had
only been against evil, it would not have been so tax-
ing. There must have been harm other than evil for the
boy to waste such energy on a shield to keep out everything. Or he acted in haste and was trapped into
his mistake.

She moved cautiously to her left knee; not so much
pain yet, the left side of her body seemed to be unhurt.
She reached her good hand to a half-burned beam and
pulled to her feet. She screamed and almost fell as her
right leg took weight. The world spun, then steadied.
Keleios stood breathing deeply, concentrating on each
movement. She whispered, "Cia, have mercy. Let me
walk this circle."

She stood away from the support beam and stood
panting, swallowing past the nausea of broken bones
and burns. She took a limping step, then another, and
another. Even as she began, the green menace flowed
toward them. She could walk the circle because she
had to. Keleios half-fell to her knees, letting the left
arm catch her weight. The first part could be done
from here. She crawled round the circle, sweeping ash
and debris clear with her left hand. The right side of
her body was a painful drag. The thing approached
once more. The chanting and clearing of ash from the
stone was all important. The flame reared in a wave
and fell upon the domed top of the spell as she dragged
to her feet, clutching ash in her good hand. She began
the ash circle. The shield bulged inward, and Tobin
cried out. The thing's weight was a heavy closeness
above her head. All thoughts went to chanting; she
could not stop now. The thing raged, feeding on Tobin's weakness. The sides gave a little, and the sunshine turned to green as the monster engulfed the

shield. The ash circle closed. Tobin gained something from it; the shield pushed outward to its original form.

Keleios eased herself down in the center of the circle, near a smoking beam. Still chanting, Keleios smeared her finger in the blood from her belly and began the first symbol. There were words that could be used, but the symbols were shorter. They were of an ancient tongue. Truth be known, they were not commonly used. Many people had perished by being unable to correctly decipher what sort of warding they were up against.

She was clumsier with her left hand, and it took longer than she wanted it to. The flame seemed to feel the nearness of the spell and rose against the shield. It threw its great bulk against the faint luminosity again and again. Tobin began to keen in a high, thin voice. The shield began to collapse. There were only two more symbols left. The stick man was easy, but the circle that rolled into infinity was more difficult. It smudged, and she had to scrape it away and try again. The shield roof was a hand's breadth above her head, and the weight of the flame made it seem lower. First the outer rim of the circle. There was a disturbance outside, a muffled sound of a dragon's trumpeting call. Keleios ignored it; the third rim was done. The flame began to lift, but the shield stayed small and misshapen. The seventh rim was a mere dot and finished. The spell took effect with a skin-prickling surge. Tobin raised his head, and with a small cry collapsed, his shield vanishing.

Outside was a copper dragon, baiting the flame. The dragon flew just out of reach but close enough to give hope and endanger herself. It was Brigette, one of Malcolm the Conjure-master's female dragons. He was a member of the council of Astrantha, and the only one who had spoken for Keleios when they took away her master rank. The dragon's scales flashed reddish-brown rainbows. Keleios sought mind-link with the dragon, wondering if she had the strength. The Astranthians bred their dragons dumb and safe. They retained the hard scales, but the magic sense, the intelligence, was ruthlessly culled to make a more manageable beast.

The dragon's mind was a jumble of chaotic thoughts, an animal's mind. Having touched Master Eroar's mind, she knew it for the blasphemy it was. Keleios projected an image of herself and Tobin, stressing the glowing ward and safety; an image of Brigette leaving the monster alone and flying high and safe followed. *Brigette, we are safe. Thank you for helping us, but leave the monster alone now, please. I have a shield up.*

The dragon gave an image of Malcolm smiling, then an image of herself flaming the monster and it dying. She swooped upon the green flame, then veered away a finger's breadth from the curling death.

Keleios gave an image of the flame beast devouring rock, fire, and people. She painted an image of a touch of green fire on dragon's wing and the result. Keleios was sweat drenched when she finished. It took control and great thought to project clear images to an alien mind.

The dragon rose a little higher.

As the dragon wheeled, her shadow fluttered over the ground. Keleios caught a glint of something. It winked again as the dragon passed overhead, a glass bottle. She concentrated and, yes, it glowed with a blaze of enchantment. Only one person made bottles to shine so: Shannie. She had been a peasant enchanter, and had made bottles to contain anything from the demon on Fidelis' shelf to storm spells. Shannie would have graduated this year.

Keleios gave an image of the bottle to Brigette. The dragon acknowledged it. Keleios formed an image of the dragon bringing the bottle near the shield.

The dragon swooped lower. Keleios sent a frantic image of the dragon flying away and coming back after the green flame had gone elsewhere.

The dragon rose above the angry flame and whirled to the east. One glistening wing showed a black burn on the webbing. Keleios was sweating and beginning to tremble from the mind contact. It was a low-energy use, but the effort of concentrating past the pain was almost too much. All she wanted was to lie down and cry and give herself over to the pain. No, she would not let Tobin die with help so close.

She half-crawled, half-dragged herself the short distance to him. He lay in a crumpled heap upon his side, his hair mostly obscuring his face. Keleios stumbled against him, pressing the broken hand into his back. She screamed and struggled to prop herself up on her left hand. She sat beside him, breathing in great draughts of air. Nausea and blackness threatened. The green flame came creeping to try her circle of warding.

It approached slowly, showing more intelligence than she had credited it with. It reached a tendril to touch the circle and jerked it away with a writhing that sent lines of orange through its green surface. Fire could not kill it, but it could stop it for a while. Keleios wasn't sure if it could ignore the pain and force the protect spell eventually or not. It stretched upward until it was thin as glass, then with a rush brought itself down to engulf them.

She watched the green wave fall. Would the fire ward hold it? A prayer whispered from her lips. ''Urle, god of the eternal flame, let this warding be hot. Let it burn the monster. Let it withstand his charge. Let it steam his . . .'' It hit.

For a moment the green lay on the tallest standing beam, draped like a tent. She thought the magic of Verm's pit was too strong. Fire. The world was suddenly flaming with good orange fire. The heat of it singed her hair. She felt in her mind the thing's screaming, a sound so high that it was like an insect's buzzing. The burned boards flamed to life again, and Keleios began to wonder if they would all die with the monster. It rolled away and began to tumble over the ground. But it did not die. She had not really expected it to, just to leave them alone.

"Thanks be to Urle, god of the eternal flame, that we are delivered and that this spell held back the destroyer of Verm."

The corruptor began to ease away as if in pain. It had evidently decided they weren't worth the effort.

Yet Keleios wasn't sure if the warding would hold against another such attack. Every warding had its breaking point.

Where was everybody? Jodda, Eroar, Belor, the children? Even the black healer, where were they?

She wanted to lie down and do nothing, just rest if the pain would let her, but Tobin needed her. He lay terribly still and was that peculiar grey color that sorcerers get when they've done too much magic at once. He had a wound on his right cheek, shallow, nothing to worry about. There was a second scalp wound, not as serious as the one Lothor had healed, but serious enough. Scalp wounds always bled a great deal, so he looked much worse than he was. There was a bandage of sorts around his right upper arm. It revealed a sword wound that had pierced his arm. Keleios was no healer to judge damage, but muscles felt torn and the main arm bones had been broken. It was the kind of wound that could deprive a fighter of the use of his arm.

Keleios began a prayer to Mother Blessen when a great flapping of wings arrived. Brigette hovered, then alit beside the bottle. She picked it up in a massive claw, gently.

Obedient to the earlier image, the dragon came closer, scuttling on three legs. The bottle was whole, undamaged, complete with a stopper. Perhaps the gods had decided to be kind.

Keleios searched for the green flame, but it was not in sight. She tested her own strength, reaching down inside to see if she could do this. The fact that she doubted it at all was a bad sign. But she had to do it, and that meant she could do it. Didn't it?

There was a flicker of green creeping over the ruins. But it was far enough away for what she had planned. She canceled the warding with one sign in the ash. The creature must have had limited magic sense because it sped its pace. Keleios used a wooden beam to drag herself to her feet, took the bottle from the dragon's claw, and removed the stopper with a word.

The creature barreled in, unheeding. Brigette took wing, but the monster was intent upon only one prey. It flowed toward Keleios in a rush of green fury, the scent of corruption riding before it like a private wind. Keleios stood, legs braced as much as possible to steady herself. She held the bottle out in front of her and spoke the words of entrapment. The thing did not slow but reared above her, a wave of green doom. The stench made her eyes water and her throat constrict. Keleios whispered the entrapment spell once more through clamped teeth. The creature hung suspended for a moment. Stretched thin as glass, blocking out the sky, it waited. She spoke the words again, and, like a high buzzing in her ear, the thing screamed. It seemed to collapse upon itself, folding inward until it was a narrow band of thick luminous green. The top of it began to bend toward the bottle.

Keleios watched the flame enter the bottle through tearing eyes. She held her breath as long as she could as the endless green line rolled into the impossibly small bottle. The clear bottle flowed green. Keleios capped it and spoke a word of strengthening.

She dropped to her knees and cried out in pain. Someone called her name. She turned slowly, the bottle gripped in her good hand.

Malcolm the Conjure-master clambered over the broken rock, his strong hands helping him where his dwarf-short legs did not. Healers followed him like a flock of carrion crows. Malcolm's face was plain as only a beardless dwarf can be, but when he smiled, his face was beautiful. He smiled at Keleios now. "Here I come to help you and you don't need any help."

She tried to smile but the right side of her face wouldn't do it. "I don't know, Malcolm. I might need a little help."

With her kneeling and him standing, they were almost the same height. His brown eyes shone with unshed tears and for a moment his face flinched as he looked at her. A familiar, freckled face appeared over Malcolm's shoulder—Larsen, Malcolm's son, his brown eyes intent on her wounds. His hands sure and deft as any healer. "Excuse me, Father, but if she can walk, we must take her to the healing area."

The dwarf nodded, looking up at his tall and very human-looking son.

"I can walk, but Tobin . . ." She tried to stand, but with nothing to hold onto, she fell heavily and screamed.

Larsen supported her, and Malcolm took the green-filled bottle from her hand. "It wouldn't do to drop it now, would it?"

She started to say, "No," but the world spun, the darkness swallowed the summer sky.

When Keleios woke again, she was lying on a blanket. The summer sky still blew overhead, but the smell of smoke was much less. Pain woke with her. The right side of her body felt as if someone had taken all the blood from her veins and poured molten fire in its place. The burn seemed to sink right to the bone. Without meaning to, she twitched her body, struggling against the pain. Someone was whimpering softly, and Keleios discovered that it was herself.

Larsen bent over her, his face concerned but with that constant cheerfulness of most healers. "I know it hurts, but I have some salve that will help the pain. You are very lucky you didn't lose the sight of your right eye." He smeared oily white cream on some clean linen and applied the cloth to her arm until the limb was wrapped in it. He laid a rectangular piece across her face, covering her right eye as well. "I have a potion brewing that will help you sleep."

The salve eased the burning, giving a measure of comfort. The whimpering could stop.

She found it easier with both eyes closed against the cloth. "Tobin, how is he?"

"He may lose the use of his sword arm without the aid of a white healer, but he will live."

She opened her left eye. "Where are the Astranthian school's healers?"

His voice came from a distance. There was the sound of a pot lid being lifted and replaced. "The High Councilman has forbidden them to aid this disaster."

"What!" She turned her head and screamed in pain. Larsen came and replaced the fallen cloth. "Please, Keleios, no violent movements."

She lay back panting. "Gladly, but how can Nesbit forbid the white healers to follow their oath?"

"Officially, the High Councilman controls the school, though it has been centuries since council has interfered with the healers. I have heard that Verrna is holding a council of her own with her fellow healers; they are taking a vote."

"If they come?"

"It will mean exile for them."

"The entire school of Astranthian healers, exiled. Every country on the continent will want them."

He agreed with her, vanishing from her sight line to stir pots once more. Keleios felt a dreaming touch—Master Eroar. She called his name and heard a sleepy grunt, but nothing more.

Larsen came back into view. "The Dragonmage is in a drugged sleep, in dragon form. He takes up quite a bit of room that way."

Keleios almost smiled at Larsen's wide-stretched arms showing just how much room, but pain was more important than smiling. "He is all right, then?"

"Breena had a look at him. She was the only one who knew enough about dragons to have a go at it."

"Where . . ." Keleios tried to look for her friend—Breena the Witch, herb healer, herb-witch, warrior, and a horrible archer. Keleios had spent most of one summer trying to teach the tall witch archery. Even Keleios had finally given up.

Larsen touched hand to her good shoulder. "Don't

try looking around. Breena is out helping search for
. . . bodies.''

There was a sound coming from behind, and she
fought warrior's training to allow someone unseen to
come upon her.

Larsen tensed, demanding, "Who are you?"

Lothor bent over Keleios. His helmet was gone, and
his platinum hair swung free in the wind, straying
across his face like mist. He looked drained; circles
like bruises were under his silver eyes. His skin looked
almost yellow. Dried blood stiffened part of his hair
and still clung in dry flakes to his face. "Will you
please tell him who I am?"

"Larsen Herbhealer, this is Lothor Gorewielder . . .
my consort."

Larsen stared down at her, his face paling leaving
his freckles stranded on pasty flesh. "But Keleios, he's
a black healer."

"I know." She closed her left eye, hoping it would
make things easier; it didn't. "He healed me last night;
he helped us banish a devil." Keleios opened her eye
and asked, "What happened, Lothor? Which devil
won?"

"The white, but Velen had regrouped his remaining
soldiers, and we were overrun." He let his head fall
forward, hair hiding his face, then came up like a man
clearing deep water. "Velen used magic on Belor; he
was knocked out of the fight early. A sword blow
stunned me. He left me for dead and dragged off the
healer."

"Belor?"

"He took him, too."

Keleios tried to think of something that could be
done, but the pain wouldn't let her think clearly. It
was enough of a struggle not to whimper aloud, like
a child, or an animal.

Larsen said quietly, "I must set that hand."

"I know."

"It will hurt a great deal."

"It already hurts a great deal."

Larsen looked across her at the black healer. "You are something like a white healer, aren't you?"

The strained ivory face smiled. "Something like, yes."

"Can you do any more healing today?"

"I had to do major healing on myself; that leaves me with very little power. I could heal very minor wounds, or I could take pain, if that's what you're thinking."

"It is."

She heard the herb healer walk away, then return. He spread a cloth on the grass and began laying things upon it. "Come over to this side, healer." Lothor stood wearily and was lost to her sight. "Grip her here." A hand settled on her shoulder just above the burns. A spreading warmth began, like a small candle against the dark. Larsen began putting the bones in place. Keleios opened her mouth to scream, and the pain leaked to Lothor.

Keleios was aware of the pain, a grinding nausea, but it was distant, muted, as if happening to someone else. A sickly sweat began on Lothor's upper lip. By the time the hand was set, his skin was almost totally yellow, a sick unhealthy shade. Larsen forced him to sip a restorative tea.

Larsen pressed an herb poultice to her side wound, exclaiming, "This is healing."

"I think a white healer did something to it while I was unconscious."

"No, Keleios, your body is healing it."

"That's impossible."

Lothor said from somewhere to her right, "Limited self-healing is sometimes a side effect of using a demonmark. It will pass."

"You're trying to make me into one of you, aren't you?"

"Don't be silly. Women can't be black healers; it's a rule."

"But I'm healing myself."

"It is temporary and will not last long enough to close the wound."

What was happening to her? The dark book, Ice, she felt the same. Keleios gathered her strength and searched herself, unbelievably weak at it. There was something more, a center of warmth. Why did something evil feel so good?

Larsen knelt over her. "You need rest to heal."

Keleios closed her eye and tried to rest, but the burns and chasing thoughts would not allow it.

A soft caressing voice came through the dark. "Keleios Incantare, so you survived."

Her stomach tightened, and fear crawled up her spine. The voice was unmistakable. She greeted without opening her eye. Keleios took a deep breath and forced her voice calm. Here was a man who hated her, and she lay nearly helpless. "Barely, High Councilman Nesbit."

She looked up. He stood tall, slim, every inch an Astranthian lord, with wavy blond curls past his shoulders, clean-shaven, this year's style in court. His doublet was black with yellow and green embroidery worked into the shapes of fantastic beasts. A square collar of white lace spilled over his shoulders. As he knelt, the edge of his dark cloak swept over her leg. "I am glad that you live, Keleios. Believe that."

Keleios found anger was stronger than fear. "Believe you? You must think me a fool."

"No, I think you a traitor to Astrantha."

"Well, High Councilman, you would know a traitor better than anyone I know."

His face flushed scarlet, then he smiled. "I hold your life in my hand."

"No, it is one thing to have me killed in a raid that you chose not to stop. It is another to have a princess executed." She turned her head with an effort to face him, choking back a scream. The cloth slid from her burn. He gasped and, as all Astranthians faced with ugliness, looked away. "You don't really want war with Calthu and Wrythe, do you?"

He spoke without looking at her. "Do not tempt me."

Groth, his healer, was just behind him. She asked, "How would you like to be a rabbit again, Groth?"

The man backed away rapidly.

Nesbit snapped at him, "She is too weak to do any harm."

Larsen came and picked up the dropped cloth. "Now you've dirtied it." He replaced it with a clean rag and admonished her not to move. "I would remind you not to upset the sick, High Councilman."

"Do you want to be exiled as well, healer?"

Larsen stood very straight. "If this is the benevolent care of council, I would be safer elsewhere."

"You could join this one in prison somewhere off the island. I have no intention of you and your compatriots being made a rallying point for the masses. Rest easy; I want no martyrs."

Keleios answered quietly, "But you already have them: everyone who died in the keep last night, everyone who was taken prisoner to be sold as a slave. In a few years your term will be up, and it is the aristocracy that votes in or out. If one keep can fall, so can others. Let them think upon it awhile, and they will fear you in office. They will seek a more trustworthy shepherd for their lands."

"That is my concern, not yours."

"Oh, but it is my concern." She wanted to look at him, but the effort was too much, so she talked looking up into the smoke-hazed sky. "You made it my concern when you destroyed this keep and killed my friends and teachers. You mark me a traitor. How can it not be my concern? You will die for this night's work, Nesbit."

"You're threatening me." He laughed, throwing his head back like a baying hound. "I will miss you, Keleios, but do not threaten me. I could still have you killed."

"I am not threatening." She struggled into a sitting position, tears streaming down her face, gasping and hating her weakness. "But you are a dead man from today on. It may not be by my hand, but someone will do it because of what you did here."

"Do you prophesy?"

She thought for a moment, trying to think through the pain and the weariness. "Yes, Nesbit, I prophesy for the High Councilman of Astrantha. I see death like a black shadow across your face." She screamed as the vision slipped away and the pain returned. "Nagosidhe, Nesbit, Nagosidhe." She collapsed to the pallet.

"Nagosidhe, what is that? Is it part of the prophecy?"

Larsen came in, forcing her to lie still. "I must ask you to leave; you are upsetting her."

Lothor's voice came smooth; only Keleios could detect the weariness in it. "Nagosidhe, High Councilman, are Wrythian warriors trained as assassins."

Nesbit left her vision and said, "What do you know of the Nagosidhe, Loltun prince?"

"Our country borders Wrythe, Councilman Nesbit. We lost three lords to the Nagosidhe before my father outlawed all raids on the elves."

"I do not believe it."

Lothor shrugged. "Believe what you like."

"But was it part of the prophecy? Will the Nagosidhe be my death?"

"I do not think so. She screamed in pain; her vision had left her. Call it a promise."

"A promise, what does that mean?"

"It means she is of elven royalty and can call out the Nagosidhe."

Keleios half-smiled. Call out the Nagosidhe—no, she could not do that. Only a pure-blooded elf could call the elven assassins. And she could never be real Nagosidhe herself, for the same reason. Balasaros Death's Master thought it unseemly that any half-elf be a Nagosidhe, even his own niece, but there were other problems to deal with before she ever saw the elven kingdoms again. And when the time came, she wanted to see Nesbit die—yes, that was what she wanted. She would not use Nagosidhe. She would do her own hunting. Keleios spoke slowly. "Where is Zeln? What have you done with him?"

Malcolm entered the clearing and answered her. "Imprisoned, but unharmed, so no laws have been broken by the High Councilman."

Keleios half-laughed and winced. "No laws broken, Malcolm."

He knelt beside her. "I know, Keleios, I know."

The councilman's smooth voice came, "You are obviously in pain. Let Groth help you, half-elf."

The grey-dressed figure knelt hesitantly, afraid. Keleios scuttled backward off the blanket, crying out in pain. "Get him away from me!"

Larsen stepped in. "High Councilman Nesbit, as you will give us no real aid, I call healer's right and ask you to leave. And take that charlatan with you."

Groth made a small protesting sound. Nesbit silenced him and said, "Very well, I will leave and take my healer. But Groth is the only help you will get on Astranthian soil, for I have forbidden any other."

A deep voice behind him spoke. "The High Councilman forgets once more that he is not a monarch."

Nesbit whirled. "Garland, how dare you?"

"How dare I." Lord Garland looked around the devastation near at hand and turned his white-bearded face to Nesbit. "How dare you force a vote on the council. I was silenced, but no more." Three healers were at his back: one white, one grey, and one black. Lord Garland worshipped Ardath and played no favorites.

Nesbit turned to look at Keleios. "Prophecy or not, half-elf, you will be imprisoned at dusk tonight; heal quickly." He turned and vanished, taking Groth with him.

Larsen helped Keleios back to her pallet and replaced the cloths. "The healing potion is ready for you."

Lord Garland asked, "Where can my healers be of greatest use?"

"Your healers are all most welcome, Council-lord." Larsen knelt beside Keleios with a warm cup. He supported her head while she drank, forcing her not to move any more than necessary. "This boy will lose his arm without quick white healing. We have found very few survivors. The other healers are out helping search for bodies."

Keleios' stomach began to knot and churn. "Larsen, I feel ill."

"I know, but the potion will help ease you."

"No, it . . ." Her spine went rigid, arching her body grotesquely. She was looking at the world through frosted glass and pain. A face hovered over her. "Jodda?" But the healer's eyes were brown as wood; her black hair, braided. Not Jodda, no one she knew.

An unusually gruff voice came from the woman's body. "Hold her so I can work."

Hands held her down, faces floating above her. There was death in her stomach, flowing through her veins in a way she had never experienced. She knew she was dying. They weren't helping her. "Aklan, tac morl, frintic aklan, aklan!"

A man's voice, "Herb healer, what did you give her?"

Larsen said in haste, "A potion for relaxation, sleep."

"What was in it?"

"Veldra, peppermint, goddess mantle . . ."

"Goddess mantle, also known as demon's bane?"

"Yes."

"You have poisoned her."

"But it isn't a poison."

"To her it is. First healer, you must remove poison from her body."

The brown-eyed healer didn't argue but laid hands on Keleios' struggling body. The arching spine and rigidity were lasting longer each time. Every sound, every movement, went through her body, jerked her muscles, sent her spine rigid. Keleios couldn't breathe until her body relaxed, and each spasm lasted longer than the last, until she could not breathe at all. The warmth of healing flowed through her body, chasing the poison. She could feel the poison being drawn from her body.

She muttered, half-gone, in pain, "Aklan."

The man's voice whispered, "Nor ac morl, nor ac morl."

The uninvited magic in her body responded to the words, calmed. Someone had understood; someone was helping.

Keleios lay still and panting, her breathing loud, her body sweat-coated.

She blinked up into a pale face lined with brown hair; two green-grey eyes stared at her. "When you are rested, I would like to speak with you in private." It was the strange male voice in the garb of a black healer.

Keleios tried to speak, but the white healer shooed them all away. "I must heal your burns and that hand. You seem to have a small ability to heal yourself. I have never touched anything like it." She shook her head. "But I will heal you, then we may talk."

Larsen was beside her. "Keleios, I didn't know. I've used the compound many times without harm."

She answered, finding her voice hoarse. "You could not have known; be at peace about it, Larsen."

Cool fingertips touched her cheek, and magic chased along the ruined skin. For a moment the pain scorched across her face. Keleios screamed and was echoed by the white healer. The healer was Meltaanian trained. No Astranthian-trained healer would have allowed the pain to increase before disappearing.

The woman sat back in meditation, and Keleios watched the burns fade from the pale face. The blackened, blistered flesh changed to angry red, then faded to pink and was gone.

The hands moved to her arm. The fire ate flesh and

the pain vanished. The healer broke contact and meditated.

The broken hand was cradled between the healer's own hands. Awake, Keleios remembered the pain—rock falling, crushing, such weight, her screaming as the pain brought her back, then dropped her in darkness.

The healer sat cross-legged for several minutes. Her face was pasty and a sick sweat dripped from her. The leg was next with its burns.

When the healer opened her eyes from the last meditation, Keleios asked, "What is your name, so I may thank you properly?"

"I am Radella of Crisna."

"Thank you, white healer Radella of Crisna."

She bent forward swiftly over Keleios' side wound. "It is a small thing, but if you go to prison tonight, I would not send you half-healed." There was a burst of warmth and pain vanished. "You will be weak for some hours, but rest and feel better."

Radella rose, leaving Keleios to marvel at her returned body.

The pain was gone; only a bone-numbing tiredness remained. She flexed her right hand, marveling at how easily it moved. Her arm bent at the elbow, raised at the shoulder; her fingers touched her face, smooth once again.

The grey-green–eyed black healer knelt with a cup. Keleios refused it politely, a part of her responding to him. He had saved her.

"It will send you into a deep healing sleep for some hours. You will wake refreshed and healed. I prepared it myself, so there will be no more inadvertent poisoning. I would greatly love to take speech with you about the demons, but you must heal now."

"I do not wish to go to prison in my sleep."

He smiled. "My lord Garland works that you may not have to go at all. But if you must go, take this so you go healed. Without this it could take days for you to strengthen."

She drank it carefully, supporting herself on one elbow. Against her will each muscle relaxed until she sank back into the pallet. Her body weighed a thousand unicorns weight. It was such an effort to move. She forced one finger to twitch and it felt as heavy and bulky as a practice sword. Keleios drifted on the verge of deep dreamless sleep.

Someone touched her. Keleios forced her eyes open. The black healer laid hands upon her, checking her breathing. The touch was a white healer's touch, healthy and good. Keleios was being forced to accept that the only difference was in the masters served, and the use made of the gift.

Breena the Witch strode into the healing station. Though only an herb healer, she seemed to bring health and heartiness with her. She was dressed in leather armor, brown hair free-flowing round her shoulders. She knelt rapidly beside Keleios.

Keleios tried to keep her eyes open, but could not. She heard the woman's rich voice from a distance. "There isn't much alive out there." She spoke an old Calthuian proverb. "The only thing more sad than a battle won is a battle lost."

Keleios let the drugged sleep sweep her under. The last thing she heard was, "Two more bodies. Where do you want us to put them?"

11

Chains

Keleios' eyes opened to dusk. The sky had been bled dark. The forest was a black bulk against a grey-silver sky where the last light of day struggled against the dark. Keleios felt refreshed. Magic was there for the calling again. Her body felt good, as if she had slept for a week. She wondered what had been in the potion the black healer gave her, for she felt remarkably well, better than she had expected.

She could see Eroar the Dragonmage curled head over tail, asleep, deep, past dreaming. She marveled at his true form. This would be only the third time she had seen it. His scales were a rich blue like the ocean far from land. His spine ridge was black, as were his claws; his true form bulked large and frightening.

Poth was a warm weight across her legs. Keleios lay still, trying not to disturb the cat. Her black and white fur was matted and dirty. She had been too tired even to groom. The cat flexed in her sleep, one ear twitching as if it caught a distant sound.

Keleios smiled in the dusk. Most wizards did not care for animals that did not earn their keep as familiar or worker. Even Keleios would never admit how much the cat meant to her.

Breena was tending the two fires, one for cooking and one for brewing potions. She fed sticks to the fire, the orange glow showing her face drawn and tired.

Carrick's nearly bald head showed above blankets. The rise and fall of his chest told Keleios he was alive. Keleios wondered if he too had been given a potion or if he would be allowed to sleep until healed. How Carrick hated magic potions.

Two men appeared, wearing the livery of the High Councilman, a black background with a red demon-spitting fire. Breena stood and was joined by the brown-haired black healer. The tallest one gave a rolled parchment to them. The witch took it. The paper sounded stiff, crinkling when she touched it, very official.

The tall one spoke in formal correct tones. "High Councilman Nesbit has decreed all surviving journeymen or teachers, traitors. We have come to ask you to ready the prisoners for moving."

Keleios had seen Breena truly angry only twice, each time glad that it was directed elsewhere. "I can read. Let me understand that the High Councilman of Astrantha has ordered injured and unconscious people imprisoned."

The guards shifted uneasily, for it was considered ill luck to interfere with a healer.

"Why doesn't he take the children, too?"

"They are young and can be reconditioned in the proper Astranthian school."

"And the weapons master, Carrick, is he to be imprisoned also?"

"No, he was doing the job he was paid to do. There is no treachery in that."

Keleios sought outward with her mind. A teleport block had gone up around the area. Teleporting was not one of her better spells but she would have risked appearing inside a tree, or another person, to escape Nesbit's net. A teleport gone wrong was a very bad way to die, but the High Councilman's dungeons were famous for making you wish for death, any sort of death. She felt strong enough to take the two guards and fight her way free. If magic were useless, then there was always steel.

Three more guards appeared.

Breena let her hand fall to her short sword. "You are not taking them like this, all unknowing."

"Please, healer, do not make us fight you."

The black healer stepped forward. "I promised the half-elf she would not go into captivity asleep." He pushed his cloak behind his shoulder and rested his hand on his sword pommel.

"I am not asleep."

Everyone jumped at the unexpected words and turned. Keleios sat up and said, "I thank you both for defending me, but I am quite able to defend myself." Poth, who had been awake for some time, stretched and leapt to the ground, yellow eyes regarding the men.

A deep rumbling voice sounded. "I, too, am awake."

Eroar's eyes caught the firelight as he raised his head. The eyes sparkled orange and fire-filled, and the dragon blew a questing breath of smoke.

The guards shifted uneasily, drawing nearer to each other like frightened children.

A smooth voice came from the forest. "There will be none of that, not unless you want to give me a reason to kill you all."

Longbowmen stepped from the concealing trees. Given a reason, they would kill all who stood in the clearing, except Eroar. It would be a miraculous shot that penetrated his scales by firelight. The wind shifted, and Keleios caught the sharp scent of crushed dragon's bane. Eroar blew another breath of smoke and stared at the men.

Nesbit stepped into the clearing. The archers did not step down. "Be reasonable, Keleios."

"I am ready to be reasonable, Nesbit. What did you have in mind?"

He motioned for an old peasant man to come forward. His blue eyes were faded to grey and his short body had bowed with age. He held chains in his hands. They rattled and clanked as he made his way across the ground. "You and all your magic friends wear these while we transport you to exile."

Keleios narrowed her eyes and hissed, "I will not wear those foul things."

"It is that or . . ." He let it trail off, but the alternatives were clear.

Breena asked, "What is wrong with the chains?"

Lothor answered, rising from where he had slept. "They are covered with runes of binding. No magic may be used against them. If you wear them, you are impotent."

Breena said, "Runes of binding are forbidden magic."

Nesbit simply smiled and stared at Keleios.

"Nesbit, I cannot; I am half-elf. The things will near kill me."

"That is the only safe way to transport such as you, and you know it."

"If I give my word not to escape, you can trust it."

"Your word is not good enough; no one's is."

"Not even your own."

Nesbit waved it away and said, "We waste time. Do you agree to exile, or do we kill you here?"

Tobin rose and stood beside Keleios. "What you ask of her is unfair, and you know it."

"I know old wives' tales; nothing more." He waited only a moment and said, "Decide, Keleios, decide now."

She realized that he wanted an excuse to kill them all. Martyrs or not, he was nervous now and wanted it taken care of one way or another. Perhaps he had overstepped his bounds, and other council members were rebelling, other aristocrats. "Very well."

Nesbit motioned the old man forward. He came tottering near, weighed down with chains. Eroar snaked his neck out, forcing the man to brush his fearsome jaws.

The old man hesitated, unwilling to pass the dragon.

Nesbit gave a short barking laugh. "These little games only waste time. The dragon will not hurt you, old man. "Go on!" The old man shuffled forward, more afraid of Nesbit than any dragon. After all, dragons did not torture a man when you displeased them.

Keleios folded her arms, afraid. The runes of binding excluded all magic. Elves were by nature magic, not merely spells, but substance. Nesbit called it old wives' tales, but those tales said runes of binding could kill elves.

"Come, Keleios, have you decided or not? Live or die."

She held out her hands slowly, fists clenched. The man's thin blue-veined hands held out a set of bracelets too big for her small wrists. The silver metal slipped round, clicked shut, and Nesbit spoke a word. The metal shrank to fit her. They snapped into place with a second spell, and Keleios was alone. Her magic was gone. She gasped, trying to bring air into her lungs. The cat screeched. Eroar bellowed, and the chain carrier stumbled backward. He fell to the ground in a clatter of chains.

"We can still kill her, dragon, so hold yourself in."

"I control myself, but there will come a day, human."

"I think not." He watched the man struggle to his feet and said, "Manacles."

"But, Lord Nesbit, she is but a girl."

"That girl could crush your skull with one hand."

The old man looked doubtful but shuffled forward and snapped them into place. Keleios was aware of it, but it didn't matter. Was this how it felt to be merely human? No, this was awful; this was a part of herself gone missing.

It was as if the world had shifted, leaving Keleios behind. She stood where she had been and yet was far away. The air was close, heavy, and hard to breathe.

Tobin was bound. He stared around at the trees as if seeing them for the first time. He whispered, "It's like being blind."

Keleios' voice was the faintest of sounds. "Worse."

Lothor stepped forward. His skin was its normal

snowy white; his silver eyes caught the fire like glass. "I am going with her."

"There is no need. You are a diplomate caught in unfortunate circumstances and are free to go."

"I cannot."

"What do you mean, cannot?"

"I am her consort. Where she goes, I go."

A look of amazement passed Nesbit's face. "Consorts." He walked to stand in front of Keleios. "Consort with a black healer, Keleios, I would never have thought it of you."

Keleios struggled to answer him, trying to draw herself back. The runes were trying to chase her from herself.

He motioned for the man to put chains on Lothor. "You do understand my position."

"Of course." A bead of sweat broke on the half-elf's brow when the chains were in place.

Nesbit turned back to Keleios. "If I had known your taste in men, we could have arranged something."

Keleios found her voice. "We could never arrange something, Nesbit."

"Don't be too sure." He came close, caressing a finger down her cheek. "I'm sure you would be just as pleasant to bed as your sister was."

She stared at him, brown eyes gone black with anger. "Methia has always had poor taste in men."

His hand traveled downward, and Breena was there jerking him backward. His sword drew with a hiss of steel, and hers answered it.

Malcolm stepped into the firelight. "I thought you had come to arrest the traitors, not harass the healers." The dwarf stepped between the two and motioned Breena back.

She spoke through clenched teeth. "He was touching her."

Nesbit said, "She is a prisoner."

Malcolm turned to Nesbit, his face blank, too blank. "Nesbit, I am allowing you to take her without a fight, but if I find that you have touched her in any way, I will challenge you to the sands.''

He began, ''Challenge me, dwarf,'' and Lord Garland stepped out of the dark.

He was naked above the waist, covered in grime and carrying a small cloth-wrapped bundle. His best-scenting hounds trailed round his legs. Garland had found few survivors. He stood beside Nesbit and forced the man to take the bundle. Nesbit held it clumsily, sword still free of its scarab. The bundle hung awkwardly, heavy in the wrong places, limp and hanging. Nesbit yelled and dropped it, leaping back from it. It hit the ground with a smack, and the cloth wrappings came loose. A child's face stared out of it, blue eyes staring impossibly wide.

Nesbit had dropped his sword and was trying to scrape at his arms as if to cleanse himself. Astranthians considered it very bad luck for a sorcerer to touch the recently dead. A stain of blood began to soak through the cloth, spreading until the child lay in blood-soaked wrappings.

''That body did not bleed while I carried it, Nesbit. You touch it but a moment, and it bleeds.''

''No, I didn't kill her.''

Malcolm said, ''The dead always know who to blame. They are very good that way.''

For the first time Nesbit looked frightened, as if expecting ghosts to appear screaming in the night.

If Belor had been there, they could have arranged something for the High Councilman, but the illusionist wasn't there, might never be with her again. Keleios had lost too much in the last few hours.

Her anger was gone, and only a cold knowledge remained. If she escaped, she would kill Nesbit. It gave her a measure of comfort.

Nesbit almost screamed, ''Enough of this!'' He drew his self-control like a cloak and picked his sword from the ground. He ran it automatically along his cloak to clean and sheathed it.

Breena had already sheathed hers.

"We will take the prisoners now."

Six guards gathered to him, swords bared and crossed on their chests. They surrounded the four prisoners. Four out of hundreds—were they all that was left? Poth ran to stand by Keleios, and the councilman laughed and let her stay. Nesbit stood and raised his arms. For the first time Keleios felt nothing save dizziness and darkness as they were teleported away.

They appeared on bare grey rock. The sea rushed and whispered along the desolate shore. White foam rode the waves like pale ghosts. Stunted, wind-blown trees formed a winter-bare forest. There was no summer on this island. A small mountain rose in the center, but no buildings could be seen.

Keleios said, "Nesbit, you cannot leave us here."

He smiled pleasantly. "Oh, but I can, and will."

She pulled at her wrists, but without the golden bracers' enchanted strength, she could not snap them. Eroar growled deep in his chest. He was magic-stripped but nothing more. He still held his dragon strength. With a word Nesbit had one of the guards train a crossbow on Keleios. "One move, dragon, and she dies."

Lothor asked, "What manner of place is this?"

Nesbit made a broad gesture to include the entire island. "This is the Grey Isle, home of Harque the Witch. Your consort can tell you all about Harque and the Grey Isle."

Keleios spoke quietly, fighting to keep panic out of her voice. "Nesbit, do you intend leaving us here, chained, without magic or means to defend ourselves?"

"It was my intent."

The guards gathered at his back. "You see, Keleios, you are right. If I execute you, I will be at war with two nations, but if you die in exile, there will be no war. I want you dead, halfling. I saw my death in your eyes. I don't want you at my back some dark night."

He smiled and looked out to sea. "And there is what will finish you."

The last brush of twilight flickered over a thick grey cloud, mottled with hints of other colors. Sickly green, the purple of bruises, a faint yellow and the sickly sweet smell of corruption came with it. It crept only yards above the sea, sending out tendrils of itself, then drawing its bulk along the tendril, coming closer. It seemed to be crawling along some invisible surface. The wind was stale, testing like invisible hands and bringing the stench with it. A smell like long-closed sickrooms and rotting things rode the wind.

The light died as they watched it just offshore. Two of the Astranthian guard began to retch from the stink.

Lothor whispered, "A moreacstrom."

Tobin asked between deep swallows, "What does moreac mean?"

"It means death storm. The thing is a minion of Verm."

Nesbit said, "Very good."

Keleios stumbled forward and fell on the rock, half-catching herself. "Nesbit, in the name of whatever you hold sacred, at least undo the chains. Give us our magic and our bodies; give us a chance."

He raised his arms. "Good-bye, Keleios Incantare, demon-named Nightseer, we will not meet again."

"If we do, Nesbit, you are a dead man."

He vanished with his guard. The stench of old death came closer.

"Can we run from it, black healer?"

"No, it can hunt over land or water."

"What can we do, then?"

"The only thing is a circle of protection." He pulled at his chains, eyes staring at the near-invisible cloud. "And we aren't going to get that wearing these."

The storm began to rain into the sea in a sickly yellow rain that made the water boil at its passing. Tobin succumbed to the wind and began to vomit onto the rock.

Lothor said, "If we can't get free, we will die."

"That I know, black healer. Tell me something I don't know. Tell me something I can use to get us out of here."

He spoke quietly. "I can't."

12

Alharzor

Flashes of odd light, like broken lighting, writhed through the cloud. The lights flashed across the rock, chasing the darkness back in bursts. The sickness of the chains tried to numb her mind, but there had to be a way. "Eroar, can you bite through the chains?"

"They are a powerful enchantment and would explode if damaged."

"Yes, yes, I know that."

Poth looked up at Keleios and meowed, one long plaintive note.

"I know, Poth, the storm is coming." There had to be a way. "Eroar, could you break them between your claws?"

"The problem remains. If I touch the runes of binding they will explode."

She nodded. "But if you touch between the runes, on the bare chain, the runes will be intact. They won't explode."

"I can no longer see magic. I cannot see where the runes are."

"Nor I." Keleios looked at the others. "Does anyone have a better idea?"

There was silence. The wind grew stronger, bringing the scent of old death.

She turned to Eroar. "I remember two runes per bracelet." She closed her eyes and said, "Here and here." She touched the metal above and below her wrist.

"Are you sure?" he asked.

"No, but I'm willing to take the risk, if you are."

The dragon nodded. He bent over her hands. His black claws, like ebony knives, hovered delicately over her manacles. Poth struck at his claws. She hissed, tail bushed, eyes wild.

Lothor said, "What is wrong with that cat?"

Keleios stared at the cat. She had never realized that her ability to communicate with animals was magic, but now Keleios was deaf and dumb, looking into the cat's yellow eyes. She didn't know what the cat was trying to say. "Tobin, hold her out of the way."

Tobin, still crouched on the ground, moved toward the cat. Poth reacted violently, striking at him.

"Poth . . ." Keleios couldn't understand this, and there wasn't time to puzzle it out.

The dragon bent over the manacles once more. The cat attacked.

"Poth!"

Lothor dived for the cat and caught her snarling and spitting.

The cat continued to yowl as Eroar started to work on the chains.

Keleios said, "Stop."

The dragon hesitated. "What is it?"

"Let her go, Lothor."

"There isn't time for this, Keleios."

"Don't you see, Poth can see the runes. Her magic sight is still working."

Eroar said, "If she could see magic before this, the cat should still be able to see the runes."

Lothor released the cat. "Our last chance is a cat's magic sight. We are doomed."

Tobin said, "Shut up, Lothor."

Poth hissed at Lothor and then walked daintily over to Keleios. Eroar touched the chains. Poth struck at him. He moved claws slightly to the right. The cat sat watching, wary but satisfied.

There was a sharp crack, and the manacle fell away. The runes were paired magic. With one bracelet off, the spell was released. The chains fell to the ground.

She stared into the cat's yellow eyes and said, "Thank you, Poth."

The leg irons were not enchanted. Keleios reached down and spelled open the lock.

Eroar nearly bugled his relief at being free again, but kept silent and began to work on Tobin's chains. Keleios freed Lothor at almost the same time, and without discussion they began to jog toward the stunted forest.

Eroar shapeshifted into his young human form and ran after them. The cloud seemed to hesitate over the land then began a laborious climb upward upon the rock itself.

The wind chased them with hungry chilling hands, telling them that the moreacstrom was still coming.

Something moved at the edge of Keleios' vision. She did not turn her head to follow the movement but whispered to the others that they were being trailed.

At least a dozen things moved like ghosts through the trees, too silent even for elves. Flashes of pale light began to wink through on either side, red, blue, and green. The colors seemed watered down, as if barely able to be seen.

Lothor said, "They are demon lights. No real harm in and of themselves, but they will report our movements and we cannot outrun them."

"I know what they are, black healer. I've been here before."

She doubled her pace and they moved to keep up, Lothor having an easier time than Tobin.

She gasped, trying not to lose too much air in talking. "There is a clearing near here where we can protect ourselves from the storm and whatever follows the lights." As if conjured by her words, they broke through to a large clearing. It was bare of all vegetation and irregular in shape, but time was short. They wouldn't find better. It looked as if it had been blasted clean. In the center of it lay a skeleton in elven chain mail with a sword still sheathed at its side. The bones were a bad omen, but there was no time to go else-

where. The wind felt like a real storm except for the
stench; bits of bark and leaves filled the air.

The sickly lights hovered round the clearing, and
Keleios fought an urge to strike at one. "Sorcery is
quick but draining, and easily broken by the more
powerful."

Eroar spoke. "Yes, herb-witchery is best, I think,
if we have the tools for it."

The first howl floated long and lonely on the storm
wind. An eerie chorus joined it until the night rang
with baying.

"The hounds."

Tobin asked, "What are you whispering, Lothor?"

"The howling, it is not dogs; it is the hounds of
Verm."

Keleios paled. "There is no time to finish an herb-
witch circle. Master Eroar, if you will erect a sorcerous circle at the limit of the clearing, I will try to back
it with an herb-witch one, but you'll need to buy me
time."

Eroar stood, and with a sweep of both arms, a shield
slipped over them.

She stared round the clearing; only bare rock
showed—no ash, no anything. "Tobin, do you have a
dagger?"

"Yes." He unsheathed it and gave it to her. It was
six inches of slim blade showing the Meltaanian urge
to overdecorate on the carved hilt.

"What are you going to do with the dagger?"

"I will use blood for the symbols; you always have
blood."

He gripped her wrist. "But there is nothing to make
the circle with. You would pass out long before you
had enough blood for it."

Lothor called, "Keleios."

He was kneeling by the skeleton, the unsheathed
long sword in his hands. He threw it to her, and she
caught it hilt first. Tobin's dagger clattered to the stone,
and she gasped. The thing was powerful. Sheathed,
she would never have seen it, but naked, it shone with

a powerful enchantment. The runes on its hilt and blade were Vallerian. Keleios traced the runes, demon, pain, death, silver, elf, and suddenly she knew what sword she held. Ache silvestri, Aching Silver, a name half-elven and half-demon, and very appropriate. It could bring true death to higher demons. The thing pulsed in her hands, alive. Though it remained quiet, she knew it was almost too powerful to be used. It was hiding now, waiting for a moment of weakness so it could control. Keleios knew better. There would be no moment of weakness, if she were careful.

Lothor said, "I have my ax. I thought you could use it."

She stared at the thing, transfixed. "Oh, yes, I can use it."

"I will not need your dagger, Tobin, or blood for the circle."

He bent and retrieved his weapon, but hesitated to ask about the sword. His own magic sense saw it for the power it was.

The baying came, and the wind rose, racing to see who would get to them first.

She gathered the sword belt and sheath and fitted them on her hips. She held the long sword, silver death, and spoke to it. "I am sorry to ill-use such a fine blade as yourself, but I need magic tonight, strong magic. Will you aid me?" It pulsed once in her hands, a dim throb, but it concurred.

She held it two-handed above her head and prayed to Urle to give strength to these two things of his art, enchanter and enchantment. The colors of the approaching storm played along the blade, and they seemed brighter in the reflected surface. Keleios plunged the blade downward to bite into the rock. With a metal scream and a shower of blue sparks, she and the sword Aching Silver began to carve a circle in the rock. Her chanting rose above the sounds of sword and rock. The circle closed, and it looked as if a thin line of fire had cut the ground. She stood uncertain, holding the blade just inches from her face. Steam rose from the blade into the cool wind. She sat in the center of the new circle, cross-legged, and drove the sword into the ground in front of her. The chant changed but remained constant. She was deep into magic and did not register the howling that came in over the twisted trees. She bent forward and sliced her arm cleanly on the sword. With blood she began the symbols. Two symbols were done when the howling erupted into the clearing. She forced memories down and continued. The spell was all important.

The first hound broke cover, pale as death. It had a naked human body covered with dirt and leaf mold. His mouth gapped open to howl skyward, exposing a horde of needlelike teeth. Fingernails like white razors clawed at the edge of the shielding. A dozen of them came sniffling and clawing around the clearing, howling in frustration. Parts of human bodies were tacked onto the hound form like grotesque jigsaw puzzles of flesh.

Lothor spoke quietly to Tobin. "Notice their claws and mouths have a yellowish cast to them, very faint over the white. It is a deadly poison to most."

"To most?"

"Yes." He seemed unwilling to elaborate, and Tobin let it go.

As Keleios traced the stick man in the dirt, she felt the pull of the sword like an invisible rope of power, a strengthening, a joining. Each mark of her finger traced a blue power, and the glow remained. She felt the sword's eagerness to join its magic to hers. She knew the sword longed for union with an enchanter as all enchanters long for a great enchantment with which to share themselves.

The hounds had quieted and lay or sat around the clearing, waiting. The winds had died down, and the stench of death was vanishing with each breath of fresh wind.

From the trees stepped the Hound Master.

He stood over eight feet tall, covered in red scales, barrel-chested, with black talons on feet and hands. A necklace of gold links draped around his thick neck. Three stones were set in it—two red that shone like new blood and one black that reflected nothing. His face broke into a toothy grin, batlike ears curling ever so slightly. The demon bent and petted one of the hounds with a floppy red and white hound ear on one side and on the other a young boy's face. "I apologize for being late. I had to reason with that mindless stinking cloud. This is too fine a catch for the storm to have." He chuckled. "Prince Lothor, are you in favor or out of favor this season?"

"Well, Alharzor, my status is one of great debate this year."

"Ahhh, someone has become ambitious, and I'll wager it is Velen the Black."

Lothor acknowledged it with a nod of his head.

"How do I know this, trapped on the godforsaken isle tending to the whims of a madwoman? Because he came here. He is very high in Verm's eyes. Velen gives orders, and I listen."

"What were his orders, Alharzor?"

"To kill you and anyone with you."

"You may find that task far from easy."

"I know, so I debate." He sat down, and two hounds crowded close to lie near him.

"Does Harque rate a minion of Verm?"

"No, but your brother does. He wanted to make sure you died, one way or another. He leaves little to chance. Fear him, prince, for he means to have you dead."

"Since you plan to kill me soon, I will not worry over Velen's ambitions."

The demon laughed. "True, true, the way I ramble on you would think that there was a chance of escape. If you defeat me, there are many others waiting for their turns."

The red demon narrowed yellow eyes and motioned to one of the hounds. The hound struggled and whined but at last flung himself on the shield. He was thrown back, stunned and burnt, but not by fire. "Ahhh," said the demon.

He stood and paused just short of the shield's glow. He closed his eyes. The concentration on his face was intent, his breathing slow and regular, as he bent hands to the shield. He was bathed in sparks of orange, blue, and white. He did not release the shield but poured more power into it.

Eroar sat calmly, unmoving, face placid, but his human shoulders shivered, and his skin began to sweat.

With a roar like close thunder, the shield tore. Eroar and the demon shrieked. Alharzor paused, shaking, then grinned.

Keleios finished the last symbol, and the witch shield pulsed in place.

The demon paused and shook his head. "Verm's wounds, this is going to be a long night."

The witch shielding had gone into place with a surge of magic. Keleios moved to take the sword from the earth, but it met her hand, leaping to her. Its life force tingled up her arm and sent power vibrating through her. The sword had had years of disuse and was wallowing in the glory of being active. She turned her face upward, and Alharzor looked full upon her for the first time.

"Ahhh, Nightseer, sister, this will not be an easy task." He peered closely, squinting. "What manner of weapon do you have there?"

"Ache silvestri, Aching Silver, painful death, the demons named it long ago."

"It cannot be."

"The great weapons protect themselves, Alharzor. It lay in this clearing for years untouched."

"It is a worthless piece of metal, nothing more."

"Look upon it. Look upon it and see it for what it is."

He pressed close to the shield. "I'll be fried, it is one of those cursed elven weapons."

The sword pulsed. The feeling was mutual.

"You are coming to us, Nightseer. You use a demon-aided sword; you endanger your soul by its use."

"Your concern for my mortal being is most touching, but you fear this weapon. You fear it in my hands."

"Perhaps, but Harque will be very pleased to find you in our net. She hates you, with a pure burning, like the sun through glass. It has burned away what was left of her senses, because your survival put her ambitions in a dilemma, to risk death for great power, or not. She is still debating whether to follow you into the pit. She hates you for offering her such power and blames you for her own cowardice in not taking it."

"She was always one to blame others for her own shortcomings."

The black jewel on his necklace glimmered. He grimaced as if in pain. "Ahhh, woe is me, she wants you all prisoners. It is hard enough to kill such magic, but prisoners. Ahh, she is mad."

"Will you disobey Velen to obey Harque?" Lothor asked.

"You see my problem, prince. I have been given a direct order by a high priest of Verm, my master, but the witch controls me through this." He pawed at the necklace.

"A necklace of obedience."

"Yes, Nightseer, and I cannot disobey her wishes."

"They are illegal in Astrantha now, for nothing can break their power once ensorcelled. Wicked evil things."

He looked ready to cry. "Can nothing break its spell?"

"There is a way. It is dangerous and may not work, but there is a way."

Hope flashed through his eyes, then died, replaced by a glittering anger. "You seek to trick me; there is no way out."

"I swear by Urle's holy flame that I speak truly. I know of one way to free you from ensorcellment."

Lothor spoke, "She follows Mother Blessen and would not lie in an oath."

"She may follow Blessen, but she holds a demon-powered sword."

Lothor shrugged.

Keleios nodded. "But you know how I come by the taint. You know that it was not choice that led me to hold this sword." She stepped close to the shielding's edge. "I was her slave then as much as you are now."

"I remember." An evil grin curled his red scaled face. "I arranged some of your entertainment on your last stay."

"But you had no choice, just as you have no choice now. You are reduced to being an errand boy, Alharzor."

Anger flared in his eyes. "I am reduced in nothing." As he spoke, he seemed to grow taller, stretching up into the sky. "I am Alharzor the red demon."

Lothor spoke. "Alharzor, no one here doubts your power, for you are a great red demon. Let us speak and come to an understanding. Let us bargain."

He shrank immediately, and it was as if the other had been illusion, which perhaps it was. "A bargain, now that is something to talk of." His eyes narrowed, and he rubbed his hands together briskly. "What have you in mind, prince?"

"We will free you from your enscorcellment, and you will free us. Is it not a fair bargain?"

"Yes, and because it is fair, you know I cannot take it."

Keleios began to protest, but Lothor waved her to silence. "Yes, I realize you will need to come off a little better than us, it is the demon way."

"So nice to deal with humans who understand from the start, saves so much time. Now do you want to go traditional? Your firstborn, a pound of flesh, a pint of blood, or a quest." He snapped his fingers and chuckled a most unpleasant sound. "I have it—you will kill Harque; that will be your quest."

"I thought ensorcellment meant that you could not even think to harm your master."

"No, Nightseer, I must obey, and I personally cannot harm or bring about harm, but I set you a near-impossible task. I truly believe you will fail, and thus no harm will come to Harque."

Lothor spoke dryly. "Bending the rules just a bit, aren't you, demon?"

He shrugged massive shoulders. "I will leave you alone to discuss your options; my pets will of course remain on guard."

He vanished.

Tobin spoke first. "Terribly cheerful for a demon, isn't he?"

"Yes," Keleios answered. "He would pull out your tongue while telling the most amusing joke about a flock of geese, a lesser demon, and a goose girl."

"You must tell me that one sometime when we have time to spare," Lothor said.

She frowned at him.

He smiled back. "Behind his back the other demons call him Smiling Aaah. But never to his face."

"Can we kill Harque, Keleios? You know her better than the rest of us," Tobin asked.

"We might, but it would be very hard, and Alharzor would be forced to fight against us."

"Is he the most powerful demon in her service?"

"He was six years ago, but things could have changed." She shook her head. "I don't trust him. To get us close enough to kill the witch, he will want to pretend to take us prisoner. He will be forced to take our weapons temporarily. Weapons gone, pretending to be prisoners and being prisoners is too close for comfort."

"Are you sure you can free the demon of his ensorcellment?"

"I don't know for sure until I explore the necklace's spell, but I believe so."

"You could simply kill him. That would free him of the spell."

"But it would break the bargain. If anyone plays traitor, let it be the demon, not me."

He shrugged. "As you like, but playing fair with demons is a narrow edge to walk."

"Agreed, but I stand firm."

Lothor sighed, but let it go.

They debated long and hard but finally came to an agreement. By the time the demon returned they had their plan. "Well, my friends, have you decided?"

"Yes," Lothor said. "We come with you."

"Splendid!"

"If we can keep our weapons."

His face fell. "Oh, my friends, that is not to be; you cannot be prisoners and retain your weapons."

Keleios said, "How fares Harque's true sight?"

He narrowed his eyes. "Why?"

"If her vision has decreased at the same rate it was decreasing six years ago, she should be almost blind by now. A small illusion should hide our weapons from her befuddled eyes, and you can supply that."

He growled low in his throat. He remained silent for a time, then said, "Agreed. Break circle and come with us. I will ready an illusion."

They stood, hands near the weapons, and Keleios swept the locking sign away with the sword point. The magic faded, and they stepped warily from the carven circle.

Alharzor spoke. "Now see of this thing round my neck, so I will not have to fight against you."

"I will look at it and see what manner of enchantment binds you." Keleios stepped forward, unsheathed sword in one hand. The others formed a semicircle around her and the demon. The hounds snuffled at their feet, perplexed. One growled at Tobin's feet.

Lothor called, "Keep them back."

The demon motioned, and the creatures fell back, whining.

There seemed to be heat coming from the demon's body, his scales glistening even in the dark with the rise and fall of his chest. Keleios fought herself to calmness, but remembered terror pushed forward. As she reached for the necklace, every muscle hummed with the need to fight or run. The gold links were cold like winter ice; that was part of the entrapment right there. The red jewels seemed just decoration. "I believe it will not be as difficult to break as I thought." Her fingertips found the black jewel. Yes, there was something here of power. She caressed it with her fingertips, eyes distant, concentrating on her inner sight.

She was not so deep into power, that she did not notice when the demon teleported with her. There was a spinning sensation as if the world had shifted ever so slightly and Keleios realized she could not feel the wind. Fear trickled through her, an undercurrent to the spell she was seeking. Alharzor had betrayed her. How very demon of him.

She continued to rub the stone, seeking its secret as another part of her sought her location. Stone walls surrounded her. Guttering torches were the only light. She whispered as if still deep in trance, "I think I almost have it." The demon bent close to hear. She gripped the black jewel and links tightly. "Yes, yes." She tensed to drive the sword upward. He saw the trick but could not break free of the necklace. The silver blade took him through the groin with a shower of blue sparks.

The hot acrid stink of demon blood filled the hallway. She drove the sword into his chest as he clawed at her. Their blood mingled on the floor, and she released him and stepped back. The leather armor hung in ribbons from her back and left side. Every claw mark began to sting and ache. If the demon had not been under a compulsion not to kill her, she would have had much worse. Blood flowed in thin streams from the claw marks.

He fell to the floor, orange-red blood pumping from his wounds. There were whispers in the corridor, "Demon slayer, demon slayer."

But Keleios saw nothing. Alharzor began to shriek, "Welcome home, welcome home."

His cries would bring others.

The sword whispered in her mind. It wanted to quench the life from the demon. It wanted death. She saw no other way to silence the demon. "Are you sure we can slay the demon? I thought you needed an evil wielder to perform that duty." It was sure. She came up behind the writhing demon out of the way of claws or sudden grabs. She and the sword lined up for a neck slice. The sword rushed eagerly, pulling her hand with it. The blade chopped cleanly, the head rolling gently to the side. Blood shot forth, and the body continued to writhe and call out. Keleios stepped aside from the blood flow. She was angry. "You said you could kill it."

It assured her that it could but not by simple methods. It whispered its needs. "That is dangerous."

"But the only way," it whispered through her head.

She stepped round the straining body and straddled the slender waist; the chest was too wide to stand across. The sword rose up in a two-handed grip, and Keleios brought it down in the demon's chest.

The demon screamed as if to bring down the very stones. The sword ate the pain, the fear, the life force of the demon. She tried to withdraw, but the sword glowed blue. The glow crept up her arms until she was bathed in it. She fought, but the power flowed through her, alien and sweet and painful. All that had been Alharzor came to her and the sword. The glow faded, and she fell, jerking the sword with her. She sat in a puddle of cooling demon blood and tried to breathe, tried to control the power rushing through her. She asked the sword, "What have you done to me?"

"Helped you kill a demon."

The sword was talking out loud. It had gained power, too. She sat and tried to understand, but a sound came from farther down the hallway. The hall curved to the left. Something was coming round that curve; something thick and wet and heavy was being dragged. She had never heard a sound like it. "What is that?"

"I think it is another demon." It warmed to the thought. "We can take another."

"No! I cannot take another so soon. You controlled me for a time, and I will not have that."

"If you do not use me, you will die."

"No." She moved to clean the sword but the blood seemed to have burned away. It continued to warn her until she sheathed it and locked it in place. The demon entered her sight, and she backed away from it. It was black and had no real shape, for it moved like thick watery mud. A trail of slime shone behind it. A single eye stayed near the middle of its head, and that eye took in the carnage, then saw her.

The black jelly split to expose a mouth that was empty except for a great red tongue. The tongue was spiked like a weapon. It dragged itself toward Keleios.

She had no intention of staying long enough for it to reach her. Keleios grabbed the bloody necklace of obedience and sought outward with her mind. She had performed dozens of teleport spells in the classroom. Each time she had come out alive, not half-buried in a wall, but four times a teacher had to help her, save her. There was no one to help this time, but if she took another demon so soon the sword might possess her. Death was better than that. She whispered to herself, "You can do this spell." She knew only one room well enough to teleport to. A slight dizziness and she stood in Harque's study. The teleport had worked, she was here, alive. The witch looked up with a smile. "I have been waiting for you, Keleios Incantare."

13

Harque the Witch

Keleios froze, waiting, sword in hand, but nothing happened. She stood near a tripod and its pentagram carved into the floor. The rectangular room was exactly as she remembered it. Harque had been nearly blind to reality six years ago and one did not move furnishings in a blind person's study. The witch sat at her desk sidewise to Keleios. Harque smiled at a point some yards in front of her near the bookshelves that covered the entire west wall.

Harque continued to smile and talk to what only she could see. "I knew you would come back for another taste of demon-ridden power." She laughed, and it rose up and down until she hiccuped. "I knew you wanted power." She seemed to lose sight of the phantom and squinted round the room. Her eyes found the real Keleios and stared. "I wanted power. I wanted it, but you took it, you took it."

Harque had been a tall woman and still in the shadow of her youthful beauty when Keleios had come and failed years ago. Now she was stooped and crippled with age. Surely just a few years could not have changed her so. The woman began to argue with herself, imitating Keleios' voice of years past. The two voices debated in well worn circles.

"I gave up my youth, my beauty, my health, for power. What have you given up?"
"I risked my life, my eternal soul, and I succeeded."
"No!"

"Yes, I did what you were afraid of doing, and now you have bargained away the youth and strength that would have let you follow me."

"Liar, you came for power; you wanted to go into the pit."

"The pit where even Harque the Witch fears to go. I was a child. I was afraid."

The witch buried her face in her hands but still spoke as Keleios. "You killed my mother. I came for vengeance, not power. Yet I who did not seek have found it, and you who have sought long have little to show for the search."

"No." Harque began to cry, and both voices ceased.

Six years ago Keleios could have killed her. Harque was strong, powerful, and evil. Now pity moved where Keleios thought she could feel none. She sheathed Ache silvestri and locked him in place; he did not want to go. Keleios crept forward, elven silent, and spread the lengths of the bloody necklace apart. She chanted silently the binding spell of the necklace. Leaving Harque alive was worse punishment. The necklace hovered over the grey head, but the witch moved lightning fast.

Harque scuttled from the chair and crouched only a few feet away; the face slipped. It was the same yet oddly shaped, and the arms grew longer, claws for hands.

Keleios unlocked Ache silvestri's sheath, backstepped to get the room's two doors in view and still not lose sight of the shapeshifting demon. The far door opened, and Harque stepped through, still tall and proudly beautiful. Her eyes were covered by two leathern patches. Her dress was cream with a soft grey cloak thrown over one shoulder, and she smiled a welcome. "Keleios, how wonderful to meet again after all these years."

The second door opened, and men came through bearing weapons. They each wore the hooded cowl of the shadow worshippers. They were only six, but magic glittered off their weapons and at least one sword dripped venom in slow heavy drops.

The long-armed shapeshifter leapt at her. She swung the necklace and caught it a solid blow across the face. It fell bleeding and stunned. She slipped the gold links across his thin shoulders, whispered words of entrapment, and said, "Aid my friends in finding me, and let no harm come to them. Now go."

The men circled warily as the little one disappeared. The necklace meant that Alharzor was dead, and that was not an easy task.

The room itself had been trapped, and she could not teleport out. Witchery locked her here, and the shadow worshippers advanced.

"Take her." Harque's impatient voice cut through their waiting.

One man said, "But she has slain Alharzor."

"Nonsense. She is an enchanter and broke the binding. Alharzor has fled home, and she kept the necklace. Do you think one lone girl could kill him?"

They didn't and were reassured, and Keleios didn't want them reassured. "Alharzor died because she told him not to kill me. He could have saved himself by slaying me, but he was bound and he died. And"—her voice changed, deepened, as she whirled the silver sword—"he is not truly gone from you. His power exists here within me." Keleios could feel Alharzor's power like a second pulse inside the sword, and all that power was hers to call upon.

They shuffled nervously, uncertain.

Harque threw a handful of powder into them, and the ones that it touched screamed. "Get her alive. All those who survive will be given unlimited freedom with the girls. I swear by Shadow."

The hesitation was gone.

Keleios tried one last thing. "No woman is worth dying for."

The one who carried the poisoned sword said, "These are."

They rushed forward, the one with the poisoned

sword closing first. Aching silver sang in her hands, cutting under the upraised blade, finding the heart and slicing through the rib cage like butter. Alharzor was there, his power strong and vital, beating with her and the sword. Blue flame flowed from the sword up to her shoulders; with each death the sword sang more sweetly. It crooned in her mind like a lover's voice, but it spoke of cutting and blood and made them beautiful. The grey-robed men fell at her feet, and she remembered little of the fight after that first kill.

When they all lay dead, she breathed as if coming from deep water. The sword sang in her head, not Alharzor's power, but the sword itself. The demon was inside the sword, and suddenly Keleios knew the sword could swallow her just as easily. In one screaming image she knew where the real danger lay. Keleios shoved every sorcerous ward she had inside her head, protection against mind-control spells. It was like crashing walls, thudding into place inside herself. She was isolated, unaware of anything but the sudden silence inside her head. She opened her eyes and her mind, cautiously.

Harque held a silver whistle to her lips. How long she had been calling, Keleios did not know, but something large was dragging itself through the near door. The demon that looked like walking mud flowed through the door. The sword sang a death song. It had never taken a demon like this one before. But Keleios didn't want to have to fight the sword again so soon.

The sword complained bitterly, but Keleios pointed her hand at the jelly mass and thought of fire. Fire that roared, gleamed, raised a sweat on her body. A fireball shot forward and splattered harmlessly. She needed more power than that. The sword promised power, but Keleios did not feel ready to trust the sword. She cleaned the blade automatically before resheathing it. Sheathed, the sword was quieter, and she could concentrate on her own magic. Fire didn't harm this demon, but perhaps cold would. Cold, cold that burns the lungs, cracks the skin, cold, ice. She drew that thought through her hands and into the demon. A double-fisted bolt of white hit the thing, and it opened its mouth to scream. It sat half-coated in ice, hurt and puzzled at this new pain.

Harque blew on the whistle, but it began to back out of the door. It had had enough for one day.

Keleios turned clenched fists to the witch when something hit her from behind. It sank needlelike teeth into her bare left shoulder. Keleios rolled, hand closing on a throat that was soft and warm. Black claws scratched at her face, seeking her eyes. A curtain of flame-colored hair blinded her, but she squeezed, digging her fingers in, searching. Something snapped in the throat, but still the thing fought on. She leapt away from its weakened grip. It was a succubus, a naked voluptuous female body topped with leather batlike wings, black claws for nails. Yellow eyes sought Keleios with hatred. With her throat partially crushed, the demon crawled after her.

The sword cried out to her, "There is only one way to truly slay a demon." Keleios had no wish to internalize the succubus' nature. The demon power raged through her now until she could hear squabbling, as if it needed more room. How many demons had the sword held before she picked it up? Through the clamor in her head she did not hear the footfalls behind her.

"Behind you!" the sword yelled.

She dove to one side. Harque's dagger thrust missed and sent the witch stumbling, blind eyes following Keleios. The succubus grabbed Keleios' ankle. Ache silvestri leapt to her hand. Keleios chopped the hand that held the dagger. It parted at the wrist and fell out of reach. Harque and the succubus screamed. Without thinking, Keleios allowed the sword to sink home in the demon and felt the power of the succubus creeping upward. She struggled to free herself, but it held.

She watched in a haze as Harque scrambled toward her, powder trickling from her remaining hand. An ax seemed to float into view, and the witch's head spun out of sight. The powder flew harmlessly, sparkling in the air.

Keleios' straining muscles pulled her and the sword backward as it freed them. She dropped the sword, but it made no sound through the roaring in her head. Tobin was there, kneeling, holding her, but only his lips moved. There was no sound but the surging voices in her head, the power of death, and a whisper of seduction.

The shapeshifting demon was there, all green now and small, the necklace winking in the lights. Keleios realized he wasn't a demon at all but an imp. No self-respecting demon would accept imps as kin, so small and weak were they. He was pulling at Tobin's arm. Lothor bent over her, but still they were far away.

A phrase slipped through. "It's the sword . . ."

Yes, of course it was. It was trying to take over, to steal her away from herself, the soul-sucking bastard. She tried to slam shields inside her mind and shut it out, but this time her sorcery would not come. Her head buzzed with the sword's presence, and the essence of the demon they had just killed. Her sorcery was nothing before the combined power. Keleios did what had to be done, accepted the power that flowed round her and the sword, and swallowed the evil and the memories of rituals that no mortal ever sees.

Slowly the world was heard again, and the sword fell silent, pouting, so close, but not close enough. Tobin helped her to her feet, and she stumbled, realizing that she was hurt. Blood seeped from a side wound. The blurred fight had taken its price. Lothor cleaned and resheathed her blade and snapped the locks in place.

"Where is Eroar?" she asked.

"He is conversing with the golden worm."

She looked a question at him, and Lothor said, "You came the easy way. We had to get by the watch worm."

"Didn't he," she asked, pointing to the green imp, "aid you?"

"Yes, your little friend aided us. But the worm was

suspicious, so Eroar showed his true shape. They are comparing notes for the last hundred years.''

''What of the demons?''

''They fled when Harque died. Can't you feel it?''

Keleios could feel a freedom, a cleanness, and yet there was something wrong with it. The place had been evil for so long; it would take time.

They swept the desk clean and laid her upon it. Poth leapt up beside her with a questioning meow, but Lothor told her to get down. She did. ''No more questions until I see to that wound.'' Lothor's slender fingers explored the wound and his face went blank, his breathing slow and shallow. The familiar warmth flowed through her, and he bent with the pain of his new wound. He healed the deepest scratches and stopped the blood loss. He stood straight, sweat beading his face. ''You will live.''

''That is comforting to know, healer.'' She sat up, carefully feeling the healed side. ''We must free the dungeon prisoners.''

Lothor shook his head. ''There is no time.''

''Harque is dead; the demons have fled. There is time. I won't leave anyone to starve in the cells below.''

He was angry but hid it fairly well and stalked off to search the study. The green imp hopped beside her. ''I did well, didn't I, Master, I did well?''

''Yes, Groghe, you did well.''

He swelled his thin chest out with pride. ''What do you want me to do next, Master?''

''Bring me the keys to the dungeon.'' He turned to leave, ''Wait. Can you guide us through the prison area? Do you know it well?''

He seemed ready to cry. ''No, oh, Master, no, I do not.''

''It's all right. Just bring me the keys and see if there is anyone left who would be a good guide. Do not bring the guide to us. Just look at the guide and tell us of him, or her. Do you understand?''

''Yes, oh, yes.''

"Then go."

Keleios slid off the desk and began searching Harque's bookshelves. Tobin leaned near the door, nervously gripping his sword. Poth had curled up on Harque's thronelike chair, yellow eyes watching Keleios.

Lothor stepped up behind her, drawing an impossibly large suit of elven chain mail from his belt pouch. He held it out toward her. "Here. With this on perhaps you won't be hurt quite so fast."

She touched the lengths slowly. They sounded like rain when they fell against one another. "It is a generous offer."

"I simply want you alive for our bargain, and you need better than ruined leather armor."

She held the chain, caressing it, and went to the desk once more. As she began to take the remains of leather off, she realized just how little was left on under it. She turned to ask Lothor to look the other way, but he was already smiling. "The price for the armor. Call it a promise of things to come."

"Urle's forge, black healer, don't you ever tire of baiting me?"

"No."

Tobin stared at the door without being asked.

Keleios turned her back on them and began to change. Most chain mail would have chafed and scraped without proper padding under it, but this was Vallerian mail. It felt light as cloth, as cool and good to the skin as silk. In the way of elven armor it fit to her body as if made just for her. Keleios belted the sword into place and she felt safer.

"It becomes you, Keleios."

"Thank you, Prince Lothor."

Tobin turned. "I have never seen such delicate workmanship."

"Nor will you outside of the elven kingdoms."

Something tugged at her magic. Something alien. The shapeshifting imp returned with the keys dangling from his wrist. Keleios complimented him on his success.

"I shaped into Harque, and the head dungeon master himself gave me the keys."

"Could you reform into Harque and maintain the shape?"

He nodded and began the change.

Again something called to her. It whispered, "Find me. Take me with you."

A perfect replica of the witch stood before them. Keleios moved around the demon and walked to a small wooden cabinet. It was locked. Keleios smashed the wood in and opened it. Inside was a squarish bundle covered in grey silk. She took it out and drew a sharp breath.

Lothor asked, "What have you found?"

"I'm not sure, but it called to me. It didn't want to be left behind."

"Keleios, only the great weapons and relics take care of themselves."

"I'm aware of that." She laid the book on the desk and unwrapped it slowly. The binding was grey. There were no runes on the cover, no warning, no instructions, no hints. She opened the front cover carefully and met a strangely yellowed page with rust-brown ink snaking across it. Keleios stepped back, rubbing her hand and shaking her head. "I'm hurt; the book struck at me." The world seemed to tilt, and she went to her knees, waiting for it to pass. When she could stand, she said, "It is *The Book of Grey.*"

"But that is legend."

"Just as Ice was a legend, and the demon-slaying sword."

He did not reply.

"There are entirely too many relics floating about lately."

"You think someone is handing them out as rewards."

"Or as weapons."

Tobin stepped close to the book. "What is this book?"

Keleios' voice fell into the singsong pattern of the bard. "Long, long ago, before the Lady of the Shadows lost her name and her body, before Verm fell from grace by the rape of his sister, when Loth was not the god of bloodshed, the three gods came together. Loth was an enchanter; the lady, an herb-witch; and Verm, a sorcerer. They joined their powers to create a great work. Verm and the Lady poured much of their power into the making, for combined they were greater than alone. But Loth only enchanted, binding their powers to a book, to pages, pages made with the rites of Verm and Shadow. For the pages they flayed skin from their most devout followers, from victims on their altars they made an ink of blood, and they began the work.

"At last it was done, but it was too great a thing and caused envy between the gods. Verm saw how powerful the book was; the essence of evil lay in it, of corruption, his essence. The Lady lay in it her substance, her lies, her power. It had been made in a bid for greater power, but now each looked to the other with fear. For the book could bring down the ruin of the other. They had allowed too much of themselves to slip into the book.

"So one night Loth stole the book and vowed that neither should have it for fear of turning against the other. At first they feared that Loth would come against them, but it did not happen. The book was lost. Until now."

The demon Harque said, "We must hurry, Master. The dungeon master might come looking for the witch."

"He is right. Lothor, you and Tobin go and free the prisoners. I cannot leave this book. And I do not know if it will allow me to pick it up again."

"I will go if you promise not to read it while we are gone."

Keleios laughed. "I am not so eager to have my mind blasted. I will not read it, you have my word."

They left, following the false Harque. Eroar appeared in the room moments later. "The Guardian Worm was badly served by the witch. An eye is infected when a little cleaning would have prevented it. The den is filthy."

"We will see what we can do before we leave."

He smiled, his human form handsome with perfect white teeth. "I promised her we would."

"Her?"

"Yes." He dared her to make something of it. She let it drop.

Poth was sniffing Harque's headless body and gave a low hiss. The flesh had begun to slip off the bones of the hand; the bones were green.

Keleios knelt beside the figure. "Verm's curse, spelled doppelganger. Harque is alive. The demons have not fled; they are in hiding. We've got to warn the others."

Eroar reached outward but couldn't get through. The protective shield was back and the room was a trap once more.

With a surge of magic, a flight of succuba appeared in the room. Like manic butterflies they swooped down, some with weapons, others with claws and teeth.

Keleios pulled Aching Silver from his sheath. Eroar sent an umbrella of cold over the demons, and they broke, shrieking in high-pitched voices. The succuba fled. Into the silence a woman spoke. "Welcome, Keleios Incantare, Elwine's daughter. I hope you have been entertained."

Harque stood near them away from any door. She was tall, straight, and handsome. Where her eyes once had been now glittered red faceted jewels.

"As always, witch, there has been nothing dull about our stay."

Harque smiled. "I am so glad. You'll be happy to know that my winged friends have gone down to visit your companions." She walked around the room to stand in front of the smashed cabinet. "I see you have found the book."

"Yes."

"Well, little enchanter, I wish you better luck than I had. I was quite mad for several years after deciphering some of the smaller spells." Her smile was wistful. "Such a price for knowledge." She stared at Keleios, and the half-elf watched life play behind the jewel eyes. Harque was in there, the jewels reflected her moods like real eyes. "And what price would you pay for freedom for you and your friends?"

"What price do you ask?"

"My, how you've changed; you've learned caution. But six years is a long time for some." She continued to pace the room, touching objects with a light caress. "What price freedom? You to be my second when I walk the pit."

Surprise flashed across Keleios' face before she could stop it.

Harque chuckled. "Yes, be surprised. Do we bargain, Keleios Incantare, or do we fight?"

Eroar spoke softly, "Is it dangerous?"

Keleios said, "Yes, but not extremely if the person passing through is strong willed. Are you strong of will now, Harque?"

"I am ready to pass into my power."

Keleios frowned at the phrasing.

A velvet cushion lay on top of the smashed cabinet and on it lay a polished globe of crystal. Harque picked up the crystal ball. "Here, see your friends; perhaps that will help you decide."

Images like fog rolled round the sphere, but Keleios sought Tobin and found him. He was naked and lost in the embrace of two succuba. He felt no danger, and Keleios moved on quickly.

Harque laughed, shaking the globe, and then calmed. "The black healer next."

The word drew the image in the crystal. Lothor was in a cell and was backing away from a copper-haired succubus. He was fighting for control, but his ax lay across the room. Another demon touched him, and he flinched away, afraid. He turned his back and began to pound the wall, gouging holes in the stone.

"That one has seen what the succuba do. He fears greatly and is strong willed." Harque smiled a lovely smile; the jewels in her face caught the light for an instant. "The succuba can drain a man to death if not kept to moderation."

She replaced the crystal on its cushion. "There are other demons and people who desire to visit your companions, many others." She smiled radiantly at them. "But then you know that better than most, half-elf."

"Yes, Harque, I remember. Free them, and I will second you."

"No, I will free them after I have walked the pit."

Keleios faced her squarely, hand clasping hilt; the sword began a soft song. "Harque, your journey will be long. In the time it takes, great harm could come to them. I will not bargain for shattered men whose minds and bodies are broken."

"True, true, but if I free them you will not bargain fairly with me."

"Then we cannot agree."

Eroar broke in. "Perhaps, if the demons were not allowed to harm them for the time it would take Harque to transverse the pit."

"No, Eroar, a demon's idea of harm is too strange. They have not harmed any of them yet, to their way of reasoning." Keleios walked forward to stand only two steps from the witch. "What if I give an oath? Will you free them before you cross the pit?"

"It would depend on the oath."

"I will swear by Verm's hounds and Loth's birds."

"A strange oath for a follower of Cia."

"These are strange times. Is it agreed?"

Harque drew a gold whistle and touched it to her lips. A red-haired succubus appeared. "Free the men after she makes this oath."

The red-haired demon pouted. "This will not be popular. They are standing in line for the white-haired one. It has been long since we have had our way with a prince of royal blood from Lolth or Meltaan."

"Why do they stand in line for the white-haired one?"

"He is most skilled with demons."

Harque waved at the globe, and it swirled to give images of Lothor with three succuba. Keleios looked away, anger and shame flushing through her. Harque laughed. "He does not fear the loving embrace; he fears his own perversion. He seems happy enough."

The succubus said, "No, master, he does not take the mindless pleasure in us that most men do. He performs wonderfully, like a well-trained animal, but he does not truly enjoy, not as the Meltaanian prince does."

A frown passed Harque's lips. "No matter, he is no longer distressed."

"Distress is a matter of definition," the demon said.

"Will you be quiet!"

The demon hung her head and said no more. The witch remembered her audience and smiled. "They will be safe for a few days."

"No, that was not the bargain."

"I don't believe I could persuade my girls to give up such satisfactory toys so quickly."

"Then there is no bargain."

"Oh, I think there will be." The lights went out. The darkness blinded Keleios, and thus was not truly darkness at all.

Eroar called out, "Keleios!"

The lights flickered on again. Where Eroar had stood was a hole, very black, through which a warm wind blew.

The silver sword leapt to her hand.

"No, half-elf, they will die if you threaten me. Their lives hang on your actions."

Keleios trembled, fighting the sword's eagerness and her own anger.

"Lay the sword on the desk. Perhaps you don't believe me. Shall I have one of them slain to prove my sincerity?"

Keleios touched the sword with her mind, telling it to be patient, that they would yet drink the demon-monger's blood. It lay silver and lovely on the desk. Keleios smoothed her hands across the chain mail, forcing herself to relax.

"Good, now look upon your dragon."

A movement caught Keleios's eye. Poth crept round the room. A chance, still a chance. "Show him to me and be done with it, witch."

"Oh, so the old Keleios still lurks within that calm facade. I will show you your dragon." She turned her gaze upon the crystal once more, and Keleios followed.

Eroar still in human form stood knee deep in black slime. Strange half shapes crowded round until it seemed the darkness itself writhed. One darted too close, a bolt of cold sent it scurrying back to the others. Keleios touched Eroar's mind cautiously. Harque did not seem to mind. *Eroar, can you teleport out to me?*

No, some magic binds me here. The image faded, and Keleios blinked up at the witch.

Poth crouched on top of the bookshelf, waiting.

Harque half-turned toward the shelf, and Poth leapt upon her. She shrieked as claws raked her face. Poth was a spitting, clawing, biting fury.

The sword asked, "Now, now?"

"Now." The blade leaped to her hand, and Keleios plunged forward.

Harque threw Poth from her and turned a bloody face to Keleios. "Cursed be." The blade slid home, seeking her heart.

Keleios drove the sword deeper as the witch dropped to her knees. They knelt face to face, and Keleios watched the life flicker in the jewel eyes. Harque whispered, "Curse you, curse you." But, there was no magic to it. Keleios watched the life slip from her eyes as it had slipped from Keleios' mother's eyes so many years ago.

Heart blood welled out of the wound, splashing the silver chain mail with near-black gore. Keleios drew the sword from its fleshy sheath. The body knelt for a moment, then slowly slid to one side. It lay crumpled and empty on the stone floor.

The sword crooned in her ear, "We bring death and vengeance."

Years ago she had come seeking the witch's death and found pain and defeat. This time she had come as a sacrifice to die and found vengeance. Was it enough for the days of suffering her mother endured? No. She cleaned her sword on a corner of Harque's grey cloak. No, it wasn't enough, but it would do, it would do.

14

A Brass Horn
Sounding

She sheathed the sword but did not set its locks and knelt beside Poth. The cat had been stunned, but her fingers found no broken bones, and Poth complained of nothing more than bruises. The cat began to lick the witch's blood from her claws and set her fur to rights again. If she was that interested in grooming, she was fine.

A length of good rope lay against the far wall with several empty packs. It looked as though Harque had been planning a trip.

Keleios went to the pit in which Eroar had fallen and knelt by the black depths. A cool warm wind blew from it. She tried mind contact and reached him. It was dark and hot. The creatures were growing bolder. *Is it hunger that drives them?*

I believe so.

Watch yourself. I am going to send down one of the bodies, then I will send down a length of rope.

Keleios selected a body near the pit and grabbed it under the grey-robed arms. She lifted from her knees up and felt the strain in her back. She had worked often enough without the magic bracers to know her own natural strength, and it was good, for a female half-elf. But a two-hundred–pound man is a two-hundred–pound man, and she was sweating by the time she rolled him into the darkness.

Keleios took out the smooth coil of rope and tied one end to the desk leg. She tested the knot and the leg itself. When satisfied, she lowered the rope. She prayed silently to Urle that the rope would reach.

Eroar, are they consuming the body?

Yes, voraciously. It is an unpleasant preview, I'm afraid.

Can you reach the rope?

Not in this form. Please throw down another morsel while I stretch my reach.

She dragged a slightly smaller guard by his robe and threw him in. A handful of seconds later and the rope became taut under her hands. The hands that scrambled to the top were huge and not the ones that had fallen in. She scrambled back from the huge bearded face that grinned at her as it pulled itself from the pit.

"Eroar?"

"Yes."

"That was unnerving."

"I had to be taller; this form is."

Poth came to peer into the hole and then backed away, hissing. "I quite agree with you, Mistress Poth, not a nice place."

"Are you hurt?"

"No, where are the others?"

"In the dungeons, we must hurry." She began pulling the rope up. "I thought you couldn't do magic down there."

"Shapeshifting is an innate ability, not a learned magic."

As the last of the rope landed on the floor, the pit began to close, the illusion becoming more solid as Keleios recoiled the rope.

Eroar shifted back to the more familiar human form and stretched. "I spend more time in this shape than my own; it's quite comfortable."

In her need to get to the others, she ordered the dragon, "Get the scrying crystal on the small table and the book on the floor. There are empty packs over there."

He stood very still, but did not move. She realized her mistake. Even in human form there was a pride, a grandeur, that no human ever quite touched. "Forgive me, Master Eroar, but time is short if we are to save the others. Will you please get the scrying crystal and the book while I coil this rope? We may need them all.''

He stood there stubbornly, hands crossed over his chest. She coiled the rope mechanically and tried to keep her temper. ''Master Eroar, if Tobin dies because you've delayed us, I will see you on the sands.''

He almost laughed, but the look in her eyes stopped him. ''You would die.''

''That is a possibility.'' They stared one at the other. She could feel his magic reaching out to her. It was a powerful, skin-prickling thing, and he had not yet cast a spell. Everything dies, even dragons, and she did not flinch. It was he who broke contact, moving to do as she asked. He touched the book and gasped, ''It pulses as if a heart beats inside.''

''It pulses with evil and is much too dangerous to leave lying about. But respectfully, Master Eroar, I ask that whatever you do, don't try to read it.''

He said nothing but wrapped the book in the table's white cloth and pushed it into an empty pack. The crystal he set upon the desk.

Keleios slid the rope in beside the book then put the crystal in beside them. She shouldered the pack, not bothering to ask the dragon if he wanted a share of its load. There was no more time for delays.

Keleios found herself holding the silver sword, blade bare and hungry. It was better to save magic if the sword would do. Eroar opened the door slowly, but the corridor was empty. Keleios took the lead. She thought Eroar would protest, but he remained silent and followed. Poth wandered ahead, cat-silent; few would bother to attack her.

Keleios remembered the corridors from Harque's study to the dungeons, for she had walked it almost daily for a month. They met one small vapor demon who was searching for the library. He had to find the library without aid of magic.

''We are on a quest also,'' Keleios said. ''We search

for two men: one tall and slender and very pale, part ice elf; the other, short with reddish hair and young.''

''A tall thin man, I know not, but the boy is in the dungeon's heart and is being deviled by many demons.''

Keleios sighed heavily. ''And our task is to rescue him.''

''You are on an entertainment then?'' He nodded sympathetically.

She continued in a sad voice, ''Yes, you are near the library. Simply follow this corridor then turn left at the second junction. The library will be the huge double doors with brass handles on the right side of the corridor.''

''Oh, thank you. One of the demons is a black fellow, very nasty looking, so take care.''

It floated down the hallway, vibrating with anxiety.

As they continued on their way, Eroar asked, ''Will he not report us?''

''No, we are both on a task. We entertain; he assumes that those in charge know what we are doing.''

''How is this entertainment?''

''That was something I never understood.''

''Why would a demon be a victim?''

''Big demons pick on lesser demons; it is the way of things.''

''You learned a great deal in a short stay.''

''Time is what you make it. These stairs lead into the dungeons. We should find Lothor down there, also, but in a cell. Only Tobin is free running.''

Groghe appeared in the corridor just in front of them. Keleios had to fight the silver sword for his life. ''Groghe, don't just appear like that. You'll get yourself killed.''

''So sorry, Master, but I escaped, for they were not interested in me. They can always torment me later.'' He fumbled with the necklace. ''I am still yours.''

''Can you change to Harque and guide us?''

''No, the other demons are suspicious and will be looking for me.''

"Then follow us invisibly and do not hinder us."

"No, Master." He blinked out. His claws scraped on the stone like mice in the night.

The stairs were wide but steep. Three large men could have walked abreast down them, but the height and pitch of the steps were not formed for human tread.

"Harque did not build this, surely," Eroar said.

"No, it was here waiting for her. Only the gods know who built it."

They came to a corridor that forked three ways. The tramp of many feet came from the left. A scream came from straight ahead; to the right was silence. "Fade back." Eroar simply became invisible for he lacked the elfish ability to blend with the surroundings.

A troop of grey-robed guards came from the left and passed into the silent right corridor. No one glanced toward the stairs; no one noticed a shadow that held other than darkness. They waited the space of five heartbeats after the last robe had vanished from sight. Eroar reappeared, and Keleios simply stepped out of concealment. Poth was nowhere to be seen.

"We go straight."

"Toward the scream."

She nodded.

The hallway stretched in a gentle torch-lined curve. It would be very hard to hide in the middle of that hallway. They went forward cautiously. She motioned for Eroar to take the left-hand side of cells, and she took the right. The first three cells were empty. The fourth held a man, curled into a small ball. She did not wait to see if he moved. Keleios tried to scan the cells without thinking about what lay inside. Just before they rounded the curve, she found Tobin's armor. It lay in a heap beside a pallet in a narrow cell. His sword was there, too. Wherever he was, he was naked and unarmed. A shriek came from up ahead, and faintly rumbling laughter.

She whispered to Eroar, "I believe Tobin will want

these back.'' She continued, ''If you can spell the door, I will scry Tobin's situation.''

''I was unlocking doors before you were hatched.''

She chose not to remind the dragon that hatching wasn't pertinent. She stood away so he could cast at the lock, and took out the crystal. The stone was smooth, cool, and flawless. She concentrated on Tobin's face. The vision came suddenly, startlingly clear. He was struggling in the grip of a very large demon, green-scaled and ivory-horned. The demon tossed him to another, who was slender and white with a spiked tail, and he threw him to the black pudding demon who caught with a tendril of ooze and covered the boy with it. Tobin struggled against it but disappeared inside the pudding. The other demons began to argue that it wasn't time to eat it yet and he better spit it out. He did reluctantly. Tobin crawled away from the pudding, retching and gasping for air. His gold-tinged skin glistened with slime. She cleared the crystal.

''The door is open. Should we . . .''

''We must hurry.''

She left without waiting to see if he followed. Eroar scowled but gathered the armor, clothes, and sword in his arms and followed.

He caught up to her in a few strides.

''Three demons are with him: one of ice, the black slime that we saw earlier, and a green-scaled demon that I don't recognize.''

The sword rose a short distance from its sheath. ''I know. The demon we absorbed earlier knows.''

''Tell me, then.''

''It is a demon of plague. In battle, if it chooses, its touch brings the dreaded spreading sickness.''

The invisible imp made a small keening sound. ''Oh, Master, he is bad, very bad.''

''Just stay out of the way, little one.'' Of all the demons to ensorcell, she had one of the weakest. Other than his shapeshifting and the limited sorcery of all demonkind, he could do little.

''That one must be taken out from a distance, then.

We can hit the slime with cold, and the ice demon with fire, but the green . . ."

The sword rose a hand's breadth of silver from its sheath. "We can destroy it."

"Safely?"

She could almost feel the sword shrug. "As safe as we can be. I cannot guarantee your safety."

She gripped the sword's hilt, testing if it could truly do what it said. "Yes. If you have no objections, Master Eroar, you could throw a fireball at the ice, and distract the slime. I will fight the green. If the green demon dies I will help you with the slime."

"If the demon does not die?"

"It will have to die."

His look was eloquent.

"I know it isn't a wonderful plan, but I don't have time for anything better. If you, Master Dragonmage, have a better plan, I'll listen."

He made no answer, but motioned her forward. "Let's go get the boy."

They waited just inside the tunnel. Eroar put Tobin's belongings on the floor, taking care that the metal did not clink. The ice and slime were to the right and the green to the left. A rack was near them and Tobin crouched on the floor near the torture device. Poth the cat crouched under the device itself. Eroar nodded that he saw her and stepped out, sending a medium-sized fireball to the ice demon.

The green strode forward to help. The sword sang in her hands, eager. The demon was not much taller than Keleios. Smooth ivory horns added to its height. It tried to move past Keleios toward Eroar, as if her drawn sword were nothing. She had to step in front of the demon and bar its way before it looked at her.

"Be gone, little female."

"Stand and fight, damn you," she said.

The demon sighed. "Very well." It turned pupilless yellow eyes full upon her. "I will kill you first."

It swiped at her with ivory claws and Ache silvestri met the hand and sliced it. The demon's other hand came out of nowhere and slammed into the side of Keleios' head. She fell, dazed. She heard the demon bending over her. The sword screamed, "Get up!" Keleios tried, but hands gripped her wrists and jerked her upright before she could move. The sudden movement sent the room spinning. Something was crushing her wrist and she opened her hand with a small gasp. Ache silvestri clattered to the floor.

"Can you see me, little female?"

Keleios blinked into the yellow eyes of the demon. She was on her knees with wrists pinned between the demon's smooth-scaled hands. "Too late to call magic, too late to use your pretty sword." He bent close to her face and flicked out a crimson forked tongue. "Time to die." The skin of her hands began to itch where he touched them, then to burn. A green sore, like mold, appeared on her right hand. The demon released her, shoving her backward. Memories of the assassin's death flashed through Keleios' mind. Of his flesh melting away. She stared as the green mold grew over her fingers, burning, itching, but no pain, not yet. It flowed over her skin like water and there was nothing she could do to stop it.

The palm of her left hand jerked, as if a muscle had spasmed. The sickness stopped spilling over her hand. It didn't go away, but it stopped spreading.

Eroar had his back to the wall. A barrier of fire kept the ice demon at bay, but the slime began to slide through the fire as if it were nothing. The plague demon just stood watching, arms crossed, back to Keleios.

A warmth, almost a fire heat started in her left palm over the demonmark. The heat rushed up her left arm and down her right until her right hand felt like it was on fire. The green spreading began to fade, as if the skin were absorbing it, the way a healer healed wounds. When the last bit of disease was gone, the burning began to fade and flow back into her left hand. Demon magic against demon magic, that was what Lothor had called it. But there was no time to marvel at her healed flesh. Eroar was pressed against the wall, backing away from the demons. They were not giving him enough time to call another spell, and what could he call? One feared fire, the other cold.

Keleios scooped Ache silvestri from the floor and rushed forward. The green demon heard her, and turned with a smile on its face. "Well, little female, are you not dead yet?" The blade took him through the ribs and up into the chest. The smile died on his face and he stood frozen while the blue glow ate over his body and up the hilt onto Keleios' hands. She didn't fight it this time; she welcomed it, drank in the power, let it wash over her and the sword. Ache silvestri cried, "We bring death to our enemies."

The demon's body sank to the floor with the sword still imbedded in its chest. Keleios turned to the other demons with wisps of blue fire still clinging to her hands. If she did not struggle against it, swallowing a demon's essence did not take very long.

Eroar was fighting both demons and being forced back. Keleios sent a burst of cold into the pudding, and it began to shamble toward her. She set her hands together, lightly touching at fingertips and base of hand, and thought of cold, the cold that numbs, that freezes the air in lungs until it burns. She drew pure cold in her mind—not snow, not ice, only cold—until the ache of it began to seep through her hands. The pudding was only feet before her when she opened her hands like a flower budding, until only the base of her hands touched, and cold came. It flowed like an icy wind to the demon. It slowed and stopped him. As the demon realized the danger, he tried to escape, but he was cold, so cold. He couldn't think, couldn't move. Still the cold came.

It was Eroar who broke the spell, shutting off the cold. "It is dead. Release your hold on the spell."

Keleios blinked at him, and broke the spell stiffly, and was surprised to find she had slipped to her knees. The slime stood like a column of dirty ice in front of her. "The ice demon is dead, let us rescue the others and begone."

She stood and began to flex her body. She had never been so stiff. There was a sound like a whimper or a quiet scream. Tobin crawled toward them. His body shook as if with ague. Keleios knelt beside him, smoothing back his hair, telling him, "You're safe now, Tobin."

He said nothing, but his eyes were haunted when they looked at her. He collapsed with a cry and clung to her for a moment, then pulled away and straightened. Keleios could feel him going through his control exercises. "I am a prince of Meltaan; I am a journeyman sorcerer, a visionary; I am Tobin." He stood straight and proud and said, "I know where Master Lothor is."

"Very good, lead us."

It was then that he seemed to notice his nakedness or perhaps he recovered enough of his self to worry about it.

Eroar fetched his armor, and while he dressed, they turned to other problems.

She walked without Eroar's aid, but it cost. "Urle's forge, but I'm shaky." She stood over the dead green demon. The tip of the silver sword pointed from its chest. Keleios bent to retrieve the sword but it struggled free itself and lifted to her hand.

It was free of blood once more, steam still rising from the blade where the blood had been heated away. She sheathed Aching Silver but left the lock off.

Tobin was fully dressed and belted his sword in place. Poth came out from under the rack, and a small skittering sound said Groghe had, too.

She asked Tobin, "Is Lothor in the far corridor?"

"Yes."

She motioned for him to lead, and they set off.

They approached the far corridor quietly; Tobin had assured them that there were more demons about. The far corridor was short, straight, and lined with cells. Keleios peered round the corner and froze as a succubus appeared and entered the open door of one cell. She ducked back around, leaning on the wall. "The succuba still play. What are we to do? They could be eating his soul."

The sword bobbed in its sheath. "If I may suggest, I hold a greater demon in me. The succuba would obey him."

"Yes, but you hold his soul, or essence, not him."

"But you are my wielder. If you desire it, you may have his knowledge, his power for a time."

"How?"

"You merely call him as if he were a spell."

"I don't understand."

"I have heard of such things," Eroar said. "Enchantments that eat souls can sometimes loan those souls to others for a time, and a price."

She stared at the Dragonmage. His dark face remained impassive; he might have been speaking of the weather, rather than using the souls of greater demons. "How safe is it?"

"It is like most spells—the success or failure depends upon how strong willed the person calling the magic is."

Tobin said, "But she is taking in the . . . essence of a demon. Doesn't success also depend on how strong willed the demon is?"

"It does," Eroar said.

"Don't do it, Keleios," Tobin said.

"I have to do something. It is only a matter of time before something worse than succuba visit these cells, or they discover the bodies."

Eroar asked, "And what if this Alharzor gains control of you?"

A cold feeling started in the pit of her stomach. "Then you must kill me and do the best you can to rescue the black prince."

Tobin protested, "No, Keleios."

"Tobin, if the worst happens, do not hinder Master Eroar. If the sword takes me, I am lost and better dead."

He nodded his agreement but frowned.

She breathed deeply, drawing her control, and the tiredness retreated somewhat. "Come to me, slayer of demons."

The sword pulsed under her hand, beating power like blood through its frame. Alharzor's anger flared through her mind, burning. His magic roared through her like fire before a wind. Power ate along her skin, spilled out of her mind. For one moment she could feel Alharzor, the sword, and herself mingle, become one. Then the sword was not there, and it was just she and the demon.

Poth backed away, spitting, able to see the power as it beat through her and out of her. Alharzor was determined to win, to control. He fought for her body, and she fought to use his soul.

Keleios accepted the demon into herself, like two hands inside the same glove, but it was her mind that moved that hand. Her eyes opened wide, and her breathing slowed, deepened. He was safely contained inside her with the help of the sword. She drew power from the sword, letting it trickle bit by bit until all of it lay contained inside her. "Stay hidden, Groghe."

The invisible demon said, "Yes, Master."

Eroar looked at her, and she said, "Touch me and search quickly."

He came forward and laid a hand on her shoulder, and his eyes met hers. His magic passed like a spring wind over and through her. "You have done it, and you have power now."

"I must bespell you both, so you will seem prisoners."

Though it was not what they wanted, neither fought her. Their eyes glazed, and their faces became blank. "Follow me," she said, and they did.

Keleios stepped into the corridor, hand on sword hilt, the men following behind her obediently. She had them wait at the head of the corridor; they obeyed perfectly. She paused at the door to the open cell. The half-elf lay under a mound of demons, their wings flexing like butterflies over a rain puddle.

Keleios drew part of Alharzor from the safety of control and let it flow through her. She sneered at the succuba. "Get off him."

They turned angry eyes and stared when they saw the body ordering them from the doorway.

One stood and began to walk toward Keleios. "And who are you to order us about?"

"Aaah, Filia, see with something other than your eyes for once."

A second joined her, and a third; all had paused. Lothor's flesh came into view. The shortest one said, "Alharzor, how did you get this body?"

"A gift from our lady witch."

"But I thought she had plans for this body."

"Is this the first time she's changed her mind?"

The demon chuckled. "No, I suppose not."

All but two of the succuba gathered round to poke and prod the new body. "Not bad, this should be able to keep up for a while."

A deep laugh came from Keleios's body. "Ooh, not at your speed, but perhaps at mine."

Lothor lay naked. Chains bound him at wrist and ankle. His body was one pure ivory color. Tiny scratches and bites marred the flawless skin. They were marks of passion rather than pain. An auburn-haired succubus curled across him. She stroked his hair and from time to time nuzzled him. His silver eyes were shut; his face turned away from her. Keleios wondered if his mind were intact.

She had been staring, and the demons noticed. A tall flame-haired one poked her arm. "Is she still in there?"

"Aaah, yes, I thought she might enjoy seeing her friends." A tittering of girlish laughter filled the room. A host of crude remarks followed.

"We could put him through his paces, or have her join us." This suggestion was met with great enthusiasm.

"Aah, girls, I am sorry, but Harque wants them all upstairs, now." A chorus of protests and whining began. "I even have to give the body back, after a time."

The auburn-haired demon left Lothor reluctantly, hands lingering on him. "We haven't broken him yet," she said. "The shame of it, Alharzor, we have to break through his control."

"I understand, girls, but there isn't time. The witch has some interesting plans for them all."

"What, oh, tell us."

"Aah, a geas."

"That doesn't sound very fun."

"It depends on where the geas forces them to go, my flame-haired beauty, and what it forces them to do."

They pouted. "It still doesn't sound fun."

"A geas to Pelrith's Isle."

They exchanged glances. One knelt beside Lothor's chained body and ran a hand down its pale length. "A shame that we won't get another chance at this one."

Keleios knew with Alharzor's memory that Pelrith's Isle was one place the succuba never visited. The demigod of the isle was too dangerous. A male being too dangerous for a succubus—that was something to think upon.

Keleios knelt beside Lothor. Keleios ran her fingers down his cheek, and his eyes opened. His eyes stared at her, intelligence untouched. Hope showed in his eyes for a second, quickly gone. She stood. "Have him get dressed, and maybe clean him up first."

A tall red-haired succubus asked, "Is she distressed to see her friend so?"

"Aah, very."

"I'll bet they were lovers," another piped.

"No, Bettia, just friends." The succubus smirked. Keleios shrugged and stood at the door to the cell.

A succubus flew in with buckets of water and hovered. "Are you all right?"

Alharzor sneered. "She is embarrassed, embarrassed to see the ice elf nude."

The succubus laughed long and rich. "She wants him, then?"

"Aah, yes, she does."

"Make time to put them together, please."

He seemed to think on it a moment and grinned wickedly, then sighed. "There just isn't time." Keleios leaned against the cell door, and the succubus slapped her behind. The succubus sighed. "What a pity." The demon carried the water into Lothor's cell.

Keleios entered and hefted his ax. "I will carry this for you, half-elf. You won't be needing it." His deep laugh echoed with the high-pitched giggles of the succuba.

Smiling an unpleasant smile, Keleios left to stand in the hall.

Gales of laughter came as the succuba began to release and clean the prisoner. Keleios, with Alharzor's memories beating through her, stood in the hall. Her eyes strayed to a large cell at the very end of the hall. It had been her home for the months she stayed here. It had been roomy enough but dank and cheerless, a very cell of a cell.

Someone whispered her name, someone who stood at the bars of that cell. His golden hair and skin glowed even now through dirt and beard. The beard was a rich reddish-gold like flame. She stepped closer, and when she looked in the golden-brown eyes, she knew who it was.

The Meltaanian noble known as Gabel Self-lover, enchanter, sorcerer, and murderer of her smithy master, Edan. He had burned him to death in front of Keleios' eyes. She could still taste the horror and rage of that moment like bile burning her throat. And somehow that rage had translated into sorcery. Keleios had called her very first sorcerous spell—fire. Fire that Edan had harnessed to shape metal, fire that burned under a pot to melt down herbs for spells, fire that glistened in the cottage to warm the food and keep the cold at bay, fire untamed and racing through the forest in a dry crackling run. Something opened in her mind

that had been locked and sealed until then. Keleios
saw the fire, true fire, flame. She drew it to her hand
and pointed at the smirking sorcerer. She had come
very near killing him.

No other Meltaanian noble had such a scar. It was
a whitened burn scar that dimpled and pitted the right
side of his face. One eye had almost been lost, and
scar tissue formed a ridge twisting the eyelid wrong.
Keleios had given him that scar. It could have been
healed but the Duke of Cartlon ruled that Gabel would
wear the scar as his punishment. Since only the physically perfect could rule in Meltaan, Gabel lost a king-
dom. Keleios was stripped of her master rank because
she had a new magic to tame. Sorcery at the age of
twenty. It was unheard of.

"Gabel." It was a hiss.

He did not flinch at the hate in the word, for the
feeling was quite mutual, but crowded close to the
bars. "Keleios Incantare, take me with you when you
go."

A great masculine laugh escaped her lips. "But Keleios is not going anywhere she wants to go."

He drew back, perplexed. "Alharzor?" But Gabel,
whatever else he was, was an enchanter and a sorcerer,
and good at each. He needed no spells to tell enchantment when he saw it. He spoke to her in a whisper.
"Alharzor does not possess you; the sword possesses
him. Take me with you when you go, or I will tell
them of your deceit."

Knowing Gabel as she did, Keleios did not waste
time being shocked or saying, "You wouldn't," because he would.

She glanced at Eroar and Tobin, who stood patiently
waiting. She stood at the door and picked the demon's
mind for the spell to the door. It was surprisingly simple. The lock crumbled in her hand like a flower.

Keleios whispered to Gabel, "If you betray us, or
bring us harm in any way, I will kill you."

He nodded. "Anything to be away from here."

A tall succubus questioned, "Why do you free that one?"

"The witch has tired of him and wishes to make an example of him to the others."

She agreed that he had grown tiresome.

A girl peered at the bars of a cell to Keleios' left. She was blond and blue-eyed, looking more like the fisherfolk than an Astranthian. She was young, fifteen at the oldest. Once she had been journeyman to the witch Harque. She had been imprisoned for failing once too often. Keleios wanted to take the girl with them, but the succuba wouldn't believe her if all prisoners were suddenly released. The gods had blessed her trickery as it was. Keleios turned her back on the girl's watching eyes and entangled Gabel in the same spell that held Eroar and Tobin. "Go stand by the others."

He moved without a word.

The succubus laughed. "A wonderful spell to quiet that one. He even talks when he ruts."

As Lothor was brought out, she bespelled him, also. His silver eyes looked into hers for a moment before they went peacefully blank. There was a terrible rage in those eyes.

They followed her quietly in single file. A guard of succuba fluttered round them to gasp at the carnage in the torture area. Keleios/Alharzor explained, "Aaah, I do not know what began this carnage, but an ice demon unknown to me slew the green demon and Slucba, the earth demon. I surprised him, and he fought me. I was forced to kill him. It was regrettable."

"Yes, red demon, regrettable." The voice was low but defiantly female. A large succubus walked into the room. She wore a golden sword and belt across her hips and a dagger in a wrist sheath on her right arm. Two straight ivory horns rose out of her skull, and her hair was the color of a good ruby, pigeon blood red. "Explain to me what has happened here."

"Elvinna, when have I had to explain anything to you?"

Her full lips drew back in a snarl, exposing ivory teeth made for drawing blood. "Since when have you been able to kill other demons without asking the witch first?" Her eyes narrowed, pupilless and yellow. "And where is your necklace of obedience?" Her sword snicked from its sheath. "Imposter." She hissed.

Keleios broke the spell on the men, slid Lothor's ax toward him, and began forcing Alharzor back into the sword. Eroar blasted Elvinna with a bolt of power that surprised her, for most humanoid males could not attack her. But Eroar was not human, and Lothor had been trained to resist. Only Tobin stood helpless.

Lothor screamed at Eroar, "Don't let her call her guard." Lothor scooped the battle-ax from the floor and began to attack the succuba. Eroar didn't ask questions but shot spell after spell at the succubus. The guards were incubi and male heroes who had worshipped her in life and they were very dangerous. But Elvinna needed at least a few seconds to call them, and Eroar was not giving her the time.

Keleios didn't have the sorcery left for a block that would defeat a demigod, but she had a demon-slaying sword. The sword swallowed Alharzor back eagerly, freeing itself for more bloodletting. Keleios called to Eroar, "I'll distract her; you put up a mind block."

The demon goddess sneered at the silver sword and the delicate attacker. Their blades met with a metallic scream in a shower of blue and red sparks. Eroar's block went up, tingling through Keleios' mind as the golden blade sought her life. The weapons recognized each other, their sentience pulsing through the hands. When the blades touched, it was like a jolt of lightning.

Keleios stumbled in a patch of melted ice, and the demon sprang forward, slashing for her head. The silver sword sprang to block with a shock that numbed Keleios' sword arm to the shoulder. She was forced to draw farther upon the sword's enchantment to attack and regain her feet. The sword's death song rang in her ears, sweet music, and she felt the eagerness as her own.

Someone shouted as she sent the demon back with a flurry of attacks. Keleios did not understand the words, and then she concentrated, letting the sword fight for a moment.

"Keleios, get away from her."

It was Lothor. She reached into the sword, forcing it back, forcing her will upon it. It struggled, nearly costing her her sword arm. Keleios feinted and made a pass at the unprotected belly and rolled over the rack to hear the golden sword bite deeply into the wood. Sword up, ready for attack, she heard a sizzling and a hideous scream. She peered cautiously round the rack to see Lothor with his ax pointed straight out. A crackling jag of white lightning came from its end and pinned the demon goddess to the wall. She writhed, glowing with heat and light.

Lothor lowered the weapon, and the light stopped. The demon sank to the floor and began to fade, snarling, "I'll remember this, black healer, and you, half-elf." She was gone, sword and all.

Lothor said, "Let us go quickly; others will come. I don't know how long it will take for her to collect enough energy to attack again—two days if we are lucky."

Tobin had been unable to attack the demons for he lacked a magic weapon. The magic of the demon goddess was too much for him, as it had been for Gabel. Tobin whispered, "So that was Elvinna. Now I know all my friends in Meltaan were lying; they never bedded that."

Keleios said, "Harque's death will slow pursuit. She was always so jealous of her power. The demons will be disorganized for a time. We must be off the island before they find a new leader."

No one argued with her. She led them out, knowing the lay of the keep, but insisted that if Gabel was to walk in back of her, that Lothor keep a weapon on him.

Tobin took offense at this. "Why did you ask the black healer and not me?"

"Because if Gabel moves to betray us, I want him killed. You, dear Tobin, would not kill someone just because I told you to. Lothor would."

There was the sound of copper bells, slightly off key, and the little green demon appeared. "I warned you first, Master, I warned first."

Keleios looked at the squat demon. "Yes, Groghe, you warned me first. Come along."

Keleios borrowed on Alharzor's knowledge and took corridors thick with dust. The torches they had taken from the dungeon area burned steadily in the stale air. They came to a branching of three tunnels. Down the center moved a single set of footprints. Keleios knelt testing, their width against her hand. "A human, soft shoes, a woman probably."

Eroar asked, "Harque?"

"Too fresh." She stood, dusting her hands off. "We need to go to the left."

Gabel asked, "But what if we meet the thing in the middle corridor later?"

"Then we do, Gabel, but we don't go chasing trouble."

They moved off into the darkness. At last a breath of wind stirred their torches, and Keleios motioned for them to extinguish the lights. She crouched at the tunnel mouth, looking out into a large cavern. The entrance of that cavern showed bright sunlight, so the hounds of Verm would not be a problem. Curled near that exit was a golden worm. Keleios had never seen such massive scales, each one as large as a knight's practice shield. The girth of the worm itself was too large for the eye to take in all at once.

Keleios whispered back, "How did you get past this thing?"

"Friendliness," came the answer.

"Well, get Eroar up here."

The dragon man worked past the rest to crouch beside Keleios. "Yes."

"How do we get past it?"

"By keeping our promise of treating its infected eye."

Keleios drew a sharp breath. "I've never seen a worm so large. Talk to it, Eroar, and I will help you treat it."

Eroar stood from the rest and walked into the cavern. He seemed to explode upward and outward, becoming dragon again. He was a mighty beast, a living mound of sapphire and ebony, but he was dwarfed beside the great golden worm.

The worm stirred and raised an eye to look at him. The rim of the black eye was swollen. Milky pus oozed from one corner. The thing's den was filthy and bare rock without a comfort to be seen.

Keleios felt anger that anyone could treat an intelligent animal in such a fashion. She nearly chuckled. With all that Harque had done, this was a small thing. It raised its massive fringed head to look with its good eye and nuzzled Eroar. They talked for a moment in common dragon. Eroar turned and motioned them forward with his blue-scaled tail.

Gabel hung back. Lothor pushed him, tumbling, down the slight slope to land at Eroar's feet. The dragon hissed at him. The deep voice said, "I may break my rule for you, Meltaanian."

He quavered, "What rule?"

Keleios answered, "Eroar makes it a rule never to eat humans." She stared at him, brown eyes distant. "Watch your step, Self-lover, or you will die one way or another."

After some coaxing, the worm lowered its massive head to Keleios. She spoke to the small green demon. "Groghe, fetch me some warm water and some clean cloths." He nodded vigorously and vanished.

Keleios noticed the frown on Gabel's face and asked, "What is the matter with you, Self-lover?"

He smiled crookedly, the left half of his face immobile. "We are risking our freedom to heal a worm."

"Our word was given."

He shrugged. "So?"

"Of course, you wouldn't understand what a person's word means."

"No, half-breed, I only understand self-preservation."

"Then get out. The cave entrance is right over there."

"No, I'll stay with you. You've always had phenomenal luck, even before you had Luckweaver." He stepped forward and said, "And where is your sword?"

Keleios said nothing.

"And no golden bracers. You are only a woman again. Perhaps I could show you what it's like to be under the scarred man. Only my face is ruined, everything else works perfectly."

Lothor placed a hand on the man's shoulder and said, "Enough."

"Let him go," Keleios said.

Lothor was reluctant but did as she asked.

Keleios drew Aching Silver from its sheath and approached the enchanter point first. "Do you know what this is?"

"A magic sword of Varellian workmanship."

"And what would it do to a man?"

"Are you my teacher now, Keleios?"

"Answer me—what would it do if used on a man?"

"It would destroy his soul. It's a soul-eater."

"Very good."

The cool metal rested against his bare neck, and he could feel the eagerness flow up from it. He could almost hear the song it sang. Fear danced in his eye, and anger.

The sword sang to her of vengeance, and she let a smile cross her lips. "If you ever come near me again, I'll use this on you."

"What would your goddess, Cia, say about that?"

"We have an understanding when it comes to you."

A bead of sweat oozed down his face. "I'm flattered."

She sheathed the sword in one quick motion. "Don't be."

She turned her back on him then and went to the dragons.

Keleios investigated the swollen eye under Eroar's direction. Dragon claws were not made for such delicate work, and the worm needed the reassurance of the dragon form. In the corner where the milky pus dripped was the head and part of the broken shaft of a spear. "Eroar, ask her why she didn't ask for the spear to be removed."

"She did, but Harque laughed and said it would teach her a lesson for nearly failing."

"But how could she keep such a beastie as guard when it must hate her?"

"Spells. It has nowhere to go, for spells block its leaving the cavern."

"Well, Harque is dead. The spells will fade and the worm will be free to leave or stay in a few days."

"She is most grateful."

Keleios drew a salve from her nonmagic belt pouch. Breena had given it to her as a parting gift. It had been brewed by Breena and had many uses, one of which was to fight infections. Groghe returned with a steaming copper pot of water and towels draped over his head and arms. He set the pot down with a small splash. "Here it is, Master, just like you asked."

"Very good, Groghe, very good." Through Eroar she warned that it would hurt, and she gripped the broken spear. When it came, she was tumbled backward. The worm reared above her, screaming in pain. A flood of unclean fluids mixed with blood flowed from the wound. The others backed away from the frightened beast.

Eroar calmed the worm after a time, and it allowed Keleios to approach again, but it was wary. She dampened one of the cloths in the water and began to clean the wound. It hurt, but it also soothed. The beast let Keleios have her way without too much trouble. When the eye was as clean as it could be gotten, she applied some salve just to the wound. "Tell her not to scrape at it. The swelling will go down if she doesn't rub it raw against the walls."

Eroar relayed the message, and the worm agreed to follow instructions.

"I wish I had bandages for that eye." Keleios shook her head and smiled. "But it would take a storeroom of cloth to do it."

The men led the way into the sunshine. Eroar waved good-bye to the worm. Groghe hopped along beside Keleios. Poth stepped daintily, not having gotten close to the worm. The scrub trees fluttered pale green leaves in the wind. When they felt enough distance was between them and Harque's keep, they spoke quietly, still alert for pursuit.

"Harque has neglected her worm," Eroar said.

Lothor asked, "How?"

"It could have been blinded in that eye if we had not come along. The giant worms are not natural, but magically created, and are susceptible to many illnesses because of it. A little extra care, and the worm would have been fine."

They broke free of the trees and began to parallel the beach toward the boats. Harque had several boats docked around the island. Using Alharzor's updated knowledge, Keleios knew where a comfortable but manageable craft could be had. A dog stood on the rock-strewn sand. It was a hunting hound of medium size, white with brown spots. As they drew closer they could see that one of its ears was missing, not chewed off in a fight, but as if it had been born without it.

Two more hounds joined it, one all white, one black and white.

Keleios whispered, "Guard yourself. I don't like the looks of them."

They passed close to the hounds now. The black one was missing an eye, and the white had a twisted foot. They stared with malice glittering in their trusting brown eyes.

Tobin asked, "What are they?"

Lothor answered, "The day forms of the hounds of Verm. And their eyes are not fooled by magic."

Gabel said, "Monstrous things."

Keleios asked, "Have you been the prey in a daytime hunt?"

"I have experienced many wondrous things since we last met."

"Poor Gabel, I was hunted through these woods when I was seventeen."

"Brave little half-breed."

Lothor said, "Enough. The hounds' powers are limited in daylight, but if they warn the others, we may fail yet."

They broke into a trot without another word. A ring of hounds surrounded the beached boat. They snarled their displeasure, and a large yellow one threatened with raised fur and bared teeth.

Lothor strode forward. "Make way for your betters." He spoke a word that no one quite heard, guttural and hissing at the same time. The hound backed away snarling and the rest slunk to a safe distance.

Keleios said, "Quickly, let us push out over the water."

Lothor asked, "But where will we go in such a small boat?"

"The fisherfolk travel from island to island in boats such as this, Loltun. Hurry."

The sea lay calm and empty. Soft waves lapped at the shore. Keleios put hands on the boat. "Push."

Poth and the green imp leapt abroad. Tobin and Eroar, in human form again, leaned into the boat. Gabel stood and did not help. Keleios spoke through gritted teeth. "The hounds will lead others to us. Hurry."

She glanced at the idle enchanter and said, "Gabel, if you don't help, you swim."

He joined the rest in putting their shoulders and arms into pulling and pushing the grounded boat into the water. The yellow hound sent a howl floating into the light, and far off was an answering horn.

"Push, push for all you're worth." The boat gave

all at once, shooting into the water, sending them floundering. Lothor fell, and the dark water swallowed him. The others climbed up the side. Keleios cursed softly as she drew the oars in the locks. "Can the black healer swim?"

"I don't think so," Tobin answered.

"Urle's forge, why didn't he ride, then?" Just before she could dive in after him, a gauntlet-covered hand grasped the boat's side followed by the Loltun prince's face. Tobin helped him up, and Keleios had to caution, "Have a care or you'll dump us all in the drink."

Lothor lay in the bottom of the boat, gasping like a landed fish.

Keleios began to row. She had Tobin grab the other set of oars and they began to move out to sea. The horn sounded again.

Gabel seemed near tears. "Why don't they simply teleport in?"

"The hounds' minds can't give a clear enough picture, and not even a demon can teleport without some idea of where and what."

Keleios whispered a prayer under her breath. "Ellil, goddess of the eternal sea, daughter of lies and humanity, you know me. I have fished and swam and trusted my body to you many times. Great Ellil, give us a wind to sail to safety." Her shoulders and arms strained at the oars. "Row, row like you've never rowed before."

Lothor sat up carefully. "I will row."

"No." It came out sharp, and his face clouded with anger. "Tobin knows how to use oars; you do not. There is no time."

If the wind did not help, neither did it harm them. Ellil was as capable of destroying their sail as filling it. She was the sea and not altogether trustworthy.

They rowed. Tobin did not turn to look back; but Keleios saw.

On the shore a group of beings could be seen, scales sparkling like jewels in the sunlight. Green, red, blue, and white the demons shone in the light. One raised a brass horn to its lips and blew a single note. The sound was clear, beautiful, and fearful.

A seeking wind blew, smelling of death and rot. The plague storm rose from the island and began to creep toward them. They rowed but could not outdistance it. The sword half-rose from its sheath. "Master, Alharzor can teleport; he is still fresh."

"No," Keleios said, "I'm too tired."

"But Alharzor is not tired."

She shook her head.

"I can teleport, Keleios," Eroar said.

She glanced at the dragon. "How many?"

"I am also tired. Three, plus myself."

Keleios sighed. "I've done one teleport today. I can't do another, but with Alharzor's power I can carry myself, Poth, and the demon."

Gabel asked, "But where to? What's within range?"

"Shut up, Gabel. Let me give Eroar the picture."

To teleport without ending part of a freshly moved chair you had know your coordinates. Keleios knew of only one thing that would be exactly the same. She envisioned piece by piece the drop of the unicorn's head as it bent to eat from low-growing dragon's blood, the stallion standing on a grey rock watching for intruders, a short bush with a rabbit hiding underneath it. She had used it as a practice point before. She asked Eroar, "Do you have it?"

"Yes."

She let the boat drift and drew demon magic inside once again, but she was achingly tired. Keleios felt as though she were swimming against a strong current, but this water was fire and burned down her skin. Alharzor was there, angry, powerful, and not tired in the least. Eroar left with the three men. Groghe leapt upon her back, and she held Poth in her arms. The cat spat at the imp, and he hissed at her.

Alharzor fought her, trying to control, to take them where he wanted to go. The death cloud crept closer, the air reeking with its smell. Keleios struggled against the demon and breathed through her mouth, fighting nausea. Poth gave a squall. Keleios said, "If you keep fighting me, we will both die."

"I am already dead," Alharzor hissed. "You killed me."

Keleios couldn't argue with him, but she had to stop him. Alharzor was a red demon; that meant fire. She thought of cold—ice to put out the fire, cold to drive back his anger. Alharzor retreated before the wave of winter magic, screaming. She held him in a prison of frost. The sword's metal froze in her hand, but the core of fire that was Alharzor pulsed through it. She had him. Keleios reached outward with his power. The cloud hovered over the boat, and Keleios glanced up once. Concentration slipped. Bits of something once alive floated in the cloud; the cloud flowed over the boat.

15

The Guardian's Isle

Keleios appeared beside the others. She half-collapsed on a bed that was shoved too close to the wall. One hand touched the wall and the rich heaviness of the unicorn tapestry. The bulk of their coming had scooted the bed crookedly. A small girl sat huddled in the bed, staring at them with wide green eyes. Groghe tumbled off of Keleios' shoulders and somersaulted past the child. The girl let out a small scream. Poth leapt free onto the braided rug that covered the floor. The nurse-maid, Magda, was defending her charge with a broom. The woman had backed the men into a corner away from the bed.

Lothor called to Keleios, "Tell this woman we are friends before I waste magic on her."

Keleios began to retch, trying to gasp in clean air. Speech was beyond her. Groghe, imp that he was, knew how to bedevil the nursemaid. He crept behind her and lifted her skirts. She screamed and swatted at him with the broom. He was too fast, and she hit empty air. The imp soon had her spinning like a top, swatting with the broom as if he were some giant green mouse.

Keleios fought the nausea, breathing in the clean, cool air. She pulled off the mailed hood, still gasping. She managed a whispery, "Magda."

But the woman was in near hysterics from the little demon's antics.

Keleios called sharply, "Groghe, leave her."

The imp gave a last swipe to the full skirts and then scuttled out of reach and sat down. He grinned at her, showing long pointed teeth.

The woman, gasping and near tears, stared at Keleios. "Are you real, or some demon-got illusion?"

"I am real, Magda."

The woman came forward hesitantly. She spoke to the wide-eyed child. "You remember your Auntie Keleios, Llewellyn."

The girl stared at the blood-coated mailed figure in front of her. The white pinched face, the matted brown hair, and the eyes—the eyes were frightening. But she had been raised properly and managed a faint, "Hello, Auntie Keleios."

"Auntie?" Lothor said from across the room.

Keleios frowned at him. "Greetings, niece Llewellyn." And knowing something of children, Keleios added, "I'm the one who brought you the metal top that spins and sings."

The child's face brightened. "It still sings for me. That was a good enchantment."

Keleios smiled. "Thank you." The door burst inward and two guards came in dressed in the white and silver of the Guardian's livery. Short swords came from sheaths at the sight of the motley group. Magda said, "Put those away. Can't you see the Lady Keleios has come home with some friends?"

The two guards looked doubtful, but Magda shooed them out of the room. "Go wake the Guardian."

At this they looked even more uncertain. One said, "It is very early for the Guardian to be up."

"No matter, her sister is here. Now do as you are bid."

They left, and the nurse shut the door behind them. Magda looked Keleios up and down and clucked her tongue. "What a mess. I'm sure there is a fine story to go with this sudden appearance, but for now, I will see to rooms for all of you, and food and clean clothes." Before Keleios could speak, Magda continued, "I will see that some men's, or rather boy's, clothing is included with yours."

"Thank you, Magda."

The woman bundled up the child into a blanket.

"Come, pet, we'll leave the room to your aunt until other arrangements can be made."

Llewellyn waved a shy good-bye over Magda's shoulder, and they were left alone in the room.

Morning sun streamed in a warm oblong across the bed. The deep rose-pink, almost red, coverings seemed tinged with gold. Slices of golden warmth invaded through the narrow windows that ran along the eastern wall.

"Where are we?" Tobin asked.

"The Guardian's Isle."

Eroar stepped forward. "You nearly had us materialize inside that bed."

"I didn't know the bed would be so close to the tapestry."

The dragon man's eyes narrowed. "You didn't know?"

"It has been over a year since I visited. Then there was plenty of room."

"You had us teleport to a point that you hadn't seen in a year, a point as mobile as a tapestry? It could have been anywhere."

"But it wasn't just anywhere; it was right here." She didn't feel like fighting with the mage today.

Gabel said, "I said that her luck was good."

Keleios settled tiredly on the bed, ignoring what the blood was doing to the bedding. Poth had curled into a rocking chair that stood at the far left corner of the room. The cat pawed the plump cushion, sheathing and unsheathing claws in the rich fabric, and, when satisfied, lay down. She curled into a black and white ball, head hidden under bushy tail. Groghe had discovered a rocking horse. The green-clawed hands gripped the baby handles at the wooden head, and his wide-scaled feet didn't quite touch the floor. He bounced his rump up and down on the wooden horse, giving a hissing laugh.

The unicorn tapestry had always hung in the nursery. A herd of unicorn ran from an organized hunt. Hounds yapped at their heels and farther back the hunters rode. The unicorns were the large white beauties of Calthu, the flowers and plants painstakingly exact. The trees were truly the Calthuian forest. Keleios wondered, as she always had, why with all the attention to detail, they had spoiled it by having the unicorns running in a herd like horses.

Gabel rested in a cushioned chair near the windows. The sunlight made his scar almost the same gold as the rest of his face. His eyes were closed, and an odd smile touched his lips.

Keleios half-wished she had left him on the island. In the boat the demons already knew. There was nothing for him to blackmail them with. She shook her head. Even Gabel didn't deserve to die at the hands of demons. Did he?

She found Gabel watching her. They stared at each other, testing wills. He turned away with a half-laugh.

Keleios watched Lothor watching them both.

There were sounds at the door. Guards entered first. They stood on either side of the door, naked swords held close to their chests.

The one on the left was tall and well muscled, but surprisingly lean. His hair was black and still fell in a tangle over grey-blue eyes. He said uncertainly, "Princess Keleios." His eyes had gone to the demon on the hobby horse shouting, "Yippee."

"It is I, Trask, returned home albeit unexpectedly and with strange companions. It is a long story." Keleios remembered him as one of the bullies who had tormented Belor when they were young.

He opened his mouth to say more, but a figure came up behind them. The figure was dressed in a woman's green cloak that fell long, giving only brief glimpses of a pale skirt as she walked. The hood was full and drawstrung so it effectively hid her face. She brushed past the guards and told them, "Put up your weapons." They did as ordered.

Gold thread sparkled along the cloak as she stepped into the sunlight. The cloaked woman stood before Keleios. They faced each other silently for a moment and then embraced. The cloak hood was pushed back to reveal a thick mane of brown hair, a fine-boned triangular face with eyes that tilted slightly at the corners and were the same gold-green as her cloak.

Except for eye color she was a mirror of Keleios. Keleios stared at her twin sister, wondering what kind of greeting she would receive.

The voice was formal. "Welcome home, sister."

Keleios answered in kind. "It is good to be home, sister."

"And who are your companions?"

She motioned Tobin forward. "Methia Twice-royal, my sister, I present Prince Tobin of Meltaan, heir to the province of Ferrian, journeyman sorcerer and visionary."

The woman extended fingertips in an Astranthian gesture of welcome. Tobin returned the touch lightly and bowed.

Methia hesitated before Lothor's black armor and pale face, one eyebrow lifting. "Sister, may I present Prince Lothor Gorewielder, sometimes heir of all Lolth, enchanter, sorcerer, and my promised consort."

The woman said quietly, "Are you, like the rest of the Loltun princes, a black healer as well?"

Lothor bowed at the neck. "I am, sister of my promised."

She seemed to wince at the last and asked, "Gore's wielder, who is Gore?"

Lothor's hand caressed the ax at his side with a cold smile.

She said simply, "I see."

Gabel was next, but Keleios said only, "He blackmailed me into rescuing him. He is the Gabel who murdered my smithy master Edan."

The harsh look that came to Methia's eyes was very like Keleios'. "Murderers are not welcome on the Guardian's Isle."

"I have been punished by the Meltaanian courts."

Keleios stepped up to him. "You still live. Edan is dead, and you still live. That has always bothered me."

He said, "And it has always bothered me that I did not have the pleasure of killing you, half-breed."

Methia motioned the guards forward. They stood to either side of Gabel.

He smiled crookedly. "I have been tried and sentenced. You cannot do it a second time; that is the law."

Methia said, "I am the law here."

He did not flinch. "But you, too, follow Cia. You will not kill me in cold blood. I have been punished, and it is not in you to harm me further."

Methia said nothing. She turned to the guards. "Take him away and guard him. I don't want him left alone at any time."

The guards bowed and led him out. Gabel had learned something of diplomacy, for he didn't protest. He stopped just short of the door. "I hope to see you later, Keleios."

"I'm sure something could be arranged."

Methia said, "No, absolutely no dueling on my island. I forbid it, Keleios."

Keleios shrugged. "You are the Guardian."

Gabel said, "Another time, perhaps."

Keleios nodded.

The guards led Gabel away.

Methia nodded at Eroar. "There is no need for introductions between us, Eroar."

"No, Methia, no introductions." They clasped hands, and Methia walked to Poth. The cat yawned, baring fangs, then stretched under the woman's expert hands. "And Gilstorpoth, I see you survived."

Methia turned to the green demon, now simply sitting on the rocking horse. "And what is this?"

Keleios motioned. The little demon jumped to the ground and scrambled apelike to squat beside her. "This is Groghe, a very lesser demon, whom I ensorcelled. He aided our escape from the Grey Isle."

Methia paled. "The Grey Isle. I heard only that you were exiled. Nesbit sent you there?"

Keleios nodded, watching her sister's face carefully. Methia chose to ignore Nesbit's treachery for something more immediate.

Methia stood very straight. "I would prefer that a demon not be in this castle."

"Understood." Keleios knelt beside the demon. "Groghe, I'm going to take the necklace back and free you." His eyes went wide with fear, and he backed away, claws clutching the gold necklace to his bony chest. "Oh, no, Master, don't free me."

"You are a demon, at least an imp. Your kind aren't supposed to like serving."

"I do not, but if you free me, I will be forced back to the bad place."

"The Grey Isle, you mean?"

He nodded vigorously.

"Why is it a bad place for a demon? Harque is dead; you are free."

"No, Master, unless ensorcelled most of us would be trapped forever." He groveled at her feet, hands encircling her knees. "Don't let me go back there, Master. I don't want to be entertainment anymore."

Keleios placed her hands on his shoulder and concentrated. "There is a geas on him, light but strong. He will be forced to return there." She pried the little demon from her. "Groghe, I will not free you for now."

"Oh, thank you, thank you, Master." He tried licking her hands, which was a sign of great abasement among demonkind.

"That isn't necessary, Groghe."

He looked like an eager puppy.

Methia said, "Well, have him stay out of sight at least."

"He will."

Methia pulled a cord by the door, and servants came almost instantly. "The servants will show you to your rooms, get you food, fresh clothes, and baths."

Methia spoke to one blond serving girl, who scurried away. Methia made it clear that she wished to be alone with Keleios, and the others were ushered out.

The door closed, and they were alone. They stood looking at each other in silence. Methia broke it. "You look awful."

Keleios looked down at the blood-stained armor. She ran a hand through her tangled hair and laughed. "Still the same Methia. Walking the corridors cloaked rather than let someone see you unprepared."

Methia smiled, but it did not quite reach her eyes. "I am the same, but you are not."

"Oh, I don't know. Isn't this usually how I came home: armored, sword in hand, bloody?"

"No."

"No." Keleios started to sit upon the bed but saw her sister wince and stood. "I am also in need of a bath and clean clothes."

"I wish to talk to you."

"I know, but we can talk later."

"Very well, I will join you in your room when you are clean and dressed. I will have food brought up to us."

Keleios nodded agreement and Methia left. She did not want to talk with Methia, not about Lothor, or demons, or anything. But when one comes home, there are always questions to answer.

She walked out the door, leaving Poth to sleep and Groghe to play with one of Llewellyn's dolls. His face was crumpled in a frown, concentrating, as he tried to undo the tiny buttons.

The bathing pools ran in precise marbled lines. It was an extravagance of magic to keep them warm and pure, but the enchantment had been set in place when the castle had first been formed. It showed no signs of giving out. Tobin was already wet, hair streaming in almost blood-red lines across his shoulders. Two serving girls helped him, and there was much giggling from all three.

Lothor sat in the hottest bath, steam rising around

him. His hair had been combed and was completely unbound. It swept in a white curtain longer than Tobin's, as long as a woman's. The tips of it floated on the water. He scowled at her and said, "I thought this was the men's bath."

Keleios answered, "We hold to Astranthian customs here, as well as Meltaan. Bath houses cater to both, and there is not room or magic to separate them."

He hunched in the water, pulling away from the two serving women. He tried to hide himself with a towel. She had to laugh at his discomfort. Two more serving woman came to help her with her armor. "Besides, Lothor, the servants are women; they see you."

"But they are servants."

Keleios understood what servants meant to royalty. They were invisible until they did something wrong. "If it will make you more comfortable, I will go farther away."

He said nothing but glared at her from one silver eye lost in a mist of platinum hair. The servants followed her, and she slid into slightly colder water than she wanted. Keleios had no wish to antagonize him further. If they were to be joined, they would at least need some semblance of friendship.

The water's heat seeped through her tired body, soaking bruises and minor cuts too small for healing. A blond servant girl began to comb the tangles from Keleios' long hair.

Keleios turned her head to look at Tobin. He was busy trying to pull a laughing girl into the water with him. Keleios asked, "Tobin, where is Master Eroar?"

The boy stopped teasing the girls long enough to answer. "He said he wanted to cleanse his real form and went off to the dragon pools outside."

Keleios settled back and let another's hands soothe away the tangles and aching. The giggling and splashing began once more at Tobin's pool.

Strong firm hands lathered her hair, and she allowed it, closing her eyes and sinking back against the side.

Warm water cascaded from a pitcher to cleanse the soap from her hair.

Strong fingers began to knead the muscles at her shoulders. Only one pair of hands was soaping her arm, one pair of hands.

She sat up, pulling away from the hands, hair streaming into the water. Lothor knelt beside the pool. There was soap in one hand, and the sleeves of his clean tunic were pushed back, baring muscled forearms. The two servants knelt a short distance away, watching all with nervous eyes.

She resisted the urge to cover herself and faced him squarely, glaring.

Keleios had never seen him dressed in anything but black—black, the color of royalty in Lolth, the color of his god. He was dressed in a silver blue with metallic thread weaving at shoulder and down arms. It softened the alien silver of his eyes, and brought a hint of color to his white skin. "What do you want, Lothor?"

"What is the matter, my beloved? Uncomfortable?"

"There are rules in the baths that must be observed. Rule one is no touching except by the servants. If that rule is not observed, we will be reduced to the days when only men were allowed in the baths."

"Ah, but I am ignorant of such customs. Forgive me."

She glared at him. "Now you know, so get out."

He set the soap in its dish and dipped his hands in the water to cleanse them.

She smashed a fist in the water, splattering him. "Get out."

He stood and the blue-grey of his knees was wet from kneeling. He began to unroll his sleeves and looked down on her, fully dressed and standing while she sat naked in the water. "There is something we must discuss."

"What?"

"I would ask we set a date for our joining."

"Then ask."

He frowned at her, puzzled, and said, "Very well, I ask that we set a date for our joining."

Keleios sighed and stared down into the water. "Must you always ask me questions when I am at a disadvantage?"

He smiled. "But my lovely princess, I enjoy it so."

She glared at him. If wishes could come true simply by thinking them, he would have evaporated on the spot. "You have a right to ask. I will talk to Methia and see how soon the feast arrangements can be made. Now, get away from me."

He fastened his sleeves and said, "I do not mean to rush you."

"Yes, you do, but I made an oath and I will keep it. I have little choice."

He hesitated a moment, then said softly, "You are very beautiful." She searched for that mocking smile, but it did not follow. There was a wistfulness to his face. He turned and walked away without waiting for her reaction.

The bath was spoiled. She shooed the servants back and finished it quickly herself. As she dried, one servant held up a dress for her to change into. Keleios had to smile. Her sister still hadn't given up on her being a proper lady. Magda would have tried to get her boy's clothing, but Methia was the Guardian. When the ruler of the land suggested something, one naturally thought it was a good idea.

She shrugged. It would probably fit, and she needed a dress for the ceremony. "I will wear this for now, but please have some men's riding clothes found for me."

They looked at each other in puzzlement. Both were too young to remember Keleios much. The older said, "As you wish, Lady Keleios."

She did refuse most of the undergarments, only taking enough so that the dress fit properly. At least the shoes had no high heel or pointed toe. They were serviceable cream-white slippers. The dress was made of cream-colored silk. The large leg-o'-mutton sleeves were slit, and cloth of gold showed through. The neck plunged to a rather daring triangle. A half-cloak had been brought and was artfully draped and pinned. The cloth was a soft brown with golden threads running through it. The cloak was pinned to the dress at hip and shoulder. It added nothing to keeping out the cold but was the height of fashion. A net of gold had been sent to hold her hair from her face. It was Methia's compromise. She knew Keleios would never consent to the elaborate hairstyle that was popular. The netting was often worn by young girls too young to put their hair up. She allowed them one thick braid, complete with cream ribbon, like a half-crown across the head.

Keleios allowed them to take the armor to have it cleaned, but Aching Silver she kept with her. There was usually no way to fasten it on over the dress, so she carried it sheathed and locked in place.

The servants directed her back to the nursery. A maid said, "The room is not quite as the Guardian would wish it. If it is all right, you shall stay in the nursery until your room can be made ready."

Keleios said that would be fine. She had wondered what, by Urle's forge, Methia could be putting in her room.

Poth lay in a bar of sunlight, flat on her side. Only the bushy tip of her tail twitched a greeting. Groghe had managed to undress the doll and had all its clothes strewn across the floor. The doll was now wearing a red ball gown.

He greeted her with, "Why does the toy have so many clothes?"

"Because there is money to buy that many. Pick it all up before my sister comes."

He scrambled to obey, wadding the expensive cloth.

"Carefully."

He tried, but a demon's idea of careful left something to desire.

A knock came at the door.

"Who is it?"

Silence and then carefully neutral, "It is Methia."

Keleios set the sword and sheath under the bed and said, "Enter."

Methia entered, bearing a silver tray laden with cheese, fruit, and cold meat. A bottle of wine was also included. "It is not Astranthian wine, but it is a good local vintage." She set the tray on a small table and drew up two straight-backed chairs. Smiling brightly, she said, "And lady Gilstorpoth, your breakfast awaits you in the kitchen." She held the door for the cat.

Poth paused uncertain and meowed up at Keleios. "Go on, Poth, down the stairs, through the big dining room, and turn left." The cat rubbed against her legs and minced to the door. She stared at Methia for several moments from her yellow eyes, then went out. The door closed.

"I don't think she likes me."

"She doesn't like being gotten rid of. Most people don't think to ask a cat to leave."

"But I am not most people."

"No." Keleios sat and had trouble smoothing the full skirt down behind. She motioned for her sister to sit also.

Methia filled two glasses with wine. "Tell me of this consort-to-be." Methia's eyes stared at the far wall, and she choked on the wine. "If the cat leaves, that thing leaves as well."

Keleios turned to see Groghe putting the last of the doll clothes away. "Go into the gardens; stay out of sight and out of mischief." He nodded enthusiastically and vanished. Keleios spared a thought for what he might not consider mischief but settled down to face the inquisition.

Methia repeated her question. "About your consort-to-be?"

Keleios bit into a piece of tart cheese, weighing her words. "He is royal, he is half-elven, he is enchanter, and a healer of sorts. I thought it was an obligation that I would take care of."

"Now, with the keep destroyed, you exiled from

Astrantha, and so many dead or missing from the keep.'' She sipped the wine and picked up a slice of apple. ''It seems an odd time for a joining. What if you get with child right away? You can't tell me you don't plan to search for your missing friends. It wouldn't be like you not to be heroic.''

Keleios shrugged, concentrating on the food. Methia had worn blue today, the color of cornflowers, light but rich. The dress's only decoration was a throw of rich blue-green, pinned with gold at shoulder and waist. It made her eyes look blue-green like shallow seawater over rocks.

''Do not lie to me, Keleios. We are all the family we have left.''

Keleios ignored the bid for guilt. That was what motivated Methia, not herself. ''All right, I gave an oath to take him as consort.''

''The last time we talked, you said, 'I wouldn't lie with him if he could get me out of the seven hells.' You were very sure.''

Keleios sighed and told Methia of the keep's fall, a fire-threatened corridor, and an oath taken.

''An oath taken under duress is not valid.''

Keleios sipped wine and tried the meat. It was good; the food was always good here. ''It was taken, and it is valid.''

The green eyes sparkled, turning a darker green, like good emeralds. ''How can you honor an oath forced from you?''

''Because of the nature of the oath.''

''I don't see . . .''

Keleios extended her right hand, exposing the palm's new scar.

''A blood oath, but even they can be broken, safely.''

''Not this one.''

''But . . .''

''Let me finish, Methia. We swore by the hounds of Verm and the birds of Loth.''

Her face paled, her eyes glittering dangerously. "That is almost unbreakable."

"It is unbreakable except at the death of one of the oath makers." She knew her sister and cautioned, "I don't want anything to happen to Lothor while he is here, sister."

"I would never do such a thing."

"No, but these people are loyal to you, and if you happened to mention your dislike, you could get somebody killed trying."

"Is he that hard to kill?"

"Perhaps, but he will be my consort, not I his. We need never cross the Loltun boder. And I raise whatever child, male or female, as I see fit."

"How did you get him to agree to that?"

"I wouldn't swear otherwise, for Tobin's life or anything else."

"There has got to be a way to break it."

"There isn't. Methia, I know the realities of this oath as well he does. I did not go in blind."

Methia stood and walked to the windows. "And I suppose your knowledge of demonlore is my fault."

"I have never blamed you for not going after Harque. We were seventeen; neither of us should have done it. You showed good sense. I almost cost Belor his life because he was loyal and went with me. Your being there would not have saved us."

Without turning around, Methia said, "I am sorry I did not go. I don't think I could go, even now, but I am sorry."

"There is nothing to be sorry for. We all have our fears, but if you need forgiveness, forgive yourself. I forgave you long ago. Come sit and don't take slight references to heart."

Methia sat with a nervous smoothing of cloth, her hands running along the rich brocade and touching the gold pins, much as Keleios touched her weapons for reassurance.

"What are you smiling at?"

"Oh, differences and likenesses."

"You can't join with him; he is a black healer."

"You joined with Councilman Nesbit. He follows the same gods that a black healer worships. And he left me chained with runes of binding on the Grey Isle, meat for anything that came along."

"No, he wouldn't do that."

"He did do that. How long has it been since he's seen Llewellyn, his own daughter?"

Methia turned away.

"It's been over two years, Methia. He isn't coming back, all because of her eyes changing from blue to elfish green, because he thinks she looks like a half-breed and no daughter of his could ever be that."

"But he's not a black healer. He can't bring pain and death with his touch. I remember that it was black healing that killed our mother, black healing that rotted her away before our eyes. What would Mother say about your joining?"

"Mother has been dead a long time. I doubt she will say anything."

"That was cruel."

"So is keeping her memory new in your heart. You've mourned long enough. Let it go."

"Who are you to tell me how long to mourn? I remember it all. I am no prophet, but it hangs on like a prophetic dream, vivid and horrible."

Keleios stood away from her sister, feeling tired and angry. "I remember, Methia, but I don't torment myself. You think I desecrate her memory by joining with a black healer?"

"Yes, don't you?"

"All right, Methia, you want to fight. Let us fight. You don't think I mourned her long enough, that my sorrow is somehow not as great as yours, because I don't still wail about it."

"Yes, may Cia forgive me, yes."

"My mourning was vengeance. I sought it and failed when I was seventeen. I asked you to come with me, but you refused. You said killing Harque would not bring Mother back. Well, neither will mourning forever.''

"Should I give up my sorrow because it is useless?''

"No, because it is a waste of energy and strength.''

Methia rose. "I see we will accomplish nothing here today.'' She turned for the door, but Keleios stopped her. Methia stood trembling but did not try to shake off the restraining hands.

"I watched the light die in Harque's eyes. I watched life flow out of her in a crimson stream. She died by my hand, and it satisfied me. It won't undo what happened, but it was enough. Lay it to rest, Methia. Harque has paid with her life, with her soul. Let it go.''

Her voice, when it came, was tight and formal. "You will join with him anyway.''

"Yes.''

"When?''

"As soon as the preparations for feasting can be made.''

Methia laughed, and it sounded bitter. "No, a feast is already prepared. It is midsummer festival tonight. Yes, we will have a torchlight procession. I will see you mated in fine style, sister. Let it be tonight; darkness will be better for it.'' She shook Keleios' hands off and left.

Keleios sat down to finish her breakfast, finding her appetite not what it had been.

16

A Matter of Magic

The armory was close dusk broken only by the glitter
of metal as torchlight struck shimmers from the weapons. Old Barrock held the torch in his wizened hand.
His long white hair was a soft crown around his bald
pate. His blue eyes were still the same clear blue, like
deep water where the fish run strong.

Keleios said, "The weapons are in good condi-
tion."

He swelled a little at the compliment. "I try, even
though no one comes back for them. I make sure they
could have them if they wanted."

Stacked and hung along the walls were all the weapons of all the fugitives who had been given refuge over
the centuries. If one intended to stay on the island,
there was no need for anything more than knives.
Magic glimmered here, alive and waiting. Keleios
stepped into the softly charged gloom with Aching Silver in hand. Her long skirts caught on a pole arm, and
she pulled back on the dress, trying not to tear it. She
succeeded and used one hand to hold the full dress
closer to her body. Barrock found an empty hanging
place between a battle-ax and a huge two-handed
sword. Keleios hung the sword in place carefully, caressing the fine workmanship. "It's a pity that the thing
is demon touched."

"Ah, 'tis a pretty piece of work. Some of the best
I've ever seen, and I've seen a lot."

They turned to go. Something fell clanging in the
darkness. The long sword lay on the floor. Keleios
hung it once more, checking that it was secure.

Through the sheath she could feel it pulse, the life beating in the metal. The lives of all that it had consumed coursed through its silver form. She tugged, and it remained. Halfway to the door it fell again.

She stopped Barrock from going back for it and said, "Let it lie there if it wants to play childish games." They mounted the stairs. Keleios nearly tripped over the sword as it appeared on the step in front of her. She walked over it, sending Barrock ahead. It reappeared two steps in front of her. Keleios squatted beside it, tugging skirts back and under. "Why won't you stay in the armory?"

Its voice came muffled and indistinct. She clasped it carefully and unlocked the blade. The sword rose half a blade length from its sheath. "I have waited for someone like you for too long to give you up."

"How like me?"

"I am elven work that needs an elven hand. I am demon powered that needs a demon hand. I am evil and need a tainted hand. My maker sought to control me by putting restraints upon who could wield me. He was an elf who had been through the pit and survived; it taints the blood." The sword rose farther until Keleios caught its hilt to keep it from falling. It pulsed and beat up her arm, singing a song of sadness and past ages. "You are half-elf who has been through the pit and survived. Do you know how rare that is? I will not give you up."

Keleios resheathed the sword and snapped the locks in place.

Barrock said, "My lady, what will you do?"

"I will find another way."

In the afternoon Keleios rode toward the sea. The white mare ran swift and sure footed along the cliff road. Someone, probably Methia, had given her the name of Snowball. Keleios chose to call her Cloudrunner. Keleios left the road when she was near Gull Cove. It was the best place to find seashells, small but fine.

She found the steep and narrow path leading down

and urged the horse to take it. The riding clothes were not exactly what Keleios had wanted. The entire outfit was blue velvet, too big, and hopelessly elaborate, but if someone didn't mind a good suit being ruined, she would wear it. Her own boots, now clean, had been kept.

The sand that stretched out before them was white and caught the light in a thousand starlike crystals. Pulverized Mirlite had gone to make most of the sand, and each grain was a tiny prism.

She let the horse walk along the beach as it pleased, reins dangling in the sand.

She had felt the call ever since she began trying to think of a joining gift for Lothor. It was customary to give something of oneself, one's own magic. Being an enchanter, there was not enough time, but being an elven enchanter, there might be.

Keleios walked just above the waterline. The waves came in dark emerald green, capped with white foam. Seaweed rode the waves in brown strands. The waves crashed upon the sand, and the tide crawled up over the ground and retreated as if pulled back. A clump of seaweed the size of a large man had been pushed up on shore. Keleios walked through the wet collapsing sand and knelt beside the seaweed. The weed was brown and heavy. There nestled in its wet fishy tendrils was the shell. It was small no bigger than the end of her middle finger. It curled to a perfect spiral and was ivory white with shades of gold sketched down its swirling length. The lip that led inside of its whispering depths was a pale pink, flushed and beautiful.

It spoke to her like raw metal could. It said that here was something of the sea's power. Here was a piece of magic given, not made. With a tiny bit of added power, it would be what she wanted it to be.

Water swirled over her boots and wet the bottom of her trousers. She stood and carefully put the shell in a small pouch she had brought for the occasion. Cloudrunner came when she called, snorting and nibbling at the salty taste of her hands. She led the horse back up to the cliff top, thinking as she went. The shell would be a charm to enable Lothor to breath underwater, for a time. Instant enchantment was not easy even for a half-elf, and given so little time, it would not be permanent. She smiled at the thought of the black healer gasping on the bottom of the boat. An adult who couldn't swim—it was unthinkable. The smile vanished. This was a joining gift, and tonight they would bed together. She shivered, half in fear and half in something she could not put a name to. Suddenly, the wind felt cold on top of the cliff.

She dropped the reins and let the mare graze. Keleios walked to the edge of the cliff. She unbuckled the sword belt, unlooped the belt from the sheath, and held it for a moment listening to the distant mutterings of the sword. It pulsed and promised power and success in battle and magic. Keleios ignored it. She drew her sorcery out and began to build it in her mind. She would put a shield between the sword and herself. A shield to surround it, a prison to keep it from her. "I cast you out; I cast you down. Let the waves have you. Let them lock you away from me." She drew all her strength and threw the sheathed sword out over the water. A thin wail sounded in her head. It spun end over end, glittering in the sun, and vanished beneath the waves.

When she returned, she was finally allowed in the room Methia had prepared for her. The bed was draped and canopied with veils and silk. The goosedown tick was so soft as to suck and hold her body when she lay on it. The coverings were done in cloth of gold and heaviest black. It was the color of mourning.

Why was it that Methia could always anger her, always? Then Keleios shrugged and laughed. Perhaps the black would make Lothor feel more at home.

Costly tapestries and hangings cloaked the walls. The scenes were all of battle, death, failed love: the failed love of Gynndon and Pestral, their gruesome suicides done in livid color; the battle of Ty-gor hill with its mounds of dead and dying. One man in particular seemed to reach out of the scene, begging for help, one hand held outward, beseeching, eyes full of horror and the coming dark. The far wall was hung with a hunt scene. The great stag fallen to its knees, blood frothing on its lips. The hounds roared down to tear at it.

Methia had the slyness of the court. She had done everything properly but in a backhanded way.

As dusk fell, Keleios stood looking out of the many narrow windows. The cream-colored dress was back on, and she had even consented to most of the under-garments, except for the stays. The things were so tight she might have passed out during the ceremony. She had left the dress plain without its half-cloak. A gold lace veil lay on the bed. Her hair had been brushed until it shone, wavy and thick, the candlelight catching hints of dark gold in it. Two thin braids, one on each side of her face, were intertwined with gold thread. It was the way a Wrythian elf would wear her hair for a wedding. No one but she would know, but then she was the one joining. Every comfort was needed.

She turned from the windows with a swish of silken skirts. Poth hissed and struck at the skirts. Keleios stooped, nearly knocking over a small table with the full dress. The cat hissed and backed away, fur stiff. "Poth, it's all right; it's still me." She sat awkwardly on the floor and coaxed the cat to her. Poth came, sniffing her hand before allowing herself to be petted.

She had tried to talk herself into acceptance. He was young, handsome, half-elven. She could have looked farther and found worse, but he was evil. Keleios was beginning to realize that she herself wasn't wholly good. The sword Ache silvestri had been evil and pre-ferred her to Lothor. Or perhaps the sword didn't feel like fighting with Lothor's ax. Yet Lothor had trapped her into this joining. He had trapped her like an ani-mal. Well, there was one more bite left in this trapped beast.

She cuddled Poth to her face. "No, I can't fight him. I break oath if I fight. But I can't just let him take me." The cat purred softly, trying to comfort, but there was little comfort to be had.

She tried to stand, got tangled in the dress, and was forced to put the cat down and crawl upwards using the bed. There on the bed was Aching Silver, painful death. It lay on the neatly made bed; nothing disturbed, but the sword was there.

There was a whoosh and crackling of flames outside. Torch poles had been put all along the road to light the procession. They flamed now, casting gold-red shadows into the night.

The sword was cold to the touch. She unsnapped the locks slowly and drew the sword. It glittered and turned pale gold in the rich candlelight. It pulsed softly and spoke. "I am yours . . . forever."

"You are cursed, a cursed sword."

The thing laughed, a strange sound without lungs to hold it. If possible, the laugh reverberated round the metal, giving a hollow sound to it. "Cursed, well, it depends on how you look at it." It went into another peal of laughter.

She shoved the blade into the sheath and locked it, its laughter still coming muffled and tinny. She tossed the sheath back on the bed.

Groghe appeared with a night-blooming flower in his claw. The thing was white and as big as Keleios' outstretched hand. The scent was heady and exotic. Methia had been using earth magic to get tropicals to grow in the winter-ruined climate. It was something their mother would never do, saying the plants weren't as happy.

"A present for you, Master, a present."

She stooped and took the flower. "Thank you, Groghe, it is beautiful."

A knock sounded on the door with a, "It is time to dress, Lady Keleios."

"Enter."

Two serving girls entered, squealing when they saw the small demon. Keleios waved them inside, suddenly tired.

The short brown-haired one began to brush at the wrinkles in the skirt, tsking. Keleios could hear the rustle of the golden veil. It was lifted over her head, and they began to bind it in place with hairpins. It fell in a point past her knees, but was mid-thigh in front. They tugged and fluffed and finally said, "Princess Keleios, you look lovely."

Keleios approached the oval mirror hesitantly. She did not recognize the creature who stared back. This person was impossibly dainty, all gold lace and silk. The brown eyes gleamed in the candle flames. She turned slowly, trying to see the back of the dress. The serving girls brought up a second mirror and positioned it. This wasn't her. Someone else had come and stolen her away and left this—this woman—in her place. Keleios had one consolation: there was a knife in a thigh hilt under all the finery. Not that she could get to it in time, but it was comforting.

She flexed the muscle, feeling the familiar restraint of the sheath. She was not gone or swept away; Keleios Incantare, called Nightseer, was still under there somewhere.

Her only comment aloud was, "It will do."

The maids exchanged glances, but it was not their place to criticize.

Groghe came closer and put out a tentative claw. "Shining," he said, "shining."

She smiled down at the imp. "It is that."

Keleios lifted the moonflower from the table. "Please have this put in water." The brown-haired serving girl bowed and took it.

Methia stepped in the door wearing the same blue dress she had worn earlier. "It is time."

"Groghe, you stay in the room while I'm gone."

He nodded and leapt upon the rocking horse. "I will do as you say, Master." Keleios followed Methia out with the serving girls crowding behind, not wishing to be left alone with the demon.

Keleios said, "It was very generous of you to move

the rocking horse in my room. Groghe is pleased with it.''

Methia sniffed. ''The demon would not leave it alone. I found Llewellyn and that thing playing together. It can have the rocking horse, as long as it stays away from my child.''

Keleios smiled behind the golden veil.

In front of the castle were four horses. Two were pure white. One was black with a white blaze down its face and one white foot. The last horse was a light golden cream with a white blaze down its face and one white foot. The cream stallion had a side saddle on it as did one of the white horses.

Tobin came down. His tunic was cloth of gold and caught the first torchlight in coppery reflections. His auburn hair looked golden-red tonight. Behind was the black healer. The silver thread in his tunic caught the light. His hair fell long and free past his shoulders, and it shimmered with a light of its own. A plain silver circlet like a prince's crown adorned his head.

Tobin and Methia stood to one side, and Lothor took Keleios' hand. A great cheer went up from the people lining the torchway. He helped her mount the cream stallion, then mounted his own black. Tobin and Methia mounted the white horses, and the procession began.

The people shouted and exclaimed over the beauty of the princesses and the exotic but handsome consort-to-be.

The temple of Urle lay in the east of the village. The procession stopped and dismounted. Lothor helped Keleios down. If he felt her reluctance, he said nothing. They walked with her left hand placed lightly on his right and entered the temple door. The only light was a fire at the far end of the darkened central room.

The rustle of silk and the tramp of booted foot was loud as they approached the priest. He was tall, broad shouldered, with a full brown beard streaked with grey. His eyes were blue, but he was not a native of the island. He wore a priest garment that draped to his feet. It was orange trimmed with brown, the colors of Urle. On the front of it was an embroidered flame and a hammer over it.

"Who has brought them to this joining?"

Methia and Tobin answered in unison, "We have."

"You have done your duty; you may go."

Lothor and Keleios stood, not touching before the priest, and he smiled down at them. "Is this a wanted joining?"

"No."

"Yes."

They glared at each other. The priest said, "You do wish to be joined?"

They both answered yes.

He stepped down and to one side, exposing the roaring pit of flame. "As fire is strengthened by each flame, let you be strengthened one by the other. As two pieces of metal are forged into one and made stronger, let it be so with the two of you. As the hammer pounds its message to the apprentice without need of words, let you both hear what the other truly means.

"It is time to give the gifts of yourself."

Keleios unwound the gold chain from her right wrist and held it out to the priest. The shell dangled small and lovely from it.

Lothor held out a ring of some kind.

The priest grasped them both and prayed, "Let these gifts be a joyous thing. Bless this joining, Urle, our god, as two of your followers join together. Let these gifts be a token of your vows to each other." He held the chain out to Keleios and she took it. Lothor had to bend down for her to slip it over his head.

"It will allow you to breathe under water for a time."

He thanked her and took his own present from the priest. The ring was woven of his platinum hair; for a jewel there was a pale red dot of his blood. She gasped as he slipped it down her finger and stared at him. He had put his life in her hands. With such tokens an herb-witch could steal the life from a man. "My hair and my blood to prove that I will never willingly hurt you.''

''Join hands.'' They did, and he had them kneel. Then he bound their hands together with a strip of leather. If it had been a marriage, it would have been a length of chain. ''Rise; you are joined.''

He unbound their hands. They walked out still hand in hand, for the crowd would expect it.

The crowd gave a mighty cry, and they were pushed apart by the crush of people. Two sedan chairs had come from somewhere, and they were carried on the backs of the crowd toward the feasting. The peasants had always had more freedom here on the isle. There were people in the crowd who had known Keleios when she was a babe. They remembered when she and Belor had gone around ambushing the island bullies for what they did to the budding illusionist one autumn. They yelled bawdy jokes and suggestions for the night to come.

Keleios caught a glimpse of Lothor's outraged face over the crowd. At least he held his tongue and did not insult them for their impudence.

Tables had been set out on the grass outside the castle, and the entire village had come to feast and dance. The crowd carried them to the dance area. It was strung with bright ribbon and marked off by white-painted poles. The ground was well trampled and nearly clean of grass. All day as Keleios and her companions had slept and washed, there had been festival. The crowd was half-drunk and already well fed. There had been much to buy and see today. There had been sacrifices of the best fruits of the field, the best catch of the day. Now the laughing throng set the new-made couple on the dance grounds and yelled for music.

When it came, it was a haunting melody, a series of rising notes that tugged at the mind but not at the feet.

Lothor frowned. He was forced to shout in her ear to be heard. ''I did not know I would have to dance. I do not know how to dance.''

''It does not matter; you would not know this

dance." She took his left hand and led him to the dance floor. She told him, "Think of it as a fight. Follow my moves, echo me." He followed her stiffly, all the grace and speed of a fight somehow mooted with his discomfort. It was a dance of fingertips and half-promised kisses. He smiled with relief when the dance ended. Keleios laughed, a full-throated sound. He looked puzzled until a lady stepped up to him and dragged him into another dance. A man grabbed Keleios' hand, and she, too, joined the dance. This was a night for peasants to dance with princes. Many, as a sacrifice to the All-Mother, had forgiven old debts, old grudges. The Mother would take a harvest of the soul as happily as a harvest of the earth.

Lothor swirled through giggling throngs of peasant-bright skirts. Keleios was grabbed by hands reddened from hauling rope and casting nets. The blacksmith, without an ounce of magic, wrapped her in a grip like the iron he worked with, still smelling faintly of the forge's burning stench. Keleios saw it all through a glory of golden spots. The veil whirled about her face, strangely hot and close. Finally, they sat down for the feasting. The tables groaned under the torchlight. There just might be enough people to eat all the food, but Keleios doubted it.

Lothor was seated at her side. A thin sheen of sweat made his skin glisten. Like some very pale human folk, he had become red with exertion. His pale skin flushed pink, and his eyes glittered from underneath near-invisible white brows. He caught her looking at him and stared at her. Keleios did not look away. He smiled, half-leering, and said, "Let us retire for the night, my princess."

She stared at him a moment longer, then nodded. A knot of tension started in her belly and climbed upward, threatening to choke her. He offered her his arm, but she refused it. They walked close together without touching, and when the crowd realized their destination, a great cheer went up.

When Keleios stumbled on the long skirt, he steadied her and she did not pull away. Good-natured cheering and rowdy jokes followed them to the horses.

She allowed him to help her mount the side saddle. She punched at the mound of skirt angrily. He raised an eyebrow and grinned at her. "Jitters, my beloved?"

Keleios chose not to answer but pushed her horse forward without waiting for him to mount.

He galloped up to her, laughing.

"You're drunk," she said.

He laughed some more. "Why, my beloved, I believe you are nervous."

"It is traditional before going to the bridal bed."

His face sobered, and he grabbed the reins of her horse. "Keleios, have you ever been with a man before?"

She jerked free of him and galloped for the castle. She heard him mutter, "Loth's blood, a virgin."

He did not chase her. She raced through the raised gates and threw the reins to a waiting squire. Somewhere in the race the golden veil had been lost. Keleios picked up the voluminous skirts, ran for her room, then stopped. He would be there eventually. She had sworn to bed him. There was really no turning back. Yet a part of her was still struggling with the idea. Until the joining ceremony, there was always hope of escape, but now, now there was nothing to do but submit.

"I won't, I won't. I'll see him dead first, no matter what the cost."

Someone stepped from the shadows. It was Magda. She spread wide her arms and said, "My Keleios, my little warrior girl." Keleios went to her and allowed the arms to hold her to Magda's plump bosom. She soothed the girl's hair. "All these years of playing with boys and housing with the warriors and you have never been with a man?"

Keleios pulled away from her and straightened. "No."

"All the talk about you being wild when you were

young, all the talk, but I knew it for envy, envy of power, position, and beauty.''

She whispered, ''Magda, what am I to do?''

''You will do what women through the ages have done. You will go through with it.''

''But how? I am so angry. He trapped me, and I can't get free this time. No sword or spell will help me now.''

''Poor Keleios, you have never had to learn the womanly art of patience.''

''I have learned some patience.''

''But you are like a man accustomed to action and controlling your own fate. Joining with any man would have been hard, but now . . . You must do your best.''

''But what is my best?''

The woman put an arm around her shoulders. ''I will give you some advice, my dear, advice from a woman who has borne five children and raised a few more.''

Keleios smiled at that. They walked down the halls with Magda's quiet voice whispering against the stone walls.

Magda had gone and taken the servants with her. Keleios waited alone in the room. The imp was gone as she ordered him to be. She hoped he did indeed stay out of trouble this night. A white dressing gown stirred along the floor as she paced. It left her arms bare but hid everything else. Keleios had decided to take Calthuian custom to heart. It was Magda's advice, for she was Calthuian. It would be a searching for body under the voluptuous cloth. She need not stand naked before him unless she wished.

Keleios felt stretched thin. Her nervousness and anger had translated into sorcery. Small things levitated near her. She was like an apprentice again, trying to control strong emotion and power.

Lothor entered with a soft tap at the door. He paused just inside the door. The air was charged, something waited like a coming storm. ''Do you intend to do me a mischief?''

She laughed, and the laughter had a wild ring to it. A hand mirror floated off the night stand. She said, almost gasping, "I am on edge tonight, Lothor. Do not toy with me."

He smiled a perfectly angelical smile. "I, toy with you? Never."

"Lothor."

"My beloved, I am a little drunk, but not so much that I would try your patience too greatly. This is, after all, the night we will bed."

She clinched a fist, and the mirror fell, shattering. "Urle's forge."

"Allow me." He waved a hand, and the broken glass vanished.

He, too, had been bathed and clothed. He wore a nightdress of white, showing no more of him than did hers. Even his arms were hidden. He bent and pulled the gown over his head in one easy motion. He was naked underneath it.

"Lothor!" She turned her back on him.

"Yes," he said mildly.

"You are not clothed."

"No, I am Loltun. We do not go to our beds trapped in cloth."

"Well I am half-Calthuian, and we do."

"A difference of opinion so soon—how sad."

She turned to glare at him and quickly turned back.

"Keleios, be reasonable. You have seen me unclothed before."

"But not in my bedchamber."

"That wasn't for lack of trying on my part."

She let out an exasperated sound, and a small vase hurled near him to shatter on the wall.

He said, "If you want to play rough, we can."

"My control is not what it should be tonight."

"These last few days have tired us all."

"Yes, I am tired."

"Then let us to bed." She heard him flop down on the bed. She turned tentatively, but he lay on top of the covers. Seeing her peek, he grinned and slipped under the mound of blankets.

She stood indecisive, hands hugging her elbows. The covers rustled, and a hand touched her arm, tentatively. "Only a sorcerer could bed you tonight. Your skin crawls with magic." The grip tightened. "Feel my magic, Keleios, feel my sorcery."

She did. It mingled, and the power crackled quietly between them. He pulled her gently to the bed, and where he touched her, magic merged and grew.

She gasped and said, "Magic."

"It will always be a matter of magic for us, Keleios. No mere rutting, no matter what you have heard of Loltun men."

There was a slight smell in the air. Keleios asked, "Do you smell sulphur?"

He tested the air. "Yes."

They looked at each other and rolled off the bed, he to one side and she to the other.

A blinding flash of light, and through spot-clouded eyes, they saw something in the room.

It was taller than a human but not much. As Keleios' vision cleared, the shape took form. There was no time for weapons as the Demon Goddess Elvinna stalked toward Lothor. He saw his danger, but his eyes were not clear. His hand went out, and an energy bolt shot from it. It went wide and fell sizzling on a tapestry.

She came on, golden sword upraised. Her voice was low and melodious. "I always keep my promises, half-elves."

Keleios closed her eyes from the distraction of her ruined sight and began to build a spell. She pulled her scattered magics inside, and Lothor yelled, "Keleios."

She went flat along the floor and felt the heat rush overhead as a wave of fire consumed the wall hanging behind her. The spell was ruined for now, but her sight was back, somewhat blurred but good enough. Bolts of power shot from the other side of the room.

The succubus screamed as some hit home, but a bed-post collapsed at a blow from her sword. Lothor tumbled near the door. A wave of flame crawled up the door before he could reach it.

Keleios crawled away from the burning tapestry. The fire, being magic, consumed the hanging but did not spread. It sputtered and died when its target was consumed. Keleios knelt and tried something simpler but more dangerous. She called sorcery to her hands without forming it in her thoughts first. It was quicker but much more dangerous. She hit blindly with power, not really sure what she would call to her hand. A ragged bolt of lighting thudded into the demon's side and knocked her backward. Keleios followed it with another, letting the lightning spill out of her hand like water. That gave Lothor enough time to reach his ax. A soul-bound enchantment could never really be separated from its maker. He had needed only a moment to call it to him.

Fire crawled up the ceiling hungrily.

A bolt of ragged white blasted from the end of his ax and drove the demon to its knees. She screamed and raged at him. A hand, shaped like a talon, struck at him. Tiny bolts of sickly green danced along Lothor's body, and he shrieked.

Keleios had drawn her spell complete, controlled and whole. Having internalized the succubus's nature, she understood now. She drew cold, not of winter winds, but of man. The coldness of an empty bed, a lonely room. The winter gale howling outside and you alone. No arms to hold you, no one to lust after you, alone. No followers to worship you. When she threw the spell, there was no icy bolt, only a faint shimmering round the demon.

Elvinna shrieked. She threw back her head and howled. She forgot to attack the man. She forgot everything but loneliness. Her cries echoed as she faded away. With her leaving, the magic flames began to die, leaving charred ruin behind them.

Lothor stayed on hands and knees, shaking his head, his ax still loosely gripped in his hand.

Keleios knelt beside him, touching his sweating shoulder tentatively. "Are you all right?"

He nodded and said hoarsely, "What was that last spell?"

"It was something against the true nature of a succubus."

"How would you know the true nature of a succubus?"

"I killed one with Ache silvestri and absorbed it."

He grinned, a pale version of his usual leer. "You absorbed the nature of a succubus. Now that should add spice in the bedchamber."

She was surprised to feel a blush creeping up her cheeks.

There was a pounding on the door. Madga's voice yelled, "Keleios, Keleios, don't kill him. You're liable to burn the whole place down." The tramping beat of guards' boots were loud in the corridor.

Someone asked, "Where is the key?"

Keleios looked around the ruined wreck of the room. All the tapestries were scorched, and one, in tattered ruins. The bed was half-collapsed and fire touched.

His smile broadened. "If bedding you is always this exciting, I shall not live out the summer."

She smiled and a giggle escaped her lips. His own lips trembled. And they began to laugh. It was good, healthy laughter, and it bubbled out of both of them. Tension flowed away on a sound of laughter.

Keleios thought enough to hand Lothor his nightshirt to cover his lap, and the door opened.

Guards rushed in and found nothing to fight. Methia strode in and nearly screamed when she saw the room. "Verm's Wyrms, sister, can't I trust you not to destroy every room I give you?"

Lothor stood and tried to explain, but the nightshirt fell to the floor and left him bare. Methia screamed, "Cover yourself!"

Lothor said, "There is no reason to shriek."

Keleios handed Lothor his nightshirt, eyes shining with suppressed laughter. He began to explain, and Methia, to yell. Keleios tugged a piece of charred bedpost from under her gown, and the laughter bubbled up full throated. Lothor and Methia turned at almost the same time.

Methia yelled, "What are you laughing about?"

Lothor winked at Keleios, behind her back.

Keleios fell backward on to the scarred floor and laughed until she cried.